She didn't move
to return to a
move, she told h
anything at all.

"I've hurt you,

She looked up at him. The fear in her eyes grew sharper as for an instant she thought he might stop, might leave her lost and alone in the strange ocean in which he'd set her afloat.

"No," she whispered. She reached up to him, wrapping her arms around him, wanting to hold him close to her, to keep the feeling. "Tonight there is no way you could hurt me."

At the touch of her lips to his, Payne pulled her close. He knew that it was insane to think he could have turned away at that moment, as mad as it would have been to think himself capable of stopping a speeding locomotive by standing in front of it.

He pressed himself to her. Aura felt herself envelope him, felt the rush of fire racing through her body . . .

A STRANGER'S CARESS

SUSAN SACKETT

ZEBRA BOOKS
KENSINGTON PUBLISHING CORP.

Chapter One

"You doubtless think I've gone completely mad, Delia, but I assure you, this really is the sanest thing I have ever done. The life this stranger offers me can not help but be better than growing old alone, another Fall River spinster, doomed to spending my days in that gloomy, depressing house.

"Just think, Delia. What chance had either of us to get out from under Father's thumb and find some other life? If I stayed, what could I possibly hope for? That some widower old enough to be my father might deign to ask me to marry him?

"Bluntly put, the two of us had the grave misfortune to be born into a family that clings to the illusion of the exclusivity of its class in an age when the young men of that class have been lost either to war or the siren call of more hospitable and far less circumscribed societies. Without the freedom to follow their lead, we are expected to content ourselves with unfulfilled, lonely lives. That may be enough for you, Delia, and if it contents you, I wish you happiness with it. I just know it would never be enough for me.

"It is no wonder to me that those sons of the mill families who survived the war choose to marry the sisters of young men from New York and Boston they meet in school. They discover a great world beyond our limited and prescribed one, and they can not be blamed if they seize the opportunity to leave when the chance appears. How can we blame them for turning their backs on us and looking elsewhere for their happiness? Why should they think of their own sisters when there are so many young women whose lives are not spent under the unpleasant shadows of those looming mills, whose childhoods were not spent under the thumbs of fathers whose major pastime is the tight-fisted counting of pennies?

"We are creatures molded by that drab and hopeless environment, Delia, and it is not enough. Even the cowardly creature you know me to be wants something more. I find I can do nothing but grasp for any means of escape. I know you would tell me that women of our class do not answer advertisements written by men seeking brides, that such truck is left to serving girls, mill workers, and poor immigrants. Frankly, I am sick to death of hearing what women of our class do or do not do. This is escape, and any escape in my mind is meet and proper. I want a husband and children, Delia, and a real life of my own. If this is the only means for me to have those things, I would be a fool to turn my back on it because of some ridiculous rule of propriety.

"I assume Father is determined not to forgive me the enormity of this sin of desertion, but if he is willing to listen, tell him I meant him no harm by leaving. I simply could not go on living there, with nothing to look forward to but a miserable old age."

Aura Statler sat back and sighed, then considered one last time the words she had written. It was all there, she thought, everything there was to say, plain and clearly stated in her painfully neat handwriting.

Her sister Delia might not agree with her, but hopefully she would understand.

She finished the letter with a request that Delia take the time to write to her soon and added the expected phrase of love. Satisfied, she signed her name. It was a relief to her to finally finish the letter, because she'd been composing and recomposing it in her mind since the morning she'd walked out of the house on Hamilton Street. She'd occupied hours searching for the phrases that would make Delia understand.

She remembered inhaling the air of freedom once she'd boarded the ship in Boston, remembered how sweet it had seemed, sweet enough to still even the nagging fear generated by the knowledge that in leaving she was cutting her ties to everything she'd ever known. She hadn't once turned back with regret, and save for this letter to Delia, she intended never to look back again. A new life was waiting for her, close enough now so that she could almost taste it. She was determined to make it a good life.

Aura folded the letter carefully and put it in the envelope she'd addressed to Delia. She would put it in the post tomorrow, as soon as the *Laura Charles* docked in San Francisco. Once she'd accomplished that last task, she'd finally be completely free of a past she was only too eager to forget.

The letter neatly sealed, Aura set it down on the small lap desk. She couldn't resist the temptation of opening the drawer in the desk's side, and staring for a moment at the heavy sheet of gray paper she kept hidden there. She reached in and touched it, almost reverently. This was all she had, this entirely too fragile link with a man she had yet to meet. It was little enough incentive to do what she had done, to give up everything she'd ever known and to have come so far.

She ought by all rights to be terrified, she thought,

poised as she was on the edge of a great precipice. It seemed a miracle to her that she'd been willing to brave a voyage around the Horn to become this stranger's wife when all her life she'd never once been able to gather enough courage to so much as voice an argument to one of her father's dicta. But strangely, she wasn't afraid, not in the least. Perhaps her cowardice had merely been part of the mantle that had been suffocating her in the house on Hamilton Street. Perhaps she'd shed it like a snake shedding his skin in that single instant when she'd walked out the door.

Whatever the reason, she was entirely collected as she reread his words to her, words that she'd long since committed to memory. He'd written that he'd been charmed by her letter, that he was a moral and sober man, with a stable business and a home, that his existence lacked only the company of a warm and loving woman to be complete. His, he said, was a comfortable life, and he was most eager to share it with her. If he could not offer her all the luxuries life in the east provided, he earnestly promised to do everything in his power to make her happy.

More than enough, Aura thought, and a good deal more than the start of many successful marriages. As for luxuries, there had been few enough of those in her father's house. Despite the wealth the mills had brought Nicholas Statler during the war, he'd never lost even the edge of his tight-fisted meanness. And in all the years she'd lived in her father's house, there had never once been a man who'd promised that he intended to make her happy. What Whitmore Randall offered her was a good deal more than she had any reason to expect ever to have if she remained in Fall River.

She closed her eyes and daydreamed, wondering what he would look like. She'd sent him a likeness of herself in her last letter, the one in which she'd agreed to come and had given him to expect her aboard the *Laura Charles* out of Boston, due to arrive in San Francisco on or about the middle of September. But there had been no chance for him to answer her letter before she'd left, and she'd had to content herself with his words alone to form her mental picture of him. A hundred times during the trip she'd conjured up an image of a tall, strong, handsome man, and she did the same thing yet again, this time letting her imagination give him deep blue eyes and wavy blond hair that inched its way onto his brow. But just as she'd done each of those times before, she didn't allow herself to linger too long dreaming over that image. Even if Whitmore Randall were to prove to be squat and round, still she would not allow herself to feel the least cheated. He offered her far too much for her to let herself be so shallow as that.

In any case, she had but to wait one day more to finally know for sure. The ship's captain had managed to make dinner that afternoon festively different from all those that had preceded it, despite the monotonous reappearance of potatoes and salt beef. He'd announced that the *Laura Charles* should expect to make port early the following afternoon, words that had been met with unfeigned joy by the *Laura Charles*'s half dozen passengers.

The end of the trip could not come soon enough for Aura. It had been a long and hardly comfortable voyage for her, memorable only for the long bouts of seasickness which had left her weak and wretched. The worst had begun when the *Laura Charles* had encountered a period of high seas and bad weather as she'd rounded Cape Horn, but it hadn't ended there. All the way up the coast the storms had continued sporadically, and through the long weeks Aura had had only

9

one thing to sustain her, the prospect of finding a real life when finally she arrived in San Francisco. Now that the time was close, she could not help but grow more and more anxious with each hour that passed.

That was all behind her now, she told herself, as she put away the lap desk. She hummed softly to herself as she returned it to her trunk, then, as she neatened her narrow bunk so that the two young women with whom she shared the cabin would have no cause to grumble about her tendency to leave her belongings scattered about in the tiny room.

Ordinarily she would have gritted her teeth as she'd gone about the chore, but today nothing seemed the least unpleasant. She even felt a hint of warmth as she considered her temporary roommates. They both had come to San Francisco with precisely the same intention as she, to marry men they had never met. But they shared a common past as mill workers, and looked on Aura, who was obviously educated and from an entirely different background, as something alien and not quite trustworthy.

From the first day they'd been guarded with her, almost suspicious, as though they considered her an enemy agent come to spy on them. And despite the forced familiarity of their shared passage, despite the fact that they'd shared bouts of seasickness and bad rations and endless wet and uncomfortable afternoons together, still they had not lost their wariness of her. As impossible as it might seem when she glanced around the tiny, crowded cabin, they had made her feel alone throughout the whole of the trip. The fact that she was about to be parted from them left her with the only sincere feeling of goodwill toward them that she'd been able to muster during the whole of the trip.

Once she'd finished her housekeeping, she made her way up to the *Laura Charles*'s deck, determined to stay there until it grew too dark to see. The evening wind was sharp, biting at her cheeks and whipping the fabric of her skirt until it snapped against her ankles. She ignored it, telling herself she would be content to endure the chill if it meant she might catch even a small first glimpse of what would soon be her home.

When she'd settled herself at the rail and turned to the east, she found there was nothing more to look at but the same gray water she'd seen for what seemed to her an endless number of days. It slapped against the *Laura Charles*'s side, the waves like tiny, grasping hands that seemed to want to hold onto the clipper ship's hull and keep her from moving forward. Silently Aura scolded them, telling them how important it was for her to reach San Francisco, how her new life waited for her there. When they seemed impervious to her silent censure, she turned her back on them, looking instead up to the ship's tall sails. Here she found something to cheer her, for the winds that filled all those yards of canvas were strong and determined. *Only one day more,* they seemed to whisper, as they slipped through the creaking cordage. *Take heart,* they told her, *only one day more.*

"So you're determined to go through with this thing?"

Whitmore Randall looked up and stared at his brother's steely blue eyes. It was more than apparent to him that his arguments hadn't put a dent in Payne's doubtful reception of the news of his intention to take a wife.

"I thought you'd be pleased for me, Payne," he said in a theatrically doleful tone. "I fear you've become a misogynist, baby brother," he added with a smile.

Payne leaned back in his chair, stretching out two

11

impossibly long legs which he then crossed. He stared back at his brother and grinned.

"I think there are a few ladies at Madame Charlotte's who might disagree, Whit," he replied.

Whit shrugged.

"Perhaps you're right," he agreed. "But try to understand, Payne. I'm not quite so young as you are. I am forced to admit I've reached that time in my life where the company of whores is not only unsatisfying, it is unsettling. I want an ordered, permanent existence, a home that doesn't always look like a barn stall. I want my dinner waiting for me when I come through the door in the evening."

"What you need is a new houseboy," Payne suggested.

Whit scowled. "I want children, as preposterous as that may sound to you. And *that* means taking a wife."

"Not just a wife," Payne grumbled. "What you're taking is some mousy little woman from back East. One who'll sweep the dust from your parlor and the joy from your days." He shook his head. "I warn you, Whit, you're making a mistake."

"You are a cynic, Payne," Whit replied. He lifted the daguerreotype that sat on the top of the thin pile of letters on his desk and stared at it. "She's not mousy at all. Perhaps not a lush, buxom beauty like your favorite at Madame Charlotte's, but she's more than pretty enough." He reluctantly handed the picture to Payne. "And she's bright and witty and well educated, I can tell that by her letters. I had no reason to expect nearly so much. You'll see in another five years or so. When you're my age, you'll want the same thing. And you'll discover you can't find it at Madame Charlotte's."

Payne growled in response and told himself he sin-

12

cerely intended never to get *that* old, but he was diplomatic enough to keep his thoughts to himself. Bright and witty and well educated, he mused, and doubtless a harridan. No family with the resources to educate its daughters would allow them to go off and marry a stranger on the other side of the country unless she was such a hag they were anxious to be rid of her. But this thought, too, he wisely kept to himself.

Instead, he dutifully leaned forward, took the daguerreotype Whit was holding out to him, and looked at it. Staring back at him in pale, sepia tones was a woman with large, dark eyes, dark hair pinned neatly back, and a slightly frightened expression. Pale, she looked, but he couldn't really be sure if it wasn't just the effect of the picture. As Whit had said, no great beauty, but then, not a fright. All in all, though, simply not his taste. Had someone asked him six months before, he'd have sworn it wasn't Whit's taste, either.

He returned his attention to his brother as he handed back the picture, wondering when Whit had grown so old and settled in his manner. Because that was what he now seemed to Payne, a dull shopkeeper with a shopkeeper's idea of how to conduct his life. Perhaps it comes to us all, he thought with a shudder that made him realize how unwilling he would be to find himself in the same position.

"If that's what you want," he muttered, "I'd be the last to begrudge it to you," he said. "It's just that this is hardly a perfect time."

"It's as good as any other," Whit countered.

"You know what I mean," Payne insisted. "Until this matter of the bank notes is cleared up, you know you're still under a hint of a cloud."

"And I also know I can depend on my baby brother to protect me," Whit laughed.

"It's not a joke, Whit," Payne told him sharply. "If

13

you could remember how you came by those damned notes, I might have something to go on. And I also might have some ammunition to use when the suggestion is made that you're part of the counterfeiting scheme."

"Damn it," Whit hissed angrily. "If you and your friends at Wells Fargo transferred the notes more often than every three months, I might have had some idea where I got those particular twenties. As it is, you only send them East four times a year. And then it takes six weeks to get them to New York, and another six for the news to reach you that a half dozen are counterfeit. How am I supposed to remember who gave me what bills sometime six months ago? Or is it that they expect me to deal only with miners back from the fields who pay for their goods with gold nuggets and send everyone with greenbacks in their pockets elsewhere to buy what I could very easily sell them?"

Payne nodded. He could more than understand Whit's anger. It *did* take too long to send the currency east. The counterfeiters doubtless knew that and were taking advantage of the fact to ensure their own anonymity. And they knew their business. It wasn't as though the bills in question had been obvious fakes.

"I can't change the system, Whit," he replied softly. "And it's not in my power to hurry the railroad."

"Well, it damn well is in Wells Fargo's power," Whit said angrily, and slapped his hand on the surface of his desk. "If they weren't so damned busy protecting the exclusive rights they now have on transferring banknotes east, they might put a bit of the money they make from the business into backing the construction of track and protecting the crews. Instead, they keep one hand on their back pockets and the other in the politicians' to make sure they'll keep their franchise."

Payne frowned. "I don't think it's that simple, Whit," he said.

"No, nothing's simple," Whit agreed reluctantly. He took a deep breath to calm himself and leaned back into his chair. "I just don't like to find myself at sea with a hole in my ship's hull. And I'm not the only one in this particular sinking boat," he reminded Payne.

That, too, was true. All the major merchants followed the same procedure Whit did, depositing a sizable share of their incomes with the Wells Fargo office, where the funds were credited to their accounts, then transferred east, where they would eventually be used to pay for the goods the merchants ordered in subsequent shipments. It was a painfully slow if perfectly reasonable and workable system, and raised little more than the occasional grumble of discontent except for the present unfortunate situation.

And the situation was unfortunate for all concerned. If Whit and the other merchants unwittingly took counterfeit bills and Wells Fargo in turn accepted them from the merchants, it was Wells Fargo that took the final loss. As Wells Fargo frowned rather vehemently on being made the recipient of fraudulent currency, the company was determined to cuts its losses by pointing a finger of guilt. Unfortunately, Whit had had the bad luck to be the recipient of the greatest number of the counterfeit bills, and so the finger was, at that moment, being temporarily pointed in his direction.

"I know, I know," Payne said, making an attempt to be placating, quite aware he wasn't succeeding.

"Then why the hell should I let it interfere with my life?" Whit demanded.

Payne shrugged. "I just don't think that getting married at this particular moment, especially to a woman you've never met, is the most intelligent thing you've ever done, that's all."

Whit leaned across the desk. "Look, Payne," he said. "I've put out feelers, and if anyone knows anything about these counterfeits, and someone in the Chinese community usually knows something about everything, then sooner or later I'll hear. I can't think of a damned thing other I can do to help you and your masters at Wells Fargo find their villains."

"I just wish you had something to give me that I could use to get to the bottom of it," Payne said.

"Well, I don't," Whit told him. "And until I do, there's nothing either of us can do but sit on our hands and wait. In the meantime, I see no reason to change my plans."

Payne gritted his teeth. "I just think the situation is damned uncomfortable. I don't need to tell you that I can't appear to be covering for you."

"Damn it, there's nothing to cover," Whit hissed. "I'm beginning to understand why our father, in his infinite wisdom, chose your name." He scowled, ignoring Payne's reluctant grin. "Look, I have no intention of changing my plans because of this," he went on. "I intend to meet the *Laura Charles* when she docks, find one Miss Aurora Statler as she disembarks, introduce myself, and take her to the justice of the peace before she has the good sense to change her mind. And if you were an accommodating brother, you'd forget all about your job, wish me well, and smile and tell me it'll be the most meaningful moment in your life when you stand beside me as my best man."

It took only a glance at Whit's expression to convince Payne that he was going to do precisely as his brother had asked. It was that overgrown puppy dog look of his, the same look that had convinced Payne it was a good idea to be an accomplice in the sin of riding

16

the neighboring dairy farmer's cows and a hundred other similar misdemeanors when they'd been boys. On the face of a man of Whit's proportions and bear-like demeanor, that look was far too incongruous to be ignored and even more effective than it had been twenty years before.

Payne couldn't keep from grinning.

"The hell with the job," he said. "See? Here I am, smiling. And I'm telling you that nothing could possibly be more important in my life than being your best man."

Whit leaned back. He returned Payne's grin.

"I always knew you'd prove to be a real brother when it came down to it," he said. "Now, why don't we go to the Gentlemen's Bar at the Palmer House and drink to my last days as a bachelor?"

"Sounds reasonable," Payne agreed. He pulled in his long legs and stood. "When did you say the prospective bride is due to arrive?"

"Any day now," Whit replied. "Her letter says sometime in mid-September. I've been going down to the docks each morning for a week and inquiring."

"So this might very well be your last night of freedom?" Payne asked with a sly grin.

Whit shrugged. "That it might, little brother," he replied.

Payne's expression grew thoughtful. "Am I correct in my assumption that it would not offend your newly acquired morals were I to suggest I treat you to a final fling at Madame Charlotte's?" he asked. He grinned again, and this time there was a slightly lewd, knowing cast to the expression. "After all," he added, "these are not only your last days as a bachelor, but also your last nights."

Whit pursed his lips in consideration of the offer as he stood and joined Payne.

"Perhaps, little brother," he replied, and then punctuated his words with that absurdly out-of-place overgrown puppy look. "Not that I'm willing to admit that I entirely approve of your chosen way of life. But I might be persuaded to allow the ladies to sing me a song of farewell. Just for old times' sake, mind you."

Payne put his arm around his brother's shoulder. Although he couldn't claim Whit's bulk, he was still tall and well muscled. The two of them made a powerful impression. They would be greeted with appropriate enthusiasm by the ladies at Madame Charlotte's, and he was well aware of the fact.

"Then we'll spend the entire evening singing *"Auld Lang Syne,"* if that's your fancy," he said. He darted Whit another sly grin. "Although you might want a bit of practice before your wedding night. It wouldn't do for the bridegroom to lack the expected prowess. Nothing worse than a disappointed bride on her wedding night."

Whit laughed, the sound a pleasant boom that filled the room.

"No fear of that, little brother," he said. "No fear of that."

Aura stood on the *Laura Charles*'s deck and stared at the pier as it moved quickly up to meet her. It was an odd feeling, the sudden awareness of having finally arrived, and she felt slightly numbed as she watched a half dozen of the crew swing down to the pier and make fast the ship's lines.

It was as though the half dozen passengers had been holding their breath until that moment. They'd been nearly silent for the previous half hour, but once the Laura Charles settled snugly up to the pier, they all began to talk at once.

"Can you believe we're finally here?"

"Oh, good luck, Aura."

"Good luck!"

Short, breathless little gasps of words, punctuated by earnestly offered hugs, quick little kisses . . . The apparent sincerity of the unexpected warmth quite bewildered Aura. It seemed that she was finally being accepted by the others, now that the *Laura Charles* had docked. Or perhaps the outflow of warmth was offered only because the ship was in port and the effort need not continue for very long. In any case, Aura accepted the embraces and the warm wishes with quite the same enthusiasm with which they'd been offered, and happily returned them. She was here, finally, and she felt much too delighted with that fact to hold onto any resentment she might feel for whatever unpleasantness was now well in the past.

As the gangway was being secured, they all turned to scan the crowd of men now gathering on the pier. As soon as the group of young women noticed them, their outburst died as suddenly as it had begun. The women stood silent and expectant as they began to consider what they saw in the faces of the men on the pier. Aura knew each of them had the same thought, each wondering, just as she was, which one might be the one she had come so far to marry.

She heard a giggle and a deep-throated whisper, "I hope he's mine."

Aura had no need to ask which of the crowd on the pier had elicited that response, for she saw him, too. He was tall, so tall he stood out in the crowd, with dirty blond hair and eyes so blue she could not help but notice them, even at this distance. As he scanned the women standing at the rail, his eyes caught hers and for an instant Aura found herself smiling at him.

Then the wind caught his hair and an unruly lock fell across his brow.

Aura found herself catching her breath in sudden surprise. The hair, the eyes, the boyish, slightly wicked grin—this was the man she'd imagined when she'd let herself daydream about the man she was coming to marry. He hadn't been a dream after all, she heard a voice inside her cry out with delight. He's real. He's the one. He must be the one.

The moment ended. He turned away just as the crewmen finished setting the gangway, turning to talk to a man standing beside him, another tall man, but this one large, with dark hair, dark eyes, and a bearded face.

Aura was left with a sense of loss which was soon supplanted by a deep feeling of embarrassment. She looked away, and then, hoping to keep the others from seeing, began to fumble with the buttons on her gloves. She needn't have bothered. They were all filled with a brittle excitement now, a feeling of tense expectancy.

Aura trotted along with the others to the gangway, telling herself that she was acting like a silly young fool, that daydreams are just that, dreams, and had nothing to do with reality. Despite her own chiding, however, she found herself mentally reviewing the outfit she'd chosen to wear for the occasion of meeting of her future husband. It was admittedly her best, and she hadn't given a thought to it before that moment, but now she found herself wondering if the sober burgundy wasn't a bit plain, perhaps even dowdy. What if the man she'd come so far to meet took one look at her and decided she did not suit him? What if he decided to turn his back on her and simply walk away?

She patted nervously at a stray curl that had escaped its pins, tucking it up and under her bonnet. She wished she'd had more of a chance to prepare, wished she'd had the luxury of a real bath and then time in front of a dressing mirror. Instead, there had been only a basin of lukewarm water, the crowded, noisy little cabin, and the nervous jostling of the others. She bit her lip. She wasn't ready. After all the long weeks of travel, she was here and she wasn't ready.

For the first time since she'd left her father's house, Aura felt real fear. She was about to face a man who would determine the whole of her future, and she was deathly afraid he would take one look at her and decide she was lacking.

She started down the short gangway, stepping gingerly, sure she was about to stumble clumsily or otherwise publicly disgrace herself.

"Miss Statler? Miss Aurora Statler?"

It was her name, no question about that, and it had been spoken in a pleasant basso. She turned, until that moment not realizing she'd been holding her breath.

She released it with a gasp. It was him, the tall, handsome man, the one she'd seen standing on the pier, the same man she'd seen in her daydreams. But this wasn't a daydream, she told herself. This was real.

She made no attempt to keep herself from smiling as she looked up at him. She was, she realized, grinning ridiculously, wearing the expression that made her look, as Delia had told her countless times, like she was all pink and white, teeth and gums.

"Mr. Randall?"

He nodded and smiled at her. But as she took the hand he offered her, Aura felt the nagging fear of being rejected return. Confused and unsure of herself, she glanced down at it, large and strong and firm, her small gloved hand looking as though it were a doll's sitting on its palm before he wrapped his fingers around it.

21

"A great pleasure," he told her.

"I can't believe I'm really here," she murmured.

She looked back up at him and realized his expression wasn't the least displeased. The fear melted away to be replaced by a wash of untarnished delight. Everything was going to be just as she'd hoped, she told herself, better. This man wants me, he's promised to marry me and make me happy. Everything she'd ever wanted in her life seemed at that moment to have fallen into her hands.

Filled with her own hopeful happiness and spurred by an improbable impulse, she pushed herself to her tiptoes and kissed him on the cheek.

As soon as she'd done it, she knew she'd made some horrible mistake. She looked at his face, saw the smile disappear, and watched as it was replaced by something quite different. She realized that he looked more shocked than anything by what she'd thought an entirely innocent gesture.

Oh God, she thought. I'm ruining it. But we're to be married. Surely he can't think the gesture inappropriate. A second glance at his face assured her he did. She would have run, fled back to the bowels of the *Laura Charles*, had he released her hand and had there been a clear path.

He grinned then, slowly, slightly deprecatingly, and Aura thought that far worse than even what had preceded it. She felt the heat of an embarrassed blush creeping over her cheeks. She looked away, not wanting to see that look, wishing she could shrink until she was small enough to hide in the cracks between the boards of the pier.

She only began to understand the depth of her transgression when he lifted his arm and called out, "I've found her, Whit." When he turned back to face her, he was still grinning, apparently amused now, if

22

still slightly superior. "Miss Statler," he said, nodding to the tall, burly man with whom she'd seen him talking earlier and who was now approaching at a run, "may I introduce you to your bridegroom and my brother, Mr. Whitmore Randall?"

Chapter Two

The embarrassment Aura had thought an instant before could become no greater grew a hundredfold. The worst part of it was that it took only the smallest glance at the man she'd mistakenly assumed was Whitmore Randall for her to realize he was not only completely aware of her discomfort, he was more than a little amused by it. His arch half grin had the effect of rousing a slowly smoldering rage that did nothing to lessen her embarrassment, yet still managed to further disconcert her.

She turned away from him, futilely trying to bury her embarrassment as she told herself she would never again allow herself to act the fool in his presence. She knew she had been momentarily enchanted by what she'd thought was a dream come to life. But now she knew he was no dream. He was superior and scornful and arrogant—everything she could only despise in a man. If she'd been weak enough to allow herself to temporarily drift off into a childish fantasy, to pretend that her mundane life had turned into the happy ending of some fairy tale, at least she was rational enough never to repeat the folly.

She forced herself to settle her attention on the man she'd come so far to marry. This wasn't the hero of her dreams, certainly, no charming prince on a white charger challenging all for her hand. Formidable, not handsome, was the first word that sprang to her mind as she considered Whitmore Randall. He seemed nothing less than that to her—very tall, with a huge barrel chest. Just standing beside him made her feel uncomfortably dwarfed. And she couldn't keep herself from thinking that he looked a good deal older than she'd expected, some ten years senior to his brother, she mused, or perhaps even more. Or maybe age was only the impression left by the thick, dark beard that covered his cheeks and chin.

She shivered slightly. That beard reminded her of her father's bewhiskered face. The similarity made her wonder how else her intended husband might resemble the autocrat of the house she'd fled eight weeks before. She panicked suddenly, wondering if she'd fled from one petty tyrant only to make herself the thrall of another.

"Miss Aurora Statler? Yes, of course, who else would you be? I see you've had the poor fortune to meet my brother, Payne. Don't worry. It may be painful, but it's never been known to be fatal."

Whit smiled broadly after he'd completed his little speech, his full lips curving up seraphically and revealing a row of even white teeth. Aura realized he'd somehow managed to extract her hand from his brother's and encase it in his own.

If her initial impression of him had left her with more than an inkling of trepidation, Aura found it quickly fading, immediately overpowered by his smile and the warmth that flowed from his hand to hers. More than that, his dark eyes were bright with good-humored pleasure, and they combined with the sincerity she sensed in his smile to dispel any illusion that he was either old or a tyrant. And there was warmth and

25

humor in his voice, both attributes she'd never found in her father. Their presence eradicated any similarity she might at first glance have found between the two.

She would like Whitmore Randall, she decided. He might not be as handsome as his brother, might not be the image of the man she'd dreamed about, but she felt an instantaneous affection for him. This man would be a good husband for her, she told herself, kind and good humored and affectionate. She had no right to ask for anything more.

"I'm afraid I mistook one Randall brother for another," she confessed with a sheepish smile, determined to put as good a face as possible on her gaffe. "You never mentioned a brother in your letters. I had no idea you had one."

"Neither had I." Whit grinned, glanced briefly at Payne, then quickly turned back to let his eyes find hers. "At least I didn't know I had one here. He appeared suddenly at my doorstep a few weeks ago for an unexpected fraternal visit. Throwing caution to the wind, I persuaded him to stay long enough to meet you, an act of foolishness for which I hope you'll someday forgive me."

Aura laughed softly. "Surely no forgiveness is needed for an act of fraternal hospitality."

Whit shook his head. "I'm not quite so sure," he confided. "He was never properly housebroken." He nodded to his brother. "However, if he promises to behave like a gentleman, I'll introduce you to him."

Aura watched him as he darted a second glance at Payne, this one pointedly sharp. A warning, she thought, but a warning for what? The intensity of that look baffled her, but she was quickly distracted when Whit returned his attention completely to her.

"Miss Statler, may I introduce my prodigal brother, Payne?" he asked with a theatrical flourish. "Payne,

26

Miss Aurora Statler, soon to be Mrs. Whitmore Randall. Now mind your manners and pretend you know how to be a gentleman."

"You slander me, Whit," Payne muttered, his expression tensely sober as he took Aura's hand again, this time briefly, barely touching it as he murmured, "A great pleasure, Miss Statler." He bowed with painstaking precision, then turned to his brother, a wry grin turning up the corners of his lips. "Do I pass muster?" he asked.

Whit ignored him. Instead, he bent his arm and tucked Aura's hand in the crook.

"I've been down here every day for nearly two weeks," he told her, as he turned to survey the easiest path through the crowd that filled the wharf. "I was beginning to worry."

"There was some bad weather as we rounded the Horn," Aura told him, in a tone that said she remembered only too clearly the misery of the trip.

Whit nodded, commiserating. A merchant could be all too well aware of the vicissitudes of importing goods by sea. Human passage, he knew, was no more reliable.

"Unfortunately," he said, "until the railroad is completed, it's the quickest way from the East, save for coming on horseback, the way Payne did." He smiled at her then, the same warm, pleased smile he'd given her the first moment he saw her. "In any case, I am only too happy that you have finally arrived, Miss Aurora Statler."

She returned the smile. "Aura, please," she told him. "My friends call me Aura. Actually, the only person who ever called me Aurora was my father."

"Then Aura it is," Whit boomed jovially, "as I want nothing more than to be your very best friend."

She smiled shyly. "I'd like that, too, Mr. Randall."

"Mr. Randall?" he bellowed. "How can we be friends if I am Mr. Randall. Whit, please, my dear Aura."

She nodded and smiled again. "Whit," she agreed.

With that, he determined their path through the heaps of off loaded cargo as well as the sundry human obstacles barring their exit and began to lead her along the length of the wharf, assuring her that he'd already seen to having her trunks forwarded to his house. He had a completely commanding manner, and if Aura found herself a bit overwhelmed by him, she realized that as long as she was with him, she would be taken care of and protected. It was, she told herself, a pleasant, decidedly comfortable feeling.

When they reached the carriage he'd hired, he didn't simply help her up, but instead put his hands on her waist and lifted her into it as if the effort involved were insignificant. Aura laughed as she settled herself onto the leather seat.

"You make me feel terribly small, like a doll," she confessed, in answer to his questioning glance. She edged over to the side of the seat to leave him sufficient room to sit beside her.

"You *are* small," he laughed, as he settled his considerable bulk beside her. "To a giant like myself, you're tiny." He grinned at her. "And pretty. Much prettier than your picture." He looked up at his brother. "Don't you think, Payne?"

Aura blushed, and looked down at her lap. She was equally pleased and embarrassed by his words, and by the sincerity she heard in his tone as he'd uttered them.

But the mechanical sound of Payne's reply, the dull, "She certainly is," offered without any sign of enthusiasm, quickly squelched her feeling of pleasure. It made her realize that she wasn't quite everything Payne Randall could possibly want in a woman, even if his brother seemed well enough pleased with her. She couldn't help but replay in her mind the stupidly gushing kiss, nor could she keep at bay the nagging embarrassment at the realization that she'd behaved quite so foolishly.

She bit her lower lip, wondering what he thought of her, wondering what she might think were she in his place. After all, in just a few hours he would become her brother-in-law. Logic told her that she ought to cultivate at least some sort of civil relationship with him.

But when she glanced up at him and saw the persistent superior glance he leveled at her, she couldn't keep from shrinking. His disdain seemed to shimmer out and settle like a mist over her. He would never forget her stupidity of that afternoon, she told herself, nor would he ever allow her to forget it. She'd be a fool to imagine she would ever be able to think of this man as her friend.

She didn't realize it, but Payne's expression was one of appraisal more than disdain. The likeness Whit had shown him, with its sepia tones, had made him expect a woman of little shading, just pale skin and dark eyes and hair. But she was far from that; her dark green eyes were of a shade he'd never seen before and her hair was a shining, brilliant auburn that glowed with sparks of gold in the afternoon sunlight. As Whit had warned him, she wasn't the lush sort of woman he admired, but she was far from being the pale little mouse he'd expected.

Of the three of them, only Whit seemed to be entirely at his ease. Oblivious to both his brother's feelings and Aura's reaction to it, he nearly glowed with the good-natured pleasure that seemed to be a natural part of his personality. As soon as the carriage started to move, lurching along the rutted street, he

29

began to point out the highlights of the city that was to be his new bride's home.

Aura was initially bewildered by his enthusiasm. At first glance, she took her surroundings to be a totally dismal landscape—dirty, mud-filled streets lined with ramshackle buildings. The complete ugliness of these streets by the wharves seemed to swallow even the sunshine and level everything to a depressing, dull gray.

But Aura soon realized her perceptions had been dulled by the long weeks at sea. Slowly she began to recognize that the wharfside streets of the young city of San Francisco were not quite the same tawdry streets she'd seen surrounding the wharves back East. They were decidedly different, and those differences mitigated the combined curses of poverty and a thick coating of grime.

Her curiosity was at first roused as she realized the buildings were peopled by a uncountable number of strange-looking men and women wearing long dark tunics and trousers, and hair that hung in a narrow braid down their backs. She couldn't keep herself from gaping as she stared out the window at them. If these streets by the wharves boasted the saloons and cheap boardinghouses that were only to be expected in places that earned their money from the wages of common sailors, there was still something decidedly unexpected, even exotic, about what she saw.

"Don't be too put off by this," Whit told her, as the carriage rolled through the muddy streets. "Up the hill, where we live, it's much nicer."

"Oh, I'm not put off," Aura quickly assured him.

The scenery had already begun to change as they left the wharves behind them, the tawdry wharfside saloons now giving way to small shops, many of them selling food, colorful heaps of produce and fish, and live chickens squawking noisily in their cages. And there were small stalls from which emanated a wealth of strange, pungent odors. She inhaled deeply, her nostrils drinking in the mystery of odors that were quite as exotic to her as the oddly dressed people. However strange, the smells were far from unpleasant.

"The Chinese come here to find work in the mines and laying railroad track," he told her. "However low the wages, it seems to be more than enough to satisfy them. One can only wonder how they lived before they came here." He gazed thoughtfully at the muddy streets and the tiny, makeshift houses. "It takes a bit of getting used to, I suppose," he cautioned Aura.

Aura turned away from the window to face him. He'd been watching her, she realized, waiting for her reaction.

"I want to see everything," she told him. "There's nothing like all this in Fall River!"

Whit laughed, obviously relieved that she wasn't disgusted by her surroundings.

"No, I suppose there isn't," he conceded. "Well, there'll be more than time enough for that. We'll leave the Chinese part of town to tend to itself today, though. Just now, we'll go to the house and let you freshen up a bit before we see the justice of the peace. And after that, there'll be a wedding celebration to occupy you."

His words sobered her. A wedding celebration. The words reverberated in her mind, over and over, reminding her that it was *her* wedding celebration. It seemed so strange to her to think that the time had come. She'd thought of nothing else for weeks, but now it seemed too quick, too pressing for her to readily consider. She swallowed uncomfortably and tried to settle herself, tried to tell herself that she'd come all

31

this way to marry this man and it was no time now to become terrified at the thought.

She forced herself to smile at Whit, hating that she could feel the brittleness of her expression and hoping he didn't notice it. This was what she'd wanted, she told herself. This was why she'd left her father's house and traveled all this way. But how could she simply marry a man she didn't know? However nice he seemed, she simply wasn't prepared to become his bride.

Stop this, she told herself silently. This is not the time to become a shrinking maiden stricken with the vapors.

She'd walked out of her father's house, knowing full well she could never return to it. Nor did she want to. She simply had no choice now but to face up to the consequences of her own decisions and get on with her life. There was certainly no going back.

"And do you, Aurora Statler, take Whitmore Randall to be your lawfully wedded husband?"

Aura had to shake herself to attention. The previous hours had passed like a dream, all hazy now and slightly indistinct. The daze had begun as surprise when she'd seen for the first time Whit's house, her house, a large rambling frame affair. She'd quickly realized that the sign, proclaiming "W. Randall—Provisions" in large gold letters, meant there was a general store filling the ground floor. Her father, she knew, would have scorned that, for what he'd termed "bringing home trade" he'd thought beneath him.

Admittedly the streets were still muddy and far removed from the cobbled streets she'd been accustomed to back East, but the houses here, further up the hill and away from the wharves, seemed pleasantly prosperous. And she'd been happily surprised to find the living quarters above Whit's store were more than comfortable, even luxurious, if a bit cluttered. Whitmore Randall was a man who obviously did not begrudge himself his creature comforts. The bedroom to which he'd shown her had been absolutely sumptuous compared to the room she'd shared with Delia in the house back in Fall River. Her father, she knew, would have derided the furnishings as extravagant and indulgent, but she thought the huge tester bed with its thick feather comforter, the large mahogany dresser and pier mirror, and the cozy little sofa tucked between the two tall windows on the far wall all simply wonderful.

Whit had anticipated her desire for the luxury of a bath after the long weeks shipboard, and had soon left her to luxuriate in an enormous tub filled with wondrously steamy water and the unheard-of luxury of French bath salts. Even after the water had grown cold, she'd hated to leave the sweetly flower-scented tub, and had only forced herself from it when she'd realized she was keeping her prospective bridegroom waiting.

And now, here she found herself, dressed in a slightly trunk-rumpled but still pretty white linen and lace-embellished dress that she and Delia had secretly sewn in the evenings before her departure. She was facing the justice of the peace, watching his lips move, but not quite certain of what it was he was saying. It was only when she realized he and Whit were both staring at her expectantly that she realized they were waiting for her.

She swallowed. Her gaze drifted in a slightly dazed bewilderment between Whit and the marginally bored justice of the peace. As it did, her eyes momentarily met Payne Randall's. His expression shook her out of her daze, that superior, knowing glance of his almost

33

screaming out that he'd known from the start that she wasn't quite what she'd presented herself to be.

She looked away quickly and met Whit's expectant gaze. Whatever her fears and uncertainties, Payne Randall's expression gave her the courage to ignore them.

"I do," she said firmly.

Whit smiled and squeezed her hand, and then slid a thick gold band on its third finger. As soon as she saw the sparkling ring, a voice inside her head began to busily distract her, a voice that was both triumphant and unsure at the same time, telling her that she was a bride now, that her fate was now sealed forever. It sobered her, and once again she felt a momentary wash of panic. Forever, the voice told her, was a very, very long time.

It was only when Whit put his hands on her shoulders that she realized the ritual had ended. The justice had told her husband it was time for him to kiss his bride.

Whit's kiss was soft and gently hesitant, as though he was afraid he might frighten her. Aura found it touching that he was so careful of her. She tasted a hint of whiskey on his lips, and realized he must have fortified himself for the occasion while she'd been occupied with her bath. Her father hadn't approved of whiskey, and this was the first taste of it Aura had ever had. She decided it wasn't all that unpleasant. And the kiss—she told herself that had not been all that unpleasant, either.

There were the words of congratulations and the handshakes, and then she found herself back in the carriage, this time, her hand with its beringed finger solidly encased in Whit's.

"We'll have a real celebration in a week or so, when you've gotten yourself settled in," he assured her. "For tonight, I can only promise you the best dinner San Francisco has to offer."

"It will be ambrosia after eight weeks of boiled salt beef and potatoes," she assured him.

He chuckled. "We'll see if we can't do just a bit better than that," he promised, before he called out to the driver to take them to the Palmer House Hotel.

Aura soon discovered that the wealth of gold first discovered at Sutter's Mill had spawned several small oases of luxury among the muddy sprawl of San Francisco to accommodate the hungers of miners eager to spend their newfound riches. The Palmer House Hotel was one of those oases.

Whit brought her to a dining room as opulent as anything she could have imagined in New York or Boston, replete with crystal chandeliers and silver buckets to hold the chilled bottles of French champagne. Couples danced to the music of a small orchestra at one side of the huge room, and sweating waiters scurried from table to table bearing huge, heavily laden trays of food and wine.

Aura stood in the entrance and simply gaped. She'd never seen anything like this, certainly never seen women dressed as the majority of the women in the room were dressed, with scandalously deep décolletage, dangerously pinched waists, and brightly rouged cheeks. There was certainly nothing like this in Fall River, at least, nothing she'd ever seen. She swallowed uncomfortably. Those laughing women with their rouged cheeks and displayed expanses of flesh made her feel lost and naive and decidedly virginal in her neck-hugging linen-and-lace wedding dress.

Whit squeezed her hand.

"I'm afraid the presence of gold does attract a number of individuals engaged in a certain unsavory vocation," he told her, when he saw her dismayed expression.

"Profession," Payne interjected. "Not vocation, profession. The world's oldest, I believe," he added with a slightly lecherous grin, as he surveyed the field of possibilities.

Whit leveled a glance that quite clearly told him to keep his remarks to himself, then ignored the interruption.

"But the food is the best by far in the city, and we can dance, if you've a mind to," he added to Aura.

She swallowed her discomfort. This was a new world, she told herself. She might just as well become accustomed to its idiosyncrasies now as later. She turned and faced him.

"I'm terribly hungry," she murmured, then added, "and I've never tasted champagne," with a small, hopeful smile.

Thick laughter bubbled up from Whit's throat.

"Then this should be a night of many firsts," he assured her.

He was smiling with pleasure as he put his hand to her waist and nodded to a harried waiter who had appeared in front of them to lead them to their table.

Aura felt slightly dizzy. Her thoughts were fuzzy and her head seemed to be growing a bit too heavy for her to hold upright. When she realized she'd allowed it to rest against Whit's shoulder, she jerked herself suddenly upright. This was not proper, a prim little voice inside her whispered up to her, reminding her that she wasn't like those painted, half-naked women she'd seen nuzzling up to drunken men in the Palmer House dining room.

36

Whit smiled down at her.

"A bit too much champagne, Aura?" he asked gently.

Aura nodded. "I'm afraid so," she replied.

She was smiling a bit foolishly, she realized, for despite the seriousness of her crime, she didn't feel the least bit contrite. In fact, she'd already come to the decision that she quite liked champagne.

"Well, no harm done," Whit assured her.

He put his arm around her shoulder, and nudged her head gently toward his shoulder. This time she didn't try to fight the inclination. This is perfectly all right, she told herself, perfectly respectable. After all, this man is my husband. She couldn't deny that she felt quite comfortable with her head resting against his shoulder, feeling the solid warmth of his bulk close to her.

She would have felt entirely contented, were it not for the fact that when she looked up she saw Payne sitting across from her, watching her with that superior glance of his. She was beginning to become accustomed to it, even beginning to think that expression wasn't reserved for her alone. He seemed to survey much of the world with a slightly bored disdain, as though he was privy to secrets that ought never to have been repeated.

Not that he'd behaved badly at dinner. On the contrary, now that she considered it, she realized he'd been quite pleasant company during the preceding hours. He'd been as amused as Whit had been at the expression she'd made after her first sip of champagne, and had offered a toast welcoming her into the family as his little sister. He'd even gone to the gallant effort of dancing with her twice during the course of the evening when it had seemed only too apparent to her

37

that he'd have much preferred the company of one of the many ladies wearing those low-cut gowns.

All in all, it had been a lovely dinner, with food every bit as good as Whit had promised—oysters and rich pâté and tender venison in a heady wine-laden sauce and a meltingly sweet chocolate soufflé, all wonders that had never once been offered at her father's dining table. And the champagne, a wonder in itself, with those impossible little bubbles bursting on her tongue and the sweet alcoholic taste that left her lips and fingers tingling.

And dancing, being held in a Whit's arms in a way she'd never been held before, as though she was something fragile and precious and a wonder herself. Were the rest of her life to be as bleak and drab as life had been in Fall River, she told herself, she would have no complaints. She now had a wonderful memory to cherish, and that was far more than life had ever promised to offer her before she'd come to this place.

The only discordant note had been the strange way Payne had looked at her, the same way he was looking her at that moment. She didn't know why, but it left her oddly uncomfortable, even a bit frightened, despite the fact that she knew she certainly had nothing to fear from him.

"We're home," Whit said.

His words roused her, and she sat up stiffly, waiting for him to climb out of the carriage and then reach up and lift her out. It was nice, she thought, to have his strong arm around her waist. She wasn't at all certain she was entirely steady on her feet.

With Payne, who'd taken a moment to pay the driver, trailing behind, they walked the length of the porch that fronted the store to the house's side door, the one that let them avoid walking through the shop. Whit unlocked and opened the door, then lit the small lantern left on the table by the entry. They were all laughing as they climbed up the steep flight of stairs, more from simple good humor than anything especially funny anyone had said.

When they were finally settled in the parlor and had shed their coats, they stood for a moment, awkward, not quite sure of the proper rules the occasion doubtless required. Finally Payne yawned.

"Bedtime, I think," he said, and gave Whit a knowing smile.

Whit cleared his throat noisily. "Yes," he agreed. "I suppose it is."

Payne leaned forward to him and embraced him.

"Congratulations, big brother," he said. He released Whit and turned to Aura. His expression was not quite so genial as the one he'd offered his brother, but he smiled at her and said, "My very best wishes for your happiness, Mrs. Randall."

Aura felt herself blush as she murmured a soft "Thank you." She certainly wasn't yet accustomed to the idea of thinking of herself as Mrs. Randall, or as Mrs. Anybody, for that matter. But it was true, she told herself. She was a wife, and hopefully would someday be a mother. She had everything she wanted within her grasp, and all it had cost her was the courage to take a chance.

And one more thing, a voice inside silently reminded her—it would require the courage to see this night to its inevitable conclusion, the courage to go to a stranger's bed. The nervousness that had plagued her since the beginning of the day returned, but this time it was far more pressing as she realized the time was now imminent when she would have to become a wife in more than name alone.

She twisted her fingers nervously in the fabric of her skirt as Payne offered his brother a last smile, then wished them both goodnight. He then immediately took his leave, drifting off to the rear of the house. It was apparent to Aura that he was only too glad to get away, and for an instant she wished she might somehow escape as well.

Once she was alone with Whit, the nervousness only grew. The two of them stood in the middle of the cluttered parlor, neither quite sure of what to say. Aura had never felt more awkward in her life.

Their dilemma was temporarily postponed by the sound of knocking on the door by which they'd just entered.

Startled by the sound, Aura nearly jumped.

"What's that?" she asked.

Whit shrugged. "I've no idea," he told her, as he glanced down the flight of stairs. "Someone at the door, but I've no idea who it could be," he told her softly. He smiled at her, wryly apologetic. "Whatever it is, I won't be long," he assured her, before he started down the flight.

Aura stood at the top of the stairs, watching him as he opened the door. He spoke softly, too softly for her to hear, but then he stood back and admitted a man. Aura was bewildered when she saw his visitor, for it was one of those strange people she'd seen early that afternoon on the way from the wharves, a Chinese man dressed in a dark tunic and pants. He glanced up and stared at her. It took her a moment to realize he became disturbed when he saw her standing there.

He turned to Whit and began to speak in a low but unmistakably agitated tone.

"It's all right," Whit quickly assured him. "The lady is my wife." He glanced up at Aura. "Go on to bed, Aura," he called up. "I'll only be a few moments."

Then he opened the door to the shop and led his visitor inside. Aura watched them disappear, then

40

turned away, crossing the parlor as she wondered what could possibly be so important to Whit that he'd be willing to entertain an uninvited visitor at such a late hour on this particular evening.

Aura undressed slowly, laying out the white dress on the small sofa, pulling on her best lawn nightgown, and tying the pale pink ribbons carefully. She could smell the odor of the bath salts that still clung to her skin, the sweetly floral scent that seemed to neatly envelop her.

She sat for a while and brushed out her hair, all the while feeling edgy, not quite sure of herself, as she stared across the room to the large four-poster bed. She kept reminding herself of how pleasant Whit had been to her, how considerate and gentlemanly. Still, she had to force herself finally to put down the brush and cross the room.

She turned down the bed cover neatly, folding it at the foot and smoothing away the wrinkles. Once that was done, she realized there was nothing more to keep her from it. She glanced nervously at the door, wondering what was keeping Whit so long.

She climbed into the big bed, feeling more than a little lost in such a huge expanse as she slipped between the smooth sheets. She leaned back against the pillows, momentarily forgetting her nervousness and relishing the comfort of the bed after the long weeks of sleeping on what had been little more than a narrow wooden ledge in the tiny cabin on the *Laura Charles*.

And then she began to ponder the mystery of just what Whitmore Randall, when he finally joined her, would expect of her.

For the simple truth was, Aura was entirely innocent. Save for an occasional dry kiss on the cheek from a disinterested cousin or uncle, the kiss Whit had given her after they were pronounced man and wife had been her first. And although her normal curiosity had been whetted by the occasional glimpse of procreation in a barnyard on the outskirts of Fall River, she had never had any opportunity to voice questions or receive answers that might have alleviated the concern that was now growing inside her.

But as the moments dragged on, the effects of the champagne and a more than ample dinner slowly eased her concern and lulled her into a fitful doze. She dreamt, of Whit and Payne and dancing in both men's arms.

And she woke to the sharp sound of pistol fire.

She sat bolt upright in bed, listening to the sound as it reverberated through the house. Then she darted up, running to the parlor and then to the stairs. The door from the entryway to the store was open, and a long shaft of lantern light slid through it, illuminating the bottom of the stairs and the body that lay at their feet.

Aura felt her stomach knot in sudden, sharp fear and she heard a scream that she did not realize was her own as she half ran, half slid down the stairs.

It was Whit—there was no question of that, she realized long before she reached him, before she knelt down beside him and touched his face and saw the dark stain of the blood that already was beginning to pool around his body.

Chapter Three

"Oh, God, no!"

Payne arrived in the parlor just a few seconds after Aura. Finding it empty, just as she had, he followed her path to the stairwell. He stood for a second staring down the narrow flight, unable to believe what his eyes told him he saw as he watched Aura lean over Whit and press her hands to his chest, unable even to recognize his own voice in the pained cry he'd uttered without realizing he'd spoken aloud.

A pale illumination snaked its way through the open doorway from the store and made the tableau below him seem unnatural, eerily unreal. A sick feeling filled the pit of his stomach, a disorientation that made it seem to him that he was on the outside staring in at his own nightmare.

But as he ran down the steps, he realized that however nightmarish it might seem, this wasn't a dream. The feel of the stair rail beneath his fingers was all too solid, the cool breeze drifting in from the open door to the outside was sharp and biting against his bare chest. And the sobering sight of his brother's body, lying limp and contorted on the floor by the open door, was far more frightening than the worst nightmare he'd ever had.

He took the stairs by twos, unable to take his eyes off Whit, unable to think of anything but Whit's body lying at the foot of the stairs. He could see no movement save for the red gush of blood, and there was a dull aching awareness beginning to grow inside him that there would never be any, that Whit was already dead. By the time he'd reached the bottom of the flight, there was no question left in his mind; he knew.

Still, he knelt at Aura's side, ignoring the sound of her sobbed cries, hearing nothing but the sickening thud of his own heart. He put his fingers on Whit's neck and felt for the pulse he knew he wouldn't find there.

He spent a horrible moment with his senses focused on the feel of the flesh of Whit's neck, the still, lifeless flesh that seemed to him already to be growing cold. The knot in his stomach grew tighter and he thought for an instant he might gag.

He drew his hand away and pushed himself to his feet, oblivious still to Aura, hardly aware that she continued to press down on the ugly red hole in Whit's chest, trying, uselessly, to stem the flood of blood flowing from it. He ran to the door and darted out into the darkness, squinting into the night, listening for some sound, some hint that whoever had done this thing was still there.

From far away there was the sharp sound of a dog barking angrily. Other than that, the night returned nothing to him but silence and darkness. He swore and told himself he was acting like a fool, that murderers do not wait about to be caught at the scene of their crime.

He returned to the entry to stand for an endless moment over Aura and Whit. He'd gone suddenly numb inside, completely empty. He wondered about that for an instant, wondered where the sharp hurt had gone. Then it struck him that a part of him was lying dead on the floor, along with his brother. Whit embodied his past to him, and now that Whit was dead, so was a good part of his life as well.

It was only then that he became aware of the sound of Aura's voice, faded now into a dull, wrenching cry. He had to force himself to focus on the words.

"You can't die," she pleaded hopelessly with Whit's body, "please don't die."

She sounded like a child who suddenly finds himself lost and alone and who has no idea of how to deal with the situation or change it. He stared at her, realizing only then that she was dressed in nothing more than a thin nightdress spattered with blood. Her face was white with shock and the cold that was snaking its way through the open door.

He knelt beside her and put his hand on hers. To his surprise, they felt warm, but he quickly realized the heat came not from her skin, but from the sticky liquid that coated them. A wave of revulsion filled him as he realized that the liquid was Whit's blood.

He felt himself fill with sheer rage, anger at the feeling of helplessness that now engulfed him, and as they finally managed to edge their way past his defenses and make an impression on him, at the sound of her continued cries.

Taking no pains to be especially gentle with her, he pulled her hands away from Whit's chest.

"It's no good," he told her sharply. "He's dead."

She quieted immediately, shaking her head, mouthing the single word *"No,"* and staring at him blankly, as though she did not believe him. She seemed about to return her hands to the wound in Whit's chest, thinking, perhaps, that she could hold the life still within him, but he refused to release them. Instead, he held them up in front of her, forcing her to see them.

45

She stared at them, then, still mute, but saying a great deal with her eyes. One glance at the blood that soaked them convinced her finally that what he'd told her was true.

She shuddered as the realization sank home, then tore her glance from her hands as Payne released them and looked up at him. Her expression, he saw, was filled with horror. The sight of her eyes, wide now and frightened, stirred an unexpected feeling of guilt within him. She was obviously terrified, he told himself, and he had no real reason to be angry with her, save for the vague feeling that had she never come, had he been alone with Whit in the house, or better yet, at Madame Charlotte's, none of it would ever have happened.

He pulled her to her feet, walked her to the stairs, and sat her down.

"What happened?" he asked.

She shook her head and sat mute and staring, not up at him, but at Whit's dead body. In silencing her cries, he'd somehow rendered her completely speechless. His anger with her returned, and all he could think was that she was purposely being obstinate. That she must know something of what had happened to Whit seemed only obvious. After all, a man doesn't leave his bride on their wedding night without giving her a reason.

He put his hands on her shoulders, not caring that his grip was so hard that his fingers bit into her flesh, and shook her.

"You must have seen something," he nearly shouted at her. "What happened?"

She cringed at the sound of his voice and whimpered softly at the hurt his fingers left in her shoulders.

He loosened his grip, and as he did, the absent thought filled him that she was cold, that the flesh he

46

felt beneath his fingers was as cold as Whit's dead flesh had been. He lowered his voice when he asked her the third time, "What happened?"

She looked down again at the slimy mess of blood on her hands. She shivered and began to wipe them on her nightgown. Payne scowled, but buried his impatience, as it was only too plain that she was trying to deal with the situation as best she could.

When the words finally came out, they sounded distant, almost mechanical, as though it was someone else who was speaking.

"A man came," she said, as she continued to rub her hands against the white material of the nightgown, even though she had by now rubbed them almost clean. "Mr. Randall," her voice trailed off for a second and she cleared her throat. "Whit," she continued, "went down to speak to him. He told me to go on to bed."

Payne stiffened. He could hardly believe that she was telling him she'd actually seen Whit's murderer.

"Man?" he demanded. "What man?"

She shook her head. "An Oriental man," she murmured.

She looked up at him, momentarily confused, wondering why he was asking her all these questions when all she could think of was the fact that she was alone now, that she had no place to turn. She closed her eyes for an instant and her father's face sprang into her mind, and with it her father's voice, smug and mocking, telling her that he'd told her she was a fool to leave his house and now she must live with the fruits of her own stupidity. She forced the image away, looking back at Payne, hoping that he would see she was giving him what little she knew, that she was trying to please him. She wished he would release her and leave her alone.

But he either didn't see, or else he didn't care.
"What did the man look like?" he demanded.

She shook her head again. She tried to remember, tried desperately, but her mind had gone blank. She remembered standing at the top of the flight of stairs and looking down, remembered seeing the black-clad figure, even remembered that he'd seemed angry. But his features had disappeared from the memory completely. This time she had nothing more to offer Payne, nothing that she might hope would appease him.

"I don't know," she cried softly. "A man. Wearing those black pajamas. I don't know."

"Damn it, you saw him," he shouted. "How can you not remember?"

She bit her lip and tried to fight the tears that welled up in her eyes, but couldn't manage to banish them. "I can't remember," she sobbed softly. "I just can't remember."

He stared down at her and found that despite himself, his anger with her was beginning to ebb. He couldn't bully her any more, he realized. She was simply too terrified and too wretched for him to consider worsening her misery.

"I'm sorry," he said softly. "It'll come back to you. Don't try to think about it now."

She looked up at him again, thankful that he seemed to have forgiven her her sin. Her gaze drifted to Whit's still body. She couldn't believe it, even looking at his body; still she couldn't believe it.

"How can he be dead?" she asked him, as though he could make some meaning of what had happened.

Her expression and the hurt Payne saw in her eyes startled him. She seemed so dazed, so completely lost, while he was becoming more and more calm, even distant, as though he were cutting himself off from the pain. She'd hardly known Whit, yet she was obviously completely shattered by what had happened. And he, despite the dully aching sense of loss he felt, was somehow regaining his wits, somehow becoming strangely withdrawn and objective.

He realized his professional training seemed to have taken charge almost without his being aware of it, pushing aside the natural inclination to mourn. He felt something hard and determined inside him, and he knew that if it was the last thing he did, he would solve the mystery of his brother's murder.

Whatever his resolve, however, and despite the infuriating sense of futility at knowing Aura had seen the man and still could not describe him, he did not press her. He could see it was useless to try to question her any further, at least for a while. He released his hold on her shoulders and straightened up.

"Stay where you are," he told her.

He stood over her, waiting for her absent nod before he turned and went into the store. When he returned a moment later with a blanket, he saw she was staring at the blank wall beside her. He understood her reluctance to look at Whit's body, even sympathized when he saw her jump as he approached her.

"It's just me," he assured her, as he wrapped the blanket around her shoulders. His hands absently touched her skin, and he withdrew them quickly, leaving her to pull the blanket tight herself. "I'm going to find someone to send for the sheriff," he told her. "I won't be gone long." He took a step back, but hesitated as he saw the empty look in her eyes. "Are you all right?" he asked her softly.

She seemed startled by the question.

"Yes," she murmured. "I'm all right."

She turned her gaze back to the blank beige wall by the stairs.

He stared at her for an instant longer before he turned and walked out into the night.

It was, Aura thought, the longest night of her life. When the mantel clock struck three, she looked up at it, completely startled. Surely it must be much later than that, she thought, as she vainly waited for the sound of the chimes to continue and found it didn't. She huddled into the warmth of the blanket. Surely it must be morning, she told herself. How can it possibly still be the same endless night?

She looked up and found the man sitting opposite her had a decidedly impatient look. She had to force herself to remember what it was he had asked her. There had been so many questions, and now they all seemed to converge in her mind into a pointless jumble.

Sheriff James Dougherty cleared his throat pointedly. "I'm waiting, Mrs. Randall," he said. "I asked what the man looked like."

Aura nodded, remembering, then bit her lips. All this was getting them nowhere, and she wondered how many more times he would ask.

"I told you," she said to the sheriff's question for what seemed the hundredth time, "I can't remember what he looked like." Her voice began to shake, and she could hear her own uncertainty. How could she be so incompetent as not to be able to remember, she asked herself. She closed her eyes and thought, picturing it in her mind, but still the stranger's face was a blank, just as it had been each time she'd tried to remember. She wished more than anything she could answer the question, wished she could give both Payne and the sheriff what they both so obviously wanted. "All I can remember was that he was Oriental, and that he was dressed in black. But that's all. I've tried, but I can't remember any more."

Dougherty scowled, obviously less than pleased. "Try, Mrs. Randall," he told her.

"I'm sorry," she murmured. "I'm trying. I really am trying."

He let his eyes narrow as he stared at her. He was a large man, with thinning red hair and blue eyes so pale they seemed almost colorless. He was obviously uncomfortable with his own bulk, and ill at ease in the cluttered parlor. He sat like a man who was afraid to move lest he turn and break something.

"Let's try it differently," he said. "Was he tall or short?" he asked, his tone dull but demanding.

Aura closed her eyes and tried to remember, but it was useless. She shook her head.

"I don't know," she said. "I was at the top of the stairs looking down at him. I had no way to judge."

"Taller than Mr. Randall?" he pressed.

She shook her head again, this time in negation. "No, not so tall as that," she replied. It was an easy enough question to answer. Save for Payne, she doubted there were many men as tall as Whit had been.

"Shorter than Mr. Randall," Dougherty repeated and made a note in a small notebook he held on his lap.

Payne hissed angrily. "My brother was six foot three," he interjected, his disgust with Dougherty's methods quite obvious. "There aren't many men in the whole of San Francisco taller than he was. And like as not, none of those few Chinese. This is getting us nowhere."

Dougherty's eyes shifted from his notes to Aura's face and then on to Payne's.

"You're an investigator for Wells Fargo, aren't you,

51

Mr. Randall?" he asked. There was a hint of dislike in his tone, the suggestion that he didn't approve of the elitism of private investigatory agencies. "Perhaps you might explain what you are doing here in San Francisco?"

Payne bristled at the insinuation in Dougherty's tone, as though he were suggesting Payne had come to San Francisco for the purpose of killing his own brother. But even through his anger he felt a pang of conscience. He couldn't shake the feeling that Whit had been killed because he'd offered to help with the investigation of the counterfeit bills. And, in a way, that made Payne responsible for his death.

Not that he had even the slightest intention of discussing the matter with Sheriff James Dougherty. Wells Fargo had very definite rules about keeping its business in its own house, and certain rules had to be followed. Even aside from that, though, Payne knew he wouldn't have offered the sheriff any information other than that which was absolutely necessary. From the minute he'd set eyes on the man, he'd realized he neither liked nor trusted Dougherty. The feeling might be groundless, but still he was not about to go against it.

"I came to help my brother celebrate his wedding," he hissed in reply to the sheriff's question.

"Well, he didn't celebrate it in the usual manner, now, did he?" Dougherty asked in a snide tone. "Most bridegrooms, to my limited knowledge, don't end up shot dead on their wedding night."

Aura shuddered at the bluntness of his words and the absent way he spoke of Whit's death. She thought he was more put out about the fact that he had been roused from bed than concerned that a murder had been committed. She pulled the blanket more tightly around her as if it might protect her from the sheer callousness that seemed to emanate from the man.

Payne noticed the shudder and the lost expression that accompanied it. He felt a sudden wash of pity, realizing how uncomfortable this must be for her. There was no question of how terrifying the experience of finding Whit's body had been. Dougherty's questions were only making matters worse.

"Surely you must be done with your questions for tonight, Sheriff?" he asked pointedly. "My brother's wife has been through a good deal tonight. It seems only civil to allow her some rest."

"I believe the grieving widow arrived here yesterday and had only a few hours to accustom herself to the role of being a wife," Dougherty replied with an unpleasant smile. "I think we can safely dispense with the fantasy that she's prostrate with grief," he added, and darted a knowing look at Aura, the sort a wolf might give a chicken he was about to make his evening meal.

"And I think you can safely keep a civil tongue in your mouth," Payne snapped. He was sick and tired of the leering looks Dougherty kept giving Aura, as though Whit's wife were now nothing more than a commodity displayed on the shelves of the store downstairs.

Dougherty shrugged, acting as though he was charitably willing to overlook Payne's comments in view of the immediacy of his loss. He studied his notes in silence for a moment, then looked up at Payne.

"You say nothing was stolen from the store?" he asked.

Payne gritted his teeth and shook his head.

"I told you," he replied. "I'm not all that familiar with the contents of the store, but from what I could see, nothing seemed to be missing."

"But there was a good deal disturbed?" Dougherty pressed.

"You saw it," Payne countered. "That's certainly not the way a neat shopkeeper leaves his domain."

"So as far as you know, then, it could be a simple case of robbery," Dougherty said.

Payne balled his hands into fists.

"No, it could not," he said through clenched teeth. "From what I could see, nothing was missing."

"Well, then, perhaps the murderer was searching for something," Dougherty suggested. "Perhaps he was looking for the cash box and was frightened off by Mrs. Randall's scream."

"Whit never kept a cash box in the store when he wasn't there," Payne told him.

Dougherty shrugged. "The thief had no way to know that. It *could* have been simple robbery."

"A robbery isn't simple if it involves murder," Payne hissed, without bothering to hide the exasperation that had crept into his tone.

"Well, now, let's consider murder, then," Dougherty returned with a mean little smile. "There's no bit of trouble your brother might have mentioned to you?" asked. "There's no one you know of who might have had a score to settle with him?"

"Whit wasn't the sort to make enemies," Payne said. "People liked him."

Dougherty smiled again, his expression as mean and unpleasant as a smile can be.

"Well, it looks like someone sure as hell didn't like him," he said, as he snapped his notebook closed.

He smiled yet again, then chuckled, apparently delighted by the unexpected wittiness of his own remark and not the least put off by the fact that neither Payne nor Aura seemed the least amused by it. Sobering, he pushed himself to his feet and then stood for a moment, staring awkwardly at what must have seemed to him a minefield of furniture in the cluttered room.

"I take it you have no more questions, Sheriff?" Payne asked.

Dougherty nodded.

"It looks to me like your brother was killed by a thief—a simple case of robbery gone wrong. There's nothing more to ask, except for a description of the thief, which Mrs. Randall seems incapable of providing at this time," he said. "If you think of anything else," he fixed a sharp glance on Aura, "or if your memory suddenly improves, don't keep the fact to yourself."

"I'm sure neither of us would dream of it, Sheriff," Payne replied with a deprecating smile.

Dougherty seemed about to say something, but then thought better of it. He stared again at the hodge-podge of furniture littering his path, then turned and threaded his way through the maze of overstuffed chairs, settees, and tables, making his way carefully to the stairs.

Aura didn't move as he left, didn't even turn to watch him go. She just sat staring at the far wall, to all appearances dazed and distant, save for the fact that she cringed slightly each time she heard the thick sound of one of his footsteps on the stairs.

She hated that man, she thought, hated his crude manners and his smug arrogance. Even after she'd heard the door close behind him and knew he was gone, still she thought she could hear his tread on the stairs echoing through the room. His odor, an unpleasant smell composed of equal parts stale beer and cigars, lingered mercilessly on in the room after him.

"A pleasant sort," Payne muttered after a long moment of silence. "And a fool. I wonder what rock he crawled out from under."

Aura stirred, forced her attention to him, and then nodded. The long interview with Dougherty seemed to have sapped away the last drop of energy from her. That, and the memory of finding Whit's body. She was beginning to feel as though she was crumbling inside, and she couldn't think of any way to remedy the problem.

Payne stared at her for a moment. Her face was still unnaturally pale, and she looked very small in the bulk of the blanket she still held wrapped around her. Staring at her, he found himself wondering why he'd become so angry with Dougherty over the sheriff's leering glances at her, wondered why he cared. After all, Dougherty was probably right—she certainly hadn't known Whit long enough to claim she felt any love for him. So why, then, he wondered, should he feel this urge to protect her?

"You really should get some sleep," he told her.

She darted a look in the direction of Whit's bedroom and he saw her pale cheeks become even whiter.

"I couldn't," she replied. "Not there."

"You can take the room I've been using," he offered. "I can sleep out here." He gestured vaguely toward the settees.

Under almost any other circumstance, Aura would have laughed. It was only too apparent that the three settees that framed the fireplace, while all thickly upholstered and unquestionably comfortable, were far too short to accommodate his tall frame. She was about to offer him Whit's bed—her wedding bed—but stopped before she uttered even a word. Even the thought seemed sacrilegious.

She shuddered and shook her head.

"I really don't think I can sleep yet," she told him.

She looks so lost and frightened, Payne thought, as he stared at her. Just for an instant he allowed himself to consider how vulnerable she appeared, how fragile and pretty. And before he knew it, he found himself wondering what the thick mass of loose auburn hair that hung around her shoulders would feel like if he touched it, wondering if those pale cheeks were as soft as the lamplight made them seem.

He swore silently, cursing himself as a treasonous bastard. He forced himself to empty his mind of thoughts of her. He might not think of himself as a totally admirable person, but he was certainly above carnal thoughts of his dead brother's wife. The last thing he intended to do was betray Whit.

He pushed himself out of his chair and crossed the room to the table that held Whit's liquor. He lifted the decanter and poured whiskey into two glasses, then returned to the settee where Aura still sat, huddled into her blanket, looking as though she was afraid to move.

"Drink this," he told her, and held out one of the glasses. "It'll help you to sleep."

She looked at the glass for a moment, as though she wasn't quite sure if it might not be poison. Then she shrugged, reached out, and took it from him. As soon as he'd given it to her, Payne turned away. She shrugged. He didn't like her, he'd made that fact clear enough from the first. She had no reason to expect him to change his mind, especially not now.

She lifted the glass to her lips and took a small taste. It wasn't at all like the champagne had been. No bubbles, no tingle on her tongue. Instead, it seemed to explode in her mouth, and, when she'd swallowed, turn to liquid fire in her belly. She gasped softly.

Payne seem oblivious to her now, as he busied himself with the contents of his own glass and lost himself to the contemplation of the half dozen framed daguerreotypes that, along with a noisy chiming clock, decorated the mantel. If nothing else, the pictures managed to distract his thoughts from Aura. After a moment, he took one of them down and returned to settle himself into the chair opposite hers.

"He was a good brother," he murmured, before taking another long swallow of the whiskey. The danger, it seemed, was past now. All he could think about was Whit. "He pretty much raised me after our mother died. My father's second wife couldn't be bothered."

Aura leaned forward and looked at the picture in his hand. It was of two boys, both dressed in their uncomfortable best. The younger, perhaps five or six years old, was seated uncertainly on a pony. The older boy, already unmistakably Whit, although much younger and far less substantial than the man she'd met and married that day, stood beside him with a comforting hand on his shoulder.

"That's you?" she asked, pointing to the younger boy, the one seated on the pony.

Payne nodded. "It was taken just before she died," he replied.

"My mother died when I was ten," Aura told him softly. "My stepmother sounds much like yours, too busy with her own life to take any bother with another woman's children." And only eight years older than she was, Aura thought, and not of the temperament to care about anyone's needs but her own.

He glanced up, startled by her words, as though he'd never considered she'd had a life before she'd come to San Francisco.

"It would seem you and Whit had something in common after all," he said.

She shrugged. "There would have been more," she said, her tone certain. "I know there would have been more. I liked him."

"He was easy to like," Payne replied. He lifted his

glass and emptied the remaining liquor in it in one long swallow. He handed the picture to her, and pushed himself out of the chair. "A refill?" he asked, before he glanced at the nearly untouched glass on the table beside her.

At his mention of the whiskey, she realized that the sensation that had originally seemed to her so much like swallowing liquid fire had moderated and left her with a not unpleasant feeling of warmth, a warmth that didn't stop in her stomach but had been slowly and comfortingly radiating throughout her body. She shook her head, rejecting his offer, but reached for the glass and took a second tentative taste of the whiskey. Braced this time for the initial heat of the stuff, she was surprised to find this second taste not nearly so fiery as the first had been, and even more surprised to find that, if she concentrated on it, she could feel the tendrils of pleasant warmth that followed as they slowly crept through her limbs. She took another swallow, this one a bit less tentative than the last.

It took her a moment to realize Payne hadn't returned to the chair beside hers. She turned, and saw he was standing once again in front of the mantel and looking at each of the daguerreotypes displayed there. Carrying the picture of the two boys and her glass, she stood and crossed the room to join him.

"You'll miss him," she murmured, as she returned the picture to its place on the mantel. She saw he was staring at a likeness of Whit as a young man and himself, now no longer a child, but a gangly fifteen-year-old.

"I already miss him," he replied. He pointed to the last in the row of pictures, this again of the two of them, only in this one the younger man was unmistakably the man who was now standing beside her and Whit had matured into the man she'd met the previous

59

day. They were both dressed in rough clothing and posed along with pickaxes and shovels. "We came out here six years ago to try our luck at mining," he told her, his tone far away, lost in memory. "It didn't take us long to realize we weren't cut out for that particular sort of misery. Anyway, Whit decided to stay here and I took half a dozen jobs before I ended back in New York, working for Wells Fargo. We didn't spend much time together after that, him here with his safe little business, me out chasing whoever my betters told me to chase, but still I always felt close, as though we were part of each other."

Much of what he was telling her passed over Aura's head. All she really heard was the pain in his words as he spoke about Whit.

"I know how that is," she told him softly. "Delia and I were never much alike, but still we've been close all our lives. The whole time on the *Laura Charles* on the way out here I kept trying to think of ways to make her understand why I left. Not that it mattered, really. It was just that I couldn't bear to imagine her thinking ill of me."

She lifted the last picture, the one of the two young men dressed in miner's clothing, and stared at the tiny sepia-toned faces that looked up at her. Payne's expression was intense, knowing, already giving a hint of that slightly superior stare she'd found so disturbing when she'd met him. But there was none of that in Whit's expression. Despite the sober expression the photographer had no doubt demanded of him, there was still laughter in his intelligent, dark eyes. He seemed to be marking a passing phase in his life, just as those earlier pictures of the two boys marked phases in growing up, and he appeared to be delighted with the adventure he'd completed and only too ready to find another.

She felt a sharp pang of regret, realizing she would never get the chance to know that man.

"He'd have taken you to a photographer in a day or two," Payne told her. "He liked to mark occasions, and his marriage would have been something he'd never have let pass unnoted."

Aura felt her throat constrict at his words, and she was struck with the absolute finality of what had happened. There would never be a picture of her standing at Whit's side now, never be a likeness to mark what ought to have been the most important occasion of her life. She felt the veneer of calm she'd somehow salvaged in order to face Dougherty's endless questions begin to slip away from her.

She returned the picture to its place and crossed the room, finally stopping when she reached the top of the stairs.

She found herself staring down at the landing below. She couldn't keep her eyes from finding the bloodstains still on the bare wood floor, obvious even in the dim light. What was worse, she couldn't keep herself from thinking about Whit's body, lying now just a few feet from where he had fallen when the bullet had stricken him, laid out in the store to await burial in the morning. But when she stared down, she could almost see him lying there just as she'd found him.

She shivered as the recognition returned to her of just how totally alone she was now. She was filled, as she'd been when Payne had told her Whit was dead, with the same sense of bewilderment, the knowledge that she was lost in a strange world with absolutely no idea of where to turn or what to do.

Chapter Four

Aura stirred. She realized she was allowing herself to sink into abject self-pity. That was stupid, she chided herself. If she was alone now, if there was no one on whom she could depend to help her, then she had better learn to depend on herself. And to put it simply, wallowing in self-pity didn't improve her chances for becoming independent and self-sufficient.

She realized she was still holding the glass of whiskey. She raised it to her lips. This time she didn't stop at a tentative sip. Determined, she took a healthy swallow of the stuff.

She waited, expecting to feel a wave of alcoholic warmth that would ease the ache she felt inside her, that would help bolster her against the sense of loss and her deep fear of loneliness. But for some reason, this time the whiskey seemed to have no effect on her.

She glanced down at the amber liquid, thinking how unfair it was that even this could not dull the hurt. She took yet another swallow as she turned her glance back to the place where Whit's body had lain. A dark ache tied the pit of her stomach into a hard knot. It was easy to tell herself she had to be strong, but something else entirely to banish the hurt.

She didn't notice that Payne had come up behind

her until he put his hands on her shoulders and turned her to face him.

"Don't look down there," he told her. "It's better if you try not to think about it."

He was right, she knew. She oughtn't to have looked, and she should try to stop thinking about it. But the image of Whit's body was indelibly printed on her memory. As much as she might want to, she knew there was no way she would ever be able to force herself to forget it.

She looked away and closed her eyes, but it did no good. Trying to escape it only made the memory that much sharper. The scene reappeared in her mind, grim and eerie in the flickering dim light, the grisly trail of blood slowly spreading itself on the bare wood floor. And Whit's body, growing pale and cold as the red stain crept from the wound. She tried to blot the memory out, but she couldn't stop thinking about it.

And despite her determination to keep herself from sinking into self-pity, she felt hot tears begin to well up inside her. Her throat grew so tight she thought she might choke. No matter her resolve. She was simply too tired and too frightened and too thoroughly miserable to try to fight the need to cry any longer. She knew Payne must think her a fool, knew that his was the far greater loss, but still she couldn't hold back the tears.

"I'm sorry," she murmured, as she felt the hot drops begin to slide down her cheeks. "I, I don't mean to."

She looked up at him, staring into the cold, deep blue of his eyes. He hates me, she thought. She bit her lip hard and looked away.

He kept his hands on her shoulders, refusing to release her despite the fact that it was obvious she was trying to escape him.

"There's no harm in it," he assured her, his tone

63

suddenly gentle and understanding. "All this can't have been easy for you."

That startled her, not only the words, but the compassion she heard in his voice. Somehow she'd not expected that from him. He might be distantly understanding, perhaps even show an aloof sort of kindness, but she'd thought real compassion beyond him.

When he put his arm around her and led her away from the stairs back into the room, she didn't protest. She wanted to be away from the sight of the bloodstains and the memories they roused. She was only too willing to let him draw her from them.

He brought her back to the sofa, and she sat, staring up at him through the mist of liquid in her eyes. This time, rather than pointedly keeping his distance and sitting opposite her, he settled himself beside her.

He was silent for a moment, and sat simply staring at her. Then he put his hand on the glass she still grasped.

"I think you've had enough of this," he told her.

She looked down at the glass as though she'd never seen it before. For an instant, she found herself wondering where it had come from, how she'd come to be holding it. She absently noted that it was nearly empty, then realized with a sudden sense of shock that she'd been responsible for nearly draining it. That was impossible, she thought. She didn't drink whiskey. Her father would not approve; there would be the direst of consequences were he to learn she'd done such a thing.

Bewildered and ashamed, she readily released the glass. Payne took it from her and put it on a table along with his own.

Aura's thoughts returned to the tears. They were streaming down her face now, and she couldn't stop them. She put the heels of her hands against her eyes, trying to force them back. She was beginning to feel confused, ashamed not only of the fact that she'd drunk so much whiskey, but of the tears as well. She told herself she had no right to tears.

"I'm sorry," she murmured again.

"It's all right," Payne told her softly.

He watched her for a while, realizing the tears didn't surprise him. The truth was, he'd begun to wonder how she'd held up as well as she had for as long as she had. The more he thought about it, the more he was coming to realize just how terrified she must be. This was certainly a far cry from the wedding night she ought rightfully to have expected.

He put his arm around her shoulders and pulled her gently to him. She resisted, stiffening and pulling away, but only for an instant. Too tired and too frightened to fight him and her own inclination, she fell against his chest and gave up trying to hold it all inside. She let herself lie against him and began to sob.

He closed his eyes as he held her. It occurred to him then that he'd not completely buried his own sense of loss, that whatever his resolve to find Whit's murderer, still it didn't diminish the empty ache that had begun to blossom inside him as the finality of death finally struck home. But the feel of Aura in his arms somehow eased the hurt.

He realized that he needed to comfort her as much as she needed comforting at that moment, that holding her let him come to terms with his own loss. He'd been so determined to deal with Whit's killer that he'd forgotten he needed to accept the pain and mourn. But with each of Aura's sobs, he felt the hard knot of hurt inside his belly begin to loosen just a bit.

The tears, Aura found, were a release that slowly uprooted the feeling of total panic that had been gripping her ever since she'd looked down and seen Whit's body lying at the foot of the stairs. She was still afraid, certainly, still aware of how completely alone she was, but the immediate gripping terror was slowly beginning to ease its hold of her.

She was dimly aware of the feeling of Payne's hands gently stroking her back, but that was something apart, almost remote. For a long while there was only the physical release of the tears and the slowly ebbing panic. Everything else was too distant to have any meaning for her, save for the feeling of warmth and protection that his arms temporarily provided.

Eventually the tears finally dried up. Aura felt drained and spent, almost too exhausted to move. Her inclination was to lie as she was, to close her eyes. It would be good, she thought, not to have to think at all, to escape, even for a little while, into sleep.

But as she began to drift off, she became aware, finally, of the feeling of warmth coming from Payne's body, the feeling of his arms around her, holding her, his hands stroking her. And with the recognition came the terrifying realization that she liked it.

Suddenly the feeling of being so intimately close to him became almost more frightening to her than the fear of being alone. She stiffened and pulled away. This is wrong, she told herself, completely wrong.

But once she was no longer supporting herself against him, she became lightheaded and disoriented. The room began spinning slowly around her, and the sensation quickly became more and more pronounced. It must be the whiskey, she realized. It had not been without effect, after all. And all that champagne she'd drunk with dinner. But no, dinner had been hours before, when Whit had still been alive, when her life had seemed finally to have found the path she'd always wanted it to follow. That had been a lifetime before. Surely the wine couldn't still be having an effect on her. Or perhaps it could. This was her first experience with alcohol and she had no idea of its potency.

She let herself fall back against Payne, humbled by the fact that her body had turned against her. It was perplexing to her to realize she couldn't order her own limbs to move, couldn't depend on her sense of balance to keep her steady. Even stranger to her was the fact that she was so close to Payne, that she could feel the warmth of his chest through the linen fabric of his shirt that had grown damp with her tears, that she could sense more than feel the dull thud of his heartbeat. Strange, all of it, and excitingly mysterious.

She didn't move, afraid that if she did she would have to return to a very unpleasant reality. For a moment, she thought, if she stayed perfectly still, she could escape the fact that she had been married and widowed that same day, could escape the fact that it was wrong for her to find pleasure in the feel of Payne's arms around her. If she didn't move, she told herself, she wouldn't have to think of anything at all. All she wanted, she thought, was to stay where she was, with her head against his chest and his arms around her, and sleep for a thousand years.

But then he stirred, and she felt a chill of loss as he lifted his hands from her back and slid them to her shoulders and then to her cheeks. He lifted her face until she was gazing up at him and began to wipe away the wet from her cheeks.

She didn't object. She began to feel a hint of the odd spinning inside her head again, and she was sure that she would have been incapable of keeping her head upright had he not been holding her.

Payne stared down into the deep green of her eyes as though he were seeing them for the first time, just as he seemed to see the thick tumble of her auburn curls as if they'd only that moment been bared to him. She was so incredibly small and fragile in his arms. He felt a thick lurch inside himself as he realized that she looked unbearably beautiful.

Perhaps it was the quantity of whiskey he'd so quickly drunk, perhaps the pain that looking at the pictures of his past had roused. Whatever the reason, in that instant his inhibitions had disappeared completely.

He found he had no desire to take the effort to search for them. Instead, he lowered his lips to Aura's and kissed her.

The touch of Payne's lips to hers was a revelation to Aura. Nothing she'd ever experienced before had felt like that, nothing had tasted quite the way that kiss had. And nothing had ever made her feel the way that kiss made her feel.

The kiss Whit had given her after the wedding ceremony had certainly been pleasant enough, pleasant in the way the champagne had been pleasant, light and gently exciting. And she'd been charmed by the way he'd seemed so tentative with her, so gentle. But Payne's kiss was anything but tentative. It burned the way that first taste of whiskey had burned inside her, sending thick rivers of molten liquid through her veins, and awakening her to feelings she'd never even imagined she might experience.

She let her head fall back, and he pressed his lips against her neck. When he did, she felt her heart begin to throb, felt her own pulse grow thick and sharp within her. Her heart had never beat like this before. For an instant she thought she was about to die.

And it was, in a way, a small death—it was a death and a birth at the same moment, for his kiss woke within her what she knew must be passion, and with its

68

birth, she also knew, must come the end of innocence.

If she'd stopped and thought at that moment, she'd have been haunted by the thoughts that she'd most wanted to avoid, the knowledge that this must be wrong. More than that was the simple fact that she'd been wed and widowed within the previous twenty-four hours, and that she was in no condition to face the consequences of yet another permanent change to her life.

But she didn't stop to think. Her mind was clouded by the alcohol she'd drunk, as well as by hurt and shock and disappointment and fear. Thought was, at least temporarily, not only impossible for her, it was also the one thing she most wanted to escape. If she didn't allow herself to think, she wouldn't be forced to remember.

And so, rather than fleeing from Payne's embrace as both prudence and propriety would have dictated, she closed her eyes and allowed herself to escape into the mysterious world to which that embrace carried her. It was an exciting, mysterious place, completely alien from everything she'd ever known. His touch left tendrils of liquid fire snaking through her body, left her buoyant and floating on waves of passion. More than that, it swept all thought of the events of the previous twenty-four hours from her mind, swept away all the unpleasant memories. It left her with only the absolute of the moment, and the searing waves that enveloped her.

She hardly noticed when he pushed the stained nightgown down and away from her shoulders, hardly noticed that he'd shrugged himself free of his own clothing. She hardly noticed anything at all save for the effect the lips he pressed against her bared breasts had on her. Her skin burned where he touched it, and yet the fire was so sweet she wanted it to go on forever burning inside her. She put her hands to the back of his neck and held him tight and close to her.

Payne had no idea where the need had come from, why it had suddenly burst forth full-blown within him, why it was so great that it seemed to overpower all rational thought. Reason would have told him the path on which he'd embarked was not only foolhardy but dangerous as well. Reason, though, he'd cast aside the moment he'd kissed her. Now he only felt the need, and the desperate yearning ache inside.

Had she pushed him away, he certainly would have contained himself—he was neither so drunk nor so lost in his grief for his dead brother that he could have salved his hurt with rape. But she didn't reject him, and more than that, he could feel the growing heat inside her, could feel the pounding wake of her pulse beneath his lips. There was no question but that the same tide was rising in her that she'd roused in him. The same need to heal the loss and the hurt with intimacy was pushing them both.

He pressed his lips to her breasts and her belly and her thighs, touched her bared flesh with his fingers, stroking the pale silk of her skin. That skin was no longer cold and pale, but rosy now, and warm beneath his hands, heated by the inner fires he stoked with his touch. His senses filled with her and the insistently growing, pounding want for her. Never had he felt the need for a woman he felt for her at that moment. Never had he felt a hunger so demanding and so strong.

When he lifted his lips to hers again, when he nudged her legs apart with his own, Aura mutely complied, spreading herself beneath him at his urging. She was unsure and slightly tentative, but completely without the will or the desire to protest. She didn't want to do anything but follow him wherever it was he wanted to lead her.

That first thrust felt to Aura like a shaft of pure fire entering her body. It snaked through her, rousing a flow of steaming lava that poured through her veins, searing her until it seemed as though the heat touched every fiber of her, entered every particle of her. She cried out, more from surprise than fear or hurt, for nothing had prepared her for either the act or the repercussion of it that radiated through her.

Payne froze when he heard that cry. He held her close in his arms, momentarily confused until he realized what it meant, until he realized what it was he'd done.

Of course, he told himself, remembering what Whit had told him, she was from a good family back East, and never married. Not a common shop girl or mill girl who might have had a small adventure or perhaps even once or twice supplemented her meager earnings the only way available to her. How could he have thought her anything but a virgin?

And he ought to have known, even if Whit had told him nothing; he ought to have known. Even if he'd had only her educated speech and manner by which to judge, it should have been immediately apparent to him.

The simple truth was, he hadn't thought, hadn't felt anything but his own aching hunger. And her wakened passion—that, too, he'd felt as strongly as he'd felt his own. He could tell himself that he'd never have gone so far had he not felt that, had he not known her to be as aroused as he himself had been. But no matter how he excused himself, he knew nothing could change the fact of what he'd done. The act was absolute and irreversible.

He'd deflowered his dead brother's bride. As much

71

as he might wish it were otherwise, there was no way to go back and change that fact.

He looked down at her, searching in her eyes for some sign of anger, a hint of disgust, some show of the loathing he was beginning to feel for himself. But there was none of that. Instead, there was wonder, and what he thought might be a hint of fear.

He put his hands on her temples and pushed away the dampened curls.

"I've hurt you," he murmured.

She looked up at him. It took a moment until her gaze slowly focused. The fear in her eyes grew sharper as for an instant she thought he might stop, might leave her lost and alone in the strange ocean in which he'd set her afloat.

"No," she whispered. She reached up to him, wrapping her arms around him, wanting to hold him close to her, to keep the feeling. "Tonight there is no way you could hurt me."

She knew she had never spoken words that were more true. There would never be another day in which she would gain and lose so much, never be another night when she'd have so much loss to mourn. Whoever had fired that bullet that evening had claimed not one, but two victims. In that single instant, he'd sealed the fate of two human beings, stealing Whit's life and robbing her of her future as well. She had nothing left to lose now, nothing but the mystifying and wondrous feelings Payne was igniting within her. The thought of giving that up so quickly, too, of having it snatched away from her just as Whit and her dreams had been, was more than she could bear.

She wanted more than anything to tell Payne that she wanted him to go on, that she wished he would never leave her, never stop touching her as he touched her now. But the words died long before she could force herself to utter them. In the world from which she came, a woman did not say such things, at least, not a decent woman, an honest woman. It was impossible for her to make so immodest an admission, completely unthinkable. Instead, she pressed herself to him, finding his lips with hers, unsure whether such forwardness would please or disgust him, but unable to think of any other way to tell him what she could never say in words.

At the touch of her lips to his, Payne pulled her close. He knew that it was insane to think he could have turned away at that moment. He wanted her, and it was obvious she was willing. Right and wrong, respect, fidelity—they all became nothing more than just sounds that had, for that moment at least, lost all meaning for him. There was only the moment, and the feel of her in his arms, and the searing need that burned inside him.

He pressed himself to her. Aura felt herself envelop him, felt the rush of fire racing through her body. Nothing had prepared her for the overwhelming flood of feeling that filled her. She abandoned herself to it, jettisoning thought and reason. She clung to him, trusting him to keep her safe in the roiling sea that surrounded her.

Aura found herself clinging to him, her hands locked onto his shoulders, holding herself as close to him as she could make herself, so close she wasn't sure where her own body ended and his began. Never in even her wildest thoughts had she come close to imagining the sensation of flesh against flesh, the taste of his tongue on hers or the heat of his lips and hands touching her. But mostly it was the feel of him deep within her that disoriented and confused her. It almost seemed as though he possessed a previously missing part of her, as though she had spent her life incom-

73

plete, waiting for this single moment. She'd never felt like this, never before felt herself so much a part of another human being.

For a fleeting instant, she wondered if it was possible that people did such things back in Fall River. It seemed impossible that even a single moment of such pleasure would ever be allowed in the constricted and joylessly dour little world into which she'd been born.

Payne moved inside her, at first helping her, guiding her movements with his hands until she realized that some knowing creature deep within her had been born with the knowledge of this ritual dance, that there was really no need for her to be taught what had been bequeathed her by Eve. Her body accepted his, welcomed his as though it was an extension of her own. And for that moment, she felt that she had been born, purposely fashioned, for this single act and no other.

She drifted, clinging to him, totally lost in the swell of passion that claimed her. She had no thought to fight the waves that buffeted her, waves that lifted her and tossed her like a bit of flotsam set adrift in a storm. They grew ever higher until finally they crashed down on her. She was sure she would drown as she felt herself being pulled into their bottomless depths.

It terrified her, that first, shattering release. If what had come before had mystified and intrigued her, this powerful explosion that filled her body frightened her as nothing ever had before. She realized she had been robbed of the last vestige of control, that whatever it was that ruled her body at that moment, it came not from herself, but from him. Whatever happened to her now, she realized, was at his whim, for she had no hope of determining her own fate.

Such a pure, sweet agony this was. Aura felt lost within herself, felt as though her body had shattered and dissolved. It seemed as though they had been melted in the same crucible, bathed in liquid fire until she was herself no longer but had merged with him, become a part of him.

This, she thought, is what it means to be a woman.

She pressed herself to him, unaware that she had begun to tremble uncontrollably. She heard a sound, something far away, a deep, low moan. She didn't realize that she had uttered it.

Payne felt her trembling release. Somehow the knowledge that he had brought her this pleasure was a greater spur to his own passion than anything he'd ever felt before. It dissolved his self control, leaving him bewildered by the powerful effect she had on him even as he gave himself up to the sweet wave of rapture that carried him with her.

They lay together, breathless and spent, arms and legs still entwined, both rapt in their own thoughts of bewildered wonder. Aura was totally lost in the moment, completely confused by the powerful changes he'd caused in her, by the strange and alien creature he'd brought to life inside her. And Payne, who had certainly not thought himself inexperienced in such matters, found himself bewildered by the realization that he had never felt anything quite so intense, quite so shattering, as he'd felt with her.

He held her close, wrapped in his arms, afraid to speak to her, sure that any words he might utter would break the spell and return him to a reality that was too painful to think about at that moment. He touched her gently, caressed her bare shoulders and back, mutely pressing his lips to hers when he thought she might be about to whisper something, stealing away the words before she could speak.

She followed his lead, so tired that words seemed an

effort greater than she could manage in any case. She was more than willing to content herself with the physical warmth, the pleasure of his body close to hers, and the protection of his arms around her. She closed her eyes and allowed herself to drift. Payne pressed his lips against her eyes, her hair, and felt himself thankful when he heard her labored breathing begin to slow until it took on the measured, even cadence of sleep.

He lay with her a while longer as a sense of contentment filled him. He let his mind lose itself in the wonder of the feel of her body, warm and soft and vulnerable, close to his. It was a pleasant lapse, almost more pleasant for him than the act, for it allowed him to play the role of protector and comforter, the loyal guard who watched over her while she abandoned herself to the exhaustion that had finally laid its claim to her.

But the feeling of contentment could not last forever. All too quickly Payne's thoughts took hold of reality and memory returned, only to be met with a painfully sharp awareness of what he'd done. A hard edge of revulsion filled him. Here he lay, naked with his brother's wife, and Whit was not yet in the ground. He thought he might drown in the poisonous bile of his own self-contempt.

He extricated himself from her carefully, taking pains not to wake her. He was grateful that she had been so completely exhausted, for the last thing he wanted was for her to waken. The thought of being forced to talk to her, the prospect of facing her and feeling the same revulsion for her as he felt for himself, was odious to him. All he really wanted to do was turn his back to her and forget what had happened between them.

He hastily retrieved his clothing, quickly pulling on trousers and shirt. Then he found the blanket in which

76

he'd wrapped her earlier, lying on the floor near the sofa where she lay. He spread it over her, pausing only for an instant to touch her cheek with the back of his hand and let himself lapse, for a last brief instant, into wonder of the unexpected passion she'd roused in him.

But the lapse was brief, and he pulled his hand away as though the feel of her skin had burned him. He'd come here to help Whit, and now he found himself facing the far from pleasant possibility that he might have inadvertently been the instrument that had caused his brother's death. And no matter how he might lie to himself, no matter that he told himself he'd only wanted a release from the pain of Whit's loss, still he knew he could never escape the fact that he'd slept with his brother's wife.

He backed away from Aura, almost afraid she might waken and reach out for him. If she did, he wondered, would he have the strength to leave her, or would he abandon himself again to the sweet escape of her embrace? It was not a question he wanted to be forced to answer.

The first dim light of dawn made its way through the parlor windows. Aura woke, opening her eyes slowly as though some part of her were afraid of letting reality come too quickly through the mists of cast-off sleep. Accustomed during the previous weeks to waking in the cramped cabin on the *Laura Charles,* she was at first completely disoriented by her surroundings. She tried to concentrate, but thought seemed momentarily beyond her. She found herself staring up numbly at the floating dust motes that were illuminated by thin shafts of early daylight.

Finally her thoughts focused, and she darted questioning glances at her surroundings, forcing herself to try to remember where she was and how she'd gotten there. It seemed some part of her was trying to keep the memory at bay, and it took several moments until it all began slowly to come back to her. When it did, she wished she hadn't been so anxious to remember.

Images passed through her mind, fleeting images of Whit's dead body lying at the foot of the stairs intermingled with others, less shocking but no less painful. And then, of course, the final image, the memory of looking up at Payne's face and remembering what had happened between them. Even the memory sent a tremor through her body and set her heart racing. But the tremor passed, to be quickly replace by a shudder of shame.

"It must be a dream," she murmured, as she rubbed her eyes.

But it hadn't been a dream. The fact that she was lying on the sofa, naked and covered only by a blanket, was enough to confirm that it had really happened.

"Payne?"

She realized that she'd barely whispered, that if he was still somewhere in the house with her, the sound she'd made was hardly enough to rouse him. But the simple fact was, she knew she hoped he wasn't there. She didn't want to see him. She felt too much shame to face him.

She sat up, then wished she hadn't. Her head swam and her stomach rebelled at the movement, making her feel as though she might retch. She sat perfectly still for a long moment, waiting for the effects to slowly ebb until she thought she could control them.

The room was cold and empty. She shivered and pulled the blanket close. For a long while she sat and stared around her at the parlor as though she was examining it for evidence. It was there, more than

78

enough evidence, only too abundant for her peace of mind. There, on the table little more than an arm's length from her, were the two glasses, hers and Payne's, one still with a drop of whiskey in it. And there were the daguerreotypes, lined neatly on the mantel, the pictures that had brought Payne so much hurt. Finally her glance fell on her own cast-off nightdress, the thin white lawn darkly spotted with the ugly stains of blood.

Suddenly she began to shiver, and no matter how she huddled into the blanket, she couldn't make it stop. There was no escape for her. All of it had really happened the night before, Whit's death, that horrible policeman, and Payne. More than anything else, she knew that what had happened with Payne was real. And the fact that he'd left her to face the cold of morning alone told her only too clearly that he was not immune to the shame and regret that had settled into a hard, uncomfortable ball in the pit of her stomach.

It was inconceivable to her that she'd done such a thing. Aura, the coward; Aura, the pale little mouse who trembled not only at the prospect of punishment, but at even the merest thought of misdemeanor. How had such a timid, fearful creature done what she had done the night before?

It wasn't her fault, she cried out silently. She must have been drunk. Surely that was why her head felt so strange, why her stomach had lurched when she'd sat up. She'd been drunk and frightened and alone. Surely it could not have been her fault.

But those were just excuses, and she knew it. What had happened, had happened with her conscious agreement. Whatever protest she might make, still she could not change the truth.

Still shivering, she stood, moving very carefully for fear she might again disturb the delicate balance in her

79

stomach. She wrapped the blanket around herself and lifted the ruin of her nightgown. The stains of Whit's blood seemed to stare up at her, like an accusing finger, reminding her of her guilt.

She made her way to the bath she'd occupied with such delighted expectation the day before, hoping she could wash away the taint of her own sins even while she was aware that mere soap and water would never wash away the guilt she felt. Still, she knew she had no choice but to try. The day promised to be far more unpleasant in many ways than even the previous night had been. There would be that policeman to face again, that horrible Sheriff Dougherty, and then a funeral to be arranged. Though she might not have been much of a wife to Whitmore Randall, she was still his widow.

She was overcome with a suffocating feeling of hopelessness. This was an alien world to her, and she was alone in it. And there was unquestionably a great deal of unpleasantness to be faced.

But the worst of it, she knew, would be facing Payne Randall.

Chapter Five

"Good afternoon."

Aura looked up and swallowed uncomfortably. She'd spent the morning compulsively tidying and worrying as she waited for Payne to return. Now that he had, she realized she'd been expecting something a good deal more dramatic than a simple exchange of mundane greetings. She wasn't sure what, but something.

Now that she considered the matter, though, she realized she had no idea what she really had expected. An avowal of undying passion, perhaps? Or a guilt-ridden plea for her forgiveness? She'd played out any number of emotional scenes in her imagination, but now it was quite obvious that those mental rehearsals had been a waste of time. Payne Randall had either forgotten what had happened between them the night before, or else did not think the experience worthy of his further consideration.

She felt a lurch in her belly, a nearly physical pain. Why, she wondered, did it hurt her to realize that he had no intention of mentioning what had happened between them? She'd already decided that it was a mistake, that she must tell him that it had been wrong and was best forgotten. Why was it so hard to accept the fact that he had already forgotten it?

She swallowed, found her tongue, and returned the obligatory "Good afternoon."

He nodded, apparently content with the cursory completion of formalities. He turned his attention to the far side of the room, to the table that held the liquor tray. Aura followed the direction of his glance. She had washed the dirty glasses, returned them to the tray, and tidied it, but when she'd wiped away the messy smudge of fingerprints, she'd been unable to wipe away the embarrassment and guilt she felt when she considered where her first experience with whiskey had led her. Nervous and ill at ease, she turned away, not wanting to think about whiskey, not even daring to look at it.

Payne, however, had no such difficulty. He somberly considered the bottles on the heavy mahogany tray and hesitated for a moment, apparently undecided. But he quickly made up his mind, dismissing whatever qualms he might have had about drinking so early in the day, and started across the room.

"I've arranged for the casket," he told her abruptly, his tone flat and without any sign of emotion.

He might have been talking about the weather. Bewildered, Aura watched him as he passed by her, then turned to stare at his back as he approached the table.

"And I've spoken to Reverend Quayle." Payne reached for the bottle of whiskey. "He offered to come pay a call," he went on, "intending, no doubt, to offer words of comfort and consolation."

How can he be so cool and distant, Aura wondered. At that moment she was feeling anything but objective. Her thoughts were a muddle of shame and guilt and hurt and anger with him because his were so obviously anything but muddled or emotional. She could barely follow the train of what he was saying.

"Reverend Quayle?" she asked numbly.

A picture of a fat little game bird had sprung into her mind, feathers tucked neatly into a dark suit, sporting spectacles and a white collar, and holding a prayerbook firmly under his wing. A silly name, she thought. Where had she heard it before?

Payne turned to face her, the bottle in his hand as yet unopened.

"He married you and Whit yesterday," he reminded her, his tone suddenly turned belligerent. "Or have you forgotten?"

A wave of hurt spread through Aura as the meanness of his words bit into her. But it didn't last long; it faded almost immediately into the undertow of a wave of anger. No wonder there had been no words of apology from him. He obviously considered everything that had happened between them to be her fault.

"No, I haven't forgotten," she snapped sharply. "A great many things happened yesterday, and they happened very quickly. I forgot the reverend's name, that's all."

"The reverend's name and the killer's face," he muttered, as he pulled the cork from the bottle and turned back to the tray to find a glass.

Aura sprang to her feet, and then stood, staring daggers at his back, full of anger but unable to find words to express it. He was accusing her of thwarting the investigation into Whit's death. And what else, she wondered. Would he next choose to accuse her of Whit's murder as well?

"I'm trying to remember," she cried angrily.

"I'm sure," he said dryly, then returned his attention to the whiskey bottle.

Aura silently swore at him. She didn't care what he

thought, she told herself. If there was blame to be allotted for what had happened between them the previous night, then he deserved as great a portion as she—or more. After all, he had given her the whiskey in the first place. And she certainly hadn't pursued him.

But it had been wrong, a voice inside told her sternly. And even if he could dismiss his part, she could not simply forget hers.

"In any case," he went on, intent on filling a glass with whiskey and completely oblivious to her anger, "I've saved you from the dire fate of hosting the good reverend's call. I told him you weren't up to visitors just yet, and he most obligingly understood. He will, I'm sure, prepare a thoroughly decent and unmemorable funeral service."

His back still to her, he lifted the glass to his lips and took a healthy swallow of whiskey. Then he closed his eyes and just stood, silent and motionless, breathing deeply.

Aura stared at his back for a moment, expecting him to turn to face her, expecting something more, doubtless something unpleasant. She swallowed the lump in her throat and decided that there was nothing she wanted to say to him. And there was certainly nothing else she wanted to hear him say to her.

She turned and stalked out of the room, wishing that there was a door to slam behind her.

Aura couldn't bring herself to look at the grave. But no matter how hard she tried, she couldn't keep herself from hearing it. Clods of thick mud, water soaked and heavy from the rain, kept breaking free from the sides of the hole and falling onto the casket with dull, thick thuds. The sound of them made her feel sick in the pit of her stomach.

This whole place, she thought, was unbearably ugly. There was no grass here, and no trees. There was nothing but a sea of thick, dark mud that clung to the hem of her dress and made her feel as though her shoes were sinking endlessly into the earth. There might, she supposed, be a pleasant view overlooking the city and the bay. That was, if the sky were ever to clear. But there was no view, thanks to the thin, dreary rain that had begun the day before and seemed determined to go on forever.

She found her mind wandering, found herself asking herself over and over again what sort of madness had brought her to this horrible place. Cowardly Aura, who'd spent her whole life hiding from shadows. Why had the first brave and venturesome act of her life brought her to such disaster?

Payne, standing beside her and holding a battered umbrella over them both, stirred, forcing her attention back to the unpleasant reason they were standing in this muddy field on a hillside just at the edge of San Francisco. The burial service for Whitmore Randall, such as it was, seemed finally to have come to an end.

Payne pressed the handle of the umbrella into her gloved hand and stepped forward, accepting the shovel being held out to him. She watched as he pushed it into the pile of dark, wet dirt and then threw the first shovelful onto the casket. Drops of rainwater slid down his face, but he seemed not to notice.

Even the anger Aura felt for him couldn't send away the ache that welled up inside her when she saw his expression. If she had nothing else to say in his favor, she did know that he had loved his brother. But he gave no indication that he felt anything as he shoveled dirt onto Whit's coffin. His face might have been chiseled from granite, his expression was so tight and hard. She knew that mask covered a hurt Payne Randall would never allow himself to show to all these strangers.

For there were a great many strangers there, men mostly, among them a good number of Chinese. She found herself looking past the others to where they stood at the back of the crowd. She couldn't stop staring at their faces. It took her a while to realize that she was searching their faces for the single one she knew she ought to be able to remember but which was still a formless blank in her mind. Despite the effort, there was nothing in their impassive expressions, nothing that jarred her memory, and she eventually gave up the effort as useless. After all, she told herself, a man doesn't kill another man, then come to pay his respects at his funeral.

"Mrs. Randall."

Something jarred her, but Aura was still having trouble keeping her concentration where it belonged and she didn't recognize what it was immediately. It was only when the stranger put his hand on her arm that she remembered that *she* was Mrs. Randall, that the good Reverend Quayle had presided over the official change of her name only a few days before. And now he was standing in front of her and talking to her.

It took all her determination to keep her mind on the matter at hand. She nodded and repaid him with a weak smile by way of accepting his condolences, but he went on talking. She pretended to listen, well aware that he was trying his best to be solicitous. Still the words were little more than a meaningless drone to her, even though she was sure his intentions were kind and he meant only to comfort her.

Reverend Quayle seemed unaware of her inattention. He went on and on, assuring her that there was

Divine Providence behind the tragedy of Whit's death, telling her that she must look for comfort in the knowledge that faith heals all wounds. When he'd finally exhausted his store of homilies, he moved aside to allow the others to approach and pay their respects to the bereaved widow.

People immediately started forward, nodding to her, murmuring a word or two as they walked past. She felt as though she was a fake, standing at a graveside dressed in black, playing the part of the grieving widow. She might have liked what little she had seen of Whitmore Randall, but she'd hardly known him. A courtship that had consisted of half a dozen letters, and those kindly but most businesslike in nature, was hardly the basis of a great passion. How, she wondered, could she be expected to mourn Whitmore Randall?

She darted a guilty glance at Payne, sure he recognized her for the fake he knew her to be, almost expecting him to shout out the truth, perhaps even tell these people that she was an adulteress. What was it the ancients did to women who acted as she had? Stone them? Perhaps that was her rightful punishment. She half expected him to shout out his condemnation and stand back to let the crowd deal with her.

To her surprise, he seemed disinterested. He looked at her, or, more accurately, through her, his expression as blank as it had been when he'd thrown the shovelful of dirt onto Whit's casket.

Now a group of a half dozen women picked their way through the oozing mud to face her. She was speechless. They looked suspiciously like the sort of women she'd seen at dinner that night in the Palmer House, their cheeks unnaturally bright, their funeral finery far more extravagant than hers, a brilliant flutter of lace and feathers and furs that not even the rain

87

and the mud could dull. They seemed to be wondering how she'd react to them, if she'd take a hand when it was offered, or even speak to them.

Aura told herself she was in no position to fault Whitmore Randall for whatever peccadilloes he might have indulged in before he'd married her. He'd certainly never had the chance to be an unfaithful husband to her. And she would be nothing less than a hypocrite were she to assign guilt to anyone else. She thanked each woman for coming and shook each hand that was offered to her.

Still, she could not help but watch these woman with studied curiosity, far more curiosity than she had been able to bring to bear on the dismal ritual of Whit's burial. She had the odd feeling that they'd repeated this particular ritual a good many times, that they were accustomed witnesses to death. Their expressions were a bit too solemn, too fixed, as they offered her their sympathies. She thanked them and then stared after them when they stood aside, waiting to find appropriate escorts to take them down the muddy slope and back into town.

"Mrs. Randall, my sincere condolences."

This voice showed none of the brisk desire to be away from the place she'd heard in those of the other mourners who'd spoken to her. It was a deep baritone, and sounded honestly concerned.

Aura looked up and saw a pair of sharp, dark eyes set in a long, thin, cleanshaven face staring down at hers.

"Thank you," she murmured. She shifted her grasp of the umbrella slightly and as she did, a splatter of rainwater fell from it onto his shoulder. "Oh," she said, "I'm terribly sorry."

He waved his hand, then brought it down on hers, patting it comfortingly.

"Please," he insisted, "there is absolutely no need to apologize. This must be terribly unpleasant for you. I do extend my heartfelt sympathies. I hope you will call on me if there is any way I can help you get past all this unfortunate trouble."

Aura glanced past his shoulder to find Payne standing a few paces beyond, staring at the two of them. Glowering, actually, more than just staring. She shivered, and turned quickly away, unsettled by the intensity of the look.

It was so strange, how they'd managed to get through the past two days, avoiding one another when they could, and when they couldn't, pretending to be polite but distant strangers. At first she'd been relieved with the arrangement, with the fact that there was no need to try to offer him explanations that she oughtn't be forced to make. But as time passed, she wasn't quite so sure that the easy path was the wisest way to deal with the situation fate had forced upon them both.

For now, though, she had other matters to think about besides Payne Randall. There was the matter of the police investigation of Whit's death, and the fact that she still could not recall the face of the killer. And there was the matter of deciding what she was going to do, now that she had no husband to provide for her.

She turned her attention back to the stranger who had approached her.

"Thank you," she murmured. "You're very kind, Mr. . . ."

"Crofton, Mrs. Randall," he introduced himself, "Howard Crofton. I was your late husband's lawyer."

"Thank you, Mr. Crofton," she repeated.

She smiled up at him. Since the moment that shot had been fired two nights before, he was the first person who seemed to truly care what happened to her, and she wanted to show him that she was grateful.

He released her hand. "I don't want to intrude on you now, Mrs. Randall. I just wanted to introduce myself to you, and tell you I'd like to meet with you as soon as you feel up to it. There are matters of Mr. Randall's affairs to be attended to."

Aura felt as though her head was swimming again. Somehow, that feeling seemed to be haunting her.

"I'm afraid I know nothing about Mr. Randall's affairs," she confessed. "And I really don't think I can consider that sort of thing now."

He nodded sympathetically. "Of course, of course. Nor should there be any need. When you feel up to it."

"Perhaps I can be of some help. I'm Payne Randall, Whit's brother."

Aura was almost relieved when Payne interrupted. Obviously, he hadn't been quite as scowlingly indifferent to their conversation as she'd thought. In fact, he seemed to have interested himself enough in the conversation to eavesdrop on it. Not that the fact disturbed her. She had no mind for business matters, and no experience whatsoever. He'd seen to the details of the funeral, the casket and the reverend and the rest of it. Perhaps it would be wisest to leave this to him as well.

Crofton held out his hand to him. "My sympathies, Mr. Randall. I was just telling Mr. Randall that I was her late husband's lawyer. There are a number of matters to be settled, and as soon as she feels up to it, I'd like to call."

Aura could see Payne's jaw harden. There was that look of disapproval with which she'd become only too familiar since the moment she'd taken her first step off the *Laura Charles*.

"There's no time like the present, Mr. Crofton," he said, as he took the umbrella from Aura and repositioned it to cover them both.

Crofton was openly surprised with his blunt manner. "But surely it would be better to allow Mrs. Randall . . ."

"Mrs. Randall," Payne interrupted him, "would doubtless like to see matters settled so that she can get on with her life."

Crofton stared at him for a moment, apparently weighing the tone of determination he heard in Payne's voice. Then he nodded.

"As you like, Mr. Randall," he replied. "I'll call on you at your brother's home later this afternoon, if that will be convenient."

"That will be most convenient, Mr. Crofton," Payne assured him.

"Until later, then, Mr. Randall," Crofton said. He nodded and touched his hand to the brim of his hat. "Mrs. Randall."

Aura nodded, mutely acknowledging his departure. Her thoughts were on Payne, though. She had no idea why he'd insisted matters be pushed this way.

But he didn't give her the chance to question him. "Unless you've a great need to stand here and accept empty condolences from the rest of this crowd," he told her, as he put a firm hand on her arm, "I suggest we leave."

"Yes," she stammered. "Certainly, if that's . . ."

Her words trailed off as her glance drifted to the group of Chinese men who were now left standing alone at the far side of the grave. One man was looking straight at her, his dark eyes fixed on hers. And Aura gasped. That was the man, she thought.

The man who'd shot Whit.

"You!"

Aura tried to cry out, but there was a thick lump in

her throat. The only sound she heard was a guttural rasping sound that lost itself in the dull thudding noises of earth being shoveled onto Whit's casket and the monotonous drone of raindrops meeting mud.

Payne, however had determined to be away from the gravesite as quickly as possible. He had no intention of waiting to give her the opportunity to protest, and was purposely ignoring her. His hand still firmly grasping her arm, he started toward the gate that surrounded the cemetery.

Her attention distracted, Aura was unprepared for the sudden lurch. She felt her feet slip in the mud underfoot as she stumbled. She grabbed for Payne's arm in a desperate attempt to keep herself upright, but it did no good—she continued to fall forward.

Payne turned back just in time to catch her and keep her from an unpleasant encounter with the sea of mud. He glared at her, his look implying that he was in no mood for whatever diversion she'd found to impede his progress.

Aura chose to ignore the look.

"I saw him," she cried softly, as he helped her steady her stance.

He gave her a confused look. "Saw who?"

"*Him,*" she insisted. "The man who came to see Whit."

Payne turned to stare at the group of Chinese men who were still standing by the grave. The others had begun to disperse as soon as Payne had taken Aura's arm and started to leave, but the group of Chinese stayed on, staring at the coffin as it was slowly being covered over by a pair of wet, mud-spattered, and magnificently dirty gravediggers.

Payne's grasp on her arm tightened.

"Which one?" he demanded.

Aura turned back to look at the group, searching

for the man who had, a moment before, so boldly stared at her. But there were no boldly staring dark eyes watching her now; there was no vaguely familiar face to shock her and bring back memories of that horrible night.

All she saw now were a huddle of dark-haired, dark-eyed men dressed in those somber black pajamas. Strangers, all of them. Only one dared look directly at her, an older man, taller than the rest and very thin, with a long, drooping moustache. She stared back at him, frustrated and bewildered.

Payne shook her arm, forcing her attention away from the moustached Chinese man. Startled, she turned back to him.

"Which one?" Payne hissed.

Aura darted a glance back at the group of Chinese men, sure that if she looked again, he would return. But it did no good. The man who had called on Whit that night, the man who was most certainly the killer, had somehow managed to disappear.

She shook her head in bewilderment.

"He's gone," she murmured. "He was there a moment ago, but now he's gone."

"Gone? Gone where?"

She glanced at the nearly empty expanse of the graveyard. There were no trees to speak of, nothing to hide behind, save for a few dozen miserable headstones.

She shook her head. "I don't know. He's just gone."

Payne stared down at her, his expression full of disdain. "If he was ever there at all," he sneered.

"He was!" she insisted, but there wasn't much determination in her voice. She was beginning to wonder if the man really had been there or if she'd just imagined it.

Payne tugged at her arm and once more started to

leave. Aura had little choice but to meekly accompany him. Not that she wanted to stay any longer. The last thing she wanted to do was listen to more strangers tell her how sorry they were for her loss. She hadn't had enough time to be Whitmore Randall's wife, and they knew it. She could only think they were laughing at her for her pose as a grieving widow.

As was Payne. The words he'd just spoken to her were more than he'd said to her in the preceding two days. She didn't realize until that moment how much his cold indifference had bothered her. The fact that she'd been as unable to meet his gaze as he seemed to be to meet hers did not mitigate the fact that his indifference hurt her. She felt more than guilty enough for what had happened and deeply regretted her part. She didn't need his barely hidden anger to enforce that guilt.

She had to hurry to keep up with his pace, tripping through the unpleasant, slippery mess of mud. By the time they reached the hired carriage, she was panting from the effort of keeping up with him and not allowing herself to slip and fall.

He handed her into the carriage with the indifferent consideration he might lavish on a sack of potatoes. Then he folded the umbrella and nodded to the driver, swinging himself inside as the carriage started to lurch forward.

He settled himself on the hard leather seat beside her and stared straight forward. It seemed obvious he did not intend to continue whatever conversation she'd begun at the gravesite. Aura stared at him for a long moment, screwing up her courage until she finally found enough of it to speak to him.

"I did see the man," she insisted, her tone defensive, angry as much with herself as with him that she needed to defend herself.

"Then where did he go?" he asked.

She shook her head. "I don't know."

"All right," he said, as he turned to face her, "let's assume, for argument's sake and the moment, that I'm willing to accept your story at face value." And he would accept it, he told himself, assuming she was able to provide him with the information he wanted. More than anything he wanted to find the man who had killed Whit, and her identification was all he had to go on. "What did he look like?"

Aura swallowed. "Like the others," she replied. "Cleanshaven, dark hair, dark eyes."

"Dressed in black," he offered, in a tone that was a shade too polite.

She nodded. "Yes. Dressed in black."

He scowled, then tried another tack. "Tall, short, young, old?" he asked.

"Perhaps twenty-five or thirty," she replied. "Not too tall, perhaps three or four inches taller than I am. It was hard to judge from the distance."

"Broad? Thin?"

"Rather slender."

"Features?" he asked. "A long nose, perhaps, or a pointed chin?"

She shook her head. "No. He had regular features. I don't remember anything unusual."

He looked at her and let his lips form a tight, uneven smile. "Let's see now, I think I have it all—a youngish man, dark hair, dark eyes, slight build and no facial hair, of average height among the Chinese, regular features, dressed in traditional Chinese clothing. Do I have it all?"

Aura nodded. "Yes," she replied.

Payne's smile disappeared.

"Does it occur to you that you've just described perhaps eighty percent of the local Chinese population?" he asked her in a tone that was thick with disgust. "Including a fair number of the women. I don't suppose you want me to go to our friend Sheriff Dougherty with that description and suggest he arrest everyone who fits it?" He smiled that tight, unpleasant smile of his again. "I could also tell him the murderer is a magician and can disappear at will," he added. "That might make the search for him a little easier."

Aura swallowed uncomfortably. She'd thought he'd be delighted that she could describe the man, and now he was making her feel like a perfect fool.

"I'm trying," she said, and then bit her lip, trying to keep herself from giving in to the sudden urge to weep.

Not that Payne would have noticed if she'd dissolved in tears. He closed his eyes and leaned his head against the back of the bench, giving a very good impression of a man who was completely indifferent to everything that went on around him.

The carriage came to a halt, and Aura looked out at the house and at the dark, empty store. She pushed the door open and got out, not wanting to wait for Payne's obligatory offer of help. Pretending to be oblivious to the rain, she pulled her skirt close and walked as quickly as she could through the mud of the street. She ran up the three steps to the front porch. The rain had become noticeably stronger than it had been at the gravesite. It was coming down now in a steady, insistent stream. She was, she realized as she stood and watched Payne extricate himself from the carriage and pay the driver, thoroughly wet and miserable.

He walked past her on his way to the far door. It seemed to Aura that he was deliberately ignoring her. She gritted her teeth. She was completely sick of his attitude. She could accept the fact that what had happened between them had been a horrible mistake, just as she could accept the fact that he didn't like her. But what she would not accept was his cavalier treatment. Even if it had been for only a few hours, still she had been his brother's wife. She deserved some modicum of respect from him, if nothing else.

"I'd like to go in this way," she told him, just as he was about to open the door by the stairs. She pointed to the door to the shop.

He turned around and stared at her as though just remembering she was there.

"Why?" he demanded.

"I want to, that's all."

He shrugged. "As you like," he said in an indifferent tone, dropping the key he'd been about to use and sorting through the key ring as he retraced his steps to the door to the store.

He found the correct key, fitted it into the lock, and turned it. The lock opened with a soft, well-oiled click and the door swung open. Payne waved her inside.

"After you, Mrs. Randall."

Aura ignored the acid in his tone and walked past him into the store. She hadn't ventured inside before, refusing to as long as Whit's body had lain there. But now the place was unoccupied, and she no longer had any reason to avoid it. She walked in and looked around.

The place was cold and damp, but that was hardly surprising, considering the weather and the fact that there had been no reason to put a fire in the large black stove that occupied a place of honor in the rear of the shop. It was also fairly dark, as the storm outside meant there was little daylight to come through the front windows. An oil lamp and matches lay in the center of the counter, and she crossed the room to it, lifted the glass, and lit the lamp.

She was aware of Payne's eyes watching her as she adjusted the flame. But she pretended not to notice, perfectly content to ignore him just as he had made a point of ignoring her in the carriage.

She lifted the lamp and looked around. The store was impressively neat, the shelves well stocked with a variety of goods, everything from foodstuffs to tools and clothing. Whitmore Randall had quite obviously been an organized and fastidious shopkeeper.

"Seen everything you were looking for?"

Aura started. He had been silent for so long, she'd almost forgotten he was there.

"I wasn't looking for anything in particular," she said, as she crossed to the thick oak counter and moved behind it. There were shelves beneath it, neat like everything else in the store, with account books, pens and ink, scissors, twine, the ordinary and usual accoutrements of a shopkeeper.

But there was one thing that wasn't ordinary and usual. When Aura saw it, she gasped softly and took a step back.

Payne edged his way around the counter to stand beside her. He looked down at the sign, staring at it blankly just as she was.

He recovered before Aura did.

"I suppose he had it made when he received your letter agreeing to marry him," he told her. "He always believed in being prepared." He read the gold lettering on the sign—"W. Randall and Sons, Provisions"— then put his hand on her arm and urged her out from behind the counter. "He told me how much he wanted to be a father," he added softly.

Aura really wanted to cry now. Every new thing she learned about Whitmore Randall made her realize just how much she had almost had and just how much she'd lost. She stared at the shop sign with its gold lettering, picturing in her mind the sons she might have given Whit, thinking of the sort of father he would have been to them. It was unfair to have been so close to happiness and have it snatched away before she could ever have the chance to taste it.

She forced herself to think of something else, something distracting. She'd had enough of tears, she told herself, and she most certainly never again intended to shed any in front of Payne Randall.

"Why did you insist that man come to the house this afternoon?" she demanded abruptly.

He turned slowly to face her, his expression showing a slight hint of surprise.

"I assumed that was what you wanted," he said. "After all, you must certainly want to be done with this unfortunate affair."

"I don't know anything about Whit's business," she objected. "How can I discuss such matters with his lawyer?"

"Don't worry," he told her. "I'll see that what needs to be done is done. And you needn't fear that you'll be cheated. You are Whit's legal wife, and I respect that fact."

"Cheated?" she murmured.

It was her turn to be surprised now. Until that moment, it hadn't occurred to her that he might think her some sort of fortune hunter, that her one concern was her claim on Whit's money.

"I've no doubt that Whit made provision for his wife as soon as he decided to marry," he told her, pointedly turning his attention past her to the rows of shelves behind her. "Once this is sold, there'll be more than enough for your passage back East."

Aura gasped. She felt as though he'd struck her.

Passage back East, that was what he'd said. He was sending her back to the prison of her father's house.

It wasn't fair, any of it. He had no right to assign motives to her actions, no right to think she'd agreed to marry Whit out of greed. And if that wasn't enough, he was making her bear the brunt of responsibility for what had happened between them. He'd treated her like a whore the night Whit had died, and now this, it seemed, was her payment, to be sent back East like an unsuitable piece of furniture or a defective pick or hoe.

It would have been kinder, she thought, if he'd left her back in that horrid cemetery, to be buried in Whit's coffin at his brother's side.

Chapter Six

Aura sat very still, all her attention riveted on what Howard Crofton was saying. She had never attended the reading of a will before, much less one in which she had a personal interest. But the more she heard, the more bewildered she became.

Crofton finally finished reading. He put the papers down on his knees, removed his spectacles, looked up at her, and smiled pleasantly. She realized he was expecting her to be pleased, not bewildered, and she wasn't entirely sure she ought to disappoint him. Perhaps she should simply return his smile and politely thank him.

But one glance at Payne's expression changed her mind. He looked smug and knowing, as though he'd expected everything he'd heard. If she simply accepted the precepts of the will, she would be proving that his evaluation of her as nothing better than a fortune hunter was right.

She turned to Crofton. "But surely there must be some mistake," she told him.

The lawyer seemed surprised by that. He lifted a brow, his expression suddenly wary.

"I assure you, Mrs. Randall, it is all according to

correct legal form," he said. "The will was properly executed and witnessed."

"I didn't mean to imply the will wasn't correctly prepared, Mr. Crofton," Aura assured him. "It's just that I don't understand the distribution."

"Just what is it you don't understand, Mrs. Randall?"

He was trying to be helpful, Aura realized, but his tone was a shade too superior, a bit too condescending. Frankly, it irked her. She had no knowledge of business, but she certainly was not an idiot, and she resented the fact that he seemed to think her one.

"It makes no sense for him to have left everything to me," she said. "It certainly doesn't seem fair. He was killed twelve hours after we were married. I don't deserve all of his fortune."

And what was more, she thought, she wanted to prove Payne had been wrong about her. She might not have any idea what was to become of her life, but somehow, for the moment at least, the future seemed less important to her than proving to Payne Randall that she was a good deal better than he seemed to think.

She turned and quickly glanced at Payne's face. For once he'd lost that smug and knowing expression that she'd begun to heartily detest. She allowed herself a slight flush of satisfaction when she saw that he seemed as thoroughly bewildered as Crofton. Why, she wondered, did these men assume she had come to San Francisco with no other intention than getting her hands on Whitmore Randall's money? Their expectations of her were infuriating.

Crofton leaned forward and smiled again, the same tolerantly deprecating smile he might offer a slightly dim child who'd made the mistake of questioning him.

"It isn't such a terribly great fortune, I assure you,

Mrs. Randall. Other than this house, its contents, and the goods in the store downstairs, there's only a small account held by the Wells Fargo office. And from what little I know of your deceased husband, I feel sure he would want you to have it all, despite the abbreviated nature of your marriage. You did, after all, come a long way to become his bride. He would not wish to see you left destitute."

"But surely his family . . ." Aura began.

"I'm all that's left of his family," Payne broke in. "And Whit's reasoning was right. I have no great need for whatever he left behind. Heavy pockets are a goad to me. I tend to feel the need to empty them on whiskey and whores."

Aura turned and looked sharply at him. She could feel her cheeks grow warm and she knew they were getting red. Surely a gentleman would never say such things in front of a lady. And the fact that he seemed to consider himself free to say them in front of her could only mean he did not consider her a lady. Nor should he, she supposed. To him she was probably no better than those whores who'd attended Whit's funeral.

She swallowed the lump in her throat. "Your personal habits are of no concern to me, Mr. Randall," she told him.

Her tone had been arch, she realized, especially when she'd addressed him. She should remain calmer, she told herself. Crofton was staring at her strangely, as though he was beginning to guess that her relationship with Payne was not what propriety dictated.

"Then accept the fact that I'm perfectly happy with the daguerreotypes and his watch, Mrs. Randall," he said, his tone as sharp as hers had been.

"It's not a question of you being content with a few

103

of Whit's personal belongings," Aura insisted. "It's a question of fairness."

"And I consider Whit's distribution entirely fair," he told her. "There's no need to discuss it further."

Before she could offer any other objection, Crofton broke in.

"I would be more than willing to make whatever arrangements need to be made for the sale of the property for you whenever you like," he told Aura. "I'd even be willing to forward you a fair price and hold it myself until a buyer comes along."

"That's very generous of you," Payne said, his tone only slightly insinuating. "I can't help but wonder why you'd make such an offer."

Crofton's eyes narrowed. It was clear that he was beginning to dislike Payne as much as Payne seemed to dislike him.

"Your brother had a respectable business here, Mr. Randall," he said. "He made a decent living from it. It only stands to reason that there'll be a buyer willing to pay a fair price for it. I only made the offer to make things easier for Mrs. Randall." He turned to Aura, the sharpness in his expression disappearing as soon as he faced her. "That way, you'd be able to leave whenever you chose." He smiled again, apparently confident that whatever qualms Payne might have, his offer would please her.

It didn't. He was thoughtfully trying to make it easy for her to go, Aura mused. Why was it everyone seemed to think she was so eager to leave? She gritted her teeth and told herself to be a bit more tolerant of them. Perhaps they really weren't thinking the worst of her. Perhaps it was just that they assumed she had someplace to go to, some home to which she might return.

"Thank you," she murmured to Crofton. "Your

offer is most kind, but I'm not ready to make any decisions just yet. You do understand?"

Crofton nodded. He leaned forward and seemed about to take her hand, to hold and pat it in the same sort of understanding way he had at the cemetery. A quick glance at Payne, however, seemed to change his mind.

"Certainly, Mrs. Randall," he said. "Of course I understand. You'll need a little time to get some perspective on everything that's happened."

"Yes," Aura nodded, "I need some time to think."

"Take all the time you need," Crofton told her. "Whenever you decide you're ready to leave, we can come to some agreement about a fair price. The details will work themselves out then."

With that, Crofton lifted a thick leather briefcase he'd left lying against his chair, carefully settled the papers inside, and then closed and buckled it.

"Can I offer you more tea, Mr. Crofton?" Aura asked, when he'd done.

She leaned forward to the tray on the table in front of her. She touched the pot and hoped he would decline. The tea had grown cold in the time it had taken him to read the will, and now she felt herself hardly capable of even so inconsequential a task as preparing a fresh pot.

The lawyer glanced quickly past her at the liquor tray, then smiled and shook his head.

"You are too kind, Mrs. Randall," he said. "Thank you, no. I've taken far too much of your time already." He pushed himself to his feet and held out his hand to her. "Whenever you're ready, please come to see me. And if there's anything I can do for you before then, anything at all . . ."

Aura returned his smile and offered him her hand.

"Thank you so much, Mr. Crofton. You've been very kind."

Crofton took the offered hand, first pressing it gently, then lifting it to his lips. This time the smile he offered her was anything but smug or superior. When he looked into her eyes, it was quite clear that he no longer was thinking of her as either foolish or childish.

"I assure you it has been entirely my pleasure, Mrs. Randall," he said. "I only wish the circumstances had been more pleasant." He smiled again, then released her hand and straightened. Aura started to rise, but he waved her back into her chair. "Please don't disturb yourself any further. I'll see myself out." He nodded to Payne. "Mr. Randall." He turned back to offer Aura one last smile. "Mrs. Randall."

With that he started toward the stairs. Before he reached the stairs, however, Payne stopped him.

"Crofton."

The lawyer turned back to face him. He eyed Payne coldly, making no effort to hide the fact that he'd noticed the slight in Payne's term of address and that he didn't like it.

"Yes, Mr. Randall?" he asked with exaggerated politeness.

Payne ignored his tone.

"I was just wondering," he said with a thin smile, "if my brother might have mentioned to you that he'd recently been the unsuspecting recipient of some counterfeit currency."

Crofton appeared to be completely bewildered by the question.

"Counterfeit currency?" he repeated. "I'm sorry, but no, I don't recall any mention of that."

"You had seen him of late?" Payne asked.

The lawyer nodded. "Yes, of course. Your brother came to me less than two weeks ago and outlined his instructions for this will. He came back the next day to sign the completed document."

"And on neither occasion did he mention counterfeit bills?" Payne pressed.

Crofton shook his head. "No, I really can't remember him saying anything much beyond the fact that he was delighted with the prospect of his forthcoming marriage," he replied.

Payne shrugged. "I suppose there would have been no reason," he said. "It was just a thought. No need to bother yourself about it."

"Well, then, I'll bid you good day," Crofton said, when it became apparent that Payne's inquiries had exhausted themselves on that one small matter.

"Good day," Payne replied. He smiled with a good deal more warmth than he'd shown the lawyer until that moment.

Crofton turned to Aura one last time, smiled, and said, "Good day, Mrs. Randall."

"Good day, Mr. Crofton," she replied. "Thank you again."

The lawyer turned and started down the stairs.

They were both silent for a few minutes, almost as though they were waiting for whatever reverberations Crofton had left behind to die away. Finally Aura noticed that it had begun to grow dark. Long shadows filled the corners and were beginning to creep across the length of the room. She stood and began to busy herself lighting the lamps.

"Nearly six o'clock," she said, after a glance at the mantel clock. "I hadn't realized it had grown so late."

"Time does fly when you're busy chatting with your deceased husband's lawyer," Payne muttered.

Aura gritted her teeth. Why, she wondered, did he continue to bait her this way? She had no answer, just more questions—why she was too cowed to fight back;

whether she'd held her tongue as long as she had because she pitied him for his loss, or because she was simply afraid to defend herself.

She decided that being meekly accepting could not comfort him for his brother's loss. And it hurt her. It was about time she started standing up for herself. Hiding her anger from him was doing no good at all.

She turned around to glare at him. He hadn't moved, so far as she could see. He was still sprawled as he had been when Crofton had been there, his long legs extended into the center of the room.

"I don't know what cause you have to be angry with me, but I've had more than enough of your vile humor," she told him. "Whatever it is you want to say to me, be done with it once and for all."

He seemed taken aback by that, as though he hadn't thought she'd take the pains to defend herself. He shook his head.

"My humor *is* vile, isn't it? I heartily apologize for it," he said. "This hasn't been entirely pleasant."

His face settled into the fixed expression he'd worn when he'd shoveled dirt into Whit's grave, but a hurt look crept into his eyes, a look that started to make her heart ache. But she steeled herself against the feeling. He was hurt, certainly, but so was she. And his hurt was no excuse to be cruel to her.

"It hasn't been pleasant for either of us," she reminded him.

"No, I suppose not," he admitted.

"In that case, your apology is accepted," she said. She turned back to the task of lighting the lamps, taking care as she crossed the room to step around his feet, as he made no effort to move them for her.

"I'd have thought you'd be only too happy to have Crofton sell the place," he said after a moment. "He seems willing to give you a fair price. That way you could leave as soon as you like."

"What makes you so certain I'm anxious to leave?" she asked, her tone weary.

She was beginning to feel empty, without any impetus to argue with him anymore, or even to try to explain. It was useless, she thought. From the first minute he'd seen her, he'd taken a dislike to her. She had come to realize finally that nothing she could do would ever change that fact. And allowing him to do what he'd done the night Whit died, she realized now, had only made it worse. For both of them.

"Nothing specific," he replied with a shrug. "I just thought you'd want to return home as there's nothing holding you here."

"Then you thought wrong," she told him, her tone sharp and tinged with anger. "I have no home to return to," she added bitterly.

"What?" he asked.

His expression showed the same bewilderment it had betrayed when she'd asked about the fairness of Whit's will. Aura got the feeling that Payne didn't especially like the fact that he didn't understand what was going on in her mind. Another item he could add to the list of her sins, she thought—the fact that he simply didn't fathom the way she thought.

She waved his question aside. "Nothing," she said. "In any case, I can't sell this house as long as you're staying here, now, can I?" That seemed a reasonable excuse, she thought.

"I can move into a hotel," he mused.

"Or you could go back to New York," she suggested.

"Eventually, I will," he told her. "When I've finished what I came here to do."

Aura stared at him in silence for a moment. That

109

wasn't right. Whit had said he'd come west to be present at their marriage.

"You didn't come here to be witness to Whit's wedding, did you?" she asked. "You came here because of the counterfeit currency."

The words had just slipped out, without any real thought behind them. In fact, she had no idea where they might have come from as she'd not given the matter any thought until that moment. But as soon as she said it, she knew she was right. And it didn't take more than an instant for her to find more than enough reasons to justify her conclusion. She was even more convinced when he pretended not to understand.

"Why do you think that?" he asked.

"Because you asked Mr. Crofton about counterfeit bills not once, but twice," she replied. "Because you work for Wells Fargo. Because coming all the way across the country on horseback is more than a man would ask of even a devoted brother."

He considered what she'd said for a moment, then he smiled.

"Whit said he thought you were bright," he told her. "It would seem he was right."

"You haven't answered my question," she insisted.

"All right," he said. "Yes, I came because of the counterfeit currency."

Aura returned to the chair she'd occupied when Crofton had been there. She leaned forward to the tea tray, and, lost in thought, absently lifted her cup.

"Did you even know he was planning to marry?" she asked.

"Not until I got here," he admitted. "He said he wrote, but I suppose I crossed the letter's path somewhere along the way."

Aura lifted the cup to her lips and took a sip. It

didn't matter to her how cold the tea had become; she was too lost in thought to think about its taste.

"Do you think he was murdered because he knew something about the counterfeiting?" she asked finally.

Now it was Payne's turn to become thoughtful. Aura could see that he didn't like the idea of explaining anything to her, that it went against every fiber of his nature to trust her.

He stood and crossed the room to the liquor tray. Aura kept her eyes on him, watching him as he lifted a bottle and uncorked it.

"Well?" she asked, when it became apparent that he intended to ignore her. "Was that why he was murdered?"

Aura could see his shoulders stiffen. She realized that she didn't need him to answer, that she'd guessed the truth, or at least, what he thought was the truth.

He seemed to have changed his mind about the whiskey. He pushed the cork back into the bottle and dropped it heavily back onto the tray. It made a loud clatter as it settled itself. He stood and stared at it as though he found the prospect of turning around to face her unpleasant.

"What difference does it make?" he demanded.

"Perhaps it makes a difference because I'd like to see my husband's murderer brought to justice," she told him. "Or does that sound unreasonable?"

"Look, you hardly knew him," he told her, as if he was imparting some deep knowledge to which she had not previously been privy. "Why don't you just go back home and forget about Whit and everything that happened here?"

Aura felt stunned. Forget it? How would she ever forget that a man had died in her arms? Did he think she could convince herself that it had been nothing more than a bad dream?

"I told you," she cried. "I have no home to go back to. My father made it plain that if I left his house, I needn't ever return to it."

She had no idea why she'd said that. It certainly was none of his business. It was just that he was so infuriatingly smug, so sure he knew all there was to know about her. The words had just slipped out.

He finally turned around to face her.

"You mean that, don't you?" he asked. "You really turned your back on your family to come here and marry Whit?"

His question found a surprisingly tender chord in her.

"Except for my sister, it wasn't much of a family," she murmured.

"And you really have no place to go back to?"

She shook her head. "I have nothing but this," she said, motioning vaguely to the room around her.

He shook his head as though he was trying to clear away cobwebs that had found their way inside it. Nothing she said seemed to make any sense to him. About that, at least, she wasn't sure she could blame him. Much of it didn't make a whole lot of sense to her, either.

"Then why were you so willing to share it with me?" he demanded.

Why had she, she wondered. Why did she care what he thought about her?

"Because it would be right," she replied.

"Right?" he muttered. "What's right? Whit killed over a few hundred dollars of counterfeit bills, was that right?"

"No, of course not," she said. "That's why you've got to find whoever it was who killed him." She let her eyes find his and stared at him for a long moment. "That *is* what you intend to do, isn't it?"

He balled his left hand into a fist and rubbed it with his right. He ought to be out doing just that, rather than sitting in Whit's parlor with her. There had to be something he could use to find the killer. But as far as he knew, all there was was her. She'd seen the man. And so far, she'd been able to tell him nothing at all that he could use.

"That might be a hell of a lot easier if you could remember what the man who came here that night looked like," he hissed.

"I told you," Aura snapped. "I saw him. I described him. He was there, at the cemetery."

"An ordinary-looking Oriental," he reminded her. "And he just disappeared."

"Yes," she insisted, "he disappeared."

He turned away. Arguing did nothing, and he knew it. Still, that seemed to be all they did, argue.

"Look, this is getting us nowhere," he told her. "In any case, it's insane to think you can stay on here. The lawyer told you Whit didn't have much money, and he was right. You won't be able to live very long on that and nothing else. And frankly, I don't have either the time or the inclination to take care of you."

Those last words were more than Aura could tolerate from him. Of all the mean and belittling things he'd said to her in the preceding days, that was surely the meanest and most belittling.

"Damn you," she shouted. "I never asked you to take care of me. I don't want it, and I don't need it."

She realized she'd uttered a profanity, and just for an instant, felt sure a thunderbolt might strike her in rightful payment. Cowardly Aura, she thought, afraid the sky will fall because you uttered a naughty word. When it didn't, her anger grew, anger with herself as

113

well as with him. Even he can see what a mouse you are, she thought. If not, why would he think you need someone to take care of you? Isn't it time you grew up?

"No, I suppose you don't," he agreed. His lips formed themselves into a tight little sneer. "Lawyer Crofton looks like he might be susceptible to a lonely young woman's charms."

What else would he accuse her of, she wondered. Why didn't he just say it out plainly? If he thought her a whore, why didn't he just call her a whore and be done with it? Well, she had no intention of trying to plead her innocence to him. He'd done nothing to earn the privilege.

"What difference does it make to you what I do?" she demanded. "You've made it more than plain that you have no interest in what happens to me."

"Damn it, I don't," he hissed. Something seemed to snap inside him. He started for the stairs, afraid that if he stayed, the anger he was feeling would start to boil over. "But before you run to the good lawyer's embrace, consider this: he lied. He knew about the counterfeits. Whit told me the day before he was killed that he'd discussed the matter with Crofton."

"That doesn't make any sense," she countered. "What possible reason could he have to lie about it?"

"What reason indeed?" he asked.

With that he turned away. He was eager enough to be away that he took the stairs two at a time.

Aura simply sat for a while, still and numb. Payne's accusations had atrophied her. The suggestion that she had been encouraging Howard Crofton left her empty of everything but rage.

But perhaps he was right, a voice inside her suggested. Perhaps she had fleetingly hoped she could

114

turn to the lawyer when it was more than apparent that she had no one and no place else to turn. Was she, she wondered, that weak? Was she really willing to give herself to a man, any man, rather than return to her father's house or face a future alone?

Her thoughts were no salve, because she realized she really didn't know what she was capable of doing. She'd begun to transgress on the values she'd been raised to accept the moment she'd left her father's house. She'd wantonly violated them the night of Whit's death. What else, she wondered, was she willing to do?

She had no idea how long it was before she finally stirred. She only knew it was a long time, because when she glanced out the window, she saw that it had grown completely dark.

At first she busied herself with mundane tasks, gathering up the remnants of the tea tray, carrying it to the kitchen, washing, drying, and returning the cups and saucers to the cabinet. That accomplished, and without any other dull chore with which she could occupy herself, she sat down beside the worn kitchen table, put her head in her hands, and forced herself to make some decisions.

Now that Payne had brought up the subject of what she was going to do, she knew she couldn't avoid it any longer. He'd said he had neither the time nor the inclination to take care of her. Nothing could have been more blunt than that. He was telling her in no uncertain terms that he was only too anxious to wash his hands completely of her.

But returning to Fall River, she knew, was simply not an option for her. And despite his accusations and her own doubts, she knew she wasn't the sort of woman who would try to trap a man into marriage simply to find a home.

She had no choice but to stay where she was and make her own way. Or else starve in the attempt.

Not that starvation really appeared to be imminent. Crofton had told her that Whit had provided for her, and she was beginning to realize just what that meant to her. He'd left her with a small amount of cash and the store. The cash would tide her over for a while, but the store was much more. It meant she wouldn't ever have to think about going back to her father's house, and it also meant she didn't need any help from Payne Randall or anyone else. Whit had left her something more important than money. He'd left her a means to earn her own keep.

And providing for herself meant she'd never have to hear Payne Randall or any other man tell her he would or wouldn't deign to take care of her. For the first time in her life, she wouldn't need anyone but herself.

That is, she wouldn't need anyone assuming she could manage a business all by herself, assuming she did not bankrupt herself by total incompetence.

And that, she knew, was assuming a great deal. Not that she considered herself completely inadequate. It was just that her schooling and upbringing had had only one goal in mind, the expectation that she would marry. She had been taught how to run a home and nothing else. She sewed and embroidered beautifully, was a better than average cook, and could be induced to a fair frenzy of housekeeping when the need arose. To those prerequisites, she also added a flair at playing the pianoforte, a decent singing voice, and the knowledge of how to set a table for company as well as how to fill it. In short, she had all those skills that would have made her a more than adequate wife.

What she was not so sure of was her ability to run the business Whitmore Randall had left to her. True, she could do sums competently, and she assumed the

116

mystery of keeping accounts, with a bit of study, would not be entirely beyond her. Still, she knew there must be a good deal more to running a business than making out bills and counting up pennies to make proper change. And the simple truth was, she had absolutely no idea what that might entail.

Well, she thought, it wouldn't do much good sitting alone in the kitchen and wondering. If she was going to run Whit's store, she might just as well begin to learn how to keep the accounts. And the most obvious way to do that, she thought, would be to look at Whit's books.

It felt good to have made a decision—any decision. And this one felt right to her, as right as leaving her father's house had seemed. For the first time since she'd looked down the stairs and seen Whit's body, she began to feel hope, tentative hope, to be sure, but hope nonetheless.

Taking a lamp with her, she returned to the parlor and started down the stairs. She hadn't ventured there in the dark since that night, and it took a bit of courage to descend the stairs and push open the door to the store.

It was pitch black inside, and her one lamp did little but draw her attention to a wealth of shadows that were almost worse than the complete darkness had been. She was tempted to turn around, go back upstairs, and leave any further venturing until the morning.

But she refused to give in to the temptation, however much she might have wanted to. If she was ever going to become independent, she told herself, then she couldn't allow herself to be terrorized by shadows. If nothing else, she had to prove to herself that she was brave enough to fight the inclination to go running upstairs and hide like a frightened rabbit.

She walked up to the counter, stepping heavily, making a good deal more noise with her heels against the wooden floor than she needed to make, but she was comforted by the sound of it. She lit the lamp that was there, turning both it and the one she'd brought from upstairs up high so that by the counter at least it was fairly bright. She glanced one last time at the shadows that clung to the corners, then turned away, determined to ignore them.

She stepped behind the counter. For an instant she glanced at the sign, "W. Randall & Sons." Just as it had earlier, it disturbed her, left her feeling as though Whit's ghost, and the ghosts of those sons he'd never had, were there in the room with her. But these thoughts, too, like her fears of the shadows, she managed to push aside. She took the sign, turned it so that the lettering faced away, and leaned it against the far wall. Then she hefted the thick account books off the shelf and onto the counter.

The first was the customer ledger. As Aura opened it, a small leaf of flimsy paper perhaps two inches square, lifted by the draft the cover made as she opened the ledger, flew out and drifted onto the counter. She picked it up and stared at it. It was pale blue and covered with what seemed to her incomprehensible squiggles drawn in ink. A strange sort of thing for a stolid shopkeeper to leave in his ledger, she thought. She wondered what it meant and why Whit had kept it.

It was, however, useless to ponder unanswerable questions. She returned the square of paper to the place she'd found it.

She began slowly leafing through the pages. Whit had had a fair number of active accounts who paid their bills monthly, and mostly promptly. Each page was headed with a name and address, and several of the names sounded to her vaguely familiar, perhaps, she assumed, because she'd heard them that afternoon at the funeral. Only one was at all unusual, that page headed with the name Charlotte O'Shay. On that page there wasn't the usual row of nearly identical signatures beside the list of purchases. Instead, there were at least a dozen different signatures, all those of women, and nearly all appended with a small missive, a little heart or an outline of a pair of lips. It didn't take her long to realize that the women she'd seen at the cemetery that morning might have had more than one kind of business exchange with Whit. At least Charlotte O'Shay paid her bills promptly, she told herself, as she resolutely turned the page.

After the page devoted to Madame Charlotte, there were a good number of pages detailing less active and less promptly paid accounts. These had no addresses listed, and the payments were usually entered in ounces, not dollars. Miners, Aura decided, who paid their bills with gold when they paid them at all.

There were a fair number of pages where payments were many months overdue. Whit had obviously been very generous with his credit, and he seemed to be willing to extend it even to miners who had long outstanding balances. He had been either a very kind man, or a sharp businessman who'd reasoned that a miner would eventually bring in enough gold to pay off his debts.

Aura decided Whit had probably been a combination of the two.

There didn't seem to be much more she could learn from the ledger, either about Whit himself or about his business. She swung it closed.

As she did, she thought she heard a sound. Imagination, she told herself firmly, nothing to be afraid of. But still she glanced up.

There was a face at the window, a man's face. She recognized it immediately. After all, she'd seen it twice before, that morning at the cemetery, and the night Whit had been shot.

It didn't take her long to realize the man had been testing her at the cemetery that morning, to see if she recognized him. And she'd failed the test. He'd learned she could recognize him, and that could mean only one thing—as a witness to a murder, she was a threat until she became the victim of a second murder. He'd come there to kill her, just as he'd killed Whit.

She screamed.

Chapter Seven

Payne walked alone in the dark. When he'd first left Aura, he'd determined to take his misery to be coddled and nursed by the ladies at Madame Charlotte's. But once he approached the house, he began to slow his pace, suddenly not so sure.

When he was finally standing at the door, he hesitated as he raised his hand to the ornate brass knocker. Rather than rap it, he stood for a long moment, listening to the sounds coming from the inside, the sounds of laughter and a slightly off-key piano. He found himself wondering if this was, after all, the way to solve the problems that were eating at him.

He was about to turn away when the door opened. A muscular-looking young Oriental man dressed in sleek black appeared and stared out at him.

"Good evening, sir," he said, as he pulled the door wide and stood back to allow Payne to enter.

Payne realized that the servant had obviously been looking out the peephole and had taken the initiative when it had appeared that he might be losing a hesitant customer. A good businessman, Payne thought. He shrugged, resigned. He told himself that it was useless to try to fight against fate.

"Good evening," he replied, and walked inside.

As soon as he stepped into the parlor, he found himself surrounded by women, virtually enveloped in a cloud of scent and lace and pale pink flesh. His arms were each entwined by soft, bare arms, and nearly naked breasts pressed provocatively close. Even Madame Charlotte herself deigned to approach him and honor him with a fluttering embrace.

"Such a tragedy," the madame moaned softly. "Your brother was such a pleasant, generous man. All the girls were so very fond of him." She gave Payne a last perfumed squeeze, then finally released him and stood back.

Payne might have come to the whorehouse wanting to be coddled, but he found the concern being showered on him well beyond both his expectations and his desires. He accepted the madame's condolences with as much good grace as he could muster.

"It was kind of you and the girls to come to the cemetery," he told her.

Charlotte shook her head, setting a wealth of unnaturally bright red curls bobbing with the motion.

"Please, don't mention it," she told him.

She refrained from adding that funerals were always a boon to business, turning men's minds to thoughts of their own mortality and reminding them to take whatever enjoyment life had to offer while blood still flowed sturdily in their veins. Still, she had to admit that she'd had no trouble enlisting a delegation to attend this particular funeral. Whitmore Randall had been generous and kind to the girls who worked at the house, and they'd been more than willing to repay his kindness by standing for an hour in the rain in his memory.

Charlotte nodded toward the young woman who had entwined Payne's left arm with her own.

"You and Molly got on well the last time you were

here, didn't you?" she asked. "Why don't you let her give you a bit of whiskey and a song to cheer you up? And your money's no good here tonight, Mr. Randall. In your brother's memory."

She smiled and swept off, turning her attention to a group of three miners who'd come to the door with heavy pockets, leaving before Payne could thank her for the generosity of her gesture. A dream come true, he thought with a feeling of hollow misery as he glanced down at Molly's smiling face. He'd just been given the run of the best whorehouse in San Francisco, and not a cent to be paid for the pleasure. All it had cost him was his brother's life.

"We know how to make you smile," Molly was saying, as she and the girl on Payne's right began to drag him toward a long red velvet-covered sofa. She was smiling up at him, her dark brown eyes bright with promises that needed no words to be interpreted. "You sit here," she said, pushing him down onto the overstuffed sofa, "and we'll make you comfortable."

Payne settled himself, unprotesting. She leaned forward and loosened his tie, then pressed a warm and decidedly friendly kiss to his lips, letting her own linger provocatively, her breath mixing with his, before she finally pulled away.

Payne stared up at her. She was pretty, he noted, very pretty, with wide brown eyes, a mass of soft brown curls framing her face and an abundant display of nearly bared breasts that seemed only too anxious to be freed of the dark green lace of her gown as she leaned forward to settle herself on the sofa beside him. But despite all that, and despite the fact that he'd considered her a quite pleasant companion on the night he and Whit had come to the brothel together, suddenly he wasn't as interested as reason told him he ought to be.

123

He darted a quick glance around the room, then looked back at Molly's smiling expression. She was talking to him, but he had no idea what she was saying. He found himself wondering what he was doing in this place, wondering why he'd come. This wasn't what he needed, a voice inside him told him. This wasn't what he wanted at all.

He forced his attention away from the voice and back to Molly, but unfortunately his eyes settled perversely on her lips. She was still talking, and as they moved, the dark red of the rouge she'd used to darken her lips began to seem to him like a smear of blood.

He had no idea where the thought had come from, but once conceived, it took on a life of its own. The image took hold, and he imagined he could almost see the red slowly begin to drip off her lips. The thought was sickening.

This is ridiculous, he told himself, finally forcing himself to shake off the preoccupation. But even with Molly's lips once again nothing more sinister than what they really were, still he could not stomach the thought of touching them.

He shook his head, trying to will away the image completely.

"I'm sorry," he admitted. "I'm afraid I wasn't listening."

She smiled archly up at him. "No matter," she assured him. She put her hand on his thigh and squeezed it. "There's no need for talk, if you don't feel up to it," she purred softly. She motioned toward the stairs.

Payne followed the motion of her hand with his eyes. A sane man, he told himself, would stop thinking and simply take this girl to bed. But at that moment he wasn't feeling especially sane. The plain fact was, he knew that if he bedded Molly, he wouldn't be thinking of her. And that wouldn't be fair, not to her, and not to him, either.

He put his hand on hers and lifted it from his thigh.

"I'm afraid this wasn't such a terribly good idea after all, Molly," he said.

"Oh," she murmured, pouting slightly, then smiling a knowing smile. "Perhaps I could make it improve. I'll bet I know how."

Payne grinned. "I'll bet you do," he agreed as he stood. "And another night I'd be curious to see how." He shrugged. "But tonight, I'm afraid . . ."

He turned away quickly, feeling more than a little like a fool, but wanting nothing more than to get out of the house. He didn't look back, afraid she might be encouraged to come after him if he did.

Once he was safely outdoors, Payne stood and inhaled the damp evening air. He felt edgy and disoriented. But one thing was absolutely certain: whatever ache filled him, he realized now it wouldn't be eased by what he would find inside Madame Charlotte's establishment.

He turned away and began to walk off, aimlessly roaming the dark streets. Eventually he found himself near the wharves. This part of town, he knew, was not especially safe, but he had no fear of whatever might find him. His size and his ability to fend for himself had long before accustomed him to feeling secure regardless of his surroundings. He even began to wish someone might approach him, to wish for the chance to vent in a fight some of the anger and whatever else it was that was eating at him. A split lip or a black eye, he thought, would be little enough to pay for the satisfaction of feeling his fist buried in some deserving bully's belly.

His wish was not to be granted. For whatever reason, perhaps simply the burning look they saw in his

125

eyes, men he encountered on the muddy street took one glance at him and then backed out of his way. No one seemed willing to tempt the fates, even with the lure of what might lie in his pockets.

Without the relief of distraction, Payne was forced to face his thoughts head on. He began to realize that the ache inside him that had begun the night of Whit's death wasn't easing as reason told him it ought to. Instead, it was growing far worse with each passing day. And he also began to realize that what he felt was a good deal more than the pain of loss. It was guilt— guilt and regret, and the sharply biting venom of a conscience that was burrowing its way through his belly.

Because he was almost certain that if he'd never come to San Francisco, if he'd never asked Whit to make inquiries that might help his investigation of the counterfeit currency, his brother would still be alive and well. Added to that was the realization that he'd used Aura to ease the hurt of that guilt, and that by using her, he'd only added to his sins.

But the worst of it was that he couldn't force himself to forget that he'd slept with her. Even more, he couldn't make himself stop thinking about what it would be like to repeat the experience, to feel her in his arms once again, to touch her naked flesh, to once again make love to her.

Because that, he knew, was why the luscious Molly and her friends had had no allure for him. Simply put, he had wanted Aura; he still wanted Aura; and he wanted only Aura. It was impossible for him to even think of a substitute.

That aching want, he knew, was what was behind the way he'd been treating her, why he was being so callous toward her. Because he knew the desire he felt for her was wrong and still he couldn't stop feeling as he did.

He also knew that it was what had so infuriated him about the way Howard Crofton had looked at her. Neither she nor the lawyer had behaved in any way that could possibly warrant his jealousy, but still it was eating at him, and logic would not send it away.

The truth was, Payne really had no rational reason to dislike Crofton, save for the lawyer's avowal that Whit hadn't mentioned the counterfeit bills to him. But he could think of several perfectly honest reasons why Crofton had denied his knowledge, first and most probable, that Whit had discussed it with him in confidence and asked him to keep the information to himself. That was what a lawyer did, remain silent about those matters his client asked him to keep to himself.

So there was no reason to brand the lawyer for his denial of knowledge—no fair reason, that is. But Payne didn't want to be fair, not after he'd seen the way Crofton had looked at Aura, like a wolf eyeing a prime young pullet ripe and ready for the taking. And it didn't help at all for him to remember that Aura had seemed more than willing to accept the lawyer's attention as though it was rain after a long drought.

Not that he could really blame her for yearning for a friendly face and a kind word. She was alone and frightened, and his own treatment of her had hardly filled the void Whit's death had undoubtedly left in her life. She'd come a long way to find a home and a husband, and reason told him that it couldn't be easy for her to contemplate facing a future without either.

Not that he had any intention of offering to provide a solution to her problems. The last thing he needed was to be tied to a wife and everything that went along with marriage. And that was what made it so unfair for him to feel this need for her, this deep, bitter need.

Because in her world, this sort of want was acceptable only when traded for a payment in vows, the kind of vows that were permanent and final. He'd have been far happier if she were the sort who recognized a different sort of currency. All he knew was that he wasn't prepared to strike the sort of bargain she'd expect.

But if he could tell himself with such certainty that he didn't want to marry her, then why did it eat at him to simply think she might turn to someone else in search of what he was unwilling to give? Why was it so painful for him to remember the smile she'd flashed so willingly at Howard Crofton?

He found it didn't help him to think. The more he turned the situation over in his mind, the worse it became. Simply put, it would have been far easier for him had she been a whore, had her affections been a simple matter of trade, as it was for the women at Madame Charlotte's. Then he'd have no reason to feel the ache of guilt he felt for having slept with her, no reason to be torn between the desire for her and the certain knowledge that he should walk away before he became so entangled with her that he'd never be able to escape.

He realized that he'd been walking for nearly an hour, and that neither the exercise nor the tenor of his thoughts had in any way improved his mood or eased the ache in his belly. He turned around, determined to return to Madame Charlotte's, telling himself that if he didn't stop thinking about Aura and Whit he'd go out of his mind. But when he found himself in front of a decidedly seedy seamen's saloon, he changed his mind. A long drink of whiskey, he told himself, imbibed in the anonymity of a dark, smoke-filled saloon—that was what he needed.

He pushed the door open, walked inside, and crossed directly to the bar. It was far from pristine—

damp and sticky with spilt beer, and, to a lesser extent, whiskey, that no one had bothered to wipe away. The floor was worse, slimy with beer and the overflow of a spittoon that appeared not to have been emptied in weeks. The air was so thick with smoke and the mixed scents of beer and perspiration that he could nearly taste it. When the barkeep halted in front of him, stared at him, and grunted, Payne ordered a whiskey and told the man to leave the bottle.

He poured his first drink to the rim of the shot glass and emptied it in a single swallow, nearly inhaling the raw-tasting alcohol. He closed his eyes and savored the burning trail it left as it made its slow way to his stomach. He returned the glass to the bar and poured himself another.

Reinforced and taking a good deal of comfort from the warmth that the alcohol generated inside him, he took the glass in his hand and turned around to face the room. It was only then that he realized that he was being eyed suspiciously. He was, he saw, dressed a good deal too well to be anonymous in such a place.

For an instant he questioned his own judgment in having come to this sort of saloon to get drunk, but when he returned a slow, steely gaze to each curious glance turned his way, he found his audience willing to lose interest in him. Satisfied, he lifted the glass to his lips and sent its contents in the same direction its predecessor had gone. Then he waited, expecting to feel a relaxation of the tight knot in his belly.

Nothing happened. His thoughts, he found, were just as miserable, and his conscience as biting, as they'd been when he'd walked in. Despite the fact that he stood by the bar and quickly emptied his glass twice more, he couldn't make himself feel any change. He continued to be oddly sober. He searched in vain for some evidence that he might soon find the oblivion of drunken forgetfulness.

It was no good, he decided. He felt a wave of miserable self-pity wash over him. Not only couldn't he face the thought of another woman or get into a fight, he mused bitterly, he couldn't even get himself decently drunk.

He dropped his glass back onto the bar, then added enough money to pay for the whiskey he'd drunk. Nothing, he realized, would make him feel any better until he did what he'd come to San Francisco to do— find the counterfeiters—and what he'd sworn to do— bring Whit's killer to justice. As for Aura, he'd simply have to live with his feelings for her and learn to deal with them.

It felt good at least to have made a decision to get on with his life. But the decision had its own problems. It left him faced with the necessity of making some sort of peace with Aura. If for nothing but the sake of Whit's memory, he had some responsibility to see to her, at least until the time she decided to return East, assuming she did finally come to that decision. And he had work to do, work that would grow more and more difficult the longer he put off doing it. There was no excuse for him roaming the streets in the middle of the night, feeling sorry for himself and trying to get himself drunk.

He turned away from the bar and started for the door, suddenly disgusted by the filth of the place and eager to be away from it. He hesitated just outside the saloon door for a moment until his eyes adjusted to the change of light. Then he started down the street, determined to return to Whit's house and make some sort of a temporary peace with Aura.

He'd walked less than a block when he realized he wasn't quite as anonymously alone on the street as he'd thought he was. He turned on his heel, the suddenness of his movement surprising the two men who had followed him out of the bar.

The one closest to Payne took a moment to get past his surprise, but then he smiled, giving every impression that he was willing to be amiable, despite the situation. He was dark headed and barrel chested, and wore a sailor's clothing, dark wool jacket and a dark stocking cap. He looked as if he hadn't bothered to shave in the previous two weeks, the stubble on his cheeks long and dark enough to make his face look as though it was partially covered with bristles. From the thick scent that surrounded him like an evil cloud, Payne decided he hadn't washed in that length of time, either.

"Some way I can help you gentlemen?" Payne asked, as he warily eyed the two.

"Now, that's a right friendly offer," the burly sailor replied. "Here I was thinkin' we could be helpin' you."

Payne didn't allow his glance to waver.

"Now, why would you want to do that?" he asked.

The sailor shrugged. "Just a thought," he replied. "Havin' a bit of trouble, are ya?" he asked, and then punctuated the question with a hopeful grin.

Payne returned his stare as he slowly shook his head. "No trouble," he replied. "Why do you ask?"

"Four shots," the man replied. "I counted. A man stands by a bar and drinks four shots fast like that usually has trouble he'd like to forget."

Payne didn't miss the hint of expectation in the man's eyes. This pair had watched him drink, taken the bother to count how much liquor he'd swallowed, then followed him out of the saloon. He wasn't nearly close enough to being drunk enough to think these two might be friendly samaritans, anxious to offer a helpful hand. Nor did he suppose they'd taken the effort they had purely out of disinterested concern for a stranger's well being.

He spread his legs and bent his knees just a bit, widening and steadying his stance, making himself ready for whatever the two might have in mind. If there was to be a fight, he had no intention of allowing himself to be caught unawares.

"You wouldn't be an associate of the Lady's Temperance, would you?" he asked slowly, keeping his eyes on the man who'd spoken to him. "Not out to save some needy, sinning souls and convert the fallen?"

The man scowled, but his companion, who resembled him in every respect save the color of his hair and beard, which were both bright red, seemed to find Payne's suggestion highly amusing. He laughed loudly, and slapped his hand against his thigh.

"Lady's Temperance," he repeated. "Now, that's just like you, ain't it, Gunny?"

"Shut up," the first man, the one called Gunny, hissed. "I ain't in no mood for jokes," he said to Payne.

"Unfortunate," Payne noted dryly.

"For both of us," came the sneered reply. "It could mean you might be findin' yourself a bit indisposed. But then, don't let the thought scare ya'. The sea air does wonders for whatever might ail a man."

Payne glanced around the street. It was unnaturally quiet. It was as if word had been silently telegraphed that something was about to happen, something that it would be wise to keep clear of.

He was beginning to get a clearer idea of what was happening. When he saw Gunny pull a short, thick club with a rounded leather-covered head from his pocket, he knew for sure. Gunny swung the club in front of him, softly hitting the palm of his hand with it, the thick sound of it striking his flesh a gentle warning to Payne of what he might expect.

Payne eyed the weapon quickly, and recognized it as a common device the seamen referred to as a sap. Properly used, a single blow could leave a man unconscious for hours. And he had no doubt but that Gunny was the sort of man who would be more than competent using it.

It was quite obvious to Payne by now that it wasn't the contents of his pockets these men wanted, after all. They were on a recruiting mission, out to fill a few empty places in their ship's complement.

A short crew was a common enough problem with merchant ships leaving the East Coast bound for the Far East. After making a few stops along the way, a certain percentage of the crew invariably came to the conclusion that a sailor's life wasn't to their liking, after all. Those who decided to end their seafaring days took the opportunity to simply jump ship in San Francisco, leaving their captains with the problem of filling their places. As a matter of simple expedience, second and third mates were usually enlisted for the task, given a small bounty for each man brought on board, and no questions asked.

It was obvious the pair facing Payne were a recruitment party, and it was equally obvious that Gunny was more interested in earning the bounty than in being especially fussy about how he filled the empty bunks. Payne gritted his teeth. He'd have only one chance, he knew. One blow from Gunny's sap and the next time he'd see daylight would be from the deck of a ship, too far out to sea to do anything about changing his condition.

Payne stared at the sap in the sailor's hand. Two against one weighted the odds, but he thought he could deal with that. The sap, however, was something else.

133

"I wouldn't make a good seaman," he said slowly, searching for an opening. "Plain fact is, I get sick just looking at a wave."

The man called Gunny smiled. "Oh, you'll be surprised how soon you'll get over those little problems," he said. "I've seen it happen hundreds of times. One day a man's lyin', pukin' his brains out, wishin' he could die, the next he's climbin' like a monkey through the riggin' an' fillin' his face with hardtack every chance he gets."

"It does sound incredibly inviting," Payne said, "but still, I prefer to decline the honor."

"Didn't your mama ever tell you that declinin' an invitation ain't good manners?" Gunny asked.

"I'm afraid I must have missed that lecture," Payne admitted.

Gunny sobered. It seemed he was becoming bored with the conversation and wanted to get on with the matter at hand.

"Now we can do this easy or we can do it hard," he said. He continued to swing the sap, and he punctuated his words with the sharp slapping sound it made as it hit his hand. "Your choice."

Payne crouched a bit, leaning forward and balancing himself on the balls of his feet.

"Most obliging of you," he said. "But the simple fact is, I'd sooner not do it at all."

Gunny smiled. Payne got the distinct impression that the sailor took a perverse pleasure in his unsavory task.

"You can't think you'll beat the two of us," Gunny sneered. "Not with the amount of whiskey we saw you drink inside you."

"I damn well plan to try," Payne hissed.

With that he kicked, not waiting for either of the sailors to make the initial move. His only chance, he

134

knew, was surprising the two by attacking first. His boot came into sharp and painful contact with Gunny's hand, sending the dangerous sap flying up into the darkness and leaving the sailor with a handful of injured fingers and even more seriously injured pride.

"That helps," Payne murmured.

"Damn you," Gunny hissed angrily, as he lunged forward, fists flying.

But contrary to his expectations, Payne really was in control of his reactions, despite the whiskey he'd drunk. He blocked all but two of Gunny's blows, and managed to land a half dozen vicious punches of his own before Gunny decided he'd had enough.

The sailor fell back, moaning, his hands grasping his belly.

Payne felt a warm drip of blood on his chin. He wiped it quickly away with the back of his hand. He didn't take the time to consider the extent of his injury, but turned his glance to the second man, who had, until that moment, seemed content to hold back and watch the negotiations.

"Care for a share?" Payne offered. He nodded toward the still gasping Gunny.

The second sailor looked at his mate. It was apparent that he'd expected his role to be a relatively passive one, and that he had no appetite for the sort of punishment Payne seemed capable of administering.

He looked back at Payne and shrugged.

"Too much bother, if you ask me," he said. Then, unexpectedly, he grinned. "I guess you ain't cut out to be a sailor, after all," he added.

"Told you so," Payne replied. "Why don't you go buy yourself and your friend a beer?" he suggested. Then, feeling suddenly effusive, he put his hand into

135

his pocket and pulled out a coin. "On me," he said, as he tossed the coin to the sailor.

The second sailor laughed as he caught it.

"You're a strange one," he said. Then he shrugged and put his hand on the arm of his still panting mate. "Come on, Gunny," he said. "You've been workin' too hard," he added, with a slightly malicious chuckle.

Payne stood where he was and watched as the two disappeared back into the saloon. His lip was cut and the taste of blood filled his mouth. Still, he didn't feel the hurt as anything but a mild discomfort. The fact was, he felt better than he'd felt in days.

He oughtn't to be so pleased with himself, he knew, but still he was. For the first time since Whit had been killed, he'd faced something straight on, no fencing, no hiding or holding back, no playing with words. It might not have been pretty or pleasant, but at least the short meeting with the two sailors had been completely honest.

He inhaled the damp night air, filling his lungs. It was time he was honest with himself. And it was long past time he was honest with Aura.

Payne was still a good distance from the house when he heard Aura scream. He had no idea how he knew it was her, but somehow he knew. He started to run.

He saw the lights in the store as he approached, the dim glow passing through the front windows and fading quickly as it met the night darkness outside. But it didn't fade so quickly that Payne missed the hint of movement at the far end of the long porch that fronted the store.

He dashed toward it and leaped forward, lashing out at the place where he'd seen the movement. As he expected, he found his hands come in contact with something warm, something that certainly wasn't the wood of the building's siding. He grasped onto it and held on as a pair of fists were suddenly turned against him. In the near total darkness, there wasn't much for him to see, but he knew he was holding onto a man's arm. It was more than enough.

His opponent was far less a match for him than the two sailors had been, and Aura's scream had left Payne far more primed for a fight than even the threat to himself had left him. He yanked on the arm, pulling his captive close, then landed one quick blow in the vicinity of what he assumed was the man's abdomen. The attack was more than enough to end all resistance. His opponent exhaled with a thick, almost liquid *"Oof,"* then doubled over.

Payne hooked his arm around his captive, then grabbed both his arms and pulled them behind him. Completely in control now, he dragged the man to the store's door.

He looked in the window to find Aura standing frozen, her expression strained and frightened, her face unnaturally pale in the lamplight. He wasn't exactly sure what he'd expected to see when he'd looked in, but the scream, he realized, had frightened him more than he'd realized. A wave of relief swept through him as he realized she was unhurt.

He tapped at the glass of the window. She jumped, frightened by the noise, then turned and peered back at him. He could tell she was about to scream again.

"Aura, it's me, Payne," he called in to her. "Open the door."

The last thing he wanted was for her to scream again. As soon as he realized she was unhurt, he began to think of a number of questions he'd like to ask the man he'd just subdued. He didn't want Aura to draw any more attention to the house than she'd already drawn. It would be a lot easier for him to ask his cowed visitor just what he'd been doing by paying a such an unconventional late night call if he could do it without the help of Sheriff James Dougherty or any of his men.

"Aura! Open the door. Now."

The second command shook Aura out of her terrorized daze. She ran around the counter to the door.

Payne groaned as he heard her fumbling with the lock. It seemed to take forever for her to get it open. He spent the time squinting into the darkness, praying that no one would happen along and see him holding a man with his arms pinned behind him. He didn't relish the thought of having to explain the situation.

Once Aura finally had the door open, Payne pushed his captive ahead of him into the store.

"Pull down the shades," he told her. When she hesitated, he repeated the order. "Do it!"

Confused, but startled enough so that she didn't dare to disobey, she hurriedly pulled down the long shades that covered the windows. When she'd done, she turned to watch Payne marshal his captive forward and force him onto the floor in front of the counter.

"What are you doing here?" Payne hissed at the cowed young man.

His captive looked up warily at Payne, and then darted a glance at Aura. His eyes narrowed as he vehemently shook his head in reply to Payne's question.

"No speakee," he muttered. He waved his hands in front of his face.

Aura crept up silently behind Payne and stared at the young Oriental. As soon as she saw his face, she felt an ache in her stomach like a cold fist clenching her inside.

"That's him," she told Payne. "That's the man who shot Whit."

Chapter Eight

Payne turned to face Aura. Her words had startled him, for the last thing he'd expected was that this cringing night prowler might be the mysterious disappearing man she'd insisted she'd seen at the cemetery.

"You're sure?" he asked.

She nodded. "Yes," she told him, her tone determined enough to make him believe her. "I'm absolutely sure. This is the man I saw at the cemetery this morning, and it was him I saw that night. He was here, talking with Whit."

Payne turned back to face the young Oriental. It was hard for him to visualize this slight, cowering youth as a cold-blooded murderer. A sneak thief, perhaps, but hardly the type to have the courage it would take to face a man like Whit and coolly fire a bullet into his heart.

Still, from what he'd seen in Aura's expression, it was more than apparent that the mere sight of the youth had terrified her. Either this actually was the man who'd come to the door the night Whit had been killed, or she was mistaken but sincerely believed it was. Payne tried to envision him facing Whit and pulling the trigger, but couldn't. There was something about his eyes, the way he looked up at Payne. This youth might be cunning and sly when the opportunity dictated, but that hardly made him a cold-blooded murderer.

Payne glowered at him and was rewarded by seeing him cringe. The reaction was enough to make him suspect the youth understood what Aura had said, despite his insistence that he didn't speak English.

"Talk!" he hissed through tight lips.

The young man cowered at the sound of Payne's voice and tried, uselessly, to back away from him. Unable to escape, he succeeded only in hitting the back of his head against the counter. Once again he shook his head and waved his hands in front of his face.

"No speakee," he murmured furiously. "No speakee."

Payne glanced back at Aura. Perhaps he was seeing something that wasn't there. Perhaps her insistence made him too anxious to believe that this might be Whit's murderer.

"You *are* sure?" he demanded.

He could see her jaw tighten. It was more than obvious she didn't like the fact that he doubted her.

"Yes," she hissed through tight lips. "I told you I'm sure."

"And you heard him speak to Whit?" he asked her.

She nodded, and slowly some of the tension began to dissipate. She realized where his questions were leading.

"I saw them together and heard them speak, but I couldn't hear what they said," she replied. "I was too far away."

Payne knelt in front of the young Oriental and grabbed a handful of his shirt front.

"My brother spoke barely a handful of words of Chinese," he said, taking no pains to hide the fact that

140

he was growing angry and impatient with his captive's lie. "That means whatever conversation you had with him was conducted in English. Now, you either stop playing games with me and tell me what it was you said to him, or I'll simply decide not to bother the sheriff about arresting you and seeing to a trial." He pulled the young man's shirt closer, carrying his torso with it, until their faces were only inches apart. "It would please me just fine to dispense with a little brotherly justice of my own. Because, believe me, it would make me feel a whole lot better to kill you with my bare hands than it would to watch you hang."

There was no longer any doubt but that the young man spoke English. His face drained of color as he listened to Payne's threat.

Aura, too, paled. She couldn't quite believe what she'd heard Payne threaten.

"You don't mean that?" she gasped.

Payne didn't even bother to turn back and face her.

"This is none of your business," he hissed. "Be quiet, or else leave."

Aura shuddered and took a step backward. But nothing Payne could possibly say was about to make her leave him alone with the young Oriental. He might not like her, might not be willing to listen to her, but still she couldn't turn her back on him and let him put a noose around his own neck. She was not about to allow him to become a murderer, regardless of the provocation.

The young man sat cowering and stared at Payne's expression for a long moment. He seemed to be weighing what he'd heard against what he saw in Payne's eyes. Apparently there was more than enough threat in the frigid blue glare Payne leveled at him to convince him he really was in danger.

He put his hand on Payne's and tried to pry his

fingers open to free their grasp. It was impossible, and he gave up the attempt. Defeated, he finally made up his mind.

"I didn't kill your brother," he said softly.

He'd dropped the pretense that he didn't speak English and along with it the false accent. Surprisingly, he'd spoken with a precise, slightly upper-class British intonation. Payne was more than a little bit bewildered by it.

"So you speakee after all," Payne hissed, mimicking the accent he'd used at the start.

The young man smiled slightly, then nodded.

"I was orphaned as an infant," he said. "I was raised by an English couple who ran a British missionary school in Shanghai." He let his eyes meet Payne's. "English was my first language, and besides, I was an excellent pupil."

"So it would seem," Payne noted. "What are you doing here?"

The young man seemed to be warming to his story. He darted a quick grin up at Aura. "I rather think the good pastor expected I'd emulate him and dedicate my life to teaching, spreading the word and enlarging the flock. I might have, too, had they not taught me the true meaning of Western compassion. You see, they left me in China when they decided to return to Britain to retire. It may have been amusing to them to have a precocious Oriental child in their home, but a grown man, now, that would be something else, especially in Morton-on-Marsh. After all, it's not something you want to spend your life explaining to the neighbors."

"No doubt," Payne growled.

"Your brother found my accent very amusing," the young man continued, punctuating his comment with a tight little grin.

Payne gritted his teeth and cursed silently. It was

apparent that the young Chinese had salvaged his composure and now felt quite secure. That definitely was not what he wanted. He knew it was much easier to get reliable information from a man who was too frightened to lie than it was to get it from one who was able to calmly meet his gaze.

He shook his head slowly. "I don't find anything about you in the least amusing," he said.

The young man now made no pretense at being even slightly cowed. If anything, his expression became a bit defiant. He looked up at Payne and shrugged.

"It was not my intention to amuse you," he said.

"Who the hell are you?" Payne demanded.

"My name is Yang Wu," the young man replied calmly. "And I assure you, I did not kill Mr. Randall."

Payne was growing angrier by the moment. The young man's manner was much too cool, too sure. Payne was now beginning to think that he might have caught Whit's killer after all.

"I suppose that's why you were at the cemetery this morning and why you came here tonight," he suggested sarcastically, "because you were just trying to tell his wife it was all an unfortunate misunderstanding?"

Wu's expression grew somber at the mention of the cemetery.

"I went to the cemetery to bid farewell to Mr. Randall," he said, "to pay him the final honor he deserved. I liked him. He was a fair and honest man, and that's a good deal to say for an Occidental."

Payne ignored the slur.

"And that's why you chose to terrify his widow and disappear," he pressed, "out of a feeling of respect for the deceased?"

Despite the threatening look Payne leveled at him, Wu remained entirely unintimidated.

"When it became apparent to me that Mrs. Randall remembered me," he said, "I thought it wise to leave before circumstances became unpleasant," he said. "After all," he added, "it would only seem logical for her to think I'd killed her husband if I was the last person she saw with him."

"And you came here tonight just to make sure you hadn't made a mistake?" Payne asked. "Or was it the thought of frightening her again that drew you?"

"I came here tonight to get something that belongs to me," Wu replied evenly.

"There is nothing here that belongs to you," Payne said.

Wu shrugged. "If it was not on Mr. Randall's body or left here in the store, then perhaps the murderer took it," he said.

Payne glared at him a moment longer, then released his hold of the young man's shirt.

"I'll give you this," he said. "You're either an idiot without enough brains to be afraid, or else you're a damn good liar."

"Or else I'm telling the truth," Wu countered.

Payne shrugged. "Or else you're telling the truth," he conceded. "Why don't you tell me your version of what happened that night, and I'll decide which?"

Freed of Payne's hold, the young man pulled back and settled himself a bit more comfortably against the side of the counter.

"What do you want me to tell you?" he asked.

"Everything," Payne replied. "Why did you come here that night?"

"Mr. Randall had asked me to get some information for him," he began.

"Why would he ask you?"

"Because I've helped him before," Wu replied. "My English makes me useful to powerful people in the

144

Chinese community. I make my living by facilitating matters for them, and that oftentimes makes me privy to information that might otherwise be unobtainable."

"What sort of information did Whit want?" Payne interrupted, although he was almost positive he already knew.

Wu met his glance, then quickly looked away to stare at Aura's feet. "That is of no matter now," he replied.

"I think it is," Payne insisted.

Wu looked up. "Then you think incorrectly," he said.

Payne gritted his teeth. This was becoming more and more difficult. He realized that each time Wu evaded a question he became just a bit more defiant. He decided it would be better to move on than to insist on hearing the answer to a question that he was sure he already knew.

"All right," he said. "Let's do it this way—Whit asked you to see if you could find out where counterfeit twenty-dollar bills were coming from."

Wu's eyes widened with surprise. He'd obviously not expected that Whit had confided that particular bit of information, even to a brother.

"Perhaps," he said.

"And this was a favor you were only too willing to perform out of the kindness of your heart," Payne continued.

The young man gave him a disdainful glance.

"Certainly not. He offered to pay me. It was a simple business proposition."

Payne shrugged. "How could I have suspected anything else?" he asked, his voice thick with sarcasm. "You might honor my brother once he was dead, but as long as he was alive, money took precedence."

145

The Oriental chose to ignore him.

"I found the answers he was seeking a bit more difficult to obtain than I originally expected," Wu went on. "What I did learn, however, was who he might go to to find his answers."

"Which was?"

The young man shook his head. "I trusted your brother," he said. "Why should I trust you?"

"Because it won't take much to push me to the point where I will gladly put my hands around your throat and squeeze the life out of you," Payne told him.

He'd spoken absolutely emotionlessly, as though he were speaking of the possibility that it might rain. And for that moment, he really believed what he said was true.

But it wasn't enough to convince Wu. He shook his head.

"If you kill me, it would only expedite matters," he told Payne. "In fact, it might be preferable to die quickly than to face what they would do to me. The people I speak of are not especially tolerant, Mr. Randall, nor are they overly burdened by scruples. If you were to go to them and let them know it was I who sent you, it would mean my life."

Payne settled back on his heels and stared at the younger man.

"It would seem you are caught between the proverbial rock and the hard place, doesn't it?" he mused. He considered Wu's determined stare. "All right," he said after a moment, "let's let that particular subject rest for a while. Suppose you tell me what happened the night Whit was killed."

Wu nodded, apparently willing to be cooperative on this matter, at least.

"There isn't very much for me to tell," he said. "I came here to relate to Mr. Randall what little I'd learned. I gave him a token that would help him gain admittance to talk to those people I mentioned. He thanked me and I left."

"And he was alive when you left?"

"Certainly," Wu replied. "What reason would I have for killing him?"

"What reason indeed?" Payne asked.

Wu leaned forward to him.

"Look," he said. "I gave Mr. Randall what information I'd managed to find, and he was grateful for what little there was of it. He paid me, rather extravagantly, I thought, for what I'd done. I certainly had no reason to do him any harm. I thanked him and then I left."

"Then how do you explain the fact that he was found shot dead a few minutes later?" Payne asked.

Wu shook his head. His expression grew thoughtful.

"The only explanation I can offer is that someone came in after I left and killed him," he said.

"And that someone must have taken a great deal of trouble to ensure his timing would be perfect," Payne muttered. "Your supposition sounds pretty far-fetched, if you ask me."

"However it sounds, that's what happened," Wu insisted. He didn't seem at all calm or defiant now. Despite the fact that Payne no longer seemed on the edge of violence, he seemed almost desperate to be believed. He looked up at Aura and stared directly into her gaze. "I swear, I didn't kill him," he said.

Aura returned his gaze for a moment, then pulled away. She glanced quickly at the ledgers that lay open on the counter.

"That token you mentioned," she said. "What was it?"

Wu shook his head. "No," he murmured. "Without knowing how it is to be used, it's useless to you. And

I don't intend to tell you how to use it. Believe me, it's best for you that I keep my own counsel on this matter."

"Yet, if you're to be believed," Payne said, "you were willing to try to break in here and steal it. That is what you said, wasn't it?"

Wu turned his glance back to meet Payne's.

"I thought it would be safer," he said. "It would seem that I was mistaken."

"And your faceless murderer," Payne continued, "what motive would he have for murdering Whit?"

Wu slowly shook his head. "I don't know," he admitted. "Perhaps to keep him from getting too close to the answers he was seeking."

"The answers he might have found had he gone to meet your mysterious and murderous friends?" Payne asked.

"These people are not my friends," Wu insisted. "And I don't know if they would kill to keep him from learning their secrets. Perhaps they would."

"Then it stands to reason that the murderer might have taken that token you spoke of, whatever it might be."

Wu swallowed, suddenly struggling with a thick lump that had sprung up in his throat.

"He might have," he agreed.

"And that means he not only knows what it was that Whit had learned about them, but possibly that you were the source of that information."

Wu shook his head. "No," he said. "If that were so, I would already be dead."

Payne smiled grimly. "You very well might be," he said, his tone ominous.

* * *

Wu's eyes narrowed. "What does that mean?" he hissed.

"It means that by helping Whit, you placed yourself in the same position he was in. Believe me, your murderous friends will eventually come to the conclusion that they did only half their job when they killed my brother."

The young man's face drained of color. Still, he remained insistent.

"They aren't my friends," he stammered. "And how would they find out I was the one who spoke to Mr. Randall?"

Payne smiled a humorless half smile. He had managed to regain the upper hand, and he knew it. Wu's pale face was proof enough of that.

"If you want to trust your life to the possibility that they have fewer resources than Whit had, I can't stop you," he said. "But believe me, you're living in a fool's paradise, a paradise that's bound to crumble. Your only hope is to help me find the source of the counterfeit bills and Whit's killer. That is, assuming *you* really aren't the killer."

"I'm not," Wu cried out. He looked first at Payne, then up at Aura, then back to Payne. "You have to believe me."

Payne shrugged. He turned around and looked up at Aura.

"What do you think?" he asked her. "Should we call our friend Sheriff Dougherty and tell him we have found his murderer for him, or should we just tell him we have a night prowler?"

"What difference would it make?" Wu asked sharply. "You know what will happen to me if the sheriff knows I was here that night. He'll decide he has his murderer, and that will be the end of it. It will be easy for him to hang a Chinese, any Chinese."

Payne shrugged, unconcerned. "Give me one reason why I should care," he said.

Aura scowled. She didn't like the offhanded manner with which he was treating Wu, especially as she was now convinced Wu was, as he claimed, innocent of Whit's murder. Aside from that, it was apparent to her that the young man was the only link that might lead them to Whit's murderer.

"Reason tells me I shouldn't, but I believe him when he says he didn't kill Payne," she said slowly.

Wu exhaled slowly. It seemed he had been holding his breath until she'd made her pronouncement.

"I didn't," he said. "I swear to you I didn't."

Aura stared at him solemnly.

"But you do know who did," she said softly.

Wu shook his head. "No, no that's not true," he nearly shouted. "When I left, Mr. Randall was still alive."

"You might not have seen him fire the bullet that killed Whit," Aura insisted, "but you know. If not precisely, you have a good idea who was responsible. And if you aren't lying, if you liked my husband, if you really wanted to honor his memory, you'd help find his killer."

Aura realized both men were staring at her, and both wore startled expressions. But Wu's was different from Payne's; the surprise she saw in his eyes was mingled with a tinge of fear. She had no idea how she had come to the certainty that Wu could point a finger at Whit's murderer, but from what she saw in his eyes, she knew she was right.

He leaned forward, toward her. It seemed to Aura that he was reaching out to her and would have grasped the fabric of her skirt had she not stepped back. When she did, he leaned back again and sighed.

"I can't help you," he said softly.

150

His voice was calm, but Aura could see something frightened, something pleading in his dark eyes. It amazed her that she had been so terrified of him. Staring down at him now, she saw that all his bravado had completely disappeared. He seemed only a frightened, bewildered youth to her.

Payne, too, saw the fear.

"Then help yourself," Payne told him.

Wu returned his glance to meet Payne's.

"You don't understand how dangerous these people can be," he murmured.

"On the contrary, I do understand," Payne assured him. "What better lesson could I have than the sight of my brother's body?"

Wu could think of no response. He sat staring at Payne, his gaze frozen and his expression resigned.

Payne waited for a moment, then abruptly pushed himself to his feet. He stood over the young Oriental, staring down at him. It seemed unnaturally quiet in the room, the three of them so still that even the air around them was motionless. For a moment Payne thought Wu might change his mind and offer to help, but as the moment dragged on and the young man said nothing, he realized he was wrong.

Finally he stood back and broke the silence.

"Leave, then," Payne said. He motioned toward the door.

Wu looked uncertainly at it.

"You're not going to call the sheriff?" he asked.

Payne shrugged. "What difference does it make to me if you're hanged for my brother's murder or killed by the counterfeiters?" he asked. "You'll be just as dead either way."

Wu hesitated for a moment more, staring up at Payne. Then he pushed himself to his feet and started for the door.

"Yang Wu," Aura called after him.

He stopped with his hand on the doorknob and turned to face her.

"Yes?"

"You can still change your mind," she told him. "I'm sure Mr. Randall would prove generous should you choose to help him find his brother's murderer."

Wu darted a glance at Payne, then turned back to let his gaze meet Aura's. She felt as though he was judging her, although she could not fathom by what standards he might evaluate her or whether or not she managed to meet his minimum measure.

"I'll give the matter some thought," he said.

Then he turned away abruptly, pulled the door open, and slipped through it to vanish into the darkness of the night.

They stood silent for a moment, both staring at the door as though it harbored some important bit of information for which they searched but which continued to evade them. Then Payne turned to Aura.

"What made you say what you did about him knowing who murdered Whit?" he asked.

Aura shook her head. The truth was, she had no idea what had made it seem so clear to her. She'd simply known.

"I don't know," she admitted. "I didn't even realize I was talking to him until I heard myself speak."

He arched a questioning brow, then shrugged in resignation.

"You were right, you know," he said.

She nodded. "Yes, he made that more than clear by his expression, if nothing else. He knows who's behind your counterfeit currency, and he also knows who killed Whit. He wouldn't have been so frightened if he didn't at least suspect."

Payne grinned suddenly.

"You aren't by any chance an undercover agent, are you?" he asked.

Aura's brow wrinkled. "A what?" she asked.

"Nothing," he said with a shrug. He followed the path Wu had taken to the door. When he reached it, he threw the bolt in the lock. It settled with a firmly solid metallic click.

"I suppose that should make me feel safe," Aura said softly.

He turned back to face her. "Hardly," he said. He considered her expression for a moment before he added, "Considering the impressive wealth of intuition you've displayed this evening, I'd think you wouldn't feel safe no matter how many locks might be on the doors."

Aura's glance found his, and she swallowed uncomfortably. His expression made it only too clear that he meant what he'd said.

"You aren't making it any easier," she told him.

"It's not my responsibility to make it easier," he told her. He stared at her silently for a long moment, feeling a hard knot of want growing inside him and hating himself for feeling as he did. Finally he turned away. "May I assume I can take it for granted that you now realize you can't stay on here?" he asked.

Aura was startled by the question. For an instant she'd been sure she'd seen something in his gaze— compassion, or perhaps even something more. And for that instant she'd let herself remember how she'd felt when he'd held her in his arms, how the touch of his hands and the feel of his body close to hers had left her weak and yearning and set her blood racing. As she remembered, the same heat started to seep through her veins.

But then he turned away and a cold settled over her, extinguishing the heat and leaving her chilled to the bone. She cursed her stupid weakness, and told herself she was a fool to let her imagination run off that way, ignoring reality. It won't happen again, she told herself; she wouldn't let it happen again.

"Why should I think that?" she demanded.

He turned back to face her. There was no possibility that Aura might misinterpret what she saw in his expression this time. It was impatience and anger.

"That young fool just got finished telling you what kind of people are involved in Whit's death," he said.

"I doubt that nice, churchgoing people usually commit murder," she sniped, pertubed by his manner, telling herself he had no reason to be angry with her.

Payne gritted his teeth. "It must be obvious, even to you, that it's dangerous for you to stay on here."

Aura shrugged, perversely pleased that she could at least rouse some show of emotion from him.

"Dangerous for you, perhaps, but not for me," she told him. "You're the one who came to San Francisco to look for counterfeiters. I have nothing to do with any of it."

She turned away from him and rounded the counter, returning to the far side. She reached for the ledger she had left lying on the counter when she first saw Yang Wu's face in the shop window. She lifted the cover and firmly shut it.

Payne crossed back to the counter. He leaned over it and grabbed her hands, holding them by the wrists, forcing her attention away from the ledgers and back to him.

She stared down at his hands for a moment. She was startled by the surge of heat that filled her at the unexpected touch of his fingers against her pulse, despite her determination not to allow him to affect her. But it was clear that this was the furthest thing from a embrace, and she told herself she was glad, that the

154

last thing she wanted from him was an attempt at seduction. She looked up at him, resignation more than anything else filling her expression.

"Whit didn't leave enough money for you to stay on here indefinitely, in any case," he said. "I've already told you that I don't have the wherewithal to take care of you. The only rational thing you can do is go back to your family."

She pulled her hands angrily away from him.

"And I've already told you, I have no family to go back to," she said. For an instant she was struck by a biting feeling of isolation as she remembered how her father had turned his back on her when she'd left. She turned the hurt against him and let it grow and change to anger. "But you needn't worry about me," she told him, her tone filled with ice. "In any case, you're the last person in the world I'd look to. I intend to take care of myself from now on."

He looked at her as if she'd suggested she was planning to sprout wings and fly.

"And just how do you intend to do that?" he demanded.

"I'm going to run this store," she said. "So you can dismiss any consideration you might have of me. As soon as you've tended to the matter of Whit's murder, you can leave, go back to New York or wherever it was you came from, and wash your hands of me with a clear conscience."

Payne felt his jaw clench. She was behaving damned unreasonably, he told himself. It was ridiculous to think she could run Whit's business alone. Inside of six months she'd ruin it, run it so far into the ground that it wouldn't be worth selling. Then she'd be left with absolutely nothing.

"Look," he said through tight lips, "you know as well as I do that you have no real right to all of Whit's

155

estate. I could take you to court, contest the will. Why don't you make things easier on both of us? Let Crofton sell the place, take the money, and go."

His tone quite simply infuriated her. She might have doubts about her ability to run a business, but he had no right to tell her she was nothing but an incompetent little fool.

"I have no intention of going," she muttered angrily. "If it bothers you to have me remain here, then that's your problem to deal with, not mine."

"You really intend to stay on and run this store?" he demanded.

She nodded. "I believe that's what I said."

"And nothing I can say will change that?"

"Absolutely nothing."

"You're an incredible little fool," he told her.

He'd made her really angry now. His certainty that she was proposing something completely beyond her only made her that much more determined.

"And you are a presumptuous, supercilious cad. Where is it written that someone who disagrees with the all-knowing Mr. Payne Randall must be a fool?" she demanded. "Doesn't it occur to you that I just might be capable of doing this without any help?"

He shook his head. "No," he admitted, "the thought never entered my mind."

The arrogance of the man, Aura thought. She wanted to strangle him.

"Well, I intend to prove you wrong."

"I hope you do," he said. "But if you don't, don't come looking for pity."

"Believe me, you'd be the last one on earth I'd go to for pity or anything else," she told him. "Now, if you'll excuse me, I have work to do." She pointedly lifted the ledger. "And unless I'm mistaken, you have something you were supposed to be doing—finding your precious counterfeiters and Whit's killer."

Payne stood back from the counter and stared at her. It was a challenge she'd offered him, and he knew it. She was telling him he had no right to doubt her when he hadn't even taken a step toward finding the counterfeiters.

He nodded to her and clicked his heels together in a passable imitation of a military bow, silently conceding the validity of her implied criticism. Still, he couldn't just let her dismiss him, he told himself, as he crossed to the hall that led upstairs. He stopped in the doorway and turned back to her.

"I have a list of merchants who surrendered counterfeit bills to Wells Fargo," he said, not quite sure why he felt a need to explain this to her, but unwilling to make the effort to overcome the inclination. "I expect they'll have a few ideas as to who might have given them the bills in payment. It's the long route, but I may be able to find a trail back to the counterfeiters. I wouldn't expect we'll see much of each other in the next few days."

"I'll suffer that disappointment," she snapped back. "I'm sure I'll have more than enough to do to keep myself busy. I doubt I'll even notice your absence."

He opened his mouth, about to say something more, but then seemed to think better of it. He shrugged and turned away.

Aura waited until he was gone before she reopened the ledger and once again began to leaf through it. It didn't take her long before she found what she was looking for, the small square of blue paper with the strange markings on it. She stared at it, fingering the paper as she considered the dark squiggles that had been written on it.

This, she told herself, was the token Yang Wu had spoken of, the free passage he'd arranged so that Whit might see those dangerous people of whom he'd spoken. She didn't know how she knew it, but the spark of intuition that had been burning since Payne had marshaled the young Chinese man into the store was glowing bright now. She was as certain of it as she'd ever been of anything in her life.

The question was, what should she do with it? Give it to Payne? If she did, and he somehow managed to use it to find those people, anything might happen. The truth was, the threats he'd made to Yang Wu frightened her. She realized she really no idea of what he was capable of doing.

Under normal circumstances he might be the most careful man in the world. Certainly Wells Fargo must trust him if they sent him so far to investigate the matter of counterfeiting. But this was far too personal for him to remain detached and objective. It was only to be expected that Whit's murder would lead him to be foolhardy.

What if she gave him this slip of paper and he discovered how to use it? What if he went to those people and told them he knew they were involved in Whit's murder? There was no doubt that the sort of ruthless people they'd proved themselves to be would not balk at the idea of causing a second death.

The thought sent a terrified chill through her. If Payne was harmed by Yang Wu's mysterious criminals, then what would she do? Even worse, what if he was killed? The possibility left a shiver of pure terror trailing down her spine.

But if she ignored this thing, destroyed it, perhaps, then she was as good as letting Whit's murderer go

158

free. This thin slip of paper, she was sure, was the only link that might lead to the killers. She stared at it, and as she did, the thing began to feel heavy in her hand. She'd stumbled onto an unexpected burden in Whit's ledgers, and it was growing heavier by the moment.

She put the ledgers away, and then tucked the blue slip into the pocket of her skirt. Payne had told her he had paths to explore. That meant she had time, she told herself, time to consider what she ought to do.

And then it struck her that it might even prove possible for her to make a few discreet inquiries of her own. After all, during the course of business of running the store, it would only be normal to ask a few questions about the many bewildering odds and ends that Whit had left unattended. People wouldn't question her motive for asking their advice. After all, she was simply a trusting widow trying to make her own way in the world.

The possibility began to grow more and more intriguing to her. It would serve Payne right if she was able to find some of the answers he was looking for, she mused wryly. Maybe then he'd reconsider his attitudes about capabilities, both his own and hers.

And as much as she wanted to, she couldn't quite ignore the small voice inside her that whispered, "Maybe then he'll realize what a fool he is by turning his back on me."

Chapter Nine

Aura raised the heavy canvas shades and stared out through the shop windows. It was a bright, sharply sunny morning, and a flood of brilliant light poured through them to fill the store. She gazed out at a street that was already busy with both foot and carriage traffic. A perfect morning, she told herself, to make her initial foray into the world of commerce.

She unlocked the door and turned face-outward the small sign proclaiming her shop open for business. Then she returned to the far side of the counter, took up the feather duster she'd been using, and busied herself by searching for any wayward motes that might somehow have escaped her attention.

She was so intent on listening for the sound of a customer at the door that when, several minutes later, it did open, the thin tinkling sound of the bell seemed almost deafening. She spun around, feather duster still in hand, and found herself completely startled by the sight of her very first customer.

"Good morning."

A wide mouthed "Oh" was Aura's less than brilliant rejoinder.

The simple truth was, Aura was a bit startled by the appearance of this particular customer. Although the woman's dark moiré skirt and jacket were in excellent taste, there was something excessive about the arrangement of ribbons and silk flowers that decorated her large-brimmed hat. Or perhaps it was just the wealth of bright red curls that peeped out from under that brim that elicited Aura's response. In any event, she'd expected she'd find it was some miner or perhaps a servant from one of the more prosperous homes standing in front of the counter facing her. It wasn't.

She reminded herself that she'd seen evidence in Whit's ledgers making it only too apparent a certain Charlotte O'Shea was a valued customer. Despite that, however, she had to admit that she hadn't really expected to come face to face with a woman who so obviously subscribed to a certain calling quite this early in her business career.

There was no question in Aura's mind but that this woman was one of the group that had attended Whit's funeral. She even had a hazy recollection of the bright red curls and the piercing look that was at that moment being leveled directly at her. And just as there had been no doubt in her mind that afternoon, she now had absolutely no question as to what role her customer played in San Francisco's burgeoning economy.

Aura felt herself shudder. She didn't need to use her imagination to know what her father would have said, had he been there. The words were silently screaming in her mind: first running away, and then taking up trade like a common shopgirl. Now dealing with whores. What next? Becoming a whore yourself?

She had to forcibly smother the words before the tyrant in her mind went on to accuse her of further sins. She certainly didn't need to be reminded that she'd slept with her dead husband's brother, or to be told that she was no better than a whore herself.

161

She focused her attention on her customer and forced herself to smile. She was a shopkeeper, she told herself, and a customer, any customer, was to be valued. Besides, this wasn't Fall River. Back East, a woman of a certain calling wouldn't dream of approaching a respectable woman, and a respectable woman wouldn't dream of acknowledging her existence. But from the little she'd seen, this customer wasn't all that unconventional here. And if she was to stay on here in San Francisco and succeed, she would simply have to adjust.

She reminded herself that she'd turned her back on her father's house and his attitudes, and told herself it was about time she rid herself of those vestiges of his prejudices that she still carried around with her. Resolve, however, no matter how strong, was hardly enough to make her feel comfortable under the circumstances.

"May I help you?" she asked, and punctuated the question with what she hoped was an appropriately welcoming smile.

Madame Charlotte glanced around quickly, her sharp eyes seeming to take in everything in the store in that single sweep, including Aura's discomposure. The corners of her lips turned up in a tight little smile. She seemed more amused than put out by the effect her appearance had had.

"I was passing by and noticed the store was open again," she told Aura. "When it occurred to me that you might be running it now, I decided to stop and congratulate you on your fortitude." She smiled again, this time slyly. "A woman has few enough means to make her way in this world."

Aura tried to swallow the lump that had formed in her throat. Despite her determination, she was, she realized, more uncomfortable now than she'd been when Madame Charlotte had walked in. The madame's reference to the limited means a woman had to support herself only sharpened her awareness of the method Charlotte had chosen to earn her keep.

"My husband left the store to me," she said, in a voice that had grown suddenly thick, as though was were talking through a wad of cotton wool. She stopped, cleared her throat, and swallowed again. "It made the decision easier than it might otherwise have been," she finished, in a slightly more normal tone.

Charlotte pursed her lips and nodded.

"Still," she said, "if anyone had asked, I'd have told them I'd thought you'd give it up and return East. You looked every bit a frightened little rabbit at the cemetery." She grinned then, this time broadly, because it was obvious that a touch of the frightened rabbit was again showing itself in Aura's face.

Despite whatever it was about her expression that made Aura the cause of Madame Charlotte's amusement, she was shocked to find she was beginning to feel just a bit less awkward. She certainly didn't know why, as their short exchange had included nothing that could possibly change the prejudices she'd spent all her life accumulating. But it was now apparent to her that Charlotte wasn't about to bite her, and she told herself a good shopkeeper did not offend a good customer. She dropped the feather duster she was still holding onto the shelf beneath the counter and started to walk out from behind it.

"I, I don't remember if I thanked you for coming to the cemetery," she said, as she approached Charlotte. "It was very kind of you."

"It was little enough," Charlotte replied. "Mr. Randall was a gentleman, and believe me, there's few enough real gentlemen in this world. It's a shame you never got to spend much time with him."

For a minute Aura thought the madame might be taunting her with the fact that she had known Whit a good deal better than his legal wife had ever known him. But a glance at Charlotte's face convinced her that the madame was simply making an attempt to be friendly, and, as odd as the situation seemed to her, she was grateful for the gesture.

"I know I shall spend the rest of my life regretting that loss," she replied.

Charlotte shrugged. "I've always thought it useless to make lifelong resolves," she said. "The best thing to do is get past unpleasantness and move on with your life. And if the good Lord put anything more substantial than feathers between your ears, that's just what you'll do. I can tell you from painful experience that it makes no sense to spend a lifetime mourning things you never had."

"No, I suppose not," Aura agreed.

"Do the most with what little you've got," Charlotte concluded.

Aura nodded. "That's just what I hope to do," she said.

"Wise," Charlotte said, her manner businesslike now that she'd completed her lecture on the fickle nature of life. She pulled the strings of her purse and opened it. "It would be only decent of me to bring my account up to date," she said. "If you have the total at hand?"

Aura nodded. "Of course," she said. She returned to the back of the counter, reached down to the shelf beneath it, pushed aside the feather duster, and pulled out the customer ledger. "There's several bolts of fine handmade lace in the cabinet there, if you'd care to look while I find the figure," she added, as she dropped the ledger onto the counter. She stepped to the side of the counter and pulled open the cabinet in question, revealing the heavy bolts of precious fabric. "They must have arrived just before Whit died. I found them still crated when I was tidying things up."

"And wisely chose not to let them languish in the darkness," Charlotte said.

Aura darted a startled glance at her. There seemed to be accusation in Charlotte's tone. Six months before, it would have been more than enough to have sent her scurrying away to nurse a hurt, but the newly independent Aura told herself she was not about to be cowed.

"It seemed good business," she said firmly.

Charlotte stared at her for a long moment, then laughed.

"I think you're going to do just fine here, after all," she said, as she walked past Aura to consider the contents of the cabinet. She eyed the half dozen bolts, then pulled one out. She fingered the heavy lace absently as she watched Aura return to the far side of the counter, open the ledger, and quickly leaf through the pages.

Aura realized Charlotte hadn't actually introduced herself, but she knew she had no need to ask for her name. There was, she knew, only one account in the ledger that could possibly be hers. She stopped at the page headed Charlotte O'Shea, the one with the half dozen different signatures and the unlikely little additions, the small pictures of hearts and lips and other oddments. She ran her finger down the column on the far right of the page, where Whit had kept a running total of the account.

"I believe your balance is thirty-three sixty-four," she said, as she looked up at Charlotte. "Does that sound right to you? If not, I'm sure I can find copies of the sales receipts."

Charlotte, she realized, had been giving her an evaluating stare, probably, she thought, wondering if she'd be astute enough to associate a name on a page with her. Not that it had really been much of a feat. But still, Aura saw her nod.

"Like I said, I think you'll do just fine here," Charlotte told her. "And you needn't bother finding any receipts. Thirty-three sixty-four sounds right enough. And I'll take a yard and a half of that lace. It will make a handsome blouse."

Aura nodded, left the ledger, and reached for the scissors. She was starting to feel an unexpected sense of confidence. She was even beginning to feel quite comfortable, especially as she was about to make her first sale. She told herself that despite her calling, Charlotte seemed pleasant enough company. Perhaps, she mused, she really ought to reconsider her old prejudices.

"Two yards would be safer," she suggested, as she began to measure out the fabric.

Charlotte laughed. "Let me know if you get tired of running a store," she said. "A good businesswoman is an asset in my business."

With those few words, Charlotte banished Aura's feeling of confidence and called up the tyrannical little ghost that had nearly managed to unsettle her a few moments before. Her father's leering face peered out at her from behind Charlotte's shoulder. What did I tell you? he seemed to be saying. Deal with a whore and then become one yourself.

Aura blushed. Even without the leering image, the suggestion horrified her.

"Oh, no, I couldn't . . ."

"No, I don't suppose you could," Charlotte broke in quickly. She smiled a tight, hard smile, but then grew suddenly very sober. "But then, you never know what you can or can't do until the time comes when you need to do it."

Aura's blush grew deeper. "I didn't mean any offense, Miss O'Shea," she said. "It's just . . ." She stopped, confused and sure that anything she said would be the wrong thing.

"It's Mrs. O'Shea, and no offense taken," Charlotte briskly assured her.

Duly chastised, Aura murmured, "Of course, Mrs. O'Shea."

She went about the business of cutting the length of lace, using the activity to hide her lack of composure. She was pleased to find that Charlotte had lost the urge to consider her every move and expression. When she glanced up, she saw the madame pull a neat roll of bills from her purse and begin to count out the amount of her bill. It was a decidedly thick roll. Charlotte's business was obviously doing quite well.

The next several minutes were spent in wrapping Charlotte's purchase and settling the account.

"I don't suppose you know of anyone who reads Chinese, do you, Mrs. O'Shea?" Aura asked casually, as she counted out appropriate change.

Charlotte's eyes narrowed. She seemed intrigued by the request, and more than a bit suspicious.

"Reads Chinese?" she asked. "Why do you ask?"

"Only because I found a few markers among my husband's accounts," Aura said, as she handed over the change. She pretended to ignore Charlotte's suspicious stare. "I'll have to have them translated if I hope to collect on the debts."

The explanation seemed satisfactory. Charlotte's suspicious stare wavered, and then disappeared.

"Perhaps my houseboy could help you," she suggested. "Ask him when he comes for the weekly order."

"I'll do that," Aura replied, with what she hoped was a completely innocent smile.

Her business completed, Charlotte tucked her package under her arm.

"Mr. Randall allowed my girls to come in and make purchases to my account," Charlotte said. "I assume there will be no problem about continuing that arrangement, Mrs. Randall?"

Aura nodded. "I see no reason to disturb an arrangement that has proved mutually agreeable, Mrs. O'Shea," she replied.

It seemed a strange sort of exchange to Aura, the Mrs. Randall and Mrs. O'Shea, especially as she knew that neither she nor Charlotte was anything like settled matrons ought to be. Still, the formality seemed fitting. She was, she told herself, behaving as a proper shopkeeper should.

Satisfied, Charlotte started for the door. When she'd reached it, she stopped and turned back to face Aura.

"Oh, please give my best to Mr. Randall's brother," she said. "My girls quite enjoyed his company."

The lump suddenly returned to Aura's throat and threatened to choke her. She bit her lip, and told herself she oughtn't to have expected anything different. She'd sworn she wouldn't think about Payne Randall any more, and now she had yet another reason.

"I'll do that," she managed to croak through tight lips.

Charlotte smiled at her, apparently satisfied that her small revelation had had the effect she'd hoped. We really can't be friends, she seemed to be saying. And there's no reason to pretend that we can.

"Well, good day, Mrs. Randall," she said.

Aura nodded. "Good day, Mrs. O'Shea."

* * *

Aura didn't have much time to occupy herself exclusively with musings about either Charlotte's revelation concerning Payne or the madame's odd expression at her mention of markers written in Chinese. Soon after Charlotte left, a slow but constant stream of customers began to arrive. Save for an occasional moment when she could consider the morning's revelations, Aura had her hands quite full trying to meet her customers' requests, find the prices of various goods, and in general, encourage sales.

She was gratified to find that many of Whit's old customers were more than willing to keep up their relationship with his widow, and even help her locate among the crowded shelves the goods they wanted to buy. She slowly began to grow confident that she actually could make the store support her.

Despite the flurry, however, whenever she could manage it, she made a point of asking her customers if they could help her find someone who could read Chinese. Generally she was met with blank stares or amused smiles. There were no more suspicious stares, no reactions even remotely like Charlotte's. As the day progressed and she had the odd moment to consider things, she began to suspect that Charlotte's odd reaction might mean that she knew something about the strange marker she'd found in Whit's ledger.

In all fairness, though, she had to admit that her judgment on the matter might be colored by her reaction to Charlotte's mention of Payne's visit to her establishment. It would suit her only too well, she thought, if Payne's whorehouse of choice turned out to be the home of counterfeiters and murderers as well as its better known residents.

By the end of the afternoon she was willing to admit to herself that she was exhausted and was more than a little pleased when she heard the tall case clock in the parlor above finally tolling six o'clock. Besides aching with tiredness, she felt exultant and depressed and bewildered all at once, a mixture of emotions that stemmed from the reasonable success of her first day of business as well as her sporadic musings about Charlotte's revelations.

She was, she told herself, glad it was time to close the store. All she really wanted to do was sit for an hour with a pot of hot tea and think about the fact that Payne had visited Madame Charlotte's house. And wonder why Charlotte had seemed so surprised and suspicious when she'd mentioned the marker. The sixth sense that had told her Yang Wu knew more than he'd told Payne was now telling her that there was something else she ought to be able to recognize, something important that had happened that she didn't yet understand.

She went to the door and turned the closed sign facing outward. She was just about to lock the door when Howard Crofton bounded up the steps and gave her a slightly pleading look that she assumed meant he wished to be admitted.

Reluctantly she opened the door and stepped back so he could enter.

"Mr. Crofton," she said. "What a surprise."

"Not too unpleasant a surprise, I hope, Mrs. Randall?" he asked.

"Of course not."

"I hope I'm not inconveniencing you," he said. He pointed to the sign. "I hadn't realized how late it was."

"No, no, certainly," Aura told him. She forced herself to smile her friendly shopkeeper smile. "A merchant is always willing to welcome a customer."

He returned the smile. "I'm afraid I'm not here as a customer," he said. "In fact, I have to admit that I was

170

quite surprised to learn you'd decided to reopen the store."

"It would seem news travels quickly here," she said.

He nodded. "I suppose it does. San Francisco is, after all, a very small town," he told her. "I'd thought you were thinking about going back East."

"As you can see, I decided instead to try my hand at shopkeeping," she said. "I hope that doesn't disappoint you."

He smiled again, a wide smile that bared a row of even white teeth.

"Not in the least," he assured her. "What does disappoint me is that you have chosen to shoulder so much all alone. I would consider it an honor to offer any assistance you might need."

"Well, I managed to survive my first day relatively unscathed," Aura told him with a small laugh. "I have every confidence that I'll be able to repeat that feat at least once or twice again. But I do sincerely appreciate your concern."

"I am stricken, Mrs. Randall," he said. "My offer of help is unwanted and, apparently, completely unneeded."

Aura laughed again, more at his theatrically crestfallen expression than anything else. His eyes, dark and bright behind his spectacles, stared down at her dolefully.

"But none the less appreciated, Mr. Crofton, I assure you," she said.

"Please, I would be honored if you'd call me Howard," he said. He reached for her hand.

Aura glanced down at his hand, bewildered by his solicitous manner. He noticed her glance, pressed her hand quickly between his fingers, then released his hold. He'd surprised her, she realized. He certainly seemed different now than he had been the day of

171

Whit's funeral. He was so much less stiff, less formal with her. She wasn't sure she understood the change.

"I do thank you for the offer, Howard," she murmured.

"Let me at least take you somewhere for dinner," he offered. "After such a day as you must have had, it would be a shame if you were forced to cook your own supper as well."

Given names, dinner? Aura wondered if this could possibly be a preamble to courtship. Nonsense, she admonished herself. No one thinks that way about a woman widowed less than a month. Not even in the wilds of San Francisco. But still, he was behaving a good deal more effusively than mere politeness required. She was bewildered now, and too tired even to think about the matter.

She shook her head.

"It's a lovely offer," she told him, "but it was a terribly long day, and I am exhausted. I confess that all I really want to do right now is drink a cup of hot tea and get some sleep."

"Certainly, certainly," he said. "It was stupid of me not to have seen that immediately." He started to back out toward the door. "I won't keep you, then."

"Thank you for coming," Aura said, following him back to the door and putting her hand on the knob, anxious to see him out so she could lock up.

"Ah, I know how I can help you," he said, stopping just as he was about to step outside. "Perhaps you might need some help collecting the outstanding accounts Mr. Randall kept. I could see that whatever markers he might have accumulated are made good. I'm sure the cash would make your first few weeks a good deal easier." He smiled down at her hopefully.

"There really aren't that many," Aura said, for some reason hesitating rather than rushing into this opening to request help with the Chinese marker as she had with her other customers that day. She pondered her reluctance for an instant, than pushed it aside. "If you happen to know of someone who reads Chinese, however, I'd appreciate it if you sent him by. There was a marker that Whit had accepted. I have no idea what it might entail."

"Really?" Crofton asked thoughtfully. "Written in characters? How strange."

"Strange?" Aura asked.

"Well, not strange, actually, I suppose," he replied. "It's just that I wouldn't have thought it likely that Mr. Randall had a great many business dealings with the Chinese. So many of them seem to slide in and out of town, you see, like a vanishing act most of the time. Mine laborers and the like. They don't stay put very long."

"Well, then," Aura said, "it's probably not terribly important."

"Probably not," he agreed. "But if you give it to me, I'd be happy to see about finding your debtor for you and collecting what you're owed."

"Oh, I couldn't ask you to do anything of the sort," Aura replied. "I'm sure it isn't a matter of very great import. As you said, it does seem unlikely that Whit would have taken a very large note."

"Still, I think it would be far easier for me to deal with the matter than for you," he insisted. "Please, let me do you this small favor. It's the very least I can do for you."

For an instant Aura was almost tempted to put her hand in her pocket, withdraw the slip of pale blue paper, and give it to him, along with an explanation of what she really thought it might be. But she stopped herself before the inclination grew too strong. This was her mystery to solve, she told herself. And she intended to do it by her own wits. Howard Crofton might be more than willing to prove himself helpful to her, but she wasn't quite sure she was ready to accept any help.

She glanced back at the counter, where she'd left the customer ledger.

"Actually, I've no idea what I've done with the thing," she told Crofton, surprised that she found it so easy to lie to him. She'd never been able to lie convincingly before in her life. "It's been such a terribly busy day."

"Well, whenever you find it," he said. "But I wouldn't take too long about it, if I were you. You stand a good chance to lose whatever it might bring you."

"I'll look for it tomorrow," she told him. "I promise."

"Excellent," he boomed jovially. "Then I'll come by again tomorrow and retrieve it."

"Oh, please, you mustn't go to so much bother," she protested.

"It would be absolutely no bother whatsoever, Aura," he said. He reached for her hand, and this time when he took it, he didn't just give it a quick squeeze and drop it. Instead, he held it firmly, sandwiching it between his two palms. "And I'll refuse to take no to a second invitation to dinner."

Aura felt awkward and befuddled. "I really don't know," she murmured.

"Please, Aura, I ask only that you take it as a testament to the fact that I am delighted you've decided to stay on here in San Francisco. There are few lovely young women such as yourself here, and I would hate to be deprived of the pleasure of your company. I know things are difficult for you just now, but I would consider it an honor if you would allow me to make them a bit easier for you."

"I'm flattered, really, Mr. Crofton . . ." she began.

"Howard," he interrupted.

"Howard," she amended.

"And I'll see you tomorrow," he went on, before she had the chance to voice any further objections. He finally released her hand and stepped quickly outside. "Until then." He pulled the door closed for her, and motioned to her to lock it.

Aura felt a little numb. She slid the bolt in the lock. When she had, he smiled at her and turned away, his long-legged gait quickly taking him to a waiting carriage. She stood watching the carriage start off down the street, then pulled down the heavy shades to cover the windows.

Life certainly is curious, she thought, as she returned to the counter and blew out the flame in the oil lamp. The store was suddenly plunged into a murky darkness.

Aura poured a cup of tea and settled herself on the sofa, facing the fireplace. A friendly fire burned in it, and she stretched her hands out to its warmth. Just sitting there seemed almost more of a luxury than she could possibly deserve.

She hated to admit it, even to herself, but standing all day in a store had made her feet and calves ache. She kicked off her shoes, pulled her feet up onto the couch, and sat cross-legged, rubbing her aching toes and arches.

She concentrated for a long moment on the task at hand, immersing herself in the lovely feeling of massaging away the cramped ache in her feet. But after a few moments, her muscles began to relax and she

175

stretched out on the sofa, leaned back against the arm, and reached for her cup of tea.

What to make of the newly evolved Howard Crofton, she mused, as she sipped her tea and stared at the flames. Once he threw aside his stiff, lawyerly manner, he was quite a surprise. Not that she was even remotely interested. At least, not now, not when Whit's body was just barely at peace. Allowing herself to be courted would be scandalous, she told herself. Back in Fall River such a thing would have been the cause of untold gossip.

But it did start her thinking about the fact that she had never really had a courtship, that the handful of letters she'd exchanged with Whit had been a poor substitute for the sort of thing most young women expect to experience before they marry. A man coming to call, bearing gifts of candy and flowers and eventually kneeling and asking for her hand, that was the stuff of storybooks and daydreams. They were all things she'd never thought she'd ever have. And now that she was forcing herself to be honest, she realized how very much she would like to have them.

Since she'd arrived in San Francisco, her life had been turned topsy-turvy, and it had all happened so quickly. Perhaps having a respectable lawyer like Howard Crofton come calling wouldn't be such an unpleasant thing, after all. He was decidedly well mannered, and although he wasn't exactly the image of the man who had haunted her dreams the way Payne was, looks certainly weren't everything. In fact, Payne Randall had very little to his credit as far as she was concerned, save for the fact that he did fit that image. And she'd learned more than enough about him since to know that he was the last thing she wanted.

Or at least, he was the last thing she ought to want. But even when she told herself he was arrogant and selfish, and as many times as she reminded herself that he'd made it more than plain that he didn't want her, still she could not deny the fact that it had pained her to learn that he'd visited Madame Charlotte's establishment. And that pain could only mean she was jealous.

It wasn't exactly a comforting thought. In plain words, she was jealous over a man who didn't want her. Of all the foolish things she'd ever done in her life, this had to be the most foolish. And it wasn't as though it was something she wanted. In fact, it was the last thing she wanted in her life, the very last thing, to feel anything for Payne Randall.

As much as she would have liked to deny it, she couldn't dismiss the small, hollow ache that filled her whenever she thought about him. Nor could she lie to herself and deny the fact that she thought about him all the time.

The chiming of the case clock startled her. She listened, counting the strokes. Eight o'clock already, she thought. She had no idea where the time had gone since she'd closed the store two hours before.

She wondered if Payne would return that evening from whatever task of stalking he'd set himself on, or if she'd be alone in the empty house for another night. She hadn't seen him since two nights before, when he'd questioned the young Chinese man, Yang Wu. She wondered if he had found any clues that might lead to Whit's murderer. And she wondered if he was spending the night in the arms of one of Charlotte O'Shea's whores.

This is inane, she told herself, sitting here feeling sorry for myself. She told herself she ought to fix herself something to eat, and then go to bed. And most definitely, she ought to push all thoughts of Payne Randall completely out of her mind.

Perhaps, she thought, the best way to do that would be to substitute thoughts of another man—Howard Crofton, perhaps. He, at least, did not seem in the least reluctant to place himself in a position to have her count on him. Perhaps a steady, well-mannered, respectable lawyer was what she needed in her life. Such a husband might even satisfy her father.

She sighed, and reached into her pocket. She withdrew the mysterious slip of pale blue paper. Why hadn't she given it to Crofton when he'd asked if he could help her? What did she really think she could do alone?

Well, she told herself, as she refilled her cup and leaned back to sip the warm tea, it didn't do any good to think of reasons or wonder about motives. At least, not now. When Howard Crofton came to call the next afternoon, she'd show the slip of paper to him and ask him what he thought of the thing. And then she'd let him know that she would be grateful for any help he might choose to offer, or any suggestions he might have that would enable her to discover what the thing meant and how it could be used.

Because it seemed only reasonable, she told herself, that when Howard Crofton came to call, she ought to take more notice of him. Perhaps he might prove to be helpful in finding Whit's murderer. Perhaps he might prove to be something more than just a polite man who'd been her husband's lawyer. Perhaps he might prove to be something far more important in her life.

She momentarily considered her decision, and told herself it seemed horribly calculating. But then she reconsidered. She had a right to be calculating, she told herself. She'd been through enough. She wanted a settled existence, a normal life.

She glanced up at the mantel, at the likenesses of Whit and Payne. She purposely chose to stare at

Payne's likeness, and as she did, her expression grew sharp and defiant. She didn't need to be clairvoyant to know that Payne had taken a dislike to the lawyer.

Well, she told herself, she didn't need to make any explanations to Mr. Payne Randall. She had a right to enlist Howard Crofton's help, if she so chose. She had a right to do whatever she wanted to do.

And now that she thought about it, she thought she might even consider accepting Howard Crofton's invitation to dinner.

Aura woke with a start. She rubbed her eyes and groaned softly. She had, she realized, allowed herself to fall asleep on the sofa, and it hadn't been just a little catnap. The oil lamp was flickering with the last of the oil, the fire had nearly burned itself out, and all that remained in the hearth was a bed of glowing embers. The room had grown cold.

There was a rumble and a flash of lightning outside. She turned to stare out the window, and realized the night had turned stormy. It was the sound of thunder, most likely, that had awakened her.

She pushed herself up and stood shivering with the cold. A glance at the clock told her it was late—nearly two in the morning. Only a few more hours and it would be time to open the store, and another day, identical to the previous one, would begin. She hadn't expected it would be easy, but she really hadn't thought running the store would be nearly so physically taxing.

Well, she told herself, she would just have to get used to it. She wasn't going to give up her independence because her first day had left her tired and her feet sore.

She yawned and rubbed her eyes again, and then

began to retrieve her cup and the teapot, determined at least to return them to the kitchen before she went to bed. But just as she reached for the pot, she heard a dull thud coming from the floor below.

She straightened up, startled and frightened by the sound. There was no rational reason for there to be any noise coming from the store, she told herself. No rational reason, that was, if it was empty, as it ought to be.

She shivered again, only this time it wasn't from the cold. What if it was Whit's murderer come back, she wondered. What if he decided to come upstairs? She was alone in the house, and hardly in a position to protect herself against a murderer.

She began to tremble, and her eyes darted around the room, looking for a place where she might hide. A sudden ache filled her belly, and her hands shook enough to make the lid of the teapot rattle.

But then she heard the sound again, and it seemed almost identical to the first noise she'd heard. Get a grip on your nerves, Aura, she told herself firmly. A murderer doesn't stand about thumping against the walls and warning people that he's entered their house. At least, a reasonably intelligent murderer doesn't.

She tried to think of some mundane reason why there might be noises coming from the store, and could think of only one. She must have forgotten to close and secure the side window, she told herself. The wind from the storm was making it shake in its frame.

She put down the teapot and lifted the oil lamp, tilting it slightly so that the wick caught the last of the oil and the flame steadied and brightened. It certainly wasn't what she wanted to do, but she realized she had to go downstairs. If she didn't, she knew she might as well as resign herself to spending her life a frightened mouse, hiding from shadows. And that meant she might just as well go back to her father's house and beg him to forgive her, to let her return to a life she hated. And in turn, that prospect, she realized, frightened her more than anything—more, even, than facing a murderer lurking in the darkness below.

She started slowly down the stairs, holding the lamp high so she could see as much as possible of the landing below.

"Payne, is that you?" she called out, hating the quivering she heard in her voice, but unable to keep it steady. "Is anyone there?"

The only response to her cry was the continued thumping sound.

When she reached the ground floor, she pulled the door to the store open quickly, sure she'd lose whatever courage had gotten her as far as she'd gone so far. She peered inside. The room seemed empty, but very cold.

She walked in, passing the counter and the closed and locked door. The sound repeated itself, a thick dull thud, coming from the far side of the store. She lifted her lamp as high as she could and moved slowly forward.

"I can hear you, so you might just as well come out," she whispered into the darkness.

She was aware that she'd barely made the words audible, and that anyone lurking in the shadows would hardly be motivated by such a complete lack of ferocity to offer himself up to the mercy of justice.

But when she reached the window and found, just as she'd suspected, that it was open, she let out a heavy sigh of relief. The thick canvas shade was being blown by the wind and it was that that had made the noise as it fell back against the window frame. A small puddle had formed on the floor just beneath the window. As she watched, a gust of wind blew in more rain and cold air, and pushed the shade forward, then faded away to let it fall back.

She put down the lamp and pulled the window closed. It wasn't quite as easy a task as she'd expected, for the wet had swelled the wooden frame and she had to tug against it to pull down the window. But once it was closed, and the wind and the storm were shut out, she felt a sense of pride. She'd overcome her fears and fought the battle of the open window, she told herself. She couldn't help but giggle at how absurdly she'd behaved. Perhaps in the future, she told herself firmly, she'd remember that most of her fears were rooted in her mind, not in reality.

The window tended to, she lifted the lamp and started back upstairs, stopping only to check the front door and assure herself that she'd at least remembered to lock it. That task complete, she let herself out of the store and climbed the stairs back up to the parlor.

She yawned again, as exhausted suddenly by the effort to contain her fears as she had been by the physical efforts of the previous day. She glanced at the teapot still on the table by the sofa and at the rumpled pillows on the sofa. She shrugged. She was too tired to tend to the minor chores of housekeeping. It certainly wasn't so great a sin for her to leave things as they were until morning. What she needed far more than a neat and orderly parlor, she told herself, was to curl up in bed and go to sleep.

So she walked past the table and the accusing litter of her meager supper, and went into the bedroom.

She hesitated as she stepped into the bedroom, something that had become a habit. She was beginning to feel less ill at ease in the room, almost as though it was becoming her own, but there still always seemed to be a ghost waiting for her when she stepped inside. It wasn't a vicious ghost, she had decided, or even an angry one. Still, she always seemed to feel that there was something there, waiting to greet her. She felt a pale shiver of a chill that quickly passed. She crossed to the dressing table and set down the lamp so that she could begin to get ready for bed.

She started to unfasten the buttons of her blouse. As she did, her glance drifted toward the mirror. Her hands froze.

There was a reflection there of a man dressed entirely in black. He realized she'd seen him, and he smiled.

Before she could turn around, before she could even think of screaming, a hand was clamped over her mouth and a strong arm encircled her.

Chapter Ten

Aura squinted and blinked several times, trying to force away the burning in her eyes caused by the sudden brilliance of the lamplight after the long period of total darkness. She would have rubbed them, but her hands were bound behind her.

The stinging eased as her eyes finally accustomed themselves to the light. She watched as a hand reached forward to untie and remove the piece of cloth that had been used to gag her. Her first thought was to cry out for help and hope someone heard her. But instead of a scream, when she opened her mouth, she found all she could do was gasp for a breath of fresh air. She inhaled deeply, hoping for a few clean, deep breaths, only to discover that the air in this place had a strange taste to it, an oddly sweet, mildly sickening smell.

She had no time to contemplate the cause of the odor, however. A hand was roughly placed on her shoulder, and then pushed her unceremoniously forward. She nearly lost her balance, and only barely managed to keep herself upright. She turned and glared at the man who had pushed her, but he was clearly indifferent to both her flare of anger and her discomfort. He raised his hand again, about to repeat the inducement.

He was Chinese, a dark-haired young man not unlike those she'd seen hurrying along the streets bent on some mundane task, but this man was different. There was no meekness in his expression, no subservience, and he hadn't turned away when she'd turned and faced him. In fact, his expression and the upraised hand were more than enough to convince Aura that her position was tenuous at best.

She meekly moved forward, to where a low stool waited in the center of the circle of bright light cast by the lamp overhead. The hand motioned downward and she sat, obeying the silent direction. The short flare of anger was gone now, washed away by a flood of fear. She was, she realized, far too frightened to think of doing anything beyond what she was directed to do. For the moment, at least, protest and rebellion were beyond her.

As she sat, a hand holding a knife reached forward. It paused in front of her, the lamplight glinting off the blade. She stared at it terrified, her imagination running wild with gruesome images of how it might be used. A face slowly slid into the circle of light beside the hand and the knife, the same leering, smiling face that had appeared so indifferent to the possibility that the shove might have sent her sprawling. It was obvious its owner recognized her terror and was, if anything, amused by it.

He ran his thumb across the blade and watched as Aura shuddered. He drew out the moment, letting her stare at the blade, taking a perverse pleasure in her fear. Then he leaned forward, reached around her and grasped her bound hands. Aura cried out as he brought the knife down.

She was still waiting for the pain, for the heat of her

own blood, as her severed wrists spewed a stream of her blood onto her hands, when the knife was drawn back. Her hands fell to her sides, and she realized the cord that had been used to tie her wrists had been severed and now lay on the floor. She breathed a thick sigh of relief as the knife was sheathed and it and its owner disappeared back into the shadows.

It took a far greater effort than she'd have imagined to lift her hands onto her lap, for her arms and shoulders were still numb from the time she'd spent with her hands bound behind her. That feat accomplished, she sat, silent and bewildered, and rubbed her sore wrists.

She had no idea where they'd taken her. Everything that had happened in the previous hour was a confused blur. In fact, the only clear memories she had were of those few frightening moments back in her bedroom, of the hands coming at her out of the darkness, reaching for her and grabbing her. They'd gagged her and bound her hands and then put that thing over her head. That had been the worst part, being forced into that tiny private dungeon of darkness. The rest of it, being dragged out of the house and put into a wagon or carriage of some sort and brought here, wherever here was, that was a haze of confusion and sheer terror.

She looked around, but saw only faint stirring movements in the dimness that enveloped the circle of light surrounding the place where she sat. There was the sound of several voices, men's voices, coming from the shadows in the corners of the room. She didn't understand so much as a word of the talk. It sounded sharp and guttural to her, and totally foreign.

"Mrs. Randall, you are most kind to accept my invitation."

It took her a moment to realize that those words had been spoken in English, that they were addressed to her, and that she understood them. She turned and peered to her side, staring into the dark place from which she'd thought the words had come. She saw nothing clearly, only shadows and the indistinct outline of dark figures that moved slightly.

"It wasn't an invitation and I didn't accept," she cried out.

It was a poor attempt to hide the fear that had made her cry out like that. But once she had done it, the fear returned tenfold, telling her she must be a fool to risk angering these people, whoever they were. She inhaled sharply, wondering why she'd been so stupid as to respond that way. What if those men standing in the shadows took offense at her manner? She thought of the knife. What would they do to her now?

As if he was about to answer that question in the worst possible manner, one of the dark forms moved threateningly forward, finally stepping into the circle of light that surrounded her. She looked up at a tall, thin figure only to find that his face was still just above the lamp's circle of light, that it was clothed still in shadows.

She could, however, see he was dressed in loose-fitting black clothing, not the typical plain dark pants and tunic she was accustomed to seeing worn by the Orientals who passed on the street by the store, but rather a soft fabric—silk, she was sure—and it was heavily embroidered, all in black, the threads of the work shining bright in the lamplight. The somberly monastic severity of the black was relieved only at the high collar of his robe, where dragons embroidered in blood-scarlet threads chased one another, heads raised upward as though they were seeking the warm sustenance that beat beneath the flesh of his neck.

"Then it was wise not to ask," he told her, his tone mild if not entirely pleasant.

187

He reached a long arm up to the lamp that was hanging from the ceiling. He took his time adjusting the flame, brightening the glow until it suited him. The circle of light grew, and his face slowly appeared, an apparition that grew out of the darkness.

It was not a friendly face, and his smile was anything but pleasant. Aura stared up at him transfixed, fascinated the way one is by something frightening and terrible, too fascinated even to turn away, although one might want to. Now she could just barely make out what it was the embroidered red dragons on his collar were seeking. One glance at his features made her wonder why the crimson creatures bothered to look for blood from a neck that seemed to her entirely devoid of it.

His skin was thin and pale, a shiny near-white layer that appeared to be stretched so tautly over the bones of his face that it seemed about to tear from the strain. It would have been the face of a skeletal corpse save for the presence of eyes and an incredibly long drooping moustache. Aura stared at it. At a time when men with facial hair were the rule rather than the exception, this moustache was still an oddity. She'd never seen anything like it. Then, as he lifted a long, bony hand to finger the moustache, her glance drifted finally upward to meet his eyes.

She shivered. His glance was uncommonly sharp, the eyes so bright they appeared to have a dark, sinister glow behind them. It seemed to her almost as though he was looking not at her, but inside her.

"Who are you?" she asked in a hoarse whisper.

He slowly waved a thin, pale finger at her.

"I ask, you answer," he told her.

His tone was sharp enough to cut. Aura cringed at the sound of it. At first, his accent had confused her, but she realized that she was beginning to understand him quite clearly now. And what she understood was that she was in no position to expect anything even remotely like consideration from him. This obviously was a man used to getting exactly what he wanted. And just now, he seemed to want information from her.

He took a step closer and peered down at her. For a moment Aura couldn't so much as breathe. She could see that he was warning her, letting her know that even his glance was much more powerful than was she.

"It is wise for you to relate location of pass."

She shook her head, completely confused.

"I don't know what you're talking about," she murmured.

She realized that her shaking, puny little voice told him she was now thoroughly cowed, just as he wanted her to be. But she didn't care if he knew. This emaciated-looking creature with his dark, sinister stare was far more frightening to her than a powerfully built man could possibly be.

He stared directly at her, and his thin, pale lips turned up just a little in what she thought might be his version of a grim smile.

"Do you not?" he asked. "I wonder."

It was the stare that made her place him. She'd seen him before, she thought. These were the eyes that had stared back at her from the group of Orientals who had stood apart from the other mourners at the cemetery. At the time, she'd been intent on looking for the face of the man who'd come to the house the night Whit had been killed, Yang Wu's face. But now the scene replayed itself in her mind, the dreary, rain-darkened sky outlining the huddle of Oriental men standing in the muck of the cemetery, all discreetly turned away save for one who boldly stared directly at her. His eyes had been the same ones that were staring at her now.

"You came to my husband's funeral," she ventured. "I saw you there."

Again the unsettling near-smile nudged at the edges of his lips.

"Most astute, Mrs. Randall," he told her. "With such a fine memory, I know you remember present location of entry pass."

Aura felt as though a cloud had settled over her, and although she understood the words he was speaking, it seemed almost as if they were foreign. Distracted, she lifted her hand to push away a thick lock of hair that had fallen across her cheek.

He reached out and pushed her hand away, then touched his finger to her cheek as he lifted the wavy auburn lock.

Aura shuddered. The feel of his fingers against her skin was like wax, ice-cold wax. It seemed impossible to her that it was the touch of a human hand.

He gave her no indication that he had noticed her reaction. Instead, he seemed intent on the feel of her hair, soft and very fine, and the pale golden glow the lamplight imparted to it. He let the strands fall slowly through his fingers, then lifted a second handful and repeated the procedure, watching it as though mesmerized by the way it drifted downward and then settled on her shoulder.

However distracted he might have seemed for that moment, he was more intent on the answer to his question than he was on the mystery of the coppery-colored, silken curls. He put his hand at the nape of her neck, silently telling her as much as he took a thick handful of her hair and wound his hand in it. Then he pulled sharply downward, jerking her head back and forcing her to look up at him.

"I asked a question, Mrs. Randall," he hissed.

Aura gasped, and a weak cry escaped her. She'd been surprised by the sudden pain, but more than that, she was frightened by the look she saw in his eyes.

"I, I don't know what you're talking about," she stammered.

"Do you not?" he insisted.

"No, no, I don't," she cried softly.

He shrugged, obviously still unconvinced. He nonetheless released his hold of her hair. He stepped back, but continued to level that unsettling stare at her.

"You admit you asked customers for Chinese translation, Mrs. Randall?" he asked.

"Yes," she stammered. "Yes, I did that."

She felt as though her brain was dazed, as though thought was, at that moment, entirely beyond her. Startled and frightened, she barely mustered enough concentration to begin to wonder how he could possibly know what it was she'd asked of her customers the previous afternoon.

"Translation, Mrs. Randall," he said sharply, forcefully focusing her attention back where he wanted it.

It came like a sudden flash of light, his words sweeping away the cloud of haze that had dulled her thoughts. She did know, she realized. In fact, she was certain now just what it was he wanted.

It was that thin piece of pale blue paper with the strange markings on it. She was as sure of it as she was of her own name. But something inside her told her that giving him what he wanted would be a terrible mistake.

She shook her head, and gathered together whatever vestiges of defiance remained within her. This man had had her kidnapped, gagged, tied, and brought to him like an animal. And now he was treating her no better than an animal, as if she had no brain

191

and no dignity and no worth. After finally making her escape from a father who'd considered her only so much valueless goods, she'd finally begun to think of herself as something more than chattel. She was not about to let this crude stranger, this foreign stranger, take that away from her.

"I needed a translation for a marker," she said, "for a debt owed to my husband."

He shook his head, sadly almost.

"A square of paper, Mrs. Randall," he said slowly. "To you, it can mean nothing. Surely it is no reason to die."

Aura couldn't believe that he would threaten her so brazenly. Until that moment, she hadn't really accepted Yang Wu's story about dangerous people among the Chinese population. There might be those who would be considered powerful among their own, for there were always those among any population who managed to achieve some eminence, some measure of control. The thought that a member of a group that all San Francisco considered servants and laborers would threaten her this way was inconceivable.

But her doubts about Yang Wu's story were being quickly eliminated, and along with them her fixed notions about racial roles, shattered the way so many of her prejudices had been shattered in the preceding weeks. This had to be the man who was responsible for Whit's death. If he had enough power to have Whit murdered, then there was no reason he'd stop at having her killed as well.

She gazed up at him, and her eyes filled with hate. This was the man who was responsible for the ruin of the future she'd dreamed about; he'd stolen away her life when he'd had Whit killed. For that instant, her fear for him paled beside the anger and loathing she felt for him.

"I don't know anything," she told him, her tone suddenly tinged with a defiant venom.

He leaned forward, putting his face close to hers. "Do you not?" he asked.

If it had just been the words, she'd have been able to maintain the defiant front. But his eyes caught and held hers, and Aura felt her will start to wither within her.

Against her will her eyes drifted downward to her side, where the pocket of her skirt seemed suddenly to press down against her leg as though it was weighted with lead. She had to force them upward, and when she lifted them, when her gaze once again met his, she knew she had given it all away.

He reached out toward her. When he did, Aura lifted her hands and struck out wildly at him, digging in her nails when she felt the skin of his hands beneath hers.

He pulled back and angrily shouted something in Chinese. In her fear and preoccupation with him, Aura had forgotten that he'd not been alone in the room, that the men who had brought her were still there and that there had been other shadowy forms moving behind him. But now she was rudely reminded of her mistake.

She found herself being roughly grabbed and pulled to her feet, and her arms were pulled up and back. She cried out, but her scream was muffled by a hand that was clamped tightly over her mouth, tight enough to make her nearly choke on her own cry.

He moved forward again, and this time there was no mistaking the smug pleasure in his eyes, nor the malicious smile on his thin lips.

"What do you fear, Mrs. Randall?" he asked her. He reached out his hand and pressed it to her breast, squeezing it tight. "Not this?"

193

It was like the hand of a skeleton had grabbed her. Aura squirmed wildly and another scream rose to her lips, a scream that was so muffled by the hand over her mouth that all that escaped was a thin little sob. Her fight was useless. She could not have escaped the hands that held her had she been ten times stronger.

The place quickly filled with the sound of laughter, lewd and malicious laughter. There were at least a half dozen men in the room, she realized, and they were enjoying what they saw. A wave of hopelessness swept over her and she felt drowned by it. She gave up her useless struggle against the hands that held her.

But now her tormentor seemed to have lost interest in the game, or else he had other interests that seemed more pressing to him. His hand slid down her torso to her left hip.

"Might this be the object of my search, Mrs. Randall?" he asked her.

He slipped his hand into the pocket of her skirt and drew out the now crumpled slip of blue paper. He glanced at it, then slid it into the wide sleeve of his robe.

"Most accommodating," he said.

Once again he punctuated his words with the unpleasant smile.

He nodded, motioning to the man who had restrained her. Immediately the hand was removed from her mouth.

"What are you going to do with me?" Aura gasped.

He didn't answer quickly, but let his dark glance meet hers and simply stared at her until she shivered.

What might he not do, she thought. All these men, and she alone and unable to fight them. And in the end, they'd surely kill her.

"What indeed?" he asked. "There are so many choices," he told her, as he once again returned his

194

fingers to her hair and raked them through the tousled curls.

Aura shivered at his touch. He seemed more pleased than put out by her reaction, for he smiled.

"I could have you killed," he told her softly, his tone calmly impersonal as though he was discussing the weather. "But that would be a great and unfortunate waste, I think. Such a commodity has much value." He seemed preoccupied with the feel of her hair in his fingers, for he finally shifted his gaze away from her eyes to stare instead at it. "To sell here, where the value is greatest, is, unfortunately, extremely dangerous," he went on, as though musing aloud to himself. He smiled then, as brightly as such a face could be thought of as smiling. "I must give thought to so grave a matter. In meantime . . ."

His words trailed off and he motioned to the man who was holding Aura's arms. He barked out a sharp order.

Aura's guard nodded silently, and turned, half carrying, half dragging Aura along with him, moving to the edge of the circle of light and toward the side of the room.

She screamed, not from hurt, but from fear of where he might be taking her, what he intended to do to her. In response, he tightened his hold of her arms and pulled them backward, hurting her terribly. She gasped with pain, but took the meaning of his warning and immediately quieted. Satisfied, he relaxed his hold slightly and the hurt in her shoulders eased.

"You learn well, Mrs. Randall."

Aura looked back. The tall, cadaverous man was staring at her, and when she turned to face him, he nodded.

"What choices have I?" she asked, in a voice that was tentative, still breathless from the hurt.

195

He shook his head. "None," he told her. "Save making your death unnecessary."

With that, he waved his hand, and her guard pushed her forward, out of the circle of light and into the darkness. She stumbled along, held upright more often than not only by his less than gentle hold on her arms.

It was a long corridor, dimly lit by tiny lanterns, and cold and damp enough to be a tunnel or a cave. Aura tried to keep up with her guard, but her pace was uncertain, and hampered by the way he held her arms behind her. She found herself slipping on the damp surface underfoot, and each time she did, he jerked her painfully upright. She'd learned a lesson, though, and she managed to keep herself from crying out, not wanting to risk the far greater hurt she knew would be the payment he'd mercilessly deliver.

Although she knew it couldn't have lasted more than a few moments, that walk seemed to Aura to go on forever before they finally reached the corridor's end. They stopped in front of a heavy, dark wooden door. Aura's guard reached out a beefy fist and rapped against it once. The sound seemed very loud in the surrounding silence.

They stood and waited. Aura was convinced there would be no answer to the summons, for she could hear no sound coming from the far side of the door. She turned and darted a quick glance at him, and saw he had been staring intently at her. She turned away immediately, afraid he would consider her curiosity enough provocation to repeat the previous lesson he'd administered. She was determined not to provoke him needlessly.

She'd had an opportunity to think during the walk, and all she could think about was how she might manage to escape. It seemed hopeless to her now, but she would not allow herself to give up. Accepting whatever these people intended for her, she told herself, was tantamount to signing her own death warrant. She was not ready to do that.

If she was to have any chance of escaping, she told herself, she would need whatever little strength and presence of mind remained in her possession. It would do her no good whatsoever to have either clouded by the hurt of her guard's punishments. She would, she decided, save her rebellion for when it might do her some good.

The moments dragged by, and Aura was beginning to wonder why he didn't turn back, or at least knock a second time. He, however, seemed unconcerned, and entirely willing to wait. Finally there was a thick, metallic scraping sound, and the door was pushed open. The doorkeeper, a small, gray-haired man, bowed and stepped away so that they might enter. He didn't give Aura so much as a glance.

Aura saw immediately why she'd heard no sound when they'd been waiting in the corridor. Both the door and the stone walls surrounding it were incredibly thick, the door six inches of solid wood and the wall at least a foot and a half of stone. The construction would keep whatever was inside, including noise, safely hidden.

Not that the room they entered was noisy. On the contrary, although there was a murmur of voices, it was a low murmur, muted, like the pale glow of what seemed to be hundreds of candles flickering in the breeze caused by the waft of air that entered along with them from the corridor by which they'd come. A fire burned in a hearth by the far wall, but a screen stood in front of it, blurring the brilliance of the flames so that the whole of the room took on a pale, nether-worldly glow from it and the flickering candles.

The only really loud noise was the sound of the door being shut behind them, a thick, dull noise, like the sound of a lid being slid onto a coffin. Once it was shut, the thin breeze was extinguished and the candle flames steadied. Aura realized that the place was quite warm, especially when compared to the corridor from which they'd come.

But it wasn't the noise or the dim lighting or even the heat in the room that immediately captured Aura's attention. It was the smell—a thick, sweet odor, so strong she could almost taste it. She recognized it as the same odor she'd caught in the air during her inter-view with the cadaverous man in black, though that scent had been but a pale hint of what was in this room. Until that evening, she'd never smelled any-thing quite like it before, and for some reason she did not understand, it seemed malign to her, as evil as the dark stare of the man who had questioned her. It hung in the air around them, a thick cloud, a floating haze of dun-colored, sticky smoke.

Aura's guard suddenly released his hold of her arms. They fell forward like broken wings. The relaxa-tion of the tension, and the elimination of the dull ache that filled her shoulders from keeping them in so un-comfortable a position, made them go nearly numb. Aura found she could hardly force her arms to move at all. Still, she was grateful for whatever urgings of unexpected kindness had moved him to release his hold on her.

She quickly found that it wasn't kindness that had been his motivation, however, but the simple necessity of picking their way through a welter of obstructions that made the arrangement by which he'd guided her thus far unmanageable. He inched past her, then grasped her wrist and tugged by way of telling her to follow.

Aura stumbled after him, no longer on her guard, but concentrating on those in the room. There were more than she could count, all Oriental men. They lazed about, lying on narrow cots or sitting on the floor or low stools. Many of them were half naked, and sweat shone dully on bared chests and arms and brows. Every man held a pipe, and the smoke that rose from those pipes, Aura realized, was the cause of the sweet, heavy odor in the air.

Most seemed hardly to notice the disturbance of a man and woman treading through their midst, even when they looked up and saw Aura being pulled along. Occasionally one smiled at her, but the smiles were distant, like idiots' smiles. There was a blankness in their dark eyes that made Aura shudder.

She didn't have much time to consider what might be the cause of that blank, absent stare. Her guard pulled her onward, and she had to concentrate on following him through the maze of bodies, to concentrate on keeping her skirts from coming too close to the candles that littered her path. It took them awhile, but eventually they'd crossed to the far side of the room and stood in front of an ornately carved door.

This time he didn't stop or knock. Instead, he put his hand against the door and it swung open, revealing a second dimly lit, overly warm room much like the one they'd just crossed. He pulled Aura inside and closed the door behind them.

Though similar to the one they'd just passed through, Aura realized this room was not identical; it was far less crowded, and she could see no bodies sprawled on the floor or hunched down onto the uncertain comfort of a bare stool. Instead, there were neat rows of cots furnished with the luxury of pillows.

199

Many cots were unoccupied, but a goodly number were inhabited by men smoking the same pipes she'd seen being smoked in the first room. Here the eyes that stared up at her through the smoky haze were Caucasian, not Oriental. This room, with its slightly more civilized accommodations, seemed to be reserved for the white inhabitants of San Francisco.

And the sight of them gave Aura her first glimmer of hope. Sure these men, however drunk or whatever it was they were, would not let her be dragged off this way. Surely they would help free a woman who was obviously behind held against her will, especially one of their own.

She glanced at the faces, searching for one that seemed less dazed and slack than the rest. And finally she found what she was seeking, the face of a young man, roughly bearded but with bright blue eyes that were not yet dazed, as the others were. He gazed lazily up at her, and when his eyes met hers as she approached him, he seemed to brighten slightly. He smiled at her.

A miner, Aura thought, as she took in his clothing, rough twill pants and heavy wool shirt. Whit had liked miners, she remembered, and he and Payne had once been miners themselves. A miner would be strong, she told herself, easily able to deal with her guard.

This was her chance. She watched the man's eyes as she approached him, and then, when she was beside the place where he lay, she pretended to stumble and then fell.

As she started forward, she dug her nails as hard as she could into the wrist of the hand by which her guard held her, hoping to free herself from his grasp. Rather than release her, however, he reacted violently, swiping forward with his free hand, lashing out at her. But when she saw the impending blow, Aura let herself really fall, and his fist slid harmlessly past her.

Her evasion, however, was not without consequence. She found herself landing heavily against the man she hoped would be her protector.

"Please," she cried. "You have to help me!"

He stared up at her, wide eyed and startled.

Aura waited for the miner to jump to his feet, to tear the guard's hand from her wrist and chase him back into the darkness of the tunnel. Surely, she thought, after the attempted blow, he could not help but see her distress. But she waited in vain. He did nothing for a long moment but stare up at her, his expression confused and distant, as though he was considering the solution of a problem beyond his capacity to solve.

The guard reached down, angrily grabbing Aura's arm and wrenching her to her feet. He shouted something at her, and although the words were entirely foreign, she had no trouble translating his tone and his expression. He raised his hand and she cringed, waiting for the blow.

It never came. A hand reached out, grasping the guard's arm and holding it.

If her chosen savior had not initially understood that she'd begged for his help, he did at least seem to instinctively subscribe to the code of chivalry that dictated that a woman is not to be stricken by a man. He stood for a moment, his glance darting between Aura's frightened face and the guard's angry one, his expression growing more muddled by the moment.

"What's goin' on here?" he growled. "What's a woman doin' here?"

"This man kidnapped me," Aura shouted. "They're

going to kill me. You have to help me get away from this place."

The miner's expression grew more bewildered.

"Kidnapped?" he asked. "They're going to kill you?"

Aura's guard seemed as bewildered as the miner. His first reaction was obviously to tear away the miner's hand and return to his initial purpose, first subduing Aura's attempt at rebellion, and then getting on with the task he'd been instructed to do. He glanced nervously at the door by which he'd entered the room, as though he was afraid that whatever laxity in his endeavors had led to this unpleasant situation had been seen. Then he let his stare meet the miner's.

He spoke, the words obviously as incomprehensible to the miner as they were to Aura. But this time he reached out and tried to pull the miner's hand from his arm.

The miner, however, refused to let go.

"What the hell's going on here?" he shouted.

His voice was loud, rising well above the thin noise of muted conversation in the room. The sound of it was more than enough to silence the talk, and save for one high, thin voice that seemed to be singing a mournful love song which continued uninterrupted, the room sank into silence. Aura could almost feel the pairs of eyes that slowly turned in their direction. She couldn't keep from smiling. With all this attention, even the dazed, drunken attention of the men in this room, there was no way anyone could force her to go where she didn't want to go or do what she was disinclined to do.

"No bother, sir, no bother."

Aura glanced up. It was the man who had questioned her, back in the small room at the far end of the corridor, somehow materialized at the doorway. He

202

was unchanged, save for his manner, which now was transformed as he hurried forward from the door, crossing the room after them swiftly, his long legs moving deftly through the maze of cots and candles and smoke. The commanding stare that had so frightened Aura was gone from his eyes as he approached the miner, and except for an unpleasant glance that he leveled at the man he'd entrusted to guard her, he seemed benign, a pleasantly smiling, overgrown, and skinny elf, eager to return his dark world to the peacefulness that was its normal condition.

"There damn well is a bother, Hung Poh," the miner growled at him. "This woman says she's been kidnapped."

The cadaverous man, Hung Poh, as the miner called him, clasped his bony hands together and lowered his head as though lost in reverent meditation.

"Mistake, mistake," he intoned softly.

"There is no mistake," Aura shouted, shaking her arm violently, trying uselessly to tear her arm free from the guard's grasp.

But Hung Poh ignored her, pretending that she'd not spoken as he addressed the miner.

"Woman works above," he murmured, and pointed to the ceiling. Then he raised his hand and tapped his fingers against his forehead. "Sick," he added, then nodded meaningfully toward Aura.

The miner released the guard's arm. The explantion, however abbreviated, seemed to satisfy him.

"Addled whore, eh?" he said. He glanced at Aura. "Shame. She's pretty, though."

"No," Aura shouted, "he's lying. You mustn't believe him."

Still acting as though she hadn't spoken, Hung Poh motioned to the guard, and he, in turn, pulled Aura close, wrapping his arm around her waist and putting his hand over her mouth to silence her continued cries. She flailed against his arm, twisting and trying to free herself from his grip, but he didn't react. He seemed as oblivious to her struggles as a stone.

As he began to pull her away, Aura saw the man who'd opened the door admitting them into the first room appear at Hung Poh's side, a fresh pipe and a long, narrow taper in his hand.

"Please forgive unfortunate interruption," Hung Poh said to the miner. He handed him the fresh pipe and held the taper to one of the candle flames to light it. "Most regrettable."

The miner seemed to hesitate for a moment, darting a questioning glance at Aura. But in the end, the offered pipe proved far more alluring to him. He took it and held it to his mouth as Hung Poh held the taper to the bowl.

As the miner inhaled a first breath of the sweet smoke, Hung Poh glanced up at Aura. He didn't need to speak for her to know what it was he was thinking.

She'd made a terrible mistake, she realized, and he would see that she paid for it.

Chapter Eleven

"Aura?"

Payne stood, waiting for an answer that he really didn't expect, and looked around the empty parlor. Finally, he stirred himself to light a lamp.

He lifted the near empty teacup, stared for a second, considering the dregs in its bottom, and then dropped it back onto its saucer. He lifted the cold pot and sloshed its contents about, then returned it, too, to the table.

This wasn't right, he thought. It wasn't at all like her to leave a dirty cup in the parlor, let alone a pot half filled with cold tea. He'd seen enough of her domestic habits to know that it would require something extraordinary to keep her from cleaning up after herself.

And even stranger still was the fact that the store was still closed, the door locked, the shades drawn and the interior dark. Nearly eleven in the morning, and the store not yet opened for business. He might have overlooked the pot of cold tea, but not that, especially considering the lecture he'd had from her about how she didn't need his help, about her determination to make her own way. A woman determined to support herself wouldn't leave a shop door closed and locked against an eager customer. At least, not an intelligent woman. And if nothing else, he had to admit that Whit had been right about that part. Aura seemed to be a very intelligent woman.

He looked around the parlor again, at the ashes in the fireplace and the rumpled pillows on the couch, then crossed to the desk. The likeness she'd sent Whit was lying there. He lifted it and stared into the wide eyes that looked out at him. He didn't know why, but an ache filled his belly, an ache that he refused to admit to himself was longing. He dropped the daguerreotype back to the surface of the desk.

"Aura?" he called out again.

Still there was no answer, nothing save the sound of his own voice echoing back at him in the empty room. The whole house was completely quiet—too quiet, he thought. And from where he stood, it felt empty all around him, as empty as the room in which he stood.

A dirty cup, cold ashes in the hearth, an empty house, and a store that ought to be open for business still closed and shuttered—hardly a litany that ought to induce panic.

Still, he found it all disconcerting, although he was not quite sure why. After all, there were a hundred explanations as to why she might not be in the store, why she might be away from the house. A hunger for fresh bread might have taken her to the bakery at the far end of the street, or the need to mail a letter could have sent her to the post office. Logic told him that he ought to assume nothing more sinister had happened to her than a trip to one of these.

But something felt wrong. There was an unpleasant ache in the pit of his stomach, and arguments to the contrary had no effect on it. Despite the logic that told him there was no need to be concerned, still he couldn't shake the uncomfortable feeling that something was terribly wrong. And whatever it was, the same instinct told him that Aura was right in the middle of it.

He started toward her bedroom, but hesitated when he reached the door. The greater part of him, he knew, wanted more than anything to enter that room and find her there, asleep in her bed. And part of him knew that the moment he opened the door, he would find something he didn't want to find, and that when he did, he'd be directing his life along a path that would allow him no return.

He put his hand on the knob, but didn't turn it. He ought to walk out of the house, he told himself, and go back to his job. He had no obligation to her. She hadn't really ever been his brother's wife, except in name. And a few hours of intimacy that had passed between them were hardly a binding contract. More than that, she'd made it plain enough that she didn't want his help, that she didn't need it or him. Whatever had happened, whatever the cause of the closed shop and the dirty teacup, it was no business of his.

But no matter how convincing the words ought to have been, they were meaningless. He had an obligation to her, and he knew it, the obligation that came with the feelings he could no longer dismiss or hide from himself. It hadn't taken long, a few days away from her. A few days spent pretending that he wasn't thinking about her. A few days learning how great a fool he could be.

The sick feeling in his belly was getting all the stronger. Something was wrong, he thought, as he turned the knob. Something had happened to her, something unpleasant. The image of Whit's dead body sprang into his mind, uncalled for and yet insistent, maliciously transforming itself into Aura's body. He stood for an instant, unable to move, unable to banish the image of her, lifeless and covered in blood, her eyes staring up at him sightlessly, her lips still and silent, and yet somehow able to accuse, to tell him that he ought to have been there to protect her.

He pushed the door open, expecting to find the worst.

The room was a shambles, bottles swept from the dressing table and broken, the shards scattered on the floor, the mirror broken, the brush that had been thrown against it lying among the pieces of glass that had fallen beneath the frame. He took one glance and felt the sick feeling settle itself permanently into the pit of his stomach. He crossed the room, glancing quickly at the bed and the floor, his only relief coming when he realized he hadn't found what he'd been dreading.

He had to forcibly detach himself, to fight the feeling of sickened panic that threatened to make him useless. He had to think calmly, he told himself. Damn it, he was an investigator. This, after all, was his job, what he was trained to do—find reason where none seemed to exist, locate clues among the chaos, and follow their path to the truth.

He walked back to the dressing table and glanced at the shards of glass. Then he turned and faced the bed once again. He realized his immediate evaluation had been dominated by his worst fears and by his first glimpse, that of all the broken glass and disarray. But now, looking at it coolly, he saw that aside from the dressing table and mirror, the remainder of the room seemed relatively untouched. The bed was neatly made, Aura's nightgown lying at the foot. Nothing else seemed inordinately disturbed, except for the chair that had been moved from its usual place beneath the window, pushed into a corner like an unruly schoolboy.

He crossed to the wardrobe and pulled it open. Nothing odd there, he saw as he did a quick survey.

Her clothing, including her coat, were hung neatly, two pairs of shoes arranged on the floor. Whatever had happened in this room had happened by the dressing table, and quickly. The struggle had not lasted very long.

He returned to stand in front of the remains of the shattered mirror, staring dully at the dozens of reflections of his own image looking back at him. They told him nothing. Whatever it was that had happened, no hint of it remained there for him to find.

But there were a few clues for him to consider, such as the nightgown left at the foot of the bed. It told him that whatever had happened to Aura, it had happened before she'd retired, before she'd had a chance to change into her nightgown, before she'd gotten into bed. He crossed to the foot of the bed and lifted the light cotton gown, fingering the fabric, thinking. Nothing seemed to make any sense.

One thing he knew for certain, however, and that was that Aura hadn't gone to the bakery or the post office. Someone had come into the house the night before, someone she hadn't opened the door to allow in, someone with whom she'd struggled. That someone had taken her away, without allowing her so much as the benefit of her coat against the night cold.

And there was one thing else which was only too apparent—she hadn't gone of her own free will, and wherever it was they'd taken her, she wasn't there by choice.

Aura huddled into the small space she'd found between two packing crates. It wasn't much warmer there, but at least it seemed a bit protected, almost hidden. Not that there was much chance she'd be able to hide in any place for very long. After all, they'd locked her into this dark underground dungeon, and they knew she couldn't possibly budge the heavy, bolted door.

Not that she hadn't tried. She'd spent the first few hours of her confinement pounding on the door and screaming. She'd kept her eyes on the tiny view a small square hole in the door allowed her, the view of a dark stone-walled place lit only by a single lantern hanging from its ceiling. It looked like a cellar to her, although she had no idea who would allow his cellar to be used to hold innocent people prisoner.

She doubted that the house belonged to Hung Poh. The cellar, or what little she'd been able to see of it, appeared to be quite large, and that indicated a substantial residence above. As far as she knew, there were no Orientals who lived in the large houses near the top of the hill that overlooked San Francisco's harbor, at least, none who were anything more than servants. And no servant would chance trying to imprison someone in his master's cellar.

Whoever it was above, she'd called out to him until she was too hoarse to speak. She'd have thought that someone would have heard her, that someone would have come to help her, but she was wrong. Either the noise she made didn't carry beyond the cellar, or else no one cared enough about the sound of a woman's screams to bother to investigate.

When finally she gave up the effort, her throat too hoarse to scream any more and her hands bruised and swollen, she also gave up the forlorn hope that someone would come to her aid. Instead, she decided she'd have to find her own path out and had spent the next few hours searching the dirt-floored room for something that might help her escape.

Even the search wasn't easy. Only a dim glimmer of light managed to make its way into the room through the small hole in the door, and she spent much of the time on her hands and knees, feeling her way. Eventually even that light failed, the oil in the lantern outside her cell burning itself out.

Plunged into complete darkness, she lost whatever persistence had kept her mind on escape and away from the hopelessness of her position. She began to sob softly. Each tiny sound she heard terrified her, and she quickly came to the conclusion they heralded the approach of voracious rats. She felt as though she'd been buried, entombed alive.

She crawled into the narrow space between the crates and pulled up her legs, trying to make herself as small as possible, hoping she might somehow escape her fears by hiding from them. Eventually exhaustion overcame her and she fell into an uneasy, desolate sleep.

She was wakened by noise and the flicker of a light coming in through the hole in the door. And with the light a small glimmer of hope returned to her. She scrambled to her feet and ran to the door. When she looked out, she saw an old woman, who'd obviously refilled and relit the lantern, busily occupied, her arms filled with two large, empty bowls. Aura called out to her as she walked past, but the woman either was deaf or she had no intention of recognizing the presence of someone imprisoned in the cellar. She totally ignored Aura's cries, walking numbly past her, then disappeared into a recess at the far side of the open cellar. She eventually reappeared, her two bowls now filled with what seemed to Aura to be potatoes and carrots.

Potatoes and carrots, Aura fumed. She had been imprisoned in someone's root cellar. And whoever that someone was, his servants were as heartless as Hung Poh.

Desolate, she returned to the small place between

211

the crates. It was now only too clear to her that when Hung Poh wanted her, he would know exactly where he could find her. He'd seen to it that she wasn't about to go anywhere without his express permission.

Assuming, that was, he didn't intend to simply leave her where she was either to starve to death or else to freeze. Starvation would come first, she told herself miserably. The air was chill, cold enough to make her decidedly uncomfortable, but it wasn't nearly cold enough to freeze her to death. Unfortunately. She'd heard that dying of the cold was like going quietly to sleep. She doubted that starvation would be nearly so pleasant.

She pulled her knees up and her skirt close around her in an attempt to keep warm, and forced herself to think. Eventually it became clear to her that it was not Hung Poh's intention to kill her, at least, not immediately. If he'd wanted her dead, it seemed only logical that he'd have had her killed once he'd found the slip of paper that had been the object of his search. No, he had something else in mind for her, or else he wouldn't bother with keeping a noisy and unruly prisoner. No matter how safe his dungeon, there was always the possibility that someone not in his employ would hear her. He wouldn't take that chance unless he had a reason for it.

She replayed the events of the previous evening, trying to remember it all, trying to find something that might shed some light on what it all might mean. Hung Poh had wanted that piece of paper she'd found in Whit's ledger. An entry pass, he'd called it.

An entry pass to what?

That place filled with the sweet-smelling smoke where all those men had been lying about glassy eyed, smoking whatever it was they were smoking in those pipes—could that slip of paper have been a means of

212

entering there? Surely something strange was happening there, something beyond anything she'd ever seen. She'd never before seen people seem so stupefied. Even the occasional drunkard she'd seen in Fall River hadn't seemed so totally oblivious to the world around him. All except for that one miner, the one who'd nearly been convinced to help her. Whatever it was that was being smoked in those pipes, it must have a strong effect, she thought, for that miner had willingly abandoned her in exchange for a fresh pipe. Whatever it was, it was powerful enough to make a man turn his back on a situation that he otherwise would have done something to change.

A drug of some sort, then, she told herself. Opium, perhaps? She'd somewhere read about the opium dens in China. After all, hadn't the English and the French fought a war in China not long before to keep their trade prerogatives there, selling India-grown opium in return for the teas, porcelains, jades, all the other Eastern goods for which Europe hungered? If smoking opium was a habit fostered by trade treaties and cultivated by the Chinese in their own country, why wouldn't they bring the habit with them when they came to California?

Many reasons, she told herself, the most important that the Chinese who came to work on the railroads and in the mines were not rich enough to afford such a luxury. They were poor laborers, men who barely fed themselves on what they earned.

Or perhaps not. The man Hung Poh had, from what she'd seen, hardly been a poor peasant. Perhaps there were other powerful men among the Chinese community, men of which she had absolutely no knowledge. After all, she was a newcomer here, and hardly an expert.

And only one of those two rooms had been inhabited by Chinese. If Hung Poh was establishing a place where men with money could cater to a dependent habit, then San Francisco was ideal. Miners with filled pockets came into the city eager to forget the misery of the days they'd spent finding those bits of gold. What better way to forget than with the help of an opium pipe?

Aura shook her head. None of it made any sense. Even if she was right about the opium, what had that to do with Whit? Why would Yang Wu have given him a pass to get into an opium den in search of information about forged currency? Because it was forged bills that Payne had come to California to investigate, not opium dens. And Payne was certain that it was Whit's attempts to help him that had led to the murder.

None of it seemed logical to her, and none of it gave her any indication of what Hung Poh might have in mind to do with her. No, the opium den, if that was what it was Hung Poh was running, had nothing to do what he intended for her. She pressed the heels of her palms into her eyes and tried to think, tried to remember.

And then something came back to her: he'd called her a commodity, she recalled—a valuable commodity. She'd been too frightened at the time to think about it, but now it came back to her, and with it, the look she'd seen in his eyes and the way he'd handled her hair. He'd told her she was too valuable to kill.

She felt a dull feeling of helplessness begin to grow inside her. A commodity was something you sold. The thought was chilling, and entirely alien. She mouthed the words to herself—Hung Poh intended to sell her. It was inconceivable and barbaric. This was, after all, part of the United States, however remote and uncivilized. Women weren't sold here. Certainly Hung Poh didn't have the power to sell her.

But she knew for a fact that he did have the power to kidnap her and hold her prisoner. And he'd had the power to have Whit murdered. Selling her seemed minor beside the crime of murder. What might a man like that do? He'd made it only too clear to her that he felt himself well above any petty laws that might apply to lesser mortals than himself.

She shivered and stared at the packing crates stacked haphazardly in the room around her. Simply more of Hung Poh's commodities? she wondered. More goods waiting for him to sell them? Perhaps there was a reason he'd left her locked up in this storeroom. Perhaps this was his way of letting her become accustomed to her new role in life.

A wave of desolate misery washed over her. She was at Hung Poh's mercy, and there was nothing at all that she could do to change that situation.

Her despair was strong enough to overwhelm her at that moment, to block out her perceptions of everything except the numbing realization of the hopelessness of her position. It was more than enough to keep her from immediately noticing the sound of footsteps approaching the storeroom.

It wasn't until the door had been unlocked and pulled open that she realized she was no longer alone. She cringed back and pulled her legs up close to her body, trying to make herself small, hoping in vain that she would somehow escape the notice of whoever it was.

For a moment she almost deluded herself into thinking the ploy had worked. She saw the light from the lamp he held move around the room and heard the sound of his voice, an angry, grating noise as he spoke. She wasn't sure if he was calling out to her or simply talking to himself, reminding himself that the room

215

was secure, that there was no possible means by which the prisoner put in his charge might have escaped.

In either case, she told herself she had no intention of answering. If by some miracle he didn't find her, perhaps he might leave the room and forget to lock the door behind him. A forlorn hope that she might actually get away from this place and Hung Poh kindled itself inside her.

But the hope was all too quickly extinguished. Eventually the light approached the place where she huddled between the crates and she looked up to see the face of the guard who'd brought her to this place however many hours before it had been. He was staring down at her, his eyes hard and mean and angry with her for the bother she'd given him. She had the distinct feeling that he'd like to strike her.

He didn't. Instead, he set a bamboo basket and a jug on the dirt floor in front of her. He uttered a few more words, then backed away.

Aura suddenly realized that he was going to leave her alone again, that he was going to close the door behind him and lock her in, leaving her to her fears and the darkness, as he had the night before. For some reason the prospect seemed worse to her than anything he might possibly do to her. Anything, she told herself, was better than to be left alone again in this cold, damp tomb. Anything was better than facing more hours of being locked up in the darkness with only her fears.

She scrambled to her feet and ran after him, catching him just as he reached the door.

"No more games," she said. "What is it that Hung Poh wants of me?"

He didn't understand her words, but she saw his expression change when he heard her utter his master's name.

"Hung Poh," she repeated, hoping to gain whatever advantage the name might buy her. "Bring me to Hung Poh."

He hesitated an instant longer, then began to turn away.

Aura reached out and grabbed his arm. An uncontrollable feeling of panic had taken hold of her. All she could think of was the terror of the hours she'd spent alone in the darkness and the fear that she would not be able to endure any more hours like them.

"Don't leave me here any longer," she cried. "What do you people want from me?"

He smiled then, and turned back to stare at her in silence. For an instant Aura thought that the smile meant she had somehow convinced him to take pity on her.

It didn't. He raised his hand to where hers held his arm and pried her fingers loose. Then he pushed her, sending her sprawling backwards as he quickly stepped outside the room.

Aura lay where she had fallen sprawled on the dirt floor as she listened to the sound of the door being slammed shut and then bolted.

She was completely still for a long moment. Then she pulled her knees up and lay in a fetal position, holding herself in a tight ball, unable to move. She began to sob in quiet misery. She was alone, and no one was about to help her. And she had no doubt but that whatever future she had to look forward to would be nothing better than an unending horror.

She heard her own voice, the sound of her sobs, and realized it was Payne's name she was crying. Payne, Payne, Payne . . . His name echoed in her ears as she cried it out over and over again. For an instant she thought that if she said it enough, he would hear her and somehow come to help her.

Eventually, she realized how inane the thought was, that he could not suddenly materialize there and save her just because that was what she wanted him to do. After everything that had happened since she'd arrived in San Francisco, she told herself, she ought to know that life did not work out as she wanted it to. By now, she ought to know that there was no such thing as a happy ending anywhere but in storybooks.

Only days before she'd sworn to herself that she would never again allow herself to live in a dream world, that she wouldn't let herself depend on anything or anyone but herself. And now she knew just how wrong she'd been to think she could survive entirely on her own. She needed Payne, not only to save her from Hung Poh, but also to fill an emptiness in her life that she'd never even known existed, apart from an absent realization that she wanted a home and a family. But now she realized she needed him for more than the security of a roof over her head. She ached to see him, to be close to him, to touch him. And now she'd never again have the chance to do any of those things. She'd never have the chance to tell him that she loved him.

She'd told him she didn't need him in her life, and that she didn't want him. She'd almost managed to convince herself that it was true. But what was far worse, he'd believed her. She'd released him from all responsibility for her, and now he was gone, leaving her to face whatever it was Hung Poh intended to do with her alone.

Payne hunched his shoulders and leaned over his beer mug as though he was trying to protect it from possible attack. Not that he really doubted a man might stick a knife in his ribs for no greater reward than the weak and watery contents of the cracked mug. He had no doubt that murders were committed for less in a place like this. It was a small comfort to him to know that his back was against a wall.

He glanced around the smoky room. It was a dirty place, more accurately filthy, one of the worst of the lot of alehouses close to the wharves. Its one distinction was that it was one of a very few establishments that catered not only to the Caucasian sailors in port, but also to those Chinese laborers who arrived in San Francisco lucky enough to have a few pieces of copper in their pockets.

The great American mercantile, Payne mused cynically, as he watched the bartender exact the pennies from his customers before he doled out their mugs of beer.

He stared down into the contents of his mug. What right had he to condemn anyone, he asked himself. After all, he'd come to this place to transact an unpleasant bit of business of his own. The only question that remained was how long he would have to wait.

He heard the door open and glanced up at it for what seemed the hundredth time. Sooner or later, he knew, Yang Wu would come through that door. He'd learned that the young man's major source of income was brokering work gangs: he helped organize groups of newly arrived laborers for the railroad and the mine owners, and took a fee for his effort. The fact that this place was one of the few where newcomers gathered meant that sooner or later he'd come here looking for fresh recruits.

Sooner or later. The words sounded strangely unpleasant to Payne. He had no idea how much time he had, but he was sure it couldn't be much. Much later might be too late for Aura. And he was just as sure that he had no hope of finding her without Yang Wu's help.

Because there was no chance that Aura would be found if he did not find her. Summoning the police had been nothing more than a wasted effort. The ubiquitous Sheriff Dougherty had examined the room, declared there was insufficient evidence to assume foul play, and suggested that if there was no word from her in a week, he'd institute a search. But Payne knew that a week was too much time to leave Aura in a kidnapper's hands. After a week, no sign of her would ever be found.

And so he'd asked his own questions about Yang Wu and then gone to the alehouse to find him. He'd been there most of the afternoon, more than long enough even to become numbed to the smell of the place. But not long enough to make him like the beer. It was awful stuff, and he was incapable of swallowing any more of it. Which only led to the unpleasantly suspicious stares the bartender periodically leveled at him. He obviously was not enthusiastic about the presence of a nonimbibing customer. Payne decided he didn't care; let the man look all he wanted. Payne had other concerns.

The foremost of which was, of course, Aura. He could think of only one reason to explain why she'd disappeared as she had, and that was that whoever had killed Whit thought she knew something. He no longer had the leisure to go about finding his counterfeiters by the circuitous route he'd been following. Yang Wu knew something, and like it or not, he was going to reveal what he knew.

For a minute, Payne wondered where his scruples had gone. After all, once he'd been convinced that the young man had had nothing to do with Whit's murder, he'd decided to take pity on him and leave him to his own devices. But the urgings of pity had been supplanted by the hard ache in his belly that had begun when he'd found that Aura was missing. No matter how reluctant Yang Wu was to talk, Payne was determined, one way or another, to convince him to tell all he knew. And if the only means of persuasion that had any effect was a violent one, then so be it. He wasn't exactly pleased with the alternative available to him, but he wasn't about to dismiss it out of a sense of nicety.

He raised the mug and pretended to drink from it, and glanced up at the door once again when it opened. This time he found himself finally rewarded by the sight of the man he'd come to find.

He sank back, out of the lamp light and into the shadows, and watched Yang Wu work his way through the crowd, chatting to the newcomers in Chinese, laughing, offering to buy them fresh mugs of the pale beer. A good number of them followed him to the bar.

He laid a handful of change on the counter, calling out to the bartender to pour his friends fresh drinks. There was a noticeable rise in the spirits of the crowd as they reached for the mugs, and Yang Wu, satisfied that he was making good progress with the group, took up one of the mugs and turned to face them, his back to the bar.

He was surprised to find that the man who had sidled up beside him was a tall Caucasian, and even more surprised when he looked up into a pair of pale blue eyes and recognized their owner.

"You," he hissed. "What are you doing here?"

"I've come for the same reason you have," Payne replied. He grinned sardonically. "To make a new friend."

Yang Wu's eyes narrowed.

"I don't think you'll find many friends here," he said.

Payne nodded. "You're probably right," he agreed. "But then, I'm not looking for a crowd. Just one friend, that's all I want."

"A man like you, why should you need to go looking for a friend?" the young Chinese asked. He spoke slowly, as though choosing his words carefully.

Payne leveled a cold, sharp glance at him.

"To help me find something that was stolen from me," he said.

Yang Wu obviously didn't like what he heard in Payne's voice. He tried to move away, but when he did, he felt something sharp had been pressed into his side.

"You make a grave mistake," he told Payne sharply. "We are on my territory now, not yours."

"So we are," Payne agreed. He lowered his voice to a whisper. "But I wouldn't suggest you try to prove any points, even here. The blade you feel pressed against your side is a good one, and believe me, I know how to use it."

"You wouldn't get out of here alive," Wu said.

"But then, neither would you," Payne countered.

Wu studied Payne's expression, then glanced down to where the dark wood of the bar and Payne's arm almost entirely hid the length of the knife.

"What is it you want?" he muttered, apparently resigned.

"I want you to take me to your friends, the ones you directed Whit to see before he was killed," Payne said.

Wu swallowed uncomfortably. "I told you, it would mean my death," he said.

"It will mean your death if you don't," Payne assured him. "They killed my brother, and now they've kidnapped his wife. And I think you know where they've taken her."

Wu looked genuinely shocked at that.

"I don't, I swear it," he protested. "I know nothing of a kidnapping."

"But you know these men. You have a good idea of what they might do," Payne said. When there was no response to that, he added, "And I don't think even the coward you would have me believe you are would sit mute and let them kill an innocent woman."

"You can't stop them," Wu muttered. "No one can stop them."

"I intend to try," Payne told him. "Now, do you help me, or do I end your miserable existence in this filthy hole in full view of all your new friends?"

Payne glanced at the group of laborers Wu had been courting. They were still laughing and talking, apparently pleased that it had been so easy for them to find a man who seemed to know his way about in this place, someone who might be of use in finding them work. They even seemed pleased with the weak beer.

"Well?" Payne prodded. "Do you help me?"

"I don't know where they have her. I can only take you to the man who knows, because I told him, that your brother might know something about the counterfeit currency. There's nothing more I can do."

"Then that will have to be enough," Payne said. He removed the blade from where he'd been holding it at Wu's side and carefully obscured it against his sleeve as he put his arm on Wu's shoulder. He saw Wu flinch as he felt the blade against his neck. "Now smile at your new friends," he said, as he nudged the young man forward, toward the door. "After all, we wouldn't want anyone to think anything's wrong."

Chapter Twelve

"Madame Charlotte's?"

Payne stood in the growing shadows at the side of a clump of bushes and stared at the big frame house at the far end of the street. It was familiar enough to him. In fact, at that moment, it seemed all too familiar.

Charlotte's residence was set apart, well back from the muddy road. The other houses seemed coolly distant, as though they were turning their backs on the whorehouse, thankful for the thick tangle of hedges that obscured their view. Only in San Francisco could a whorehouse exist two hundred feet from the homes of the proper citizenry, he thought. But then, few of the proper citizenry were so totally oblivious to the baser hungers that fueled the young city's thriving economy that they could afford to ignore them. After all, most of them made their living one way or another from the proceeds derived from those hungers.

From where he stood, Payne could see a woman moving about in the parlor, stopping to light the lamps in preparation for the first of the evening's customers. As the light in the room was turned up, the outlines of furnishings came into focus, the deep burgundy red of the flocked wall paper, the careful arrangement of couches, the piano against the far wall,

MORE PASSION AND ADVENTURE AWAIT... YOUR TRIP TO A BIG ADVENTUROUS WORLD BEGINS WHEN YOU ACCEPT YOUR FIRST 4 NOVELS ABSOLUTELY *FREE*
(AN $18.00 VALUE)

Accept your Free gift and start to experience more of the passion and adventure you like in a historical romance novel. Each Zebra novel is filled with proud men, spirited women and tempestuous love that you'll remember long after you turn the last page.

Zebra Historical Romances are the finest novels of their kind. They are written by authors who really know how to weave tales of romance and adventure in the historical settings you love. You'll feel like you've actually gone back in time with the thrilling stories that each Zebra novel offers.

GET YOUR FREE GIFT WITH THE START OF YOUR HOME SUBSCRIPTION

Our readers tell us that these books sell out very fast in book stores and often they miss the newest titles. So Zebra has made arrangements for you to receive the four newest novels published each month.

You'll be guaranteed that you'll never miss a title, and home delivery is so convenient. And to show you just how easy it is to get Zebra Historical Romances, we'll send you your first 4 books absolutely FREE! Our gift to you just for trying our home subscription service.

BIG SAVINGS AND FREE HOME DELIVERY

Each month, you'll receive the four newest titles as soon as they are published. You'll probably receive them even before the bookstores do. What's more, you may preview these exciting novels free for 10 days. If you like them as much as we think you will, just pay the low preferred subscriber's price of just $3.75 each. *You'll save $3.00 each month off the publisher's price.* AND, your savings are even greater because there are never any shipping, handling or other hidden charges—FREE Home Delivery. Of course you can return any shipment within 10 days for full credit, no questions asked. There is no minimum number of books you must buy.

TO GET YOUR 4 FREE BOOKS WORTH $18.00 — MAIL IN THE FREE BOOK CERTIFICATE T O D A Y

Fill in the Free Book Certificate below, and we'll send your FREE BOOKS to you as soon as we receive it.

If the certificate is missing below, write to: Zebra Home Subscription Service, Inc., P.O. Box 5214, 120 Brighton Road, Clifton, New Jersey 07015-5214.

4 FREE BOOKS

FREE BOOK CERTIFICATE

ZEBRA HOME SUBSCRIPTION SERVICE, INC.

YES! Please start my subscription to Zebra Historical Romances and send me my first 4 books absolutely FREE. I understand that each month I may preview four new Zebra Historical Romances free for 10 days. If I'm not satisfied with them, I may return the four books within 10 days and owe nothing. Otherwise, I will pay the low preferred subscriber's price of just $3.75 each; a total of $15.00, *a savings off the publisher's price of $3.00.* I may return any shipment and I may cancel this subscription at any time. There is no obligation to buy any shipment and there are no shipping, handling or other hidden charges. Regardless of what I decide, the four free books are mine to keep.

NAME

ADDRESS _____ APT

CITY _____ STATE ____ ZIP

TELEPHONE ( )

SIGNATURE _____ (if under 18, parent or guardian must sign)

Terms, offer and prices subject to change without notice. Subscription subject to acceptance by Zebra Books. Zebra Books reserves the right to reject any order or cancel any subscription.

ZB0394

the tall mirrors that made the room seem as a large as a small ballroom. The parlor of Madame Charlotte's house was as close to real luxury as most of the men who visited there would ever come.

But Payne wasn't interested in the gaudy furnishings Charlotte had chosen to enhance the seduction of her paying guests. He had already seen all he needed to see of the whorehouse. He was in search of something other than amusement at the moment, and he was not in the mood to have Yang Wu try to misdirect him. He turned and glared at the young Chinese.

"This is your secret information?" he asked. "A whorehouse?"

"You must enter this way," Wu told him.

"I'm not in the mood for games," Payne growled. "If I wanted the company of a prostitute, I damn well wouldn't need you to guide me to it."

"No," Wu replied, "you do not ask for a woman. You tell them someone told you about the den. Say you heard about it from some miner. Tell them you want to visit the parlor."

"What the hell are you talking about?" Payne demanded.

He stared at Wu's expression, expecting to see the small, slyly absent smile that would tell him the young man was trying to play him for a fool. But Wu's face showed no hint of amusement. If anything, there was fear written on his features.

Payne reconsidered his opinion. Perhaps Wu wasn't trying to play with him, after all. Perhaps he'd just lost his grasp on reality. Wu saw his expression and scowled.

"The man you seek is named Hung Poh," he told Payne. "He is the proprietor of an opium den."

"Opium den?" Payne asked, genuinely puzzled. He

225

shook his head. "Opium is the Manchu's devil. There aren't any opium dens in San Francisco."

"There is one now," Wu assured him. "Hung Poh came here from China six months ago, bringing with him a good store of the powder and a great deal of money. Since then he has come to control much of the commerce that is conducted among the Chinese community. Commerce and more, much more. About three months ago he somehow convinced the madame of this fine establishment that it would be profitable to her to provide this service for her customers. I am told it is starting to become quite popular with the miners."

"How can one man can do all that in half a year?" Payne muttered. He was clearly unconvinced.

"A single, powerful man can do all that and much more," Wu insisted.

"And all this happens under the nose of the stalwart Sheriff Dougherty?"

Wu shrugged, obviously as unimpressed with the local representative of law and order as was Payne.

"Perhaps Hung Poh has escaped the good sheriff's notice," he suggested, his tone slyly insinuating. "Perhaps he has found some means to keep himself free of scrutiny. I do not know."

"You're suggesting he buys off the sheriff," Payne said.

"I suggest nothing," Wu replied. "I only warn you that Hung Poh is a most formidable man. It is whispered that he even arranges the smuggling of wives for the miners, but of this I have no sure knowledge."

"Wife smuggling?"

Payne almost laughed. The thought seemed entirely too ludicrous.

Wu gave him the sort of look that suggested he was wasting his time trying to instruct a slow schoolboy.

"A poor farmer sells a daughter because he cannot

226

afford to keep her or pay the dowry to marry her. A broker buys her and sells her to a man who needs a wife. It is common enough in China."

"This is not China," Payne snorted.

"Isn't it?" Wu asked him with a sly smile. "In the hills to the north and east, with the work gangs, how do you know what it is?"

Payne opened his mouth but didn't speak. He had to admit that he really didn't know what it was like on the bleak hillsides where the mining gangs labored, moling their way into the mountains. But despite that, Wu's suggestion still seemed impossible to him. After all, the War Between the States had settled certain matters, and the selling of human beings was one of them. He shook his head.

"I don't believe it," he muttered.

"Believe what you like," Wu told him. "I can only tell you that a woman is valuable property where there are few and many men. It could be a very profitable business to someone willing to take a few risks."

"Like this Hung Poh?" Payne asked softly.

"Perhaps," Wu said.

"But even if all this is true," Payne demanded, "what has it to do with Aura?"

Wu shrugged once more. "Perhaps nothing. Perhaps a great deal. If you are careful, perhaps you can learn something from Hung Poh. I told you, secrets come to his ears."

"And I'm supposed to go to Charlotte's whorehouse, tell them I want to visit the opium den, and then find this man Hung Poh? Isn't that a roundabout way of finding this man?"

Wu pointed to the outline of the stables behind the house.

"If you were Chinese, it might be easier. My people

go in that way," he said. "But you must enter through Madame Charlotte's."

As he spoke, the doors of the stables opened and a cart with a half dozen crates in its rear was driven out, down the path, and onto the street. Payne watched as it as it passed, aware that the driver glanced at him with almost as much curiosity as he was leveling at the whorehouse.

When the cart had passed, Payne was still silent, considering what Wu had told him. It occurred to him that San Francisco had changed a good deal in the years since he and Whit had quit mining. In those years, the worst trouble a man with a few ounces of gold in his pockets could get into was a whore's bed or a high-stakes poker game. He wasn't sure but that he thought things ought to have remained as they had been.

"And you believe this Hung Poh is responsible for Aura's disappearance?" he asked finally.

Wu shook his head. "I do not have any knowledge of your brother's wife," he said. "Nor do I hold any opinions on the matter. But it was to Hung Poh that I directed your brother the night he was killed. I can only tell you what I told him, that secrets somehow find their way to Hung Poh's ear, that if anyone knows about the counterfeiting, then that person is Hung Poh. It was an entry pass to the opium parlor that I gave him that night."

"And that's what you came to steal the evening I caught you?"

Wu nodded. "It seemed safer if it was not to be found," he said.

"Then perhaps this Hung Poh is responsible for Whit's murder," Payne mused softly.

Wu was silently thoughtful for a moment or two. Then he looked up at Payne.

"No," he said, finally, "even knowing what he is capable of, I doubt Hung Poh would have ordered such an act. Not that he would be morally indisposed to murder. But not the murder of a Caucasian. That would be far too risky. It would call too much unwanted attention to him. But if anyone knows who is responsible, he does." He looked pointedly at the knife Payne was still holding at his side. "I have done as you asked," he said. "I have nothing more to offer you. I expect you will keep your word and allow me to leave now."

Payne considered the younger man's expression for a long moment, then withdrew the knife and slid it into a leather sheath under his jacket.

"If you're lying to me," he said, "I promise you, you won't find a safe place where you can hide."

Obviously relieved, Wu hurriedly turned and took a few steps away. But then he paused and looked back at Payne.

"It seems we must trust each other," he said softly. "If Hung Poh even suspects how you learned about him, I will have no more need to fear either him or you. Dead men have no fears."

"Mr. Randall, this is indeed a surprise. You're a bit early, but if you don't mind waiting, I'm sure we can manage to find some way to accommodate you."

Payne pushed himself out of the overstuffed chair and took the hand Charlotte offered him. After insisting that he be admitted despite the fact that it was not yet normal business hours, then demanding to see the madame personally, he was aware he had made a scene. He was beginning to wonder if he wasn't making himself a bit too obvious.

Charlotte's stare seemed a bit fuzzy, her eyes puffy

and red, as though she had just awakened from a nap. Payne grinned as pleasantly as he could and hoped his expression was the one he wanted, the proper naughty schoolboy look that was usually received with such pleasure by women of a certain age.

"Oh, I wouldn't think of disturbing any of your ladies, Miss Charlotte," he replied and repeated the grin. "It's just that a miner I met told me about a," he hesitated and offered her a final grin, "a room here . . ."

Charlotte, he realized, wasn't buying his act as easily as he'd expected. She stared at him, her eyes narrowing.

"A room?"

Payne cleared his throat. He was beginning to feel almost as awkward as he was pretending to be.

"This miner, he said a man could get something to make him forget his problems," he replied.

"And did this miner happen to have a name?" she demanded.

"I suppose he did, but I don't think he mentioned it," Payne told her, and punctuated the words with another grin. "To tell the truth, we were both a little drunk at the time."

"Didn't anyone ever tell you it doesn't pay to believe the word of a drunkard, Mr. Randall?" Charlotte asked.

It was clear to Payne that it wasn't going as easily as it ought to. Charlotte seemed to suspect he wasn't simply a bereaved brother trying to come to terms with his sibling's untimely death. Still, he knew he had no other cards to play, at least, not at the moment.

He looked down, pretending to stare at his feet. It occurred to him that he was carrying the naughty schoolboy act a bit too far, but he'd begun with it, and it seemed that changing in midstream would be a mistake.

"Since Whit's death," he said softly, "well, I've a few things I'd like to forget. I was hoping that what that miner said was true, because nothing else seems able to help."

It was the mention of Whit that seemed to pave all roads in San Francisco, he realized, at least in Charlotte's domain. The madame's expression softened as soon as she heard him speak his brother's name.

"We all have our own painful memories, Mr. Randall," she said softly. "Perhaps I can help you deal with yours, after all. But I warn you, it won't be cheap."

She smiled then, finally sympathetic rather than suspicious.

"The miner warned me about that," he replied. "I can pay."

Charlotte nodded. "Very well," she said.

Payne breathed a sigh of relief as she turned and called out to the servant, the man who'd admitted Payne to the house, who must have been waiting for the summons, because he appeared in seconds. He was a tall, powerful black man with watery eyes and an entirely unconvivial expression. But more than that, he had arms and a chest that made him look to Payne as though he was strong enough to rip rooted trees out of the ground with his bare hands. He glanced at Payne with a look that implied he would be more than happy to return him unceremoniously to the street.

"Ma'am?" he muttered, addressing Charlotte.

"Conduct Mr. Randall downstairs," the madame directed him.

"Downstairs?" he repeated, his tone suggesting he had expected to be given entirely different directions.

"You heard me," Charlotte snapped. She turned

back to Payne. "Once again, Mr. Randall, my sincere sympathies. Should you require any other service later, please return. We'll be more than happy to accommodate you here."

"I appreciate your kindness," he told her.

"Not at all," Charlotte murmured, as she turned away.

It seemed to Payne that she nearly fled from the room, as though she was telling him she had no further responsibility in what he was about to do. Odd, he thought, how genuinely sorry she seemed to be about Whit. Surely there hadn't been any great store of feeling between the two, and yet she gave every indication that she was deeply disturbed by his murder.

He shrugged. Whatever motivated Madame Charlotte's sympathies, he was grateful for them. He dismissed her and turned his attention to his obviously less than enthusiastic guide.

"Well?" he demanded.

The man sneered. "You'se a fool to play wit what ye don't understan', man," he said.

"Do you understand?" Payne asked him.

"No matta what ah do and what ah don't," he said. With that, he turned and motioned Payne to follow.

He led Payne out of the parlor and along a hallway leading to the rear of the house. He stopped before he reached the kitchens, though. As the man took a lantern from a peg on the wall, Payne sniffed at the scents coming from beyond the kitchen door. Roast beef, he decided, the aroma strong enough to make his mouth water. Madame Charlotte's girls ate well.

The servant lit the lantern, adjusted the flame, then pulled open a door revealing a flight of steep stone steps.

"Watch yer step, mind," he said. "Stones is sometimes slick."

Then he started down.

Payne grinned, realizing the man had lisped slightly with the string of sibilants. Even giants have their weaknesses, he told himself, as he started down the stairs after his guide.

The basement, when they reached it, was cool and dim. Several storage cellars, all neatly secured, suggested that Charlotte's house was well enough provisioned with vegetables, flour, and liquor to endure a considerable siege. He passed by them, glancing into the rooms through the small openings in their shut doors.

Despite the wealth of provisions, however, Payne could not see anything that would remotely suggest the sort of place Yang Wu had told him was here. He was beginning to think he had been the butt of a not too nice joke, after all.

"Dis way," the man said, interrupting his thoughts.

Payne returned his attention to his guide, watching as the man pulled open a thick door at the far side of the cellar. Much to his surprise, it was not an opening to the expected side stairs to the outside. Once opened, it revealed instead a dark, walled tunnel.

"You're Hung Poh?"

Payne made a conscious effort to keep the surprise out of his tone, because the tall, thin man standing in front of him hardly seemed capable of being the monster of which Yang Wu had spoken. Save for this man's eyes, which were sharp and disturbingly piercing, there was nothing even remotely powerful looking about him. On the contrary, he was tall and painfully thin, almost cadaverous. Payne had the feeling that were he to touch the pale flesh it would crumble.

Nor was there anything about this room that might

233

suggest an opium den. In fact, except for the fact that its stone walls gave the appearance of yet another extension of the cellar of Madam Charlotte's house, the windowless room was quite comfortable. Both he and his host sat on chairs, ornately carved of some dark wood, and between them was a small desk, also of the nearly black wood and handsomely decorated with incised figures. It was hardly the environment he'd have expected a villain of the sort Yang Wu had described to occupy.

"Please, sir, you will be kind enough to tell why you ask?" his host questioned.

He smiled, but Payne could see the look was far from genial.

Payne shrugged, from all external appearances unruffled, careful to display little more than a touch of idle curiosity.

"Because the miner I spoke to said to ask for a man named Hung Poh," he replied. "He said Hung Poh would see I was well taken care of."

"Man? What man?"

"A miner," Payne answered quickly. "Tall, big fellow, with a taste for whiskey. I don't recall his name."

"But you remember name of Hung Poh," the cadaverous man prodded. He smiled again, with no more warmth than before.

"Because he repeated it enough times," Payne explained. " 'Hung Poh,' he said. 'Good fellow, Hung Poh. Knows what a hardworking man really needs.' " Payne grinned. "That's what he said, anyway."

Hung Poh lowered his head slightly, the suspicion not quite gone from his glance, but his manner begrudgingly becoming more obliging.

"I have once or twice had the honor of obliging a gentleman like yourself with the favor of a soothing pipe," he said softly.

"That's just what this miner said," Payne said.

Hung Poh raised a warning brow.

"Unfortunately," he said, "the special sort of mixture in pipe is most difficult to obtain in this country. It is very costly. I regret I myself am unable to bear expense purely out of regard for the gentleman in question and the dictates of hospitality."

He lowered his head once again, apparently willing to wait for Payne to reach his own conclusion as to the meaning of the small speech.

Payne took the cue. "I understood that the stuff was expensive," he quickly assured him. "I can pay." He put his hand into his breast pocket and withdrew the twenty-dollar bill he'd placed there before entering Madam Charlotte's.

Hung Poh barely glanced at the bill. Once he'd determined it had been duly deposited on the table in front of him, he seemed to lose all interest in it. He looked up, for the first time letting his gaze fully meet Payne's.

And as soon as their eyes met, Payne knew that Hung Poh was everything Yang Wu had warned him he was, all that and more. He had thought that as soon as they were alone, he'd do what he'd come to do, ask a few questions, and hopefully find some meaning in whatever answers were offered to him. But now he quickly changed his mind.

There was something incredibly malign behind the man's dark stare, something Payne could only describe as evil. More than that, Payne had the sick feeling that Hung Poh knew more about Aura's disappearance than a few whispered words might bring to his ears. He decided that what he really ought to do was look around and see for himself if Hung Poh didn't have more hidden away in his underground lair than what Yang Wu had given him to expect was there.

235

Hung Poh was the first to look away. Payne had the feeling that the protracted stare was a test of some kind, a test he had apparently passed. In any event, Hung Poh waved away the man who'd been his guide. He waited in silence until Charlotte's servant had exited and closed the door behind him before he moved. Then he pushed himself to his feet.

"Be so kind as to follow, please, sir," he said, and he motioned to a door to the rear of the place where he sat.

Payne hesitated for a moment, wondering what it was about the way Hung Poh spoke that made the hackles rise at the back of his neck and made a warning voice silently shout out to him that the only sensible thing to do was to bolt, to get away as fast as he could. Because despite the extreme politeness of Hung Poh's words, still there was something threatening about the way he spoke them, and the coldly vicious look never left his eyes.

But Payne didn't bolt. Instead, he watched as Hung Poh moved toward the door, noting the deliberate way he walked, his long, thin legs moving like carefully controlled stilts, the shiny black silk of his clothing whispering softly with each step. Payne cast a quick, regret-filled glance at the bill he'd put on the desk, before getting to his feet and following.

"My God," Payne said softly, as they stepped into the next room.

"Please, sir?" Hung Poh asked.

Payne shook his head. "Nothing," he muttered. "This is a good deal more impressive than anything I expected," he said. "I'd never have thought anything like this could have existed beneath Madame Charlotte's garden."

Hung Poh rewarded his statement with a tight little smile, and for the first time Payne thought there was actually a hint of real amusement in the smug expression.

"We are industrious people," Hung Poh explained, expansive with the encouragement of Payne's amazement. "Men who earn their rice hollowing whole mountains have little trouble to make such a place as this."

Put that way, it sounded reasonable enough to Payne. A mining work gang wouldn't need very long to hollow out a space like this from the rocky soil of the hillside overlooking the harbor, but still he couldn't help but be impressed by it. Not that it was so large, but it was completely unexpected, and made more so by the relative comfort of its furnishings. There were carved screens that divided the space into small, almost private compartments, and it was surprisingly warm in a place that, since it was underground, ought to be cool and damp. The place seemed oddly exotic. Even the air had a strange scent to it, thick and heavy and sweet.

The room seemed empty save for Payne and Hung Poh, but he could see there were places for a dozen or more customers, each furnished with a narrow cot covered with a toss of plump pillows. It seemed that Hung Poh's customers were given a reasonable comfort in which to pursue their pleasures. More than that, he quickly calculated that at twenty dollars a head, a good evening would bring Hung Poh two hundred and fifty dollars or more. It was clear that the opium business was even more profitable than mining gold. And, he told himself wryly, it required the expenditure of a good deal less sweat.

Hung Poh waved toward one of the cots.

"Make self comfortable, please, sir," he told Payne. "Servant will bring all that is necessary." He paused and smiled a sharp, sly smile. "Enjoy self, sir."

With that, he took a few steps back and pulled one of the carved screens forward, effectively setting off the small area Payne was to occupy and making it discreetly private.

Payne hesitated a moment, then seated himself. This wasn't exactly what he'd planned to do when he'd knocked on Madame Charlotte's door. But if he was going to find anything, he knew he had to be exactly what he was pretending to be, at least, for a long enough time to keep from rousing any suspicion.

Because no matter how much Yang Wu had insisted that Hung Poh was simply a source of information, Payne found he couldn't shake the feeling that there was more to this place than an unexpected method of fleecing money from miners eager for a thrill. A sick ache filled his belly as he found himself wondering if Aura wasn't here someplace, hidden away in some dark hole dug into the ground, waiting for whatever fate Hung Poh had decided for her.

One thing was certain, though. Before he could look around, he'd have to make himself seem innocuous enough to be ignored.

The man who appeared a few minutes later bearing a long, white ivory pipe was a good deal less disturbing in appearance than Hung Poh had been. Shorter, with a long braided pigtail of dark hair down his back, he was the model of obsequiousness. He handed Payne the pipe, then lit a taper from the flame of a candle he carried. He held out the small flame, waiting for Payne to bring the bowl of the pipe to meet it and light its contents.

Payne did just what he assumed was expected of him. He held out the bowl of the pipe and drew on it when the taper was touched to the mixture of tobacco and opium. He inhaled his first breath of the smoke and held it for an instant. The smoke was strong, but

238

more than that, its effect was a good deal more powerful than he'd expected. He gasped and exhaled.

His reaction seemed quite amusing to the man. He laughed heartily, then motioned to Payne to watch, pantomiming the act of drawing on the pipe, holding the smoke in his lungs for fully half a minute, then slowly exhaling. When Payne nodded that he understood, the man checked to see that the pipe was properly lit, then turned and left.

Payne sat for a moment listening to the sound of his footsteps moving away, waiting until they finally faded entirely. He sat for a while longer to be sure that the servant would not return, then carefully set the pipe down on the stone floor. A thin line of smoke rose up from it, sweet scented and ominous.

Payne stood. He moved away from the trail of smoke, trying to keep from inhaling too much of it. He wasn't really sure how much of it he could breathe before becoming affected by it. The single breath he'd taken had been enough to make him feel slightly lightheaded, as though he'd drunk a healthy swallow of whiskey. He had no intention of allowing himself to become careless by breathing too much of it.

He stood and walked silently to the screen. He glanced around it, making sure that he was not being watched before he started his little exploration. It seemed that he had been left alone to enjoy his first foray into the world of opium dreams. From what he could see, the place was quiet and, except for himself, completely empty.

He hesitated for a moment, considering the room around him. From what he could see, there were only two doors, the one by which he'd entered, and another on the opposite side of the room. He told himself he already had an idea of what was behind him. He started across the room to the door at the far side.

Being careful to make as little noise as possible, he crossed the room only to find another space quite similar to the one he'd just left, if a bit more crowded with furniture. More space for revelers, he told himself. Perhaps poorer ones, or even the Chinese who Yang Wu had warned him came here. But here, too, he saw no one. He stole through the room, surprised at how easy it was to wander around Hung Poh's domain undetected.

When he pulled open the door at the far side of the second room and found himself facing a long, dark tunnel, he hesitated. If Hung Poh or one of his servants were to find their only paying visitor had disappeared, they'd be sure to start a search. But he didn't really have much of a choice now. If he was going to find whatever lay hidden at the far end of the tunnel, he couldn't go back and play with a pipe filled with opium.

He listened, and once he'd decided there was no sound in the tunnel, he stepped into it, pulled the door closed behind him, and started out at a loping sprint. The faster he got to whatever it was that lay at the far end, he told himself, the better.

Moving underground was disorienting, and once he realized that the tunnel curved slightly, he gave up trying to figure out precisely where he might be. When he finally came to the end of the tunnel, he found he didn't care.

This space gave no indication that it was anything grander than a cellar. No candles, no comfortable chairs, no carved desks. But when he lit the lantern that hung from the ceiling and turned up the flame to illuminate the whole of the room, he found himself whistling in amazement.

The center of the room was empty except for a stool that had been set beneath the lantern, but all around him was printing equipment, a press, racks for drying, and tables for cutting the finished product to size. He crossed to the press and found it empty of plates, but there was evidence of smears of dark green ink. The racks, too, showed dark green smudges.

He was, he realized, most likely looking at the press that he'd come to San Francisco to find. He had little doubt but that it had been used to turn out the counterfeit bills that had brought him to California in the first place. Whether or not he had realized it, Yang Wu had directed Whit in precisely the right direction to find the source of the counterfeit currency. And whether or not he'd known it, he'd also given him directions to meet his murderers face to face.

No, that couldn't be right, Payne silently amended, as he looked around. Whit had never gotten to the opium den, never gotten to see Hung Poh. Whoever had killed him had done it before he could learn anything certain about the counterfeiters.

But if it hadn't been Hung Poh, then who was it who had ordered Whit's murder? And if Aura wasn't hidden away here someplace in this underground maze, then where was she? He might have found the answers to the questions that had brought him to San Francisco, but he still didn't have the answers to the questions that were really important to him now.

"Ah, Mr. Randall, so sorry to disturb. And great disappointment to learn mistake to trust you."

Payne spun around. Hung Poh was standing in the entrance, staring in at him. And he was flanked on either side by two extremely large, unpleasant-looking men whose expressions reminded Payne of those of trained attack dogs.

Payne pretended nonchalance.

"I seem to be a little lost," he said and grinned.

Hung Poh shook his head.

"No good, Mr. Randall," he said. He produced the twenty-dollar bill Payne had given him and held it up. "Not that the return of this was needed to recognize a spy."

Payne swore to himself. He'd known before he'd left Hung Poh's office that it had been a mistake to pay with one of the counterfeit twenties, but by then it had been too late. And now he had only himself to blame for the consequences of his own stupidity.

Chapter Thirteen

Aura gradually came to a misty consciousness. For a long while she had been drifting in and out of a series of bizarre dreams, most of them terrifying and completely irrational, and her first conscious thought was that this was just another of them. It took her several minutes to force her thoughts to focus. They seemed determined to skitter back off into the foggy dream world. Eventually, however, she realized that wherever she was, it wasn't a dream, but only too painfully real.

Her head hurt, her shoulder ached sharply, and for a moment she thought she was blind. But once she had managed to still the panic those realizations evoked, she realized that she was lying on her side with her arms pulled behind her, and the position was achingly uncomfortable. And wherever she was, it was ominously dark.

She tried to move, to shift herself into a less strained position, but found herself immobile. Her wrists and ankles hurt. She realized they were tied, hands behind her back, ankles crossed.

Something bumped and her shoulder knocked into the wall behind her. She was moving, she realized, or, more accurately, she was in some vehicle that was moving. It was a carriage or cart of some kind, she told herself, and it was traveling over an uneven, rutted road. The jagged movement made her head swim.

It came back to her slowly, being locked in the damp cellar room, lying on the floor, alone in the tiny prison, sobbing until she was left with no more tears to cry. And then there had been the odd realization that she was hungry, that despite her fear and misery, her body was behaving as a normal, healthy young body was supposed to behave and demanding that it be given fuel.

She remembered feeling ashamed as she opened the small bamboo basket that had been left for her, feeling almost that by giving in to her hunger she was admitting defeat to Hung Poh. Still, she dipped her finger into the small mound of sticky rice and fish and tasted it. It was far too salty, and she hadn't eaten much. But she had emptied the water jug. At least, she thought she'd emptied it.

They must have put something in the water, she told herself. That was why she could remember nothing after drinking it. And that would probably explain why her head felt so odd, why what little moments she could remember of her dreams were so frighteningly horrifying. They'd drugged her and put her in this dark box, and now they were taking her somewhere. The knowledge brought her absolutely no comfort whatsoever.

But they hadn't gagged her.

She didn't stop to think what that might mean— that if they were afraid her cries would bring her help, they would have taken the effort to see she was unable to cry out. The logic of all that seemed, for the moment at least, beyond her grasp. She began to scream.

"Help! Let me out of here! Help!"

Whatever effect she'd hoped the cries might have, she was disappointed to find that they seemed to produce no discernible result whatsoever. Still, she kept at it until she was hoarse before she gave up, breathless and exhausted. Whoever was out there, she realized, he had no interest whatsoever in the cargo he was carrying.

Cargo—that was what she was at the moment. A sack of flour or a crate of barrel staves would have had as little effect on their fates as she was having on hers.

But a sack of flour couldn't think, she told herself, nor could a crate of barrel staves act on those thoughts. She had the ability to do both.

And the first thing she had to do, she realized, was somehow get out of whatever it was they had imprisoned her in.

She slowly edged her way around until she was lying on her back. The position made her arms hurt even more, but she told herself that there was nothing to be done about that. She lifted her knees as far as she could and began to kick with all her might.

At first, it seemed all she was accomplishing was hitting her feet, making them hurt with the force of the blows. The contact of them with the wooden lid of her private little coffin sent shivers of conveyed hurt upward and through her legs. But she refused to stop. She told herself she was not about to allow herself to become a compliant sack of flour, not about to let herself accept the condition Hung Poh seemed to think himself able to impose on her.

She was in an uncomfortable position, and it was hard work to kick upward as she was doing without even the room to fully lift her knees. She found after a few moments that she was breathless. She stopped and rested, but once she'd caught her breath, she started once again.

She kept up in this fashion for what seemed an endless amount of time, kicking fifteen or eighteen times, then stopping to rest her legs and shift her position slightly. She tried to ignore the fact that her hands and arms felt like they were filled with pins and needles and that her shoulders ached miserably. This was all she could do except give up, she kept reminding herself. And she was not about to do that.

Eventually she began to think she was having some effect. There was a soft cracking noise now when her feet came into contact with the wooden top of the crate. And she realized she could see a small sliver of light where the lid met the sides.

She paused and thankfully considered the thin shaft of light. It was daytime, then, she told herself. It was daytime, and she was in a cart that was moving over a rough road, probably well away from the city. And whoever was driving either could not hear the racket she was making or else seemed to think his captive was secure, because there had been no attempt to silence her or keep her still.

All the better, she thought. Whoever was out there probably assumed it was impossible for her to escape. And that, she told herself, could definitely be useful to her if she was careful to make the most of her meager advantage.

She decided it would be foolish to go on kicking. Sooner or later the driver would be bound to notice that the top of the crate was splintering. Instead, she steadied herself as well as she could, lifted her knees as much as possible, and began to press against the lid of the box.

Slowly, ever so slowly, the line of light began to widen. The kicking had begun to loosen the nails that held the lid, she realized, and now, with the pressure she was exerting against them, they were slowly being worked out of the wood. A little more pushing, and she ought to be able to lift it off entirely.

It was a good deal harder than she'd anticipated. She had to stop twice and let the muscles of her thighs loosen from the cramps that developed in them, but eventually she did work the nails at the foot of the box free. She took a deep breath and pressed upward one last time. There was a soft tearing sound, and then the lid of the box rose up.

Aura nearly laughed out loud with the knowledge that she'd done something finally to help herself. She lay still for a moment to catch her breath, and listened for any sound that would tell her someone had noticed what she'd done. All was silent, and she began to think she might actually avoid detection, might somehow escape. She took one long, deep breath, then pushed the lid off the box completely and sat up.

She heard a rumble of low laughter from behind her, but she didn't turn to find its source. She was too startled by what she saw around her even to move.

There were women, young Oriental women, a dozen of them, sitting in a row on either side of her, their bodies swaying slightly with the motion of the closed wagon. For she wasn't outside, as she'd thought, and the light she'd seen coming through the crack in the lid wasn't daylight at all, but a dirty glow from a hanging lantern fastened to the ceiling overhead that swayed with the motion of the wagon.

But the fact that she was inside a wagon didn't amaze her nearly as much as did the presence of these women. They were, all but one, fairly plain-looking, with round, flat faces and slightly dull eyes that stared out at her from beneath heavy fringes of nearly identical dark bangs. The one exception was smaller than the others, her oval face delicate, her dark eyes wide and expressive. All of them, however, wore identical expressions of surprise as they stared at her. And one by one, twelve pairs of dark eyes were lowered as Aura's glance met theirs.

"Who are you?" Aura murmured in surprise. "What's happening? Where are we going?"

There was no response from any of her companions. They looked away, carefully ignoring her, all too obviously pretending that she wasn't even there.

Once again, she heard the low rumble of laughter from behind her.

This time she turned around and looked at the source of the laughter she had evoked, only to be rewarded with the unpleasant surprise of realizing she recognized the man's face. It was Hung Poh's man, the same guard who had brought her the food and drugged water and left her in that horrible cellar, letting hunger and thirst drive her to administer her own soporific.

"You," she mouthed softly.

He was smiling at her now, looking at her with an expression that told her he'd been aware of her struggle, that he'd been waiting for her either to exhaust herself or extricate herself from the box. She had the distinct feeling that he'd enjoyed the whole of the tedious performance immensely.

Aura didn't stop to think. She lurched forward to her knees, struggling to get as far away from him as possible.

"Help me," she cried out to the women around her.

Unable to ignore her now, they stared at her in mute bewilderment.

The guard's smile disappeared. He reached for her, caught her by the shoulder, and pulled her back.

Aura landed heavily against the side of the crate, the sharp edge of the wood biting into her forearms and back with a breath-stealing blow. She started to cry out but found herself mute with the hurt.

She couldn't get away, she realized. She'd deluded herself into thinking she might, but everything she'd done had been nothing more than an amusing display for this sadist of a man. Whatever had been planned for her, she was powerless to affect it in the least.

Aura dozed and woke and dozed again. Each time she woke she could think of little more than the aches in her neck and arms and shoulders and back. But the monotonous swaying of the lantern light was hypnotic and inescapable, enough to drain away even thoughts of her discomfort.

Not that her companions didn't provide enough of a mystery to her to give her sufficient material to ponder. None of them seemed to be under duress as she was, at least as far as she could see. Their wrists and ankles were not tied as hers were, and none of them appeared to be frightened or desperate.

More than that, from all indications, they were totally mute. Not one uttered so much as a word, to her or the guard or even to each other. Not even when the wagon's lurching sent them sliding along their benches to bump against their neighbors did they speak. Never in her life had Aura been in the company of women who were so completely silent for such a long time.

She sat as mute as the others when she wasn't dozing, resigned to the fact that there was nothing she could do to change her circumstances, at least for the moment. Not that she was giving up, she continually promised herself. When the time came, she would try again. She swore to herself that she wouldn't stop trying as long as there was breath left in her.

But for the moment at least, it was more than apparent that there was nothing she could do. She smiled at the woman seated next to her, hoping to find, if not an ally, at least a friendly face. The effort was useless. The woman turned away, ignoring both Aura's smile and her presence, leaving her to feel ostracized and alone.

Eventually the wagon drew to a halt. This, at least, seemed to rouse some interest among the women. They fidgeted nervously in their places on the hard wooden benches and glanced toward the door at the rear of the wagon, but none of them made a move to rise until the guard barked out a few short words at them.

Given permission, they knelt and each fished out a small, cloth-wrapped bundle that had been stowed beneath the benches. Armed with this pitifully small baggage, they stood and faced the rear of the wagon. After a moment, the door was pulled open, and the women, still silent, filed out.

Aura had watched this performance with an absent curiosity. But once the women were outside, she turned and looked at her guard. He muttered something incomprehensible but managing to convey a general impression of anger, then drew out a small knife.

He held out the blade, smiling at her, waiting. Aura could see he expected some reaction, expected to see her fear. But she rememnber that he'd played this game with her once before, in that strange, dark room with Hung Poh. She was not about to give him the satisfaction of letting him play it a second time.

She narrowed her eyes and retured his stare.

He leaned down and slit the rope that had bound her ankles.

This is the moment, Aura thought. Kick him. Surprise him. Get away somehow.

But the thought was easier to come by than the reality. Her ankles might be free, but her legs were numb from hours of constraint. When she tried to lift them, she found they barely moved.

Her guard stood quickly back, as if he anticipated she might try to strike out and had determined not to give her the opportunity. He grasped her arm, hauled her unceremoniously to her feet, and began to push her toward the door. Pins and needles filled her feet and calves as the numbness in them slowly eroded with returning circulation, and she stumbled, nearly falling. He tightened his grasp and dragged her out of the wagon.

It was night, she realized, the sky a dark, moonless blue spotted with an impressive scattering of brilliantly sparkling stars. She stood at the side of the wagon where her jailer had pushed her, staring up at the immense, deep blue bowl of the heavens, thinking that it had never seemed quite so beautiful to her before.

Nor had it ever seemed quite so cold and distant. Perhaps it seemed that way because the night air was cold, especially after the hours she'd spent in the closed wagon. She inhaled the fresh, clean air, at first grateful for the mind-clearing briskness of it, but after a moment wishing it were just a bit less chill. One thing it did tell her, however, and that was that they were nowhere near a city or settlement. There was no hint of wood smoke or food cooking or any of the other scents that accompanied human habitation. The only odor in the air was a clean scent of fresh pine.

It took her a moment to become accustomed to the darkness, but as her vision slowly improved, she realized that she hadn't been entirely right in thinking they were in the center of complete wilderness. She could see the outline of tress around them, certainly, but there was also a large, rectangular shadow, a shadow that soon gained dully glowing, square eyes. Wherever she'd been brought, she realized, there was shelter.

She didn't have long to consider that fact. Her

guard pushed her forward, toward the structure, and she had all she could do to keep herself erect. The numbness was slowly leaving her feet and legs, but she was not yet entirely normal, and her balance was less than perfect.

He pushed her into the cabin, and Aura saw that the light inside came from two lanterns that had been lit by a second man, the driver of the wagon, presumably, who'd preceded them. The two men watched the young women file inside, spoke a few sharp words to them, and left. The door was swung closed and there was the dull thud of a bar being lowered into a slot to ensure that it stayed that way.

Once the men were gone, it was as if a spell had been broken. The dozen women, so placid and mute the whole of the time in the wagon, suddenly became quite animated. They spoke to one another, nodding and laughing. One strode around the cabin with her shoulders back and her arms swinging, making a face that reminded Aura of the guard, although there was really no physical similarity between the two. She barked out short, sharp commands to the others. The rest tittered with halfheartedly stifled laughter. It was obvious that, like her, they were not entirely fond of the guard.

She took their reaction as a good omen. Perhaps, she thought hopefully, without the guard's presence, they might behave with a bit more friendliness.

"Who are you?" she asked, addressing the group as a whole. "Where are they taking us?"

They quieted suddenly and turned and looked at her as if they'd forgotten all about her. Then they turned away and began to unfasten their bundles, each mutely shaking out a thin bedroll and settling it on the floor.

Resigned once again to her status of nonentity, Aura watched them settle themselves down to sleep. Without benefit of bedroll, she sat with her back against the wall, feeling cold and uncomfortable and completely miserable. She found a rough projection in the wood of the cabin wall, and eventually she began to scrape at the cord that still bound her wrists. She could at least free her hands, she told herself, as she rubbed the knot against the bit of sharp wood.

She'd been working halfheartedly at the cord for perhaps three-quarters of an hour without a great deal of progress when she realized that a shadow had fallen near her feet. She looked up. One of the women, the small, pretty one, was standing in front of her, facing her.

"What . . . ?"

The woman put a finger up to her lips, motioning Aura to be silent. Then she knelt down beside her and began to untie the knotted cord around Aura's wrists.

"Thank you," Aura said as the knot began to loosen.

"Must be quiet," the woman whispered as she untied the last of the knot and pulled the cord away. Then she nodded toward the others and the door. The sound of a snore rose from somewhere in the middle of the room, and one of the now sleeping women turned and groaned.

Aura stared at her unexpected friend, suddenly feeling very dull with amazement.

"You speak English," she whispered back, although that fact was more than apparent to them both and hardly needed to be verbalized.

The woman nodded. "Young lady seminary, Canton," she whispered in reply and smiled.

Before Aura could say anything more to her, she turned away, stepping carefully through the maze of sleeping bodies to where the lantern hung. She reached up and lowered the flame until it was a pale, low glow. The sound of the sleeping women's breathing became slower and more even as they drifted into a deep slumber.

Aura sat and rubbed her stiff wrists and shoulders, trying not to think about how much they hurt, telling herself that once the circulation returned, she'd feel better. She watched the young woman carefully pick her way back through the sleeping bodies that littered the cabin floor, wondering why she'd made the effort to help, why she'd bothered to untie the cord. It was obvious that the others had no interest in her, and most probably had been given orders not to try to communicate with her. The young woman's friendly overture was, most likely, an infraction of whatever rules governed their behavior.

Aura saw her stop when she'd covered perhaps half the distance between them, and she thought the woman had decided that she'd taken all the risk she intended to take and would now do as the others were doing, curl up in her blanket, sleep, and pretend there was no stranger among them. Instead, she stooped and lifted her blanket from its place on the floor, then continued her carefully silent journey until she was once more standing in front of Aura.

She seated herself with her back to the wall at Aura's side and spread the blanket over herself, holding up a corner, obviously offering to share. Gratefully, Aura took the offering and tucked the blanket around her shoulders.

"Who are you?" Aura whispered, once the young woman seemed to have settled herself. "What are you doing here?"

"My name Jei Mailee," she whispered in reply. "We both here same—to make wife."

Aura was literally speechless, at first sure she'd misinterpreted, then afraid that she hadn't. She started to

254

speak, but words failed her and for a long moment she sat mute, with her mouth open.

"What?" she finally managed to croak.

"Wife," Mailee replied. "Miner wife. Go north, to gold mine, make wife to miner."

Aura stared at her with disbelief.

"Wife?" she nearly shouted. "Miner?"

Mailee's expression became immediately alarmed. "Shh," she warned Aura in a sharp whisper, and touched her hand to Aura's lips. "Too much noise." She looked around, her expression clearly indicating that she was afraid of the consequences if Aura had wakened one of the sleepers.

Aura was duly chastened. She hadn't realized that she'd allowed her voice to rise, but now she thought she heard its echo, ringing acusingly in her ears. She glanced around at the sleeping women, waiting for one to sit up, see that Mailee had transgressed, and shout out to the guard.

Mailee's obvious reluctance that they be discovered talking together made her even more aware that their guard had most likely warned the Oriental women to stay away from her. There was no doubt in her mind now that Mailee was courting punishment merely by speaking with her.

"I'm so sorry, Jay Molly," she whispered. She paused, realizing she'd mangled the other woman's name horribly. She hoped she hadn't behaved in so insulting a manner that she'd be abandoned again.

But Mailee was more amused than insulted by Aura's linguistic incompetence. She giggled softly.

"Mailee," she said, then repeated it slowly, separating the syllables of her given name so that Aura could not possibly miss it, "Mai-lee."

"Mailee," Aura repeated, this time pronouncing the name nearly correctly.

Mailee nodded and smiled encouragingly.

"You?" she asked and pointed to Aura.

Aura realized that she'd been so shocked by Mailee's statement about being sent to become miners' wives that she'd entirely forgotten to offer her own name.

"Aura," she replied quickly. "Aura Randall."

"Oh-ra-ran-del," Mailee repeated. She smiled and nodded, obviously delighted for the opportunity to display her knowledge of English custom and language. She held out her right hand. "Most pleased, Oh-ra-ran-del."

Aura couldn't help but smile. She took the offered hand.

"Just Aura," she said. "And I'm most pleased as well."

The two sat for a moment smiling at one another, both feeling just a little bit awkward to be shaking hands, formally introducing themselves as though they'd both been invited to the same tea party. But this wasn't a tea party, Aura told herself. They were a long way from anything remotely resembling a tea party.

Once the absurdity of the situation had dulled, she could think of nothing but what Mailee had told her. The short explanation had given rise to far more questions than it had answered.

"What miner?" she asked for the second time.

Mailee shrugged, her expression suggesting that the question had no real significance.

"Whatever miner have money," she replied.

"Money?" Aura repeated, a sick feeling filling her as she began to realize what it was she was being told.

"Money to buy wife," Mailee replied.

She let Aura consider this bit of information as she settled herself onto the floor, tucking the blanket around her shoulders. She looked up at Aura and motioned to her to follow.

"Sleep now, Oh-ra," she whispered. "Talk later."

Aura followed her example, sliding down beside Mailee, gratefully accepting the portion of the blanket the young Oriental woman seemed only too willing to share with her. But she knew she couldn't sleep. Her mind was too filled with questions to let her simply drift off.

Finally she could contain herself no longer. She touched Mailee's shoulder.

"What do you mean by a miner with money?" she demanded in a breathless whisper. "You can't mean they're going to sell us to miners?"

Mailee didn't move for a moment, as though she was trying to decide if she would rather simply pretend she was already asleep. But she seemed to come to the conclusion that Aura wouldn't let either of them get any rest if she didn't answer.

"Women come China," she explained. "Miner see, like, buy wife."

"That's barbaric," Aura gasped.

Mailee frowned, obviously not recognizing the word.

"Father poor farmer," she explained. "No dowry, no husband. Not happy father, not happy daughter. Sell daughter."

"To send them here to be sold to some stranger?" Aura hissed. The very thought filled her with revulsion.

"Father get money, fifty, maybe hundred yuan," Mailee explained. One look at Aura's face told her she was not being quite convincing enough. "Daughter get husband," she insisted, trying to make her argument more acceptable to Aura. "Make happy."

"Happy? Women sent off to be bartered like cattle?"

Aura demanded. "How could that make them happy? Why don't they run away?"

As soon as she'd posed the question, she realized that it wasn't as foolish as it might have seemed at first glance. There were a dozen of the women locked in the cabin, and only two guards. If they were to band together, there was a good chance they could actually escape. If she could get them to organize, to fight for their freedom, perhaps they might all escape.

"Barter?" Mailee frowned. It was obviously another word she'd never encountered in the young lady's seminary in Canton, and for the moment at least, its meaning posed a more pressing question than the possibility Aura was suggesting.

Aura waved away the question, too busy with the sudden flood of thoughts about organizing a mass escape, about finding a means to get away from Hung Poh's men and getting back to San Francisco and pressing charges.

"There are only two guards," she went on, ignoring the bewildered stare Mailee directed at her. "We can fight them. We can get away."

Finally it dawned on Mailee just what it was Aura was suggesting. Her expression changed from merely puzzled to completely appalled. She stared at Aura as if she'd suggested they all grow wings and fly.

"Daughter obey father," she said flatly.

That seemed to end the matter as far as she was concerned.

"But . . ."

Aura's objection died before she could voice it. From what she could see of Mailee's expression in the dim light, the matter of disobeying the instructions of a father was simply not to be considered, not even by a daughter whose father had sold her. These people were indeed different, she thought, different in ways she doubted she would ever even begin to understand.

She retrenched.

"But you aren't the same as the rest," she insisted.

Indeed, it was obvious from both Mailee's appearance and the fact that she was educated that she hadn't spent her childhood laboring on some poverty-stricken bit of farmland. Pale and delicate, with tiny feet, she was as different from the others as was Aura.

Mailee frowned slightly.

"No," she said softly. She spoke very slowly, as though she regretted having to make the admission. "Father merchant, in Canton."

"Then why are you here?" Aura demanded.

Mailee bit her lip, silent for a moment. When she did answer, she nearly spat the words.

"Mailee shame father," she said.

She stared at Aura, her expression suggesting that that was explanation enough, that she ought to understand. But Aura just stared back at her with a puzzled expression on her face. She sighed, then turned over, lying with her back to Aura, and began, in a very soft whisper, to explain.

"Two year past, Mailee marry. Husband not nice man."

"What do you mean," Aura asked warily, "not nice man?"

Mailee didn't answer, and Aura immediately regretted the question.

"I'm sorry," she whispered. "I shouldn't have asked. I don't mean to pry."

She waited, and for a long moment Mailee still remained silent. Aura had come to the conclusion that her curiosity had completely alienated her from the one friend she had at the moment, and was wondering how to go about apologizing, when Mailee spoke.

"Husband hurt Mailee," she whispered slowly.

259

"Oh," was Aura's only response. It was apparent that Mailee was not about to say any more about the matter, and she could only imagine what those three words might mean.

Mailee went on quickly then, obviously wanting to be done with the story.

"Husband family not nice," she said. "Accident, bang, bang, husband die. Husband family not so rich as father, not wish lose bride money. So husband brother offer make Mailee second wife. Father agree."

She paused there and Aura could hear her sigh. "And then?" she prodded softly.

"Mailee refuse," came the reluctant reply. "Shame father."

Aura pondered those four words. She had felt brave and proud when she'd defied her father, but it was obvious that Mailee had felt nothing but remorse and regret.

"How could such a thing shame your father?" she asked. "How could he expect you to marry a man you disliked?"

Mailee turned back to face Aura.

"Father give word. Mailee disobey, shame father," she said, her words softly spoken but determined, as though she was trying to convince not only Aura, but perhaps herself as well.

"But surely," Aura insisted, "if you had explained to him . . ."

"Not for daughter explain to father," Mailee interrupted. "Father tell daughter, daughter obey."

Aura understood perfectly what Mailee was telling her. Her own life had mostly been spent under the roof of a petty tyrant who'd felt the lives of those in his household were his to direct. It was Mailee's determination that bewildered her. The Chinese girl had been raised to believe certain roles were ordained, and it seemed obvious to Aura that although she'd disobeyed, still she had not abandoned those beliefs. She might have been unable to bring herself to live the sort of life they dictated she ought to live, but still she believed in them.

"So your father sent you away to be sold to some stranger?" she asked. She felt an aching well of pity rise as she realized that Mailee actually believed this punishment fitting for her crime of disobedience.

Mailee nodded. "Mailee shame father," she whispered. "No more father."

Aura watched as a half dozen tears slowly trickled across Mailee's cheek. She understood now, or thought she did. After all, she'd seen her own father turn his back on her, heard him tell her never to return to his house again, and all because she proposed doing something that didn't quite fit his image of what a daughter of his ought to do. If she could not understand a culture that demanded such complete and slavish obedience to a father's wishes that even those who broke the code still believed in it, she could all too easily identify with the abandonment Mailee must feel.

"I think I understand," she whispered.

She put her hand on Mailee's cheek, wiped away the tears, and was rewarded with a shaky smile of thanks. And then Mailee turned away, obviously embarrassed that she'd cried in front of a stranger, that she'd said all she'd said.

Aura lay silent, staring up at the ceiling, thinking how much she and this young woman from the opposite side of the world had in common. Perhaps she and Mailee were not so very different, after all. They had both been wed and widowed, and disowned by proud fathers who held their positions more dearly than they held their daughters. And both of them seemed doomed to face the same uncertain fate.

Chapter Fourteen

Payne stood mute and stared at Hung Poh's confident expression. He had to admit to himself, however reluctantly, that he really wasn't completely taken by surprise by the fact that he'd been found out. He'd known all along that it wouldn't take long for Hung Poh to realize he wasn't exactly what he'd presented himself to be and mount a search for him.

What disturbed him were the circumstances of his discovery. He quickly scanned the room. Hung Poh had him trapped in a space with just one way out, and it was only too obvious that he was as aware of that fact as Payne. The two thugs Hung Poh had brought with him, who now stood by the only door, gave the impression of being, both of them, small mountains. Payne needed only a glance at them to recognize that he couldn't hope to fight his way past them.

"This is why you come?" Hung Poh asked him now, holding out the counterfeit twenty Payne had given him and waving it gently in the air.

Payne shrugged, refusing to give the bill so much as a second glance, refusing to let himself dwell on the enormity of the error he'd made in using it.

"I don't know what you're talking about," he insisted, playing for time. "I just got lost, that's all."

Hung Poh was unimpressed with his explanation. More than anything else, his thin smile told Payne that he was even a bit amused by it. His smile widened and he actually laughed a short, nasty laugh.

"If that were true, it will be a great misfortune that I must have so innocent a man killed," he said softly. "Luckily, you lie."

"Killed?" Payne asked, feigning shocked surprise. "For getting lost?" He took a step forward, trying to position himself so that Hung Poh was directly between himself and the two impressive-looking guards. When Hung Poh stepped back, he stopped and stared at the man's remarkably piercing eyes, and said, "Oh, I see, this is your idea of a joke. I don't mind telling you, I don't think it's very funny."

Payne ventured another step forward and this time Hung Poh did not react. A few feet more, he told himself, and he would be close enough to Hung Poh to use him as a shield.

"Not a joke," Hung Poh told him.

He smiled again and took another step back, his eyes narrowing as he considered Payne. He seemed to be saying that he knew what Payne was planning, that he knew everything. He motioned to his two men.

The two started forward into the room, past Hung Poh and toward Payne. Their approach was wary, and they kept their eyes glued to Payne's expression. He didn't move, making it plain that he had no intention of fighting them. They seemed disappointed by his calm, as if they were hoping that he would give them the opportunity to display their pugilistic skills.

But that was the last thing Payne intended to do. He didn't want to give them an excuse to beat him senseless when there was no chance that he might escape them here. Instead, he offered Hung Poh a wry smile as they took places on either side of him. It was some small satisfaction to him to see how confident they were of themselves, to note that they didn't make any attempt even to hold onto his arms as long as he made no threatening move. Let them think him a coward or a weakling, he thought. When the time came, their underestimation of his abilities could be used against them.

"It would seem you're just too smart for me," he told Hung Poh, reason dictating that if feigned ignorance was of no use, perhaps feigned admiration might serve him better. He spoke the words with reluctance, pleased that he sounded so sincere, that he managed to edge his tone with just a hint of admiration. "I'd never have expected to find this little mint of yours here, right under the noses of the upright citizens of San Francisco, in the cellar of the sheriff's favorite whorehouse. A stroke of brilliance."

"Now I fear your flattery, Mr. Randall," Hung Poh told him. "I ask self, does this flattery have a motive?"

"Perhaps it does," Payne agreed slowly. "Perhaps I just want some answers."

"Answers?" Hung Poh asked. "Why should I give you answers?"

"To satisfy my curiosity, of course," Payne replied. "What could be crueler than sending a man to his maker still filled with questions?"

Hung Poh shook his head and smiled. "You are an amusing man," he said. "It is a great shame we must be enemies."

"Enemies?" Payne countered. "I have absolutely no desire to be your enemy, Hung Poh. I only want to know what happened to my brother's wife."

"That is your reason to be here?" Hung Poh asked. "To learn the fate of a woman?" There was no questioning the surprise he showed at the possibility.

264

Payne nodded and grinned, thinking that in a way, Hung Poh's amazement mirrored his own.

"However surprising that fact may be to both of us," he said, "it is nonetheless true." Then, quickly sobering, he added, "It is the one reason that seems to have meaning to me just now."

"Meaning?" Hung Poh asked.

Payne shrugged. "I really don't know," he admitted. "But we digress. Where is she?"

Hung Poh pursed his lips in thought. Then he smiled.

"As you will soon die, no harm can come from answers."

"Then you know where she is?" Payne asked.

"Perhaps I have heard word of her," Hung Poh admitted.

"But you know more than what a stray word could bring you, don't you?" Payne pressed. "You know precisely where she is."

"Alas, such precise knowledge is beyond the abilities even of Hung Poh," came the solemn reply. "No man can know where a butterfly goes when he watches it take flight."

Payne scowled. Hung Poh was playing a game with him, playing games for no greater reason, he supposed, than that it was amusing to him.

"But this particular butterfly didn't exactly take flight, now, did she?" he insisted. "You kidnapped her."

"Hung Poh is a peaceloving man, Mr. Randall," Hung Poh replied. "Surely you can not believe me a common abductor of women?"

"No, I suppose not," Payne agreed. "There's nothing common about you at all, Hung Poh. You're not a man who dirties his own hands. You just had her abducted." He nodded toward one of the guards. "Perhaps by one of these gentlemen?"

"Abduct is so unpleasant a word," Hung Poh replied. "I merely received commission to see Mrs. Randall makes no problem."

Payne glared at him.

"What does that mean?" he demanded.

Hung Poh only shrugged.

"See that she makes no problem?" Payne went on, his voice rising with a sudden spurt of emotion he could not control or hide. "Is that what you were afraid my brother might make, problems? Is that why you had him killed?"

"You wrong Hung Poh," came the reply. "I had no hand in the death of your brother."

Something about his expression made Payne feel that his words had the ring of truth about them. Perhaps Hung Poh really was innocent of Whit's death, he thought. But even if that was true, he'd as much as confessed to Aura's kidnapping. Thoughts of Whit receded and fear for Aura sent a shiver of hatred through him.

"And his wife?" Payne demanded, his voice rising to a near shout. "Where's Aura? What have you done with her?"

Hung Poh's expression filled with scorn.

"You are a fool," he hissed.

Payne knew that his self-control was crumbling, but there was no way he could contain it. Nor did he want to. All he wanted was to know what had happened to Aura, where they'd taken her, and it seemed obvious that Hung Poh wasn't going to tell him. Anger overpowered every thought, even those that might protect him. He totally forget about the two mountainous thugs. All he could think about was putting his hands

266

on Hung Poh's throat and forcing the answers he needed out of him.

He started forward, darting toward Hung Poh, oblivious to the probable repercussions of such an act. Hung Poh's two men didn't wait for him to reach their master. They set on him, landing a half dozen quick, punishing blows to his stomach before he could so much as think about defending himself. Then they finished with a single sharp blow to the back of his head. Payne staggered with the pain and fell to his knees.

The two were about to continue when Hung Poh barked a single warning order to them. They darted disappointed glances in Payne's direction, but obediently fell back immediately. Hung Poh advanced, moving forward until he stood directly in front of Payne, and stared down at him.

"Hung Poh is a generous man," he told Payne. "As such, I will satisfy your curiosity before you die, Mr. Randall. Your brother's wife is not here. She is sent north, to provide some worthy miner pleasure and me great profit. A worthy bargain, do you not agree?"

"You bastard," Payne growled, and started for him, but Hung Poh's men quickly grabbed his arms.

Hung Poh nodded to his men and spoke to them again. Then he returned his attention to Payne.

"I tell them to take you away and kill you, Mr. Randall," he said. He smiled unpleasantly. "A man with satisfied curiosity should find comfort in death."

With that, he turned and left, leaving Payne to the less than tender attention of his thugs. If Payne hadn't been otherwise occupied, he would have heard the sound of Hung Poh's laughter echoing back at him through the underground passage.

* * *

Payne inhaled slowly, trying to get past the burning hurt in his belly. Hung Poh's men might not be fastidious, but they were effective—at least, effective enough to leave him feeling less than certain that he would ever be able to draw breath normally again. Each time he inhaled he felt a wave of pain ripple through his stomach and send shivering echoes throughout him.

But they weren't quite as thorough as they ought to have been, he thought, making an effort to detach himself from the pain and try to look at the situation as an objective professional might. They hadn't taken the effort to search him, and that, as any objective professional knew, was a grave mistake.

They hadn't found his knife.

He could feel it when he pressed his arm against his torso, the hard blade flat and comfortingly solid, lying in its sheath against his side. Given the slightest opening, it might even matters considerably, or, if not exactly even them, at least give him a fighting chance. All he needed was a few minutes to catch his breath and the opportunity to retrieve the knife from beneath his jacket.

He didn't look up, didn't give the two of them the chance to know how quickly he was recovering from their attack. That had been stupid, he told himself, to give them reason to do this to him, to lose his control so completely. But the thought of what Hung Poh had done to Aura had set loose a kind of madness inside him, had robbed him of all rational thought. All he'd wanted to do was put his hands around that smirking bastard's neck and press the life out of him.

And he'd gotten nothing more than a very effective beating for his effort. If nothing else, at least the pain had served to sober him. He supposed he ought to be grateful for that, but somehow, even though the ache in his belly was slowly growing duller, gratitude still evaded him.

The two guards spoke to one another, apparently convinced that Payne was completely subdued and not bothering to so much as look at him. After a moment's conversation, one of them started for the door. Payne supposed he was leaving to make whatever arrangements had to be made for their unsavory task.

As he watched the guard disappear out the door, Payne thanked whatever lucky star had taken pity on him at that moment. Even armed, he knew he would have had a hard time against the two of them. But one against one, that seemed more than reasonable to him. He waited until the remaining guard reached down and grabbed for his arm. He looked up and nodded.

"All right, all right," he muttered, slowly pushing himself to his feet, pretending the effort cost him a good deal more pain than it actually did.

As he started to rise, he put his hands to his stomach, hoping his guard would accept that the movement wasn't threatening, that it was just the pain that had prompted him. The man seemed unconcerned, and yanked on Payne's arm, nudging him to hurry. As he did, Payne slid his right hand beneath his jacket and grasped the handle of the knife.

As the guard pulled him to his feet, Payne pulled the knife free of the sheath. He took a deep breath and then swung swiftly around, lifting the weapon and swinging wide. There was the satisfying sensation of the solidity of contact and a gasped cry as Hung Poh's man released his hold. Payne pulled the knife away and stepped back.

He had, he realized, opened a fair-sized gash on the man's arm. Hung Poh's man stared down at the wound, his face showing nothing more than dull surprise as he saw the line of red that spurted across his

269

arm. He slowly turned his glance to Payne, then his eyes narrowed and he grunted his anger. But he'd hesitated a moment too long before gathering his wits. That hesitation was his downfall.

Freed, Payne had no intention of losing his advantage. Before his adversary could regroup, Payne darted forward and grabbed the man's wounded arm, pulling it behind him and and then sharply and painfully upward. At the same time, he pressed the blade against the man's neck. It all happened in a second, before the guard so much as realized how completely he'd lost control.

"Well, now, it looks like we've got a different game to play, eh?" Payne hissed into the man's ear.

The guard grunted in reply, and tried to twist around to face Payne. Before he made any progress, Payne pressed the knife slightly into the flesh of his throat. A thin line of dark red blossomed from the shallow cut. It had its effect, however. The threat was quickly acknowledged. The man quieted immediately.

Payne glanced quickly around the room. He had at his disposal the means to kill this man, but he had no desire to do that. Despite what he knew Hung Poh had ordered the man to do to him, and despite the fact that he had little doubt but that those orders would have been carried out to the letter, still he did not relish the thought of slitting another human being's throat. But Payne knew he couldn't just walk away and leave him behind.

The printing press gave him his answer. He nodded toward the side of the room.

"That way," he said sharply. "Move."

The guard quickly took the hint, despite the fact that the English words meant nothing to him. He moved slowly as Payne had directed, his attention obviously firmly planted on the blade pressed to his neck.

The man murmured something and Payne smiled.

"I suppose you're telling me that I'll never get away with this," he said. He found himself smiling, although he realized that there was nothing even remotely amusing about his position. "Well, truth is, for a while there, I didn't think I'd get this far, so let's just say I'm already ahead of the game." He edged the man back against the printing press. "Now, you behave in a nice, cooperative fashion, and we'll both live to tell our grandchildren about our little adventure."

And while Hung Poh's man was busy puzzling over the words he quite obviously couldn't understand, Payne jabbed him sharply in the side with his elbow, then quickly grabbed the heavy wooden arm that was used to press the paper over the printing plates. He swung it smartly against the back of the man's neck, stepped back, and waited.

For a moment Payne thought he'd made a terrible mistake by releasing his hold of the guard. The man stood unmoving, his eyes wide with surprise but to all appearances otherwise unaffected. Payne held his breath, waiting for him to attack.

But then the man's body shuddered and he slumped forward, sprawling onto the floor. Payne breathed a thick sigh of relief as he knelt beside him and felt for the pulse in his neck.

"I'll bet you have a hell of a headache when you wake up," he told the unconscious man with a satisfied grin. "You needn't bother to thank me. Just think of it as a little something to remember me by, a momento of our fleeting acquaintance."

Satisfied that he'd neither killed the man nor left him able to do any more mischief, at least in the near future, Payne silently slipped out of the room. Once in the corridor, he stood for a moment, darted a glance in either direction, and listened. There were noises, he

271

realized, the sounds of someone coming from the direction of the opium den.

"Didn't want to go back there anyway," he muttered softly to himself. Then he turned his back on the sounds, moving toward an opening in the corridor ahead of him. Whatever it was, he realized, it was his only choice. He couldn't go back.

Once he reached the opening, he found it was a flight of stairs.

A flood of relief filled him. Up toward the surface was at least the right direction. It might even mean safety.

Now, this is convenient, Payne mused as he started up the stairs. He hoped it wasn't too convenient, that he wasn't running directly into the arms of Hung Poh's men.

He started up the stairs, taking them two at a time, but the ache that remained in his abdomen reminded him that he was, if not permanently injured, at least seriously bruised. He was, he realized as he slowed to a more sedate pace, in no shape to begin a foot race. He hoped that condition wouldn't prove to be fatal.

When he approached the top of the flight, he realized he might be saved from the effort of having to run any races, after all. The scent of the place was unmistakable. He was entering Miss Charlotte's stable.

Whatever elation he felt at that realization, however, quickly disappeared. Standing not twenty feet in front of him, busily placing a bit in a horse's mouth in preparation to hitching the animal to a wagon, was the second of Hung Poh's henchmen.

Payne slipped his knife back into its sheath and silently lifted a large, flat shovel that had been left resting on the side of the stall nearest where he stood.

It had obviously been used recently to shovel out the stalls. It was heavily coated, and a thick odor of fresh manure rose from it.

Taking great care not to make any noise as he moved, Payne started forward. Behind him, a horse stirred in his stall and snorted at the presence of a stranger. Payne didn't have time to wonder if Hung Poh's man would turn around to find out what had disturbed the animal. From behind him, somewhere near the bottom of the flight of stairs, came the sound of a shout.

Payne didn't have time to think. He lunged forward, swinging the shovel with all his might. It landed with a thick thud against the shoulder of Hung Poh's man just as he began to turn around. The shock of the surprise blow staggered him and sent him sprawling backward. A thin shower of manure splattered over his tunic.

Payne dropped the shovel, letting it fall with a clatter. He could hear the sound of the voices behind him, and they were quickly growing much louder and closer.

He had only one way out, and the thought that it might label him a horse thief wasn't nearly enough to keep him from grabbing the lead of the horse that was being readied for the harness. He took a thick handful of mane, and, grunting with hurt, pulled himself up onto the animal's bare back. He felt dizzily unsteady, but despite the pain, he managed to keep himself from falling. He dug the heels of his boots into the horse's flank with a sharp kick, then leaned forward and shouted, *"Git,"* into his ear.

The horse reared at the treatment, then started forward to the stable doors at a gallop. Payne had all he could do not to lose his seat. He leaned forward and clung on for dear life, giving the animal his head, letting him take the hurdle of the wooden half gate like a practiced steeple chaser. In one heart-pounding second they were over the gate and out of the stable.

More shouts followed him, but Payne didn't stop to look back and take count of the number of Hung Poh's men who were pursuing him. He turned his stolen mount toward the street, letting him trample unchecked through Madame Charlotte's flower garden.

Despite the fact that he realized they wouldn't continue the pursuit through the city streets, that Hung Poh's methods depended on stealth, still Payne didn't stop until he was halfway across the city, into the crowded street that fronted San Francisco's best hotel, the Palmer House. He pulled the horse to a stop about a block away from it, slid off his back, and gave him a grateful pat on the neck.

"Sorry to ride and run, fella," he said softly. "But I think it's best you and I part ways here."

With that, he tied the lead to the hitch in front of a rather noisy saloon, settled his rumpled jacket as best he could, and nonchalantly walked across the muddy street to the Palmer House.

First, he told himself as he climbed the hotel's front steps, he needed a stiff drink to help him settle his nerves. Then he would decide what he would do next. Because from what little he'd learned from Hung Poh, he realized that he had to do something about finding Aura, and he had to do it fast.

But first things first. His hands were still a bit unsteady, and he was honest enough with himself to admit that he had to calm down if he expected to think clearly. Besides that, his belly hurt like hell.

He pushed opened the etched-glass door of the

Palmer House. A lobby, large by San Francisco standards, boasted a good deal of dark red velvet upholstered furniture and a welter of potted plants. But Payne wasn't interested in either sitting or admiring the flora. He crossed the lobby directly to the entrance to the gentlemen's lounge.

"Lounge" was probably a complimentary term for it, for it was nothing more than a common saloon with polished brass, rather than tarnished pewter, spittoons. The air was filled with the scent of cigar smoke and a slightly alcoholic haze. Payne inhaled thankfully and then made his way directly to the long mahogany bar.

He ordered a double whiskey, and when it was served to him, he immediately lifted it and took a healthy swallow. Then he turned around to face the room, casually surveyed the crowd, and began to weigh his options as he let the trail of alcoholic warmth work its way into his bruised body.

It was more than obvious to him that riding north and trying to search the mining camps alone would be an endless and no doubt fruitless task. There were dozens of mines that employed the cheap labor of Chinese work gangs. Aura might have been sent to any one of them.

But the longer he thought, the more he realized that there couldn't be more than one or two places where Hung Poh could organize an illegal human auction site. The mines all had overseers, and it would be next to impossible to carry on such a business without an overseer at least being aware of it. Even if some of them might wink at the illegal arrangement among the Chinese, Payne doubted there'd be many who'd permit the sale of a Caucasian woman. Hung Poh would have to be certain that wherever it was he sent Aura, she was not only far enough away from the city to

275

make any attempt at escape futile, but he had to know that those not directly involved in the business could be trusted never to talk about it or try to interfere.

It was clear that there was no way he could again approach Hung Poh or any of his minions and expect to remain alive for very long, so whatever little information he already had from that source was all he was about to get. And trying to take Hung Poh to the law would be similarly useless. If what Yang Wu had told him was true, Sheriff Dougherty was already in Hung Poh's pay. There would be no use trying to accuse Hung Poh of kidnapping if he had no real proof of what had happened to Aura. The only way he'd ever get Dougherty to act would be to present him irrefutable proof of the kidnapping, proof that couldn't possibly be ignored, even by a crooked sheriff. At the moment, absolute proof was one thing he didn't have in abundance.

He could, he supposed, bring the sheriff around to institute a search for the press that had turned out those counterfeit bills. But he had no doubt that Hung Poh had already hidden the incriminating machinery and would keep it well hidden until he felt it safe to use it again. He doubted if charges would be brought. Besides, even if he was lucky, even if the press was found, it wouldn't help Aura. At that moment, it was more important to find her than to see the counterfeiting at an end, at least as far as he was concerned.

So that left him with only Yang Wu. Not that he relished a return to that wharfside bar, or the wait that would probably face him there. Nor did he anticipate with any pleasure the thought of forcing the young Chinese man to place himself in a difficult situation. But he couldn't see any other way of finding out where Hung Poh might have sent Aura. Yang Wu had hinted his knowledge of the practice of selling wives. There was not a doubt in Payne's mind but that he knew a good deal more that he hadn't cared to reveal.

Payne sipped the remainder of the whiskey slowly, letting his mind wander for a moment to the pleasant sensation of warmth that filled his belly. He still hurt, but he was beginning to find the pain a good deal less distracting. He had some idea that it was probably the effects of the alcohol rather than any great curative powers that dulled the hurt, but he wasn't about to dispute what seemed to be working.

When the glass was finally empty, he looked at it morosely and thought how much he would have liked another. He didn't, however, permit himself to motion to the bar man. Enough to dull the pain, he told himself, not enough to dull his brain.

He set the glass down on the bar, fished enough coins out of his pocket to pay for the drink, and dropped them beside the glass, then reluctantly pushed himself away from the bar. He'd wasted more than enough time, he told himself. He had to find Yang Wu.

He was approaching the door to the lobby when it opened and Payne found himself standing face-to-face with Howard Crofton. For an instant the two men stood silently eyeing one another, and Payne realized there was no way to ignore the feeling of animosity that flowed between them. He was asking himself why he disliked the lawyer as much as he did when Crofton nodded at him.

"Randall," he said. "I see you're still in town."

"No place to go just now," Payne replied.

"Sorry to hear that," Crofton noted, with just the slightest hint of a sneer. "But don't let me keep you," he said, as he started forward into the bar. "You will send my very best regards to that lovely sister-in-law of yours, now, won't you?" he threw back over his shoulder, as he wandered into the smoke-filled room.

Payne found himself unconsciously gritting his teeth as he left the bar and started across the Palmer House lobby. He hadn't grown any more fond of Crofton since the day he'd first met the man at Whit's funeral, nor did he appreciate the tone that the man had used in referring to Aura. Crofton wore his ambition like a mantle, Payne told himself, and there was something about the man that made Payne believe his ambition was the sort that would drive him to just about anything to be satisfied.

And there was something else, he thought, a feeling that made him equally sure Crofton had included Aura in his plans, whatever they were. However irrational the reaction, he realized that what he felt when he looked at Crofton was nothing more than simple jealousy. Even if Crofton was as pure as the driven snow, Payne knew he wouldn't like him any better.

For a minute he almost considered enlisting Crofton, telling him about what had happened to Aura and asking the lawyer to use whatever contacts he had in San Francisco to help locate her. That would be the logical thing to do, he told himself, the rational thing. But something kept him from turning around. He told himself that he might regret it, but he couldn't bring himself to go back into the bar to find Crofton.

Crofton was wrong, he told himself. He didn't know what it was, and he didn't have the time to search for it just now, but he knew if he turned over the right rock he'd find something unpleasant the lawyer would just as soon keep hidden.

He had to find Aura. Once he'd done that, there would be more than enough time to take care of Lawyer Crofton.

And if he didn't succeed, then Crofton wouldn't matter anyway.

Chapter Fifteen

Aura woke with a start. She looked up, disoriented and, for a moment at least, not understanding why she wasn't staring at the ceiling of the bedroom above the store.

It came back to her, then, in a distasteful rush of remembrance. She closed her eyes and tried to wish it away, but when she opened them, she realized that wishing would do her no good. She was here, in this wretched cabin, surrounded by a dozen young women who were stirring now, just as she was.

She hadn't slept very well, and what little sleep she did manage to get during the night had been filled with less than pleasant dreams. She told herself the dreams were grim enough so that she ought to be grateful for the daylight that glinted past the grime-covered windows and the grunts and growls of reluctant wakening that filled the cabin.

She sat up and wrinkled her nose with distaste. The cabin stank. Not that she ought to have expected much else. Thirteen women in the single, closed-up room, none having been given the opportunity to wash the night before, and all forced to use the one large pot that had been left for them by the door. The air was thick and foul.

Beside her, Mailee sat up and rubbed her eyes. Aura noticed that her nose, too, wrinkled with distaste at the less than pleasant bouquet, but she said nothing, just smiled at Aura and then went about the business of rolling up her blanket as the others were doing.

Aura stood at the side of the cabin, watched her, and tried to think of something other than the sharp pains of emptiness inside her stomach. She was hungry, so hungry she thought she could feel her stomach walls touching one another. She'd eaten nothing since the meal that had drugged her early the previous day, and very little of that. Hunger hurt, she realized with a vague start of surprise. She'd never even imagined how very much it hurt.

By the time the women had all finished turning their bedding into the same small packages Aura had seen them carry the night before, the door was pulled open and the women's keeper barked a few words at them. Then he motioned them outside.

It was obviously a ritual they were well accustomed to following, for they filed silently out of the cabin directly to the fire that had already been started. With a minimum amount of whispered discussion, they went about the business of cooking their own and their keepers' breakfasts, measuring and stirring, setting the pot on the fire, retrieving bowls and spoons from the bundles of gear tied to the side of the wagon.

Aura watched them, surprised that there was so little talk, half expecting them to indulge in a bit of the sort of chatter and joking they'd shared the night before as they'd settled themselves for the night. Under the watchful eyes of the two men, however, they were as diligent and as unswervingly hardworking as drone bees.

Only Aura remained relatively idle. When she approached the women preparing the food, they turned away from her, ignoring her as they had the day before. Mailee ventured a smile, but then she, too, hurriedly went about her task.

Given the leisure to do nothing more than observe, Aura noticed that Mailee was not entirely accepted by the others. The women seemed stiff with her, almost suspicious, as though they understood the differences in their backgrounds separated them from her, and made them wary of her. Perhaps, Aura thought, Mailee had needed a friend as much as she had the night before. Perhaps it had been need as much as pity that had prompted her to those painful moments of sharing.

Aura grew uncomfortable the longer she stood idle and watching, both ill at ease and cold. She wrapped her arms around herself in a vain attempt to keep warm in the early morning chill, wishing she'd been allowed a task that would have kept her closer to the fire. She sniffed the air for the scent of food, and thought how nice it would be not to feel her stomach grinding with emptiness. Waiting for the contents of the pot to be finally ready seemed to her a vicious sort of torture.

When the food was finally ready, Mailee and one of the other women each took a bowl and brought it to the men. The other woman handed the bowl she carried to the driver, who sat ready and waiting for his food. But the guard pretended to ignore Mailee. She stood in front of him, waiting and obviously awkward, holding the bowl. He persisted in ignoring her.

"Chaou Li," she finally ventured.

So that was his name, Aura thought.

He looked up at her, and Aura could see the satisfaction in his eyes. He was enjoying the fact that he had been making Mailee uncomfortable. Now he spoke to her, his tone sharp, chiding her, Aura assumed, for disturbing him. He took the bowl finally, and, thankfully freed, Mailee bowed and backed away from him.

The women all stood now and watched the men eat. They lifted their bowls to their mouths and used a pair of sticks to push the contents forward. When they emptied their bowls, one of the women hurried forward and refilled it. As he ate, Chaou Li talked and joked with the driver. The two men seemed oblivious of the women who were waiting for their own meal.

Finally the two men finished with their meal. It wasn't until their bowls were taken away that they finally gave the women leave to start eating.

Aura was given a bowl along with the others and a pair of sticks like those she'd seen the men use. She sat as the others did, in the grass around the fire, relishing the warmth. She stared at the contents of the bowl, at first a bit put off by the looks of it, a thick, soupy mix of rice and small bits of vegetables and dried fish. It was hardly the sort of breakfast she was accustomed to eating, a far cry from country ham and eggs and toast. And she was disgusted by the prospect of pushing food from the bowl to her mouth with a stick. It seemed coarse and uncivilized to her.

Still, she was far too hungry to be fussy for long. Her stomach was so empty she'd have eaten the grass she was sitting on, if that had been all that was available.

She glanced at the others, at Mailee, who daintily used the pair of sticks to lift bits of food to her mouth, and at the others, who ate as the men had, pushing the food directly from the bowl to their mouths. At first she tried to emulate Mailee's technique, but discovered it was a good deal more difficult than it appeared. In the end, she gave up, lifted the bowl to her lips, and used the sticks to push the food forward.

Once it began to settle into her stomach, she decided that it wasn't all that bad. It was warm and filling, if a bit bland. And she was hardly in a position to complain about it, she reasoned, as she silently directed the thick liquid into her mouth. No one would have listened even if she'd tried, nor would they have understood even if they'd listened.

It was gone all too quickly. If she'd dared, she'd have tried to ask for more, for she certainly could have consumed another bowl. She scraped up the last bits from the bottom of the bowl and carefully swallowed them as she glanced longingly at the pot where it sat by the fire. If one of the others got up to get some more, she told herself, she'd do the same.

But they didn't. They all seemed satisfied with the contents of a single bowl, or, if not satisfied, at least accustomed to it. Aura glanced at her own scraped-clean bowl and thought ruefully of the admonitions she'd heard endlessly in her childhood, that a lady always "left a bit" on her plate, that it was only good manners, and manners separated a real lady from the rest of the world.

She scowled at the memory. The only thing that separated a lady from the rest of the world was the fact that she'd probably never been really hungry, Aura told herself. She noticed that the rest of the women were as conscientious about cleaning their bowls as she had been. The absence of a meal the previous evening and the way they all finished every last grain of rice made her think that this might be the only food they'd be given all day. She immediately began to anticipate the return of the hunger pains in her stomach.

She told herself she ought not to think about it, but she couldn't force the thought out of her mind. She wanted to ask Mailee, but there was no chance for her to get close enough to whisper a few words, and there was no one else with whom she could speak, even had she not been so pointedly persona non grata.

Funny, she thought, how easily one's thoughts tend to center on the barest of necessities. A few weeks before, it wouldn't have entered her mind to wonder if she would have enough to eat during the course of a day. Regular meals were something she'd always simply taken for granted. When she thought about the way her stomach had felt an hour before, she realized that that had been the first time in her life she'd actually felt real hunger. There had been times when she'd had a healthy appetite for her dinner, certainly, but never before had she felt her stomach so completely empty for so long that it was physically painful. It hadn't been pleasant.

When the meal was completed and the women began climbing back into the wagon, however, even the question of food fled her mind. She edged her way to Mailee's side.

"Don't they let us wash?" she asked in a horrified whisper.

Mailee looked as thoroughly unhappy about the situation as Aura was.

"Not every day," she whispered in reply.

She quickly turned away, afraid their guards would see her talking to Aura. Aura wanted to go after her, to question her more, but wisely decided that would be foolhardy. Mailee's position was, she thought, only a bit less tenuous than her own. And she had the lessons of a lifetime to frighten her away from the prospect of disobeying those who had power over her. After all, the single attempt at defiance she had made in her life had cost her her family and sent her away from her home in disgrace.

It was only surprising that Mailee had ventured to

talk to her at all, Aura told herself, as she reluctantly climbed into the wagon along with the rest.

Aura glanced out the open wagon door, peering outside at the faces of the men waiting there. They stared at the women as they filed past, their attention riveted, their expressions, if not exactly rapt, certainly deep in consideration.

Their eyes narrowed as each woman climbed down and past them, their expressions, speaking of weighty decisions. These, then, she decided, were the mine laborers who hoped to buy a woman at the bride auction. They stood in the insistent drizzle, subdued by the cold and the wet, patiently waiting to get a first glimpse of the merchandise that would be offered for sale. Aura could see their eyes move as they inspected the women who climbed down from the wagon, as they considered the relative merits of each, deciding which would be the stronger worker, the better cook, the most eager to anticipate and accommodate a man's needs.

Their faces were as dull and barren as the dark mud of the hillside behind them and as bereft of comfort as the cluster of rickety shacks huddled at the slope's foot. These men were much like the women in that, she thought, for they appeared to be as drained of life as the poor farmgirls who had been sent to become their bedmates and their servants. There was no sense of the anticipation of pleasure about them, or even an expectant hint of happiness. They looked as though they were driven more by need than anything else, Aura thought, as though they were deciding on the weighty question of which piece of meat or which coat offered for purchase would be most deserving of their painfully earned money.

Sad, lonely, hardworking people, she thought. None faced a life that held much promise. This decision was nothing more than yet another requirement forced on them by the press of their body's needs, as consuming and yet no more personal than the requirement to replace a pair of old, worn shoes or fill their bellies.

But as Mailee climbed out of the wagon, those expressions altered suddenly, first with surprise that changed to pleasure, and then, finally, to pure lust. These men had never considered the possibility that they might someday have a woman as lovely as Mailee, Aura decided, and the fact that they were suddenly being faced with that possibility shook them out of the businesslike lethargy with which they'd been considering their prospective purchase.

When the guard motioned her to climb down and join the others, Aura was still intent on surveying the men's awed expressions. But once they laid eyes on her, the awe was transformed into bewilderment tinged with shock. If Mailee was a surprise to them, she, she realized, was a far greater surprise.

Surprise, however, was not to be the exclusive province of the mine workers. Aura was next dealt her own share as she turned and saw a man standing at the side of the wagon, a tall Westerner, thickly bearded and burly. Her first thought was one of relief, that here was one of her own kind, someone to whom she might turn for help.

His eyes were still glued on Mailee, his pleasure at what he saw only too obviously written on his face. Aura wanted to shout out to him, but something held her tongue. Perhaps it was the far from gentle hold Chaou Li had on her arm, perhaps it was the memory of the miner back in the opium parlor. Or perhaps, and more likely, it was the simple logic that told her this man knew exactly what was going to happen to these women, and he was, most likely, party to the whole horrible process.

In any event, she waited until he tore his glance away from Mailee and let it drift in her direction. She met his glance evenly, hoping to find some hint of outrage in it, some possibility that he might be incapable of standing silently aside and watching her being sold along with the others. And suddenly she felt a burst of elation when she saw him glance angrily at Chaou Li and start after her.

The guard reached for her, wrenching her arm back sharply and encouraging her to move along with the others in his own sadistic fashion. But there was no way he could push her away fast enough. The miner was on him in only a few seconds.

"What's this that Hung Poh thinks he's doin'?" he demanded, as he grasped the guard's arm. "I never agreed to nothin' like this."

Fury filled Chaou Li's eyes, but he made no move to shake off the other man's hold.

One of the Chinese men rushed forward and began to speak to the guard, apparently translating the miner's words. But he'd barely gotten a few words out when the miner pushed him aside.

"He speakee just fine himself," he said. "There's no way Hung Poh would send out a wagonload of valuable cargo with a man who didn't speak the lingo." He stared at Chaou Li, challenging him with his look.

There seemed to be an unnatural silence as the two men stood glaring at each other, even the sound of the wind died away as if it were waiting to see what would happen. And then Chaou Li smiled.

"Hung Poh say Jack Duran smart man," he said slowly. He smiled again and bowed his head slightly.

Aura was bewildered, entirely puzzled. This man

had pretended complete ignorance of English, had pretended he couldn't understand a word she spoke. Now she realized it was all a lie, and the only reason she could think he might have had for it was simply to intimidate her, to make her feel alone.

The miner, however, didn't seem either impressed or surprised by the revelation. He nodded toward Aura.

"The agreement I have with Hung Poh doesn't include this," he hissed.

Chaou Li was, apparently, prepared for the objection. He put his hand into a pocket in his jacket and removed an envelope. He handed it to the miner.

"For Mister Duran, from Hung Poh," he said, pronouncing each word very carefully.

Aura watched Duran take the envelope, stare at the neatly written letters of his name on it. She had no need to see the bills inside to know what it was Hung Poh had sent. After all, this man had to be as much in Hung Poh's employ as the guard who'd brought her, she told herself. The contents of the envelope could only be a little extra to keep him from raising any objection about business that clearly deviated just a little from the norm.

She was right, she saw. Duran released his hold of Chaou Li's arm after only a glance at the contents of the envelope, and was about to turn away.

"There are people in San Francisco who will pay handsomely for my safe return," she shouted at him, before he took a half dozen steps.

She had no idea what had prompted her to make such an offer to him, for there was no one in San Francisco or anywhere else, for that matter, who would make good on her offer, who would even care if she fell off the face of the earth entirely, a realization that was far from pleasing to her. In the previous six months she'd alienated the whole of her family, and, with the possible exception of her sister, Delia, they'd washed their hands of her. There had only been Whit in San Francisco, Whit and Payne. Whit was dead now, and Payne had made it only too clear that he had no interest. She'd certainly managed to make a thorough mess of her life, she thought, and there was no one she could blame for the fact but herself.

But those thoughts were fleeting in the face of far more immediate needs. She had to get away from this place, she told herself. She had to get back to San Francisco and a world where she at least understood the rules. Once she'd done that, she could see to rectifying the mistakes she'd made. For now, though, she couldn't afford to think about them or let herself feel sorry for herself. If she did, she'd be lost.

This miner could be bought, she told herself. He'd proved that by accepting money from Hung Poh. And by promising him a reward, she'd given him a reason to help her, however false. Now she had to make him believe it was true.

When Duran turned back to face her, she could read the greed in him, could see it in his eyes, could feel it settle like a cloud over him.

"What did you say?" he asked.

She had him, Aura thought, as she filled with a smug flush of success. She'd learned her lesson back at the opium parlor—a man could be talked out of chivalry and she'd be a fool to expect to depend on anything so transitory. But greed, that was something else again, something far more immediate, more visceral.

Chaou Li didn't give her much of an opportunity to gloat. He didn't like the fact that Duran was taking an interest in her, and he had no intention of letting her pursue the matter with the miner. Before she could answer, he pushed her away from Duran, shoving her toward the other women who waited, patient and silent, huddled into a damp, uncomfortable group. Unused to attention of any kind, they weren't happy to find themselves surrounded by so many wondering eyes. They stared down at their feet, pretending rapt interest in watching them slowly sink into the dark mud.

This was what Chaou Li expected of her, Aura realized, what he considered decent female humility. She was not about to show it. Instead, she turned back to the miner.

"Help me," she called back to Duran, as she was being pushed away from him, "and you'll be well paid for the effort."

She was rewarded for her own effort by another sharp shove from Chaou Li. This time his anger was strong enough to overcome whatever minor constraint he'd shown until then. He pushed her hard enough to send her slipping through the mud. Aura struggled with her balance for an instant, then lost it completely. She fell to her knees.

She didn't move, didn't try to climb back to her feet and get away from the cold wet of the mud. Instead, she stayed where she'd fallen, kneeling in the muck, and stared up at Duran, letting her eyes meet his.

Chaou Li moved toward her, his eyes filled with hatred. It was clear enough to Aura that the fact that she ignored his authority infuriated him. He'd had enough of her, that was obvious. Had she been a Chinese woman, she had little doubt but that he'd have intimidated her into submission by now. But she refused to behave with the sort of humility he expected of her. She refused to allow herself to become as cowed as the group of farmgirls who expected nothing better from their lives than the fate to which Hung Poh had sentenced them. She'd fought hard for the right to think of herself as an independent human being; she wasn't about to throw away that belief and surrender herself to the role that relegated her to a position no better than that of a head of cattle.

She continued to stare at Duran.

And for a moment she thought the miner might actually make a move to help her. He seemed to lean toward her, to glance at Chaou Li as though he was weighing his chances of besting the man if the need were to arise. But he hesitated with indecision, and indecision led to resignation. Chaou Li needed only to turn to him and glower, muttering under his breath. The threat was open and more than clear enough for Duran.

The miner shrugged and turned away. He motioned to the workers, calling out to them to get back to work, telling them to move, or they'd never earn enough money to buy a wife. The Chinese man who had attempted to serve as his translator with Chaou Li now had his opportunity to fulfill his task. He not only repeated Duran's words, but mimicked his motions as well, waving his arms and motioning up the barren, rocky hillside to the mine entrance and the projecting wooden sluice that looked like some misshapen, deformed appendage protruding from it. The group of men reluctantly turned away from the women and started climbing the rocky, mud-slicked slope toward a gaping hole in the hillside.

It was only too painfully obvious to Aura that Duran wasn't about to jeopardize whatever arrangements he had with Hung Poh, even for the promise of a reward that she held out to him. She felt as though something precious had been stolen from her, snatched away while she stood helpless and watched.

She didn't even look up at Chaou Li as he grabbed her arm and yanked her back to her feet. He called out to the women, and, like a herd of obedient sheep, they began to move toward a wretched-looking building a few hundred feet away. As they walked away, the dismal drizzle turned suddenly into real rain, a steady, thrumming downfall. It struck the sodden earth, and finding no home there, quickly accumulated to run down the hillside in filthy rivulets, soaking the women as they marched along the base of the hill.

Aura walked as silently as the rest, letting herself think only of the necessity of lifting her foot from the mud carefully lest she lose her shoe entirely in the muck. She absently puzzled at the speed with which their footprints filled with rain. It was best, she told herself, not to let herself think of anything else.

She was beginning to grow very numb inside. Just as the rain soaked her and slid down her face, so, too, all feeling seemed to be sliding away from her. It was no good, she told herself. Each time she'd dared to hope, the chance she'd hoped for had been squelched all too quickly.

She told herself it wasn't worth hoping any more. There was no chance that she'd ever get away, no possibility that a white knight would suddenly ride up and save her.

She choked back a sudden ache in her throat and a desire to cry. All feeling hadn't died after all, she realized. All she wanted now was to see Payne again, to have him hold her in his arms and make her feel safe.

And she knew it would never happen.

It wasn't much of a cabin, even to judge by the standards of the place where they'd spent the previous night. It was ramshackle, shoddily built, with chinks in the walls large enough to let cold gusts of wind and the occasional splash of rain into the room. But it was equipped with a wood stove, and even the stingy fire

292

that had been lit in it seemed a great luxury to the cold, rain-soaked women.

And more than that, this cabin was supplied with barrels of water, ample water, albeit cold, for all of the women to wash. This they did with more enthusiasm than expertise, first stripping off their wet clothing and giggling with embarrassment at the need to expose themselves to one another. They soon lost their discomfort, however, and began to make a game of the process, splashing and laughing at one another. When they were done, they occupied themselves with combing one another's hair and passing a single small mirror among themselves in order to practice the application of rouge to ruddy, suntanned cheeks.

Aura and Mailee stood aside, washing and watching the others.

"They look like schoolgirls preparing for their first dance," Aura muttered.

She was suddenly angry with those women, she realized, angry that they seemed so eager to become merchandise in Hung Poh's market, angry that they were willing to take pains to please.

They were, Mailee told her, going to the effort in order to make themselves as attractive as possible. The more a man paid for a woman, the wealthier he must be, they reasoned.

"All want rich husband," Mailee finished.

Aura's tongue itched to say that husbands were not found at public auctions, that wives were not purchased, that this arrangement spoke of something else altogether. Nonetheless, she kept her own counsel, reminding herself that her opinions were of little value here, that somehow she'd managed to wander into an alien world that held to rules different from her own.

But as she watched the women, she began to feel her own determination, determination she'd thought she'd lost, grow and strengthen. She would not give up her own values and simply try to adjust, try to become complacent and content, as they were.

She certainly had no intention of trying to make herself more presentable, she decided. She considered her mud-caked, soiled, and rumpled clothing and weighed the benefits of washing them against the possibility that the act might be perceived as one of capitulation. In the end she decided to wash her blouse and underthings, but leave the mud-encrusted skirt just as it was. It would, she hoped, put off any man from thinking she might make even a passable wife.

"When will they hold the sale?" Aura asked.

"I hear Chaou Li say tomorrow," Mailee replied. "He say many men come tomorrow."

Tomorrow, Aura thought, as she scrubbed her underthings. She let her eyes rove around the cabin, considering the chinks in the walls that let gusts of damp wind blow through. This place was not nearly so well built as the cabin they'd spent the previous night in, she decided. And once again, despite her temporary determination that hope was useless, she found herself thinking about the possibilities of escape.

"Well, I don't intend to stay here that long," she muttered to Mailee.

Mailee turned and stared at her as if she'd lost her mind.

"What choice have you?" she asked.

"Look at this place," Aura told her. "It barely keeps the wind out. And unless I was seeing things on the way in here, I'm sure the latch that bars the door is barely attached to the side wall. If I can't get out of here, I deserve nothing better than to be sold like the rest of these sheep."

Mailee scowled slightly, and Aura wasn't sure if she'd taken exception to the word or if she was simply mulling over what she'd heard. She didn't care, Aura told herself. She wasn't about to take lessons from a woman who'd spent a lifetime believing that women were nothing better than chattel.

"But where you go?" Mailee whispered.

"I don't know. If I can, I'll steal a horse. Or I'll walk, if I have to. But the wagon we came in needed a road of sorts to bring us here. I'll follow it back to San Francisco." She looked at Mailee, her eyes narrowing as she saw the indecision in the Chinese woman's eyes, the hint of yearning. "You can come with me," she offered. "It would be easier for two of us than it would be for one alone."

Mailee's brow furrowed with indecision as she looked around at the others. "How would we escape?" she asked. "They follow, bring back." She shuddered at what punishment that particular procedure might elicit.

"Not if we leave when the others are asleep," Aura told her. "The rain will keep Chaou Li and the driver inside tonight. No one will even know we've gone until tomorrow, and by then it'll be too late for them to find us." She looked at Mailee and grasped her hand. "Come with me," she said. "You don't belong here any more than I do, and you know it."

Mailee was silent for a moment as she stared at the other women and thought. Aura could almost read the fear in her, not that she could blame her, for she felt her own share of that. When a seemingly endless moment had passed and still Mailee had said nothing, Aura told herself that it was foolish of her to expect to change a lifetime of beliefs in a few moments.

"I understand," she said slowly. "Just promise me you won't tell them what I plan to do."

But then Mailee turned back to face her. She shook her head.

"No," she said. "Mailee go, too."

Aura smiled and breathed a sigh of relief.

"After dark, then," she said. "When the others have gone to sleep."

Aura lay tense and alert in the darkness. She'd been listening to the sound of breathing coming from the other other women, and now, finally, it seemed to have sunk into that peculiarly regular drone that indicated slumber. She touched Mailee's shoulder.

"It's time," she whispered.

Mailee nodded and sat up. She carefully folded her blanket as Aura made her way through the maze of sleeping bodies to the door, then silently followed. Aura was kneeling by the door, peering out into the darkness through the gap between door and wall when she reached her.

"We go, Aura?" Mailee asked in a frightened whisper, and gestured toward the door.

Aura looked up at her and smiled. She nodded. "We go," she said, her voice, though carefully kept low, was unmistakably defiant.

"How?" Mailee insisted.

Aura put her finger to her lips, warning Mailee to silence.

"Stay here," she whispered.

Then she edged her way to the side of the cabin where the last of the fire was slowly dying in the stove. She remembered that one of the women had sat here slowly combing her hair just before she'd finally given in to her exhaustion, wrapped herself in her blanket, and gone to sleep. And just as Aura had hoped, the comb still lay clasped in her half-closed hand.

Moving very carefully, Aura grasped the end of the comb and slowly slid it from the sleeping woman's grasp. It was an easy theft. The sleeping woman, exhausted from the day's excitement and dreaming

296

dreams of her future husband, didn't move as Aura slipped the bone comb from between her fingers.

Mailee didn't seem to like the deceit, but Aura ignored her look of disapproval.

"I'll return it in a minute," she promised, as she knelt beside the door.

Then she turned all her concentration to the task at hand. Slipping the comb through the gap between door and wall, she carefully lifted it until she felt it come into contact with the latch. She'd been right about the loose latch. It slid easily upward when she pushed.

There was a soft metallic scraping sound, and for a moment Aura froze, afraid the noise might have awakened one of the women. But she quickly realized the sound had been minor compared to the moaning of the wind and the constant drumming of the rain on the roof. From what little she could see, none of the women had been wakened by it.

With the latch free, the door swung open. Aura had to hold onto the knob to keep it closed and keep the elements safely at bay.

"Here," she told Mailee. "Hold this and wait for me."

Mailee did as she asked, and stood holding the door to keep it from being pulled open by the wind as Aura returned to the side of the woman from whom she'd taken the comb. She silently placed it on the floor by the woman's hand, and then returned to Mailee.

"Ready?" she asked with a breathless smile.

Mailee nodded.

"Ready," she said.

Aura took the knob, then slowly pushed the door open. All she could see around her was the rain, pouring down in thick, endless sheets.

She slipped outside and motioned to Mailee to follow. Then she pushed the door silently shut behind her and returned the latch to its place.

Mailee already looked miserable, cold, and wet from the downpour.

"Don't worry," Aura told her with an encouraging smile. "The rain will help hide us. We couldn't ask for better weather."

She put her hand on Mailee's arm, and together they began to trudge through the downpour and the streams of mud, following the edge of the hillside until they were close enough to the wagon to see it despite the darkness and the rain. There was noise coming from inside, the raucous sort of sound men make when they've drunk too much and still go on drinking more.

"Chaou Li and the driver seem to be celebrating," Aura whispered.

Mailee nodded in agreement. "They finish job."

"Careful now," Aura warned. "We don't want them to hear us."

They skirted the wagon in silence and quickly came on the rutted road they were looking for, unmistakable because of the shallow river of rainwater that swirled along its path.

"You afraid, Aura?" Mailee asked. There was fear in her voice, there was no mistaking that. "Can still go back."

Aura turned to face her. "You go back if you want," she said. "I'd sooner die out there in the wilderness than go back."

Mailee darted a glance at the wagon and the cabin, nothing more than shadows in the darkness. She nodded.

"Mailee, too," she said. She darted a look around the camp. "A horse?" she asked.

Aura also looked around. She felt suddenly indecisive. She had no idea where the horses had been left

298

hobbled, she could see next to nothing in the dark, and the rain and wind drowned out any noise the animals might make.

"We'll have to search for them in the dark," she replied.

"No," Mailee insisted. "Best to leave."

Aura hesitated. They'd travel much more slowly on foot, but the chance of being caught while they made their search of the camp was more than she wanted to consider. It might be better to get away as quickly as possible.

"You're sure?" she asked Mailee.

Mailee nodded. "Sure," she said.

With that, the two of them began to tramp through the mud and the swirling rivulets of rain.

Aura was so tired she could barely think. Every muscle in her body ached; she was soaking wet and completely chilled through. The rain had temporarily slowed just before dawn, but that had done little to mitigate what the rain had done to her hair and clothing. She was actually beginning to think that perhaps Mailee had been right, perhaps it had been simply foolhardy to think they would ever escape Hung Poh's men.

"Please, Aura, please, rest now?"

A glance at Mailee told Aura that she was more than merely tired. Unused as Aura was to this sort of exercise, it was clear that Mailee was a good deal less accustomed to the sort of exertion required by tramping through the woods in a rainstorm. She looked as though she was about to keel over and was upright only by sheer force of her will.

"Yes, we need to find someplace where we can rest for a few hours," Aura agreed.

She began to scan the wooded area that bordered the wagon track. At first glance it seemed hopeless, for everywhere she looked there was little more than fir trees dripping rain onto the sodden mud at their feet. But the countryside was hilly, and after a few minutes more walking she saw a rise with a rocky overhang less than twenty feet from the path.

"There," she said to Mailee, and pointed at the place. "There ought to be a protected place there."

Mailee muttered something Aura took to be a small prayer of thanks, and they left the path and started for the small hillock. Pine needles underfoot, crushed by the pressure of their passage, emitted a fresh, sharp odor, the first pleasant thing Aura could remember having encountered since the awful adventure had begun.

"There," she said, once they'd reached the place. She pointed to a small niche beneath the overhang, not dry certainly, but a good deal better than the mire they'd been hiking through all night. "We'll be snug and safe here, I should think." There were leaves and grasses, and Aura looked at them with as much anticipation as she would have looked at a featherbed a few weeks before.

Mailee sank gratefully down onto the ground, and slid back to the relative comfort of the niche. She looked up pointedly at the blanket Aura held under her arm. They'd taken turns carrying it, even though Aura had considered it a useless burden, for it was soon as soaked as they were. She handed it to Mailee, more grateful than not to be relieved of the effort of holding it.

"Tell again about San Francisco," Mailee said, as she spread out the blanket.

Aura sank down beside her. "San Francisco," she repeated. She was beginning to think she knew as little

300

about the place as Mailee did. But one thing she did know: what Hung Poh had attempted to do to her was against the law. She'd go to the sheriff and see that he was arrested and unable ever to do again to anyone what he'd tried to do to her. "I own a store," she told Mailee. "You can work there, if you like, and stay with me as long as you want. And no one can sell you or tell you who you have to marry. This is the United States and we have laws here, laws against that sort of thing."

Her voice trailed off. Funny, she thought—even the wet blanket didn't feel nearly as cold as she'd thought it would. It kept away the wind, and she was beginning to feel so sleepy that she could barely keep her eyes open.

She didn't fight the feeling. She let her eyes drift closed and was almost immediately lost in a dream about Payne, a pleasant dream where they somehow had forgotten all the things that were wrong between them, and clung only to those things that were so wonderfully right.

And so it was even more painful for her than it otherwise might have been to feel a hand shaking her shoulder and rousing her from the dream that she would certainly have wished to make last longer. But the disappointment of waking was nothing compared with the shock she felt when she opened her eyes.

She found herself staring into the face of Chaou Li.

Aura couldn't believe what she saw. She lifted her hands and rubbed the heels of her palms against her eyes. It wasn't nearly enough to make Chaou Li disappear. Worse, Jack Duran was standing behind him, and both men were smiling in a very unpleasant way.

"I told ya they'd folla the wagon track," Duran was

301

saying. "No place else for them to go. And those prints in the mud were easier to folla than a trail o' bread-crumbs."

Duran's gloating satisfaction seemed to have no effect on Chaou Li. He continued to stare at Aura with a decidedly nasty look in his eyes, a look that told her only too clearly that he intended to make her pay for the trouble she'd put him to.

"Aura," Mailee wailed softly. "What happen, Aura?"

Aura shook her head. She had no answer for Mailee, none that made any sense to her. She had been so sure their absense wouldn't be discovered until the women were wakened to make breakfast. And there was no way the men could have trailed them so quickly. It was only a few hours after dawn.

But she did feel responsible. She'd encouraged Mailee to come with her, promised her that they'd get away, that they'd be safe. Only she'd been wrong, as wrong about that as she seemed to have been about everything else of late.

Duran reached for Mailee's arm and pulled her away from the rock.

"Now you two ladies have ruined our night of fun," he said, as he pulled Mailee to her feet. He leered at Mailee. "I had special plans for the two of us, darlin', and when I went lookin' for you, you was gone. That wasn't nice, now, was it?"

And with Duran's words, Aura understood what had happened. The mine overseer, it seemed, had the privilege of a night with his choice of the women. Her and Mailee's absence had probably been discovered shortly after they'd left the cabin.

Mailee whimpered miserably as Duran began to maul her, obviously intent on making up for what he'd lost.

"Stop that, you animal," Aura shouted, but as Chaou Li grabbed her, she realized he had no intention of letting her interfere.

As a matter of fact, it soon became only too plain that he had his own plans for her.

realized, the sounds of someone coming from the direction of the opium den.

"Didn't want to go back there anyway," he mut-

Chapter Sixteen

Aura heard herself gasp as a sharp pain filled her, a pain as numbing as any hurt that had been caused by a physical blow could have been. This pain, however, was caused not by a blow, but by fear. Nothing seemed more real or immediate to her than the threat she saw in Chaou Li's eyes, and nothing as inescapable. She couldn't keep herself from cringing.

Her reaction seemed to please Chaou Li. He lifted a hand as though he were about to strike her, but held back for a moment as he watched her eyes. He seemed almost to feed on her fear, and the taste of it pleased him. When that pleasure finally began to pale, he brought his hand down slowly, relishing her useless struggle to pull away before he slapped her face briskly.

Aura felt the biting sting and the heat of her blood rushing to her bruised cheek. Much as she wanted to, something kept her from crying out. She wouldn't give him the satisfaction, she swore, wouldn't let him have that pleasure as well. She bit her lip hard enough to cut it, but managed to swallow the cry.

When she turned back to look at him, she realized that she'd been right, that what he'd wanted was to hear the sound of her scream. Her defiance had incensed him.

The first time, he'd slapped her because it amused him to demonstrate to her that she was at his mercy and because it pleased him. But now he was angry. He raised his hand and slapped her again and again, not stopping until he heard a scream of terror and pain.

It wasn't Aura's scream he heard, but Mailee's cry of terror. Duran had pushed her to the ground and fallen on her, his hands reaching to push up her tunic as she struggled uselessly against the weight of him. Her fists flailed, striking his back and arms, but he took as little notice of her struggle as he might have taken of an insect that dared bite him.

Still clutching Aura, Chaou Li turned and watched them, for a moment seemingly hypnotized by the scene in front of him. Then he shook himself, stood, and pulled Aura to her feet. His attention was still glued to Duran and Mailee.

Pulling Aura along with him, he came to stand over the miner, looking down at him and Mailee. Aura struggled to free herself from him, sickened by the thought that he might stand there and watch the act to its end. Even worse was the prospect that he might make her watch as well.

But it seemed he had other intentions.

"Later," he said suddenly. He kicked Duran's leg. "Get up."

The order surprised Aura, and she grew puzzled as she considered what might have prompted him to hold Duran back. One thing was perfectly clear to her after a glance at his expression, however, and that was that he had no intention of being ignored.

His tone, a sharp, terse command, froze Duran.

The miner turned and looked up at him. His eyes were glazed with bewilderment and lacked focus.

"What?" he asked.

"Later," Chaou Li repeated. He pointed upward to where a dim daylight struggled, trying vainly to work its way through the unending gray haze of the sky. "Go back now."

There was no question but that Duran was unhappy with this pronouncement. He pushed himself to his knees and, still straddling Mailee, glared at Chaou Li.

"There's time," he hissed.

Chaou Li returned his stare through hooded, threatening eyes. He shook his head slowly.

"I say later," he insisted.

"And I say now," Duran returned.

Chaou Li gave him no further opportunity to protest. He leaned back, and in one incredibly fast, fluid movement, turned slightly, raised one foot, and kicked. The heel of his boot came into painful contact with the side of Duran's head. There was a dull sound, then a grunt of pain as Duran fell beside Mailee on the wet ground.

"I say later," Chaou Li repeated, this time very slowly. He glowered at Duran, daring him to make a countermove.

The miner lay where he was staring up at Chaou Li for a moment, and Aura could see the sly look in his eyes as he evaluated his position. Duran was certainly the larger of the two, but Chaou Li had given him ample evidence that he was faster and stronger. It was clear that in a contest between the two, Chaou Li would be the winner.

Aura wasn't the least surprised when Duran pushed himself slowly up, first to his knees, and then to his feet.

"Later," he muttered in reluctant agreement.

He reached down for Mailee and pulled her, whimpering, to her feet.

"Ya hear that, darlin'?" he asked her with a frozen smirk. "We'll have our fun a little later, you and me."

Aura was still dazed by the sudden, if temporary, reprieve. Whatever unpleasantness was to come, she and Mailee would have a few hours to think about it, to anticipate it. She wasn't sure but that Chaou Li hadn't decided on that particular course on purpose, knowing that the time spent wondering would be a punishment in itself.

She and Mailee were pushed toward the men's waiting horses, then summarily dragged into the saddles in front of the men. Aura could feel the heat of Chaou Li's body against her back, the unyielding restraint of his arm around her. There was no escape now, she told herself. And she had no one to thank but herself.

She turned and glanced at Mailee. Duran, she saw, was doing more than merely holding her firmly with him on the saddle. He was letting his hand range against the young Chinese woman's body, giving her no respite from what he'd promised.

And she was the cause of that as well, Aura told herself. Now she had not only to bear her own punishment, but to acknowledge that she was the cause of Mailee's punishment as well.

It was nearly noon when they rode into the mining camp, not that there was any warmth or sunshine to indicate the hour. On the contrary, the rain had begun once again, not quite as pounding a downpour as the one that had soaked Aura and Mailee the preceding night, but a steady, monotonous rain that made the ride a sodden, muddy misery.

Chaou Li seemed completely oblivious to the weather, but Jack Duran was not nearly so complacent. As they rode into camp, he stared up at the dark mudslides beginning to ooze from beneath the under-structure of the sluice that protruded from the entrance to the mine. The hillside had turned into a slowly shifting river of mud. What he saw did not please him.

He gritted his teeth and muttered angrily, "The damn underpinnings are being washed away. There'll be a hell of a job to fix it, and no ore to show for the work."

Chaou Li barely listened to his complaint. He was too intent, as was Aura, on surveying the crowd of men that had flooded the camp. If she'd thought the group of thirty or so that had greeted the women's arrival the day before was large, it was nothing compared to the group that had gathered now. Word had spread, Aura realized. Many of the men were as wet and as mud spattered as she was, probably from having walked most of the night to arrive in time for the auction.

It was a quiet, well-ordered throng. They hunkered in the rain at the edge of the hillside, waiting patiently for the sale to begin. Others continued to arrive, small groups of two and three at a time, and joined those waiting, jostling for a place as close as possible to the temporary platform that had been set up just a few dozen feet from the cabin in which the women had been housed for the night.

Aura surveyed the small sea of heads with their flat, conical, rain-slicked hats. There had to be close to three hundred of them, she thought—three hundred men and only a dozen women. They looked up at her and at Mailee, and began to nudge one another and whisper.

"Many customers," Chaou Li murmured, obviously pleased with the turnout the auction had elicited.

Duran was not nearly so delighted.

"Damn lousy weather," he replied. "There ought to be more. The bidding will be sluggish."

It was an orderly crowd, one that grew eerily silent as Duran and Chaou Li drew the two horses to a stop at the side of the cabin. Duran's factotum, the man who had served as his interpreter the day before, came running up as the men slid down from their mounts.

"Auction begin now?" he asked Duran nervously. He motioned to the crowd of men crouching in the wet of the hillside. "Men anxious."

"Hell with 'em," Duran muttered. "Bring me some hot coffee," he ordered, as he pulled Mailee down from the horse.

Chaou Li, however, was a good deal more intent on business and far less concerned with Duran's animal comfort.

"We start now," he said, pointedly overriding Duran's instructions.

He casually lifted Aura from his saddle and dropped her, indifferent to whether the act left her on her feet or sprawled in the mud. She slid in the muck, struggling to maintain her balance while he waved to Duran's man and spoke a sharp order that sent the translator scampering onto the platform and calling out to the crowd for silence.

Satisfied that the preliminaries had begun, Chaou Li took Mailee's and Aura's arms and guided them with more haste than concern to the door of the cabin. He pulled the door open, then pushed them inside before following after them.

The women seemed momentarily frozen by the blast of cold air that entered from the opened door. They turned and watched Aura and Mailee enter, and then Chaou Li stalk into the cabin. They pointedly backed away from the two returned escapees as though they were afraid proximity might breed contamination, might somehow mark them with undeserved guilt. Then they turned hopefully to Chaou Li and waited patiently for his instructions.

They'd changed considerably, Aura noted. Their clothing was fresh and clean, their hair was neatly combed and braided, and all of them had applied a bright blush of rouge to their cheeks. Chaou Li walked past them, inspecting each one silently, Aura and Mailee apparently temporarily forgotten in the face of more pressing matters. His decision finally made, he pointed to one of the women. Without so much as speaking to her, he turned on his heel and walked to the door. The woman he'd chosen silently followed after him, her head bowed shyly, her cheeks bright red with a blush of anticipation that managed somehow to overwhelm the blotch of bright rouge.

Mailee crept to the wood stove and stood by it, trying to warm away her fear with its heat. But Aura followed the woman to the door, watching as Duran's man offered her the shelter of an umbrella, covered her head with a large, bright red cloth, and then led her toward the platform. The rest was left to Aura's imagination when her view was summarily cut off as the door was slammed shut. The impatient murmurs of the crowd suddenly ceased as hopeful bidders centered their attention on Chaou Li and the goods he offered for sale. The auction was finally begun.

Aura turned to consider the remaining occupants of the room. The other women had gathered into a small group at the far side of the cabin, making it only too plain that they had no intention of permitting any communication whatsoever with the two miscreants. But Aura wasn't interested in them; she was interested in Mailee.

The young Chinese woman was standing by the stove, her back to Aura, but her stance was more than enough to convey her sense of desolation. Aura approached her slowly, not sure how an overture would be received, sure only that she deserved whatever anger Mailee might care to turn on her. After all, she'd been the one who'd thought of running away, and she had urged Mailee to join her. She had been the one to promise that they would be safe.

"I'm sorry," she whispered. "It's all my fault. I'd never have asked you to come if . . ."

"No," Mailee interrupted, and turned finally to face her. "Not your fault, Aura. No one's fault . . . fate."

She smiled a worn, tired smile, one meant to convey compassion and the warmth of an unexpected friendship. Assuring Aura of her forgiveness, however, did not in any way relieve her fear. Tears welled up in her eyes and slid slowly down her cheeks, and she started to turn away.

But Aura put her arms around her, and the two women hugged. Neither knew what the immediate future would bring them, but both knew that it would be far from pleasant. And each knew how frightened the other felt, for both were fighting desperately to control their own fears.

"They not beat us," Mailee sniffed.

Aura pulled away.

"What?" she asked.

"Not beat us," Mailee repeated. "Bruises bad business."

Aura put a trembling finger to her bruised cheek, touching it gingerly. It hurt, the slightest pressure sending a sharp throbbing that spread from her cheek to her neck. She could only imagine how ugly the bruise must be. At the thought of it, she suddenly began to laugh. It grew until she shook with laughter, fairly choked with it. From the far side of the cabin the other women turned and gaped at her in disbelief.

Mailee, too, stared at her in amazement, for there was nothing even remotely amusing about their situation, so far as she could see.

"Aura, you sick?" she asked gently.

Aura shook her head. "Look at us," she managed to gasp through her laughter. She motioned to her own bedraggled appearance, her soaked, matted hair, her filthy clothing, her bruised cheek. "No one will want to buy us in any case. It'll serve Chaou Li right."

Pensive, Mailee looked down at Aura's wet and mud splattered skirt, comparing it to her own far from pristine clothing. And then she smiled.

"Bad choice for wife," she agreed solemnly. Then she, too, started to laugh.

But their laughter soon died. The cold, silent stares of the other women reminded them of their isolation, of the fact that they were alone and without any hope of finding help anywhere. And the memory of the look in Chaou Li's eyes when he'd struck her sent a chill shiver through Aura, a shiver that dissolved all sense of amusement and replaced it with shuddering fear.

The auction was a protracted procedure, the selling price of each woman carefully guided upward by Chaou Li's attentive urgings and a constant drone of cajoling by Jack Duran's translator. Inside the cabin the noise sounded like little more than a muted, meaningless clatter to Aura, but from time to time Mailee listened and explained what was being said. It was a demeaning experience for the woman, Aura decided, as she listened to Mailee's translation of the litany that promised strong shoulders, round breasts and sturdy hips. It seemed almost as if Chaou Li was selling cattle.

Once a woman was taken from the cabin, she did not return. Aura watched at the door as the next was led to the platform, and caught a glimpse of the previous winning bidder leading his purchase away in the rain.

As the number of women remaining in the cabin dwindled, those that waited became more and more agitated and nervous. They walked around the room, and peered out through the cracks in the boards, trying to get a glimpse of those men who were bidding on the women. For it seemed that most of those who'd gathered on the hillside had come, not with the expectation of actually buying a wife, but merely to observe, to catch a glimpse of a woman of their own kind, to remember, perhaps, what life had been like for them before they'd left their homes.

In any event, it was late when finally the last of the farmgirls was taken out of the cabin, leaving only Aura and Mailee behind. The two sat for a moment, numbed by the probability that this was, most likely, the last time they would have, realizing that they would never see one another again. They both felt awkward, each wanting to thank the other for the unexpected gift of friendship, and neither knowing what to say.

"Cold," Mailee murmured finally.

Aura nodded and looked around. The room, she realized, had sunk into a dull grayness, and the fire in the stove had died completely.

"I suppose they'll come for us soon," she said.

Mailee wandered to the largest chink in the wall, the one that had served as as peephole on the process of the auction.

"Almost night," she said. "Rain much worse."

Aura joined her and peered through the chink to watch the dismal procedure of the sale. She could see that lanterns had been lit and set on the platform, that both Chaou Li and Jack Duran stood with rain streaming down their faces as they stubbornly pushed the proceedings along. The ranks of bidders had dwindled considerably, for even the prospect of diversion had been dampened by the insistent downpour.

"There'll be no one left to buy us," she ventured.

Mailee turned and looked up at her. "That good?" she asked.

Aura shrugged. She knew what Mailee was thinking. If they were sold, at least they would have an unknown with which they would have to deal. But if there were no buyers, then it was Chaou Li and Duran who would determine their fates. Aura thought of the way Duran had promised Mailee they'd have their "fun" later, of the vicious promise in Chaou Li's eyes when he'd struck her.

"No," she said softly. "I think that will be very bad."

She didn't have to say anything more. Mailee nodded agreement.

"Very bad," she repeated slowly.

Aura tried to swallow the lump that filled her throat, but it refused to disappear. She watched with a dull feeling of dread as the final bid was offered. Chaou Li spoke, urging the remaining bidders to raise their offers, but the incessant rain and the growing darkness seemed to have eaten away the last of their enthusiasm. Chaou Li nodded to the successful bidder, and the sale was complete.

Aura expected Chaou Li to start toward the cabin, but he didn't. Instead, he spoke to the remaining men who stood now in a small knot in front of the platform, the group huddled close against the rain and the wind.

"What did he say?" Aura asked Mailee.

Mailee didn't answer immediately. She looked up at Aura and bit her lip.

"What is it?" Aura demanded.

"He tell them come back tomorrow," Mailee replied. "He tell them two more women to sell tomorrow."

"Us," Aura murmured.

"Us," Mailee agreed.

"And that leaves tonight," Aura said, her voice a hoarse whisper.

"Tonight," Mailee repeated softly.

A night for Duran and Chaou Li to have their fun, she thought numbly. A night for them to take their revenge on the two women who'd dared to try to escape.

The door of the cabin swung open and Jack Duran soon filled the space it had occupied. He looked around the dim cabin until he found Mailee.

"I told ya we'd be getting to have our fun, darlin'," he said, as he started forward. "And this time there ain't nothin' goin' to stop us."

Mailee cringed back against Aura and for a moment Aura felt a ripple of mutual terror pass between them. But then she took a step forward and faced Duran. This was her last chance, she told herself. It might well be useless, but there was nothing now that could make her position any worse than it already was. She might just as well try.

"What do you want to take us back to San Francisco?" she demanded, doing her best to imitate the tone her father had always taken with servants and anyone else he considered his social inferior. "Whatever it is, I'll see you'll be paid it."

Duran gave her a slightly dazed look, then slowly grinned.

"Ain't we gettin' high now, darlin'?" he muttered.

Aura ignored him.

"How much?" she repeated.

He shook his head.

"You do surprise me, darlin'," he said slowly, "and I must admit it grieves me, but I find I'm forced to decline your kind offer."

"Name your price," Aura insisted.

"There ain't enough money in the world," Duran told her. "Ya see, Hung Poh and his friends would skin me alive, and even your sweet promises ain't enough to make that fate appealin'."

"Hung Poh can't hurt anyone if he's in jail," Aura insisted.

Duran grinned again.

"And you'd arrange that, too, I suppose?" he asked.

"He had me kidnapped," Aura fumed. "There are laws in this country."

"Laws that would put me behind bars as well, darlin'," Duran insisted.

"No," Aura assured him. "I'd tell them you didn't know anything about it, that when you saw what was happening, you helped us get away."

"That's what you'd tell them, eh? I have your word on that?"

"Yes," Aura insisted. "That's all, I promise."

A low chuckle escaped Duran's lips.

"You almost sound like you mean all that, darlin'," he said. "But the plain fact is, I have a nice thing goin' here. The mine owners pay me to see that the coolies pull gold out of the mountain, and Hung Poh pays me to turn my back every once in a while and I get a pretty little piece of the money the auctions bring in." His eyes narrowed slightly as he considered Aura. "And, beggin' your pardon, darlin', cause I do hate to call a lady a liar, but I have a real nasty feelin' that you don't have so much as a pot to your name."

"I have a friend," Aura insisted, "a very rich friend."

Duran held up a hand and shook his head.

"Sorry, darlin'," he said flatly. "If you don't mind, you just step aside now, and me and this little lady will start gettin' to be friends."

He reached out for Mailee's arm and grasped it. And as he did, Aura realized that he'd been almost polite with her, perhaps even his idea of gentlemanly. He'd never touched her, or spoken harshly to her, while he seemed to have no scruples whatsoever about his treatment with Mailee. The difference, she realized, was that she was one of his own kind, and Mailee was not.

"Let her go," Aura shouted at him. She began to pummel his arm with her fists.

Duran released Mailee and turned to face Aura. His cheeks above his beard grew blotched with anger, but still he restrained himself as he put his hand on hers and held them to keep her from striking him again.

"You are makin' me real angry with you, darlin'," he told her through a clenched jaw. "And it ain't nice for a gentleman to get angry with a lady."

"Gentleman?" Aura spat back at him. "You're no better than a barbarian!"

She had, she realized, finally crossed the line. He pushed her angrily aside.

"What the hell do you care what happens to a Chinee?" he hissed at her. His eyes narrowed and he spat on the floor. "They ain't no better than a herd of dumb sheep." He spat again. "And you, I'm startin' to see you ain't much better."

Finally Aura understood how he could do what he'd been doing, how he could do what he was planning to do. The Chinese who labored in the mines, the women Hung Poh sent to this forsaken place to be sold, they were all the same to him. In his eyes they weren't even human, no better than animals. And it didn't matter what a man did to an animal. He might still have had some scruples about raping Aura, but Mailee was Chinese, and that made her unworthy of his concern.

He turned away from her in disgust, reaching down to Mailee. And when he turned his back on her, Aura saw the knife sheath hanging from the side of his belt. She bolted forward, driven by rage more than by reason, reaching for the knife and grabbing it, shouting at him to stop as she raised the weapon.

He turned to face her, and his eyes narrowed as he saw the glint of the knife in her hand, his knife.

"You ain't goin' to use that," he hissed. "Not over some Chinee."

"I will," she shouted. "You let us go, or so help me, I'll plunge it into your rotten black heart."

He hesitated an instant, and then his eyes relaxed and he began to smile.

"No," he said softly. "I don't think you will be doin' any such thing, darlin'."

Aura inhaled sharply. She had never thought herself capable of doing anything like this, but suddenly it seemed the only way out. If she stopped Duran, she and Mailee could try to run again, only this time Duran wouldn't be able to track them, to lead Chaou Li to follow after.

Mailee paled with horror and she screamed.

Aura closed her eyes and brought the knife down with all her might.

The knife never found its target. Suddenly there was a sharp pain in Aura's arm and she dropped the knife harmlessly to the floor. As it slid from her fingers, two massive arms surrounded her and pulled her backward so sharply that her breath was forced out of her. She dully realized that Mailee's scream had been a warning, a warning that had come too late.

From a place just behind her ear came the rumble of Chaou Li's voice.

"Take her," he ordered Duran. "Go."

There was disdain in his voice, and Duran looked at him with as much hatred as his fear of the stronger man allowed him to show. But he quickly sloughed it off, letting his anger center instead on Aura.

"You be havin' a pleasant evenin' yourself, now, darlin'," he hissed, as he once again grasped Mailee's arm and began to pull her toward the open door. "I spect you'll be a bit less high and mighty, come mornin'."

Aura felt the last of her resistance seep out of her. Chaou Li's arms held her as she watched Duran drag Mailee from the cabin, but even if they hadn't, at that moment she had no strength left to try to fight. She would have stood and stared numbly, even if there had been nothing to restrain her.

And then the cabin door swung closed behind them, and she realized that she was left alone with Chaou Li. His hold of her loosened, and finally he released her. She turned around and faced him.

And found he was smiling at her, relishing every gesture, every hint of her fear.

Her blood seemed to turn to ice inside her. Her whimpering submission, her cringing fear, she saw now that those were the things he wanted from her. Reason told her that she should give him what he wanted, that it would go easier on her if she did. But deep inside her some part of her rebelled. She could almost hear it shout out, "No!"

Whatever he intended to do to her, she refused to give up and meekly become his victim. No matter what she felt, she told herself, she wouldn't give him the satisfaction of showing him her fear. If she had nothing else, still she had some vestige of her own sense of worth.

"On your knees, woman," he hissed.

She saw the cruelty in his eyes, saw the way he anticipated the pleasure her pain would bring him. And from outside the cabin, she heard Mailee scream. The sound galvanized her.

"To hell with you!" she shouted, and she lunged forward, falling to the floor, reaching out and grabbing the knife she'd stolen from Duran that lay, still, where he'd forced her to drop it.

He scrambled after her, but it had taken him a moment to realize what it was she was doing, and that had been a moment too long. By the time he reached her, she had the knife in her hand.

She turned and twisted, jerking away from him, stabbing with the knife as she tried to escape him. And due more to luck than any skill with which she handled the weapon, the blade eventually found a target, meeting the muscle of his upper arm. He fell back, releasing her, a thick ribbon of red sliding out of the line of the cut.

Aura scuttled back and away from him, as shocked to see the line of red blood on his arm as she was to realize that she had been the cause of it. She stared numbly at the red-tinged blade in her hand.

Chaou Li was even more surprised than she was to see the wound. He stared down at it for a long instant, stiff with disbelief, unable to accept the fact that a woman had done such a thing to him. And then he lifted his eyes to meet Aura's.

He pushed himself to his feet and started for her. Aura edged back and away from him, but she couldn't move fast enough to escape him. She realized now that the wound had been little more than a scratch, that what she'd really struck with the knife had not been muscle and sinew, but something far more fragile, his pride.

He was standing glowering down at her, towering over her.

Aura brandished the knife. "Get away!" she shouted, although by now she harbored no hope that the knife would be much of a deterrent.

His eyes narrowed and he smiled viciously, already relishing what was to come. Then he leaned forward slightly and kicked the hand with which she held the knife.

Aura cried out, her hand burning with the pain of the contact of his boot. She could do nothing but watch the knife as it flew into the air. It landed at the far side of the cabin, skittering across the rough wooden floor before it finally came to rest by the wall.

"Now you pay, woman," Chaou Li hissed, as started for her. "Now I make you pay."

Chapter Seventeen

Payne pulled his horse to a stop when he realized the wagon road through the woods had finally opened into the clearing of a mining camp. He arched his back and stretched. He felt as if he'd been in the saddle for weeks. Every muscle in his body ached, and he knew the condition stemmed not from the twenty-four hours he'd spent riding, but from his fears for Aura.

Yang Wu let his horse sidle up next to Payne's.

"It's a good thing we're here," he said. "It's too dark to go any further."

"It's been too dark to go any further for more than an hour," Payne countered. It was true, he thought. He'd been risking the horses on that muddy, rutted path, riding in near total darkness, and he knew it. But he couldn't have given up for the night if he'd wanted to, and he hadn't wanted to, not with thoughts of Aura filling his mind. "You think this is really the place?" he asked Yang Wu.

He squinted through the rain and the darkness at the dull outlines of structures in the clearing that lay in front of them. It was, at best, a desolate, filthy place, perhaps not the worst he'd seen in the last twenty-four hours, but certainly close. It made him think of the years he and Whit had spent mining, and the memories did little to ease his tense mood.

The young Chinese man nodded. "The men in the other camps," he replied, "they all said the same thing. The auction is here."

Payne didn't feel nearly as sure. But considering the fact that it had been Yang Wu who'd spoken directly to the Chinese workers, he was hardly in a position to question the pronouncement.

He prayed Wu was right. If he didn't find Aura in this mining camp, then that would mean Hung Poh had rid himself of her in another, entirely final, way. The possibility made him sick with a sense of loss.

He looked around. Save for a few dim lines of light that managed to work their way past the dirt on the windows of the cabins, there was little sign of life in the camp, no noise, no movement. Under other circumstances, that fact would hardly have surprised him. A half dozen days of nearly incessant rain would justify any sane man taking to his bed whenever the opportunity arose. But still, the prospect of a wife auction— reason suggested that ought to rouse the interest and the spirits of even the most demoralized and sodden member of a mine's work gang.

"It doesn't look right," he muttered. "There ought to be noise, activity of some kind. Lonely men don't take to their beds as soon as the sun sets on the night before they'll lay eyes on the first women they've seen in months. They stay up drinking and boasting and pumping themselves up for the feats they tell each other they're about to do."

Wu nodded in depressed agreement. It *was* too quiet, just as Payne had said. The small cluster of cabins of the camp seemed to cling to the mud in silent resignation, cringing against the elements.

"Perhaps it's already over," he suggested.

He gave Payne a sidelong glance, well aware that the possibility would not please him. Not that he harbored any real fear of Payne any longer; that was long since past as he'd come to know him. Nor did he feel that he'd shortchanged him in the bargain they'd struck. He'd found the place where the auction was to be held, and he'd promised nothing more.

It was simply that he was beginning to feel a bit responsible for the fate of Whit Randall's wife, beginning to think that perhaps he ought to have been more cooperative with Payne from the start. After all, his British missionary upbringing had left enough of an impression on him to make him find the wife auctions distasteful. More than that, there was something about Payne's desperate search that touched him. He wondered what it would be like to feel so strongly for another human being that reason would take second place to the search to find her. Love might make a man crazy, but he was beginning to think it was a craziness that might not be so very terrible to endure.

"I could go into one of those shacks and ask the miners a few questions," he suggested.

Payne shook his head, rejecting the offer.

"No, I go in this time," he said. "If the auction's already over with, then there are some questions I want to ask personally."

He dug his heels into his horse's side. The animal began to move a bit more quickly toward the dim lights leaking out of the cabin windows.

"And hope to get an honest answer," Wu added, as Payne's horse started to move ahead of his own.

Payne turned and darted a glance at him. "Oh, I'll get an honest answer," he said. "One way or another, I'll find out where she is."

Wu shrugged. Something about the determination he'd seen in Payne over the previous twenty-four hours left little doubt in his mind but that Payne would do precisely what he said. The only thing left for him to do was wait. If he was lucky, the woman would still be in the camp, they'd arrange to buy her back from whoever had purchased her, and the whole unpleasant episode would be over.

He reluctantly prodded his own horse to follow after Payne's, promising himself that he would remain discreetly out of sight should there be any possibility that matters couldn't be handled in a peaceful and rational manner.

But Payne suddenly pulled his mount to a stop, turned, and stared into the shadows behind them.

"What was that?" he asked.

"What?" Wu asked.

"I heard someone cry out," Payne muttered. He turned in the saddle, squinting into the darkness.

"I heard nothing," Wu insisted.

He was lying and he knew it. He *had* heard a scream. He simply didn't want to think of it or the unpleasantness it might eventually lead to. He'd envisioned this little excursion as entailing nothing more threatening than the miserable weather. A scream did not bode well for his expectations.

"I heard it, I tell you," Payne hissed angrily. He turned his horse around, away from the cluster of cabins that had been his initial goal and toward a single dark shape a short distance away, along the edge of the hillside. "It came from that direction," he added, as he started toward it.

Wu gritted his teeth. He didn't like any of this. Women's screams were definitely not the sort of omen that pointed to a peaceful conclusion of business. In his experience, women's screams more often than not led eventually to the forcible application of men's fists.

The darkness and the discomfort of the wet, along

with the prospect of possible violence, was doing a good deal to undermine whatever sense of obligation he might have felt a few moments before. He was accustomed to living by his wits. He'd managed to survive as well as he had in San Francisco by avoiding confrontation of any sort. If he'd considered from time to time that that particular habit made him a coward, then he'd countered the accusation by reminding himself that he was at least an alive and thriving coward. He didn't relish the thought of following Payne into the sort of situation that he'd spent the previous three years taking the greatest care to avoid.

He darted a glance toward the dark trail through the wilderness that had brought them to this filthy mining camp. He could, he told himself, simply turn around and take that path back to San Francisco.

He played it over in his mind, reminding himself that he owed the Wells Fargo man nothing more. Whatever debt he'd incurred over Whitmore Randall's death he considered long past canceled. And the payment he'd been promised for this unpleasant ride through the countryside had been well enough earned to keep his conscience clear.

He told himself he would incur no loss of face were he to leave quietly. And to hell with Payne Randall and the dead Whitmore Randall's wife. To hell with all of them. After all, he had his own interests to look after; a man's primary responsibility was to himself.

He cursed silently. His stalwart missionary upbringing had done more than teach him excellent English, he told himself; it had also corrupted his Oriental soul, that part of him that told him his duty was not to himself, but to his family, to the honor of the ancestors who had come before him and to the betterment of the progeny yet to come. Honor dictated that he go with Payne, he told himself firmly.

But he knew nothing about his ancestors, he silently argued, and so there was no way he could dishonor them. And going with Payne might mean he would never live long enough to father any offspring. In this case, self-interest served not only him, but the generations he hoped would one day call him ancestor.

He'd made his decision, he told himself, the only rational decision. He turned his horse and started it walking toward the dark sliver of a path through the trees. But he hadn't gotten very far before he pulled the animal to a halt. The thought of facing all that darkness alone in the downpour was as unappetizing as whatever Payne might be leading him into. He sat for an instant, sullen with his own indecision.

In the end, it was the scream that settled it for him. There was pain in it, and fear, so much fear that he knew he would never be able to live with himself if he turned and ran. He might be a coward, but he was not a base coward.

He turned his horse back and started after Payne, squinting into the darkness in time to see Payne slip from the saddle and dart after a man who was dragging a woman through the thick mud. Perhaps there won't be much to it, he told himself. Perhaps the man would be too weak to fight, or clumsy enough to get himself bested quickly. Perhaps they wouldn't all end up dead.

Please, he silently prayed to the endless stream of his unknown ancestors, please let us not all end up dead.

From the start, Payne knew it wasn't Aura. She was too small, and the long hair that hung loose down her back was far too dark and straight to be her auburn curls. But he could no more turn his back on a woman who cried out with such terror than he could wade an ocean. He slid down from the saddle and sprang after the two, reaching for the man and swinging his fist before the other had a chance to realize what was happening.

It wasn't much of a fight. Duran had been far too intent on hauling Mailee away from the cabin to his own even to notice the soaking figure approaching him until it was too late. Payne struck him twice, hard, once in the belly and once on the chin. The breath knocked out of him, Duran released his hold of Mailee and fell to his knees in the mud.

As soon as he'd freed her, Mailee ran blindly away in panic. She had no idea where she was going, no idea what had happened, except that she'd somehow been freed. When she found herself being chased by a man on horseback, her confusion and panic only increased. In the back of her mind she knew there was no chance she could escape him, but still she slipped and struggled through the heavy mud. Duran hadn't been her only monster. Now it seemed monsters were everywhere she turned.

"Stop. I won't hurt you!"

The assurances did Wu little good, and he was forced, finally, to slide down from the saddle and push her to the ground to stop her.

"I won't hurt you," he repeated, this time in Cantonese. When she continued to struggle, he held her hands and stared down at her, repeating the words in every dialect he'd ever learned.

Mailee quieted finally and stared up at him, bewildered by the intensity she saw in his eyes, surprised to realize that he seemed to be pleading with her, not demanding anything.

"Who are you?" she asked in precise Cantonese. "What do you want?"

Wu released her and pulled back. From what little

he could see through the mud and the incessant rain, she was beautiful.

"My friend needs your help," he said, as he scrambled to his feet and offered her his hand to help her up. "He's looking for a woman."

"Every man in this godforsaken place is looking for a woman," Mailee hissed angrily. But she took the hand he offered and allowed him to help her to her feet and then lead her to the place where Payne was standing over the still groaning Duran.

"I don't know nothin' about no woman," Duran was insisting, as they approached.

"You do know," Payne corrected, as he reached forward and grabbed the other man's collar. "Her name is Aura Randall. She was brought here with a group of Chinese girls. Now, you tell me what happened to her."

Duran looked up at him and sneered. "Ain't no Chinee girls here," he said, his expression suddenly sly.

Then he turned, sliding onto his side and kicking Payne hard in the leg. The unexpected blow sent Payne sprawling in the mud as well. He growled with anger, and threw himself at Duran.

Wu held Mailee out of the range of the two thrashing men, confident that Payne's determination would make a quick end to the struggle. He was right. There was a brief melee, and then Payne landed two quick, sharp blows to Duran's chin. Duran quieted and Payne pushed himself to his knees.

"Where is she?" he demanded. He took Duran by the shoulder of his coat and shook him, but it did no good. He reluctantly released his hold and the miner fell back and lay still in the rain and the mud. "Damn," he hissed. He hadn't meant to knock the man unconscious. A knot of fear filled his belly. What if he was already too late? He looked around at the

329

dismal huddle of shadows that constituted the camp. "Where the hell is she?"

"Perhaps she can help," Wu offered. He motioned to Mailee.

Payne nodded. "Ask her," he said.

Wu began to speak, questioning Mailee in Chinese, but she cut him off with a motion and instead turned to Payne.

"You come help Aura?" she demanded.

Payne inhaled, the knot in his belly beginning to ease. He got to his feet, Duran forgotten, all his attention centered now on Mailee. She knew Aura, that was clear. And with any luck she could lead him to her.

"Where is she?" he asked.

Mailee lifted her arm and pointed to the solitary cabin, its outline little more than a dark shadow sulking in the rain.

"There," she said. "Hung Poh's man there, too."

Payne didn't take the time to listen to her last words. Instead, he took off at a run toward the cabin, ignoring the warning Mailee called after him. She turned to Wu.

"Chaou Li there with Aura," she told him. "You must help."

Wu hesitated. He looked at Mailee and swallowed uncomfortably. What she expected was only too painfully clear to him, and he felt himself wavering, despite the fact that logic told him what she wanted was the last thing he wanted. When he looked into her eyes, he found an irrational urge to give her anything so long as she would continue to stare at him that way. But that didn't change the fact that the thought of one of Hung Poh's henchmen sent shivers of fear through him.

Mailee saw his uncertainty.

"Chaou Li *yakutsa*," she insisted. "You must help."

330

"Yakutsa," Wu repeated numbly. A warrior trained in killing, a man who sold his services to the highest bidder. In short, the last person he'd care to face in a fight, even if he wasn't alone.

Had she not been there, had she not been staring at him with those wide, expectant eyes, he knew he'd have turned away and let Payne Randall deal with Hung Poh's creature himself. But she was there, and if he could simply walk away from Payne Randall, there was no ignoring the fact that he suddenly found himself completely incapable of walking away from her.

This is insanity, he told himself as he started after Payne, aware of the weight of Mailee's eyes on his back.

Payne raced to the cabin. He had a rifle strapped to his horse's saddle, but he didn't stop to think that he might need it. Aura was inside that cabin, and she was in danger, and there was no room for any further thought than that.

He pushed open the door of the cabin and stormed inside. What he saw when he entered was as bad as his worst nightmare.

Chaou Li had pushed Aura to the floor and was holding her pinned as he pushed away the fabric of her skirt and groped at her thighs. She kicked and squirmed, fighting in any way she could, unaware that he enjoyed her resistance as little more than a precursor to the certainty that he would eventually take what he wanted of her.

Payne charged forward, his anger outweighing his logic, a logic that would have told him that facing a man of Chaou Li's build and character unarmed was in the least foolhardy. He lunged forward, grabbing

Chaou Li's shoulders and pulling him back and away from Aura.

Chaou Li fell back, for a moment dazed at the unexpected interruption. Then he turned and stared up at Payne and his eyes narrowed and grew darkly vicious.

"Yankee fool," he hissed, as he pushed himself to his feet. He crouched forward and glared at Payne. "Whoever you are, you have made a grave mistake."

Payne glanced at Aura and sighed with relief when he saw that she had backed away and crouched now with her back against the wall. She was staring at him with the sort of look that she might have had had she seen a ghost. He would have grinned at that had she looked less terrified.

He turned his attention back to Chaou Li. There was nothing to grin about what he saw there. Hung Poh's man was behaving strangely, moving carefully on his toes, making strange motions with his hands. This, he realized with an uncomfortable premonition of what was to come, was not going to be the average barroom brawl; this man was a trained fighter.

"So this is what Hung Poh's great warriors are," he hissed, as he steadied his own stance, crouching forward slightly, bracing himself for the first blow. "Nothing better than a swine that brutalizes an unarmed woman."

"Your words are brave, Yankee," Chaou Li hissed, as he edged a bit closer to Payne. "Or perhaps they are merely stupid."

He moved then, his body fluid, almost snakelike, and repeated the maneuver Aura had earlier seen him use on Duran. He turned swiftly and kicked forward, this time raising his leg and aiming his foot at Payne's belly.

Too late, Payne saw the kick coming. He tried to step aside, but he wasn't nearly fast enough. The heel of Chaou Li's boot caught him in the side and he felt his breath forced out of him in a thick gasp of pain.

Chaou Li smiled, pleased with himself. He edged back again, sure a second blow would put a fast end to Payne's resistance and enable him to deal with the unexpected interruption at his leisure.

But this time Payne was ready for him. He jumped away in time, escaping the brunt of the blow and managing to catch Chaou Li's heel with his hand. He pulled up and back before he was forced to let go, but it was enough to unbalance Chaou Li.

Chaou Li tumbled backward, landing heavily but still in enough possession of his wits to keep himself rolling when he hit the floor and then push himself back to his feet in a single, incredibly smooth movement.

"It would seem not entirely stupid," he muttered, when he once again stood facing Payne.

Payne eyed him, impressed with the way the man had recovered so easily, impressed enough to feel a wave of doubt. He watched the way Chaou Li kept his feet moving, the way he stared. He knew Chaou Li's stare was intended to distract and unsettle him, that the man was waiting for an opening. Payne refused to give him the opportunity he was looking for, refused to let his attention stray. When Chaou Li lunged forward, he was waiting, anticipating the move.

This time he sidestepped the blow completely and managed to deliver a swift succession of sharp jabs before Chaou Li could regain his balance. Once again Payne stepped out of Chaou Li's range as he darted forward, his arms traveling in a swift, wide arc, and once again he landed a short series of blows in the few seconds of confusion that followed the effort.

Now, when Chaou Li's eyes found his, Payne was grinning. He was aware that he was infuriating the man, that his gloating as much as his success in avoiding Chaou Li's attacks were beginning to undermine the Chinese man's assurance.

Keep close, Payne told himself as he darted forward. Don't let him have the room to swing his arms and legs. Stay with him a little while longer and he'll defeat himself.

Chaou Li was beginning to breathe heavily now, and there was a shiny line of sweat on his forehead.

"You fight well, for a Yankee," he muttered.

Payne let a slow smile turn up the corners of his lips.

"New York City street fighting," he replied. "Not quite so pretty as whatever it is you do, but not so bad, either."

"But not good enough," Chaou Li countered, as he made it clear he had no intention of making things easier for Payne. He lunged forward, jabbed Payne sharply in the belly, then leaned slightly to the side and kicked once again.

This time Payne could not move quickly enough to avoid the contact. He doubled over, his hands clutching his belly as he groaned with the sudden pain of the blow.

Aura had gone numb. She kept repeating to herself that Payne had come for her, that she meant enough to him for him to seach for her and somehow he'd found her. The realization stunned her, because she'd completely convinced herself that he'd washed his hands of her. She was almost afraid to believe what her eyes told her was true.

But when she saw Chaou Li lumbering toward him, fists raised and ready to deliver a final blow, the numbness disappeared. She sprang to her feet, darting after him, grabbing hold of his arm and pulling it aside.

Chaou Li gave her a quick, furious glance, then turned on her, delivering a single, sharp blow that sent her reeling backward. The distraction, however, had been enough to let Payne regain his breath. He lunged forward, grabbing Chaou Li's shoulder and turning him, then pushed his head down at the same time he brought his knee up. The contact was enough to deliver a wave of pain that radiated through Payne's thigh. It was also enough to send Chaou Li sprawling senseless on the floor.

Payne stood over him for a second, his breath coming in sharp, panting gasps, his fists ready for another attack. But Chaou Li didn't move, and he gratefully turned his attention to Aura.

He ran to her, wrapping his arms around her, pulling her close to him.

"You came after me," she murmured. Her throat was tight, and she felt the bite of tears stinging her eyes. "How did you find me?"

She couldn't believe how good it felt to be in his arms. She'd never thought to see him again, and here he was, a wet but triumphant white knight come to save her. She closed her eyes and drank in the feeling of him, the scent of him. She pressed herself close to him, afraid she might wake up and find he was no more real than a dream.

"There'll be time to talk later," he told her as he reluctantly released her. He stepped back and stared at her, taking in her disheveled appearance, her dirt and bloodspotted clothing. "Are you hurt?"

She shook her head.

"I have never in my life felt better than I do at this moment," she assured him.

He couldn't understand why, considering her general appearance, but no woman had ever before seemed so beautiful to him as she did just then. He wanted more than anything to hold her in his arms, to drink in the feel of her body close to his, to kiss her until both of them forgot every cruel word they'd ever spoken to one another. But all that, he told himself, would have to wait until a more propitious moment.

"I think we'd better get out of here," he told her.

He held out his hand for her. But she didn't take it. Instead, she screamed, "Payne, look out!"

He turned in time to see Chaou Li's lunge, but not to avoid it. The weight of the Chinese man's body pushed Payne backward, into the wall. The back of his head struck the wooden planks, and he stumbled, dazed, to his knees.

Chaou Li pressed his advantage, bringing the side of his hand down against the back of Payne's neck. Payne moaned and then fell to the floor. He lay still and unmoving as Chaou Li stepped back and lifted his foot, ready to deliver a kick to his abdomen.

Aura darted forward, her hands flying, her nails sharp against Chaou Li's cheek. Unruffled, he turned to face her, catching her hands in his, jerking her arms back and holding them behind her.

He slowly wiped away the blood that was slowly seeping from his nose, the result of Payne's final blow. Then he glanced down at the cut in his arm that she had given him.

"Your debt grows, woman," he hissed at Aura. "But before you pay it, you can watch the man die."

With that he shoved her away, sending her stumbling across the room. She fell against the wall, dazed and aching.

Chaou Li bent over Payne and raised his hands once more, this time intending to strike the side of his neck and kill him.

"Not so quick, *yakutsa.*"

Chaou Li turned and straightened. He seemed unsurprised. His eyes narrowed as he stared at Yang Wu.

"A whole army of gnats come to irk me," he hissed. He lifted his hands and motioned to Wu. "Come here, little gnat," he said, "and I show you what I do to insects that dare to bother me."

Yang Wu's eyes settled on Chaou Li's face. The man looked like a crazed demon, with blood dripping unheeded from his nose, a half dozen scratches lining his cheek, and eyes that glowed dark with unfocused hatred. He'd been a fool to follow after Payne, he told himself. None of this was any interest of his. There was no reason for him to die.

For the first time he remembered the rifle that was strapped to the saddle on Payne's horse, and he cursed himself for a fool for not having thought of it before. What did he think he could do against a trained warrior, a man who could kill with nothing more than his hands? Had he been able, he'd have turned and run.

But by now Chaou Li was circling him, and there was no place for him to run. He let his eyes drift for an instant away from Chaou Li's face as he glanced first at Payne, then at Aura, and then at the knife that lay on the floor not ten feet from where Aura had fallen. If he could manage to stay alive long enough to get to it, he might stand a chance.

He looked back at Chaou Li and saw the man's smile. He knew that Chaou Li saw what he had seen, knew that he realized what it was he planned to do.

"Go ahead, little gnat," Chaou Li told him. He motioned toward the knife. "Pick it up." He laughed. "It will do you no good."

Wu glanced again at the knife, then raced to it, falling to his knees and sliding across the rough floor to grab it. And just as he felt it in his hand, he felt a sharp throb of pain and saw it fall to the floor in front of him. The pain in his hand seemed to scream through his arm. He hadn't even seen Chaou Li move. He was sure every bone in his hand had been broken.

He pulled back and cradled his hurt hand. When Chaou Li kicked the knife so that it slid close to his leg, he could do nothing more than stare dumbly down at it.

"Pick it up," Chaou Li sneered.

Wu looked up at him. He had been a fool to think he could stand up to a man like this, he told himself, a fool to come racing in here for no greater reason than the look he'd seen in the eyes of a woman he didn't even know.

Chaou Li was smiling at him now, enjoying the cowed and frightened look in Wu's eyes.

"Beg me to kill you quickly, little gnat," he snarled.

Those were the first words Aura heard as her thoughts slowly came back into focus and she began to realize what was happening. And as she did, she knew that the more evil Chaou Li did, the more superior and inflated he became, the more invulnerable he would be. It seemed as though there was not a place in her body that did not ache, as though there was not a spot that hadn't been prodded and bruised. But the hurt generated by each movement she made seemed dull and distant as she pushed herself away from the cabin wall to grasp the knife.

Chaou Li glowered at her.

"You need more proof that this is futile, woman?" he sneered.

He leaned back, slowly preparing to kick once again, letting her anticipate the blow. But Aura didn't wait. She sprang forward and stabbed.

There was a second when she could feel the slight resistance as the blade struck his clothing, and then it seemed to slip forward, deeper than she'd have thought herself capable of forcing it into his body. She

338

released her hold of the handle and jumped back, terrified by what she'd done.

Chaou Li stood for a moment, his expression dazed with disbelief as he looked down and saw the handle protruding from his shoulder. His eyes grew wide with pain and hatred, and then he put his hand to the thing and pulled the knife free.

He turned his stare on Aura. The bloody knife in his hand, he started for her.

She knew then that she had made a horrible mistake, that the wound she had given him wouldn't stop him, that nothing would stop him except death. And he was showing her just how far he was from death at the moment. He was letting her think about what he was going to do with the knife.

She darted a glance at Payne. He was still unconscious, unable to help. And he would probably never wake up, she realized. Chaou Li would see to that.

She asked herself how she'd done so much evil. She'd never meant to hurt anyone, and yet she'd been the cause not only of her own misery and Mailee's, but Payne's death and Yang Wu's as well. It seemed too great a burden to carry to her grave.

She looked up at Chaou Li's hate-filled eyes and screamed.

Chapter Eighteen

Mailee stood in the downpour and watched Yang Wu follow Payne into the cabin. When he'd disappeared, she glanced down at the unconscious body of Jack Duran. She had no idea which of the gods had decided finally to smile on her, but she knew she would be eternally thankful for the abrupt change in her fortunes. Something inside her seemed to swell up and burst. She was free, she told herself. For the first time in her life, she was totally free.

Her glance drifted then to Payne's horse, standing forlornly in the downpour less than twenty feet from where she stood. She turned her back on Jack Duran, first giving a him a final distasteful glance and then daintily stepping past the place where he lay spread-eagled in the mud as though she was avoiding a heap of garbage that had been thrown in the gutter.

She could climb on that animal's back, she told herself as she approached the horse, she could climb on his back and ride away. She need never look back, never again think of Hung Poh or Chaou Li or Jack Duran. The horse shied away slightly as she approached, but he was a well-trained animal and soon quieted.

She reached up for the pommel, and for a moment

her hand lay on it, shaking with fear, fear of fleeing mixed with fear of staying. Go, she told herself, get away from this horrible place while you can.

But as much as she wanted to, she found herself incapable of climbing up onto the horse's back. She told herself that aside from Aura she had no friend in this strange, vast country, that flight from here would leave her with even less than she had at that moment. And rather than flee, she instead unstrapped the rifle from the saddle.

The thing seemed alien and unnaturally heavy in her hands, something far removed from the orderly progress of her normal life. But everything that had happened to her since she'd been sent to this place was well beyond the experiences of the life she'd known in China. And it was not as though she had never seen a rifle fired. The time for meek acceptance had long since past, she told herself. She started walking toward the cabin.

She had just reached the door when Aura screamed. One glance told her more than she wanted to know. She raised the rifle and tried to sight it as best she could at the hulking form that was moving threateningly toward her friend.

As Mailee stared down the barrel at Chaou Li's back, she thought of all those things that had wrongly befallen her. She'd spent a lifetime learning that it was a woman's duty to accept silently whatever life brought her, to follow obediently the dictates of those men who held in their power the right to rule her existence. And not once had she questioned the wisdom of those teachings, at least, not until she'd met Aura.

Aura hadn't meekly accepted, and that did not make her immoral or wicked, as Mailee had been taught her own disobedience would make her. Aura had bravely fought against what she'd held to be wrong, even though she'd had little chance of winning. In Mailee's eyes that rebellion made her brave, if foolish. It was time, Mailee told herself, that she became brave and foolish as well.

She thought of the monsters in her own life, of the stranger her father had chosen to become her husband, a man who had beaten and abused her, and of the father who had turned his back on her when she most needed him. Then she sighted the rifle at the back of the monster who was about to strike at Aura. When she squeezed the trigger and fired, she wasn't just firing at Chaou Li, she was firing at every man who had ever mistreated and failed her.

The recoil shocked her, slamming into her shoulder and nearly sending her reeling backward. She had to fight to keep herself on her feet.

Her aim had been better than she could have hoped. Chaou Li arched backward and tottered for a moment. Then he clenched the knife and reached out viciously toward Aura as he fell forward, determined to take his revenge on her even he had to do it in death.

Aura screamed as he started to fall toward her, then wildly pushed herself forward, toward Yang Wu. The blade of the knife slid by just inches behind her and then Chaou Li fell against her, the weight of his body pinning her against the wall. He didn't move.

When she turned her head she found herself staring into Chaou Li's sightless eyes. She began screaming, or at least tried to scream, but no sound escaped her. It seemed an eternity to her before Wu and Mailee managed to pull Chaou Li's body off her.

She was shaking so hard she could barely stand, but not so badly that she could not see Payne's still body lying on the floor at the far side of the cabin. She could see no movement, and a terrified voice inside her shrieked out wildly that Payne was dead, that the blow Chaou Li had delivered to the back of his neck had broken it and killed him.

She pulled herself away from Mailee and started toward him. She felt as though the very air around her was holding her back, and she struggled forward, every step taking all her concentration and every ounce of her strength.

It seemed to take her forever to cross those few feet, but finally she reached him. He was completely still, too still. She fell to her knees at his side and reached out to him, her fingers trembling as she touched his cheek.

She was sobbing now. She could hear the sound of it, a remote keening noise of which she would never have thought herself capable before that moment. He was dead, she told herself; Chaou Li had killed him. She wished that she hadn't fought so hard, that before he'd died, Chaou Li had killed her as well. It had been one thing to fight against fate when she'd thought Payne hated her. Now, kneeling beside his still body and knowing he cared enough about her to come after her, to die for her, it all seemed unbearably futile.

She'd never before felt the sort of emptiness, the complete desolation, that filled her at that moment. Payne had come after her, he'd found her and fought for her. He cared for her, cared enough to do all those things. And now he was dead.

It seemed so unutterably unfair that the bitterness of that moment threatened to overwhelm her. She'd never had the chance to tell him that she loved him, she told herself miserably. Nothing else mattered, not their arguments, not their differences, only that she loved him . . . and needed him. Despite her determination to be independent, she realized now that whatever she achieved in her life, it would mean nothing to

343

her without him. The pain of losing him now seemed unbearable, of knowing that she'd never even have the chance to tell him that she loved him.

She said it now, the words little more than a vague whisper on her lips, each achingly filled with regret: "I love you, Payne, I love you."

And then he groaned.

She stared at him through tear-blurred eyes, not quite sure she could believe that she'd heard him make the sound.

He moved his head slightly, then winced and opened his eyes. For a moment he simply stared up at her. Then he smiled.

"You're alive," she mouthed in disbelief.

"You needn't look quite so disappointed," he muttered, then started to push himself up, wincing with pain. He put his hand on the back of his neck where Chaou Li had struck him. His head was suddenly a weight he was incapable of supporting. "What the hell did he hit me with?" he asked, as he rested his head against the wall behind him and took a few deep breaths.

"You're alive," Aura cried, aware that she was smiling inanely now as she stared at him.

He grinned and reached out for her, grasping her shoulders and pulling her to him. Dazed, she fell forward, her eyes still blurred with tears and lost in his.

"Can I take that foolish grin to mean that particular fact doesn't disappoint you?" he asked her.

He didn't wait for her to answer, but put his hand at the base of her neck and pulled her to him, pressing his lips to hers.

Aura felt a shiver of sweet liquid fire pass through her as his lips found hers. This is madness, a voice inside her told her. After everything that has happened, to let yourself feel like this is madness.

344

She didn't listen to the voice, didn't care whether it was madness that made her feel like this. A moment before, when she'd thought him dead, she'd been certain her heart would stop and never beat again. But now it was throbbing wildly in her chest. If it was madness, she told herself, she never again wanted to be entirely sane.

"You're alive," she whispered, when his lips had left hers.

"It wouldn't be much of a rescue now if I wasn't," he told her. He glanced across the room at the bloody heap that was Chaou Li's body. "Not that I quite anticipated all the minor details." He looked up at Wu and grinned. "Remind me to express my gratitude at a more appropriate moment," he said.

Wu approached him and offered a hand to help him up.

"Your gratitude belongs elsewhere," he said, and nodded toward Mailee. "But in the meantime, may I suggest we leave this place? As much as that man deserved killing, I really don't think it would be healthy to be here when his body is found."

Payne took the offered hand as Aura scurried to her feet. Then he pushed himself slowly to a standing position. He took one step and nearly fell.

He put his hand on the back of his head as Aura and Wu caught him.

"What did he hit me with?" he murmured, repeating the question he'd jokingly asked a moment before.

"Chaou Li *yakutsa*," Mailee said.

Payne gave her a bewildered glance.

"A warrior," Wu explained, "a man trained to kill with his hands. You're lucky he didn't kill you with the first blow to the neck."

"I don't feel all that lucky just at the moment," Payne muttered.

"And I don't think Hung Poh is going to be very happy when he learns about this," Wu said. He looked at Chaou Li's body with, if not exactly regret, then certainly reluctance. He knew that even were they to get away from the mining camp without further problem, still the matter would not forgotten.

"Hung Poh has a few things of his own to answer to," Payne said.

Wu scowled. It was obvious that the thought of facing Hung Poh didn't appeal to him in the least.

"We'd better leave now," he pressed. "I have a feeling if we don't, we won't live long enough to have to worry about Hung Poh."

Aura put Payne's arm around her shoulder and her own around his waist.

"Lean on me," she offered.

His fingers squeezed her shoulder.

"I think I'm feeling better already," he told her with a wry grin.

"That fact, friend, does bring me a great feelin' of comfort, I assure ya."

Mailee gasped when she heard the voice, and the three others looked up, startled, to find Jack Duran standing in the doorway. He was holding a pistol, and it was pointed directly at Payne's heart.

"You drop that rifle, darlin'," Duran told Mailee. When she hesitated, he shouted, "Drop it!"

Startled, she did as he ordered. The rifle fell to the floor with a dull thud.

Duran smiled. "Now, that's better," he said. "Get back against that wall," he ordered them, and motioned with the gun.

It was only when all four were standing against the wall that Duran entered the cabin and crossed the room to where Mailee had dropped the rifle. Keeping his eyes on Payne, he knelt and retrieved it, then wandered to the opposite side of the cabin and glanced down at Chaou Li's body.

He smiled and then turned his attention back to his captives.

"Now, ain't this a shame?" he asked, although there wasn't the least hint of regret in either his tone or his expression. "Such a kind, generous soul he was, sent so young to meet his ancestors." He glanced at Mailee. "That is the right expression, isn't it, darlin'?" he asked her. "Sent to meet his ancestors?" When she refused to answer, he shrugged and nodded toward the body. "No matter. I'm sure we agree his death is a great loss to us all."

"What are you going to do?" Payne demanded.

"Now, *that* is a question to ponder," Duran mused aloud. He put his foot on Chaou Li's shoulder and pushed, turning the dead weight of the heavy body with obvious difficulty. "It pains me to find that such a likable group as you all have turned out lawless enough to have done cold-blooded murder."

"Call for the federal marshal," Payne suggested. "We'd have no objection."

"No," Duran mused, "I don't suppose you would. But I'm afraid that under the present circumstances, I don't find that particular choice at all appealin'."

Aura knew what he was thinking, that a federal marshal would find more to interest him in the mining camp than in Chaou Li's death. There were the small matters of kidnapping and holding her against her will, not to mention the illegal sale of human beings, all of which had occurred with Duran's knowledge and cooperation. She could easily understand why he'd be reluctant to have a federal marshal looking into those activities.

"You can get out now, Duran," she told him. "If

you leave, no one need know what part you've had in all this."

Duran smiled, as if he was amused by the suggestion, and then shook his head.

"You never fail to surprise me, darlin'," he told her. "Now, why should I run away when there's no real need? No, the real problem as I see it is decidin' what to do with this here unfortunate body. Too bad we can't just dig a hole and put him in it, but I'm afraid Hung Poh wouldn't like that." He glanced at Chaou Li's body, then back up at Aura. "Like I said, the problem is decidin' what to do with Chaou Li. And then, I'm afraid, decidin' what to do with you."

"You can't expect four murders would go unnoticed," Payne told him.

"No, I suppose that'd be more than it would be reasonable to hope for," Duran agreed.

"In fact, you'd never succeed in killing all of us," Payne went on. "Four of us, rushing you at the same time. We'd get to you, and then we'd be forced to kill you. It isn't a good bet." He took a step forward. "Of course, you could just come back to San Francisco with us, nice and peaceful," he suggested, as he took another step.

Duran lifted the pistol and fired. The bullet struck the wall just to the side of Aura's head. She screamed in terror.

"Get back," Duran shouted at Payne. "Get back, or the next one will kill her."

Payne knew he was cornered. He might have tried to face Duran down if he'd been alone, but he wasn't about to risk Aura's life as well as his own. He did as he was ordered, backing up to wall again, reaching for Aura and holding her, then gently pushing her behind him and out of Duran's sight.

Unfortunately, he didn't get far enough.

348

Duran fired a second bullet, and this one grazed Aura's arm. This time, it wasn't just fear that prompted her cry, but pain as well.

"Move away from her," Duran shouted. "Do it or I'll kill you both now."

Payne stared down at Aura, every fiber of him filled with regret that he'd been the cause of her hurt.

She pushed him away. "It's all right," she assured him, as she glanced at her arm. It stung terribly, but it was clearly nothing worse than a cut in the flesh. It wasn't even bleeding very much.

Payne turned to Duran. "All right," he hissed. "Leave her alone. What do you want from me?"

Duran seemed delighted at this admission of defeat, however reluctant.

"Now that's better," he told Payne. He even smiled. "All I want is that you do as you're told," he said. "Not much to ask. And just now, that means you get down on your knees and put your hands behind your head." When Payne glowered at him, he screamed, "Do it!" and fired again, this time just above Mailee's head.

"Stop it, you bastard," Payne shouted. He knelt and put his hands behind his head.

Duran nodded. "Now that's just right," he said. "Now I want you to do nothin', absolutely nothin'. I don't want to see you move again. If I do, I'll be forced to make the little lady pay for it, an act that I'm sure both of us would regret. You understand?" When Payne didn't respond, he lifted the pistol and aimed it at Aura. "I asked you a question," he snarled at Payne.

Payne nodded. "I understand," he replied.

Duran smiled. "Good," he said. "Now, where were we?" he mused. "I think I was about to thank you." He smiled again. "Ya see, you folks did me a bit of a favor here. It pains me, but I have to admit I didn't like this arrogant, uppity Chinee, not one little bit. I thought once or twice of puttin' a bullet in his heart myself. But unfortunately, I have business dealin's with his master, and that makes this whole thing a bit sticky, if you get my meanin'."

"What are you going to do?" Aura murmured.

"The first thing I'm gonna do is ask you to join me, darlin'," he said. He motioned with the pistol. "Come here."

Aura shuddered.

"Leave her be," Payne told Duran.

Duran raised the pistol and made a show of aiming it. "I thought you and me had come to an understandin'," he said. "Do we need another lesson?"

The ache in her arm reminded Aura just how little she relished the thought of another of Duran's "lessons."

"No," she said as she stepped forward, "that's not necessary."

Duran took a few steps back from Chaou Li's body. "Good," he said. "Now what I want you to do, darlin', is unbutton our friend here's jacket. Open the pocket you will find there and remove the contents."

Aura looked at Chaou Li's body and shuddered.

"You can't be serious," Payne hissed.

"Perhaps I'll just kill you first," Duran suggested as he repositioned the pistol. "It might prove a good lesson to the rest."

"No," Aura cried. She stepped forward. "I'll do whatever you want."

"Now, that's real smart of you, darlin'," Duran told her. "You know, I think I'm startin' to take a bit of a likin' to you."

Aura knelt besides Chaou Li's body. The smell of blood seemed to hang over it, and the dark smears of

350

red on his tunic revolted her. She touched the heavy cotton fabric warily, trying to avoid the sticky splotches of red. The body was still warm to the touch, but Chaou Li's face was unnaturally pale and slack, and Aura soon found she couldn't avoid touching the blood. As soon as she began to unbutton the tunic, she started to gag.

"Now, that just won't do, darlin'," Duran told her. "You just take a deep breath and get about your business."

"For God's sake," Payne muttered.

"I thought you was keepin' yer mouth shut," Duran told him. His eyes narrowed as he fingered the trigger of the pistol.

"I'm all right," Aura told Payne.

She wasn't, of course, but the sight of Duran threatening Payne with the pistol did seem to partially cure her squeamishness. She returned to the business of the buttons, and unfastened enough of them to turn back the front of the tunic in less time than she'd have imagined possible. Beneath it, Chaou Li's naked chest was pale and unmoving.

"There," Duran told her, "on the right side."

She swallowed her distaste, then carefully reached inside the pocket, taking care not to touch Chaou Li's naked flesh. She withdrew a fairly large silk bag from the pocket. It was heavy, surprisingly heavy for its small size. She held it up for Duran's inspection.

"That's it, darlin'," he told her. "Now, you just throw it here."

She did as he told her, tossing the bag to him. He caught it and hefted it in his left hand.

"Better than three pounds, don't ya think?" he asked her. He grinned at her. "There was to be more, when you and your Chinee friend there were sold. But I'll have to settle for this, I suppose."

"That's the money paid for the other women," she murmured in disbelief.

Three pounds of gold nuggets, she mused, was that the value of a dozen human lives? Less than fifty ounces at fourteen dollars the ounce, she quickly calculated, came to not quite seven hundred dollars. Human life, female Chinese human life, in any case, was valued less than cattle or sheep.

He nodded. "Gold. Stolen gold, if you must know. Those Chinee buggers are constantly sneakin' off with a few nuggets when you're not lookin'. If I owned this here mine, I'd be real unhappy with that fact."

"Twice stolen now," Payne ventured. "First from the mine owner, and now from Hung Poh."

Duran nodded and grinned. "Twice stolen from twice removed," he replied. "Seems fittin', don't it?"

"Now what?" Aura asked.

"Now comes the moment of decision," he replied. He motioned with the pistol. "You can be gettin' back there with yer friends now, darlin'," he told her.

She scrambled to her feet and retreated quickly, glad to be as far away from both him and Chaou Li's body as she could be. But when she was standing beside Payne again, she wasn't so sure she ought to have hurried.

"It looks to me like you four will have to pay for your crime, after all," Duran told them. "A shame I had to kill you to keep you from killin' me like you did my dear friend Chaou Li here."

Panicked, Aura realized that Payne had lunged forward. When she looked up at Duran, she found he was aiming the pistol and pulling back the trigger.

It started just an instant before Duran fired. The cabin seemed to shudder, the floor shook for an in-

352

stant before it seemed to slide out from beneath her. Disoriented, Aura tumbled forward. Her scream combined with Mailee's, and together they were almost loud enough to compete with the sound of the pistol fire.

Aura fell against Payne, her weight carrying the two of them to the shifting floor. The bullet struck the wall, just at the place where Payne's chest had been an instant before, but neither of them noticed it. The beams of the cabin were crying out, making loud, cracking protestations. It was only too clear that whatever was happening, the structure was not nearly well enough built to withstand whatever the forces were that had been thrown against it.

Payne pushed himself up to his knees and for an instant listened to the chaotic noises that filled the cabin. Then, with barely a glance at Duran, he got to his feet.

"We have to get out of here," he shouted at Aura. He grabbed her arm and started pulling her toward the door.

As shaken as were the others, Duran stared at them for a panic-filled instant, but when he realized they were about to get away, his fear of what their escape might mean to him outweighed his fear of whatever it was that happening around him.

"Not so fast," he shouted at them, and pointed the pistol.

By now Mailee and Wu had also scrambled to their feet and were racing toward the door, the threat of possible bullets forgotten in the terror of being caught in what seemed the certain collapse of the cabin. Duran fired, but the floor seemed to be sliding about beneath them. The shot went wild.

Payne tugged at Aura's arm, but she was too dazed to react. With no time left to try to reason with her, he put his hand around her waist and half lifted, half dragged her forward, to the door.

"Get out of here, you fool," Payne called back to Duran as he half ran, half tumbled out of the cabin.

Duran was confused. He realized by now, just as the others did, that the cabin was about to collapse around him. Panicked, he started after them, running toward the door, only to find himself falling to the floor.

He had enough time to look around and see Chaou Li's hand clinging to his ankle.

Duran shrieked. He'd been sure Chaou Li was dead, and his first thought was that the dead man was trying to stop him from stealing the gold. But then he turned and looked at Chaou Li's eyes and saw them staring back at him. The eyes were wild, but very much alive.

Duran shuddered at the clawlike grip on his ankle. He tried to shake it free, but the hand tightened its grasp. The rafters above him groaned and then began to split. Duran watched them fall, bringing bits of the roof along with them.

Duran realized then that Chaou Li knew he was going to die, and he was determined to take a victim with him to the grave. There was only one way out for him, he told himself, only one way he could get away before the cabin collapsed completely.

He turned the pistol to Chaou Li and fired.

A bright red, jagged circle appeared on Chaou Li's arm. That's it, Duran thought, as he tried to pull his foot away. He couldn't believe it when the grasp on his ankle tightened to a viselike grip, couldn't believe the maniacal look in Chaou Li's eyes. He screamed and raised the pistol to fire a second time.

He pressed the trigger again and again, but the pistol didn't fire. Too late, he realized he'd already spent all six bullets.

He looked up and saw the roof begin to cave in.

He opened his mouth to scream, but never had the chance.

Aura had only a glimpse of the cabin collapsing in on itself. Her attention was drawn away from it by a thunderous noise coming from the top of the hillside.

She looked up, and even though her vision was obscured by the rainfall, still she could see the river of mud that was slipping down the hillside. It was a mudslide that had toppled the cabin, she realized. And it was continuing, and even growing, the dark viscous flow creeping steadily down the side of the hill.

She stood, staring at it, mesmerized with the horror of knowing it was headed straight for the place where she was standing.

"Run," she heard Payne shout. "Run for the trees before we're caught in it!"

But she couldn't run. She couldn't move her feet. They were rooted, caught not so much in the mud but in the realization that flight was futile, that there was no chance they could escape that enormous flow.

"Run," Payne shouted again, and grabbed her arm.

His touch startled her, waking her out of the reverie of death the sight of that mud flow had settled over her. She started forward, slipping and sliding in the muck, but with Payne's help she kept on her feet and kept moving. She caught a glimpse of Mailee and Wu, some thirty feet ahead of them, fleeing into the relative safety offered by the line of trees at the edge of the camp.

I can't give up now, she told herself. She felt Payne's grasp of her arm, steady and sure. He hadn't given up on her, she reminded herself. She wouldn't give up on herself now.

Rain streamed down her face and mud splashed up with every step, but she was unaware of any of that. All she knew was that Payne's hand was holding hers, and nothing else seemed to matter, no adversity seemed insurmountable, not even the mountain of mud steadily slipping toward them.

And then suddenly there were tree trunks around them, a virtual wall of pines. Payne released her arm and then put his arms around her and pulled her close.

"We made it," she gasped.

He nodded. "We made it," he said.

She could feel his heart beating, the thick thud matching the sound of her heart's heightened beat. She reached up for him, wrapping her arms around his neck, shaken and lost with relief at the knowledge that they'd somehow escaped.

He lowered his face toward hers, the rain dripping from his cheeks onto hers, and she almost laughed with the sheer joy of knowing they were alive and together. She looked up into his eyes and eagerly waited for his kiss.

The thick cracking sound she'd heard while they were still outside the cabin thundered a second time off the hillside. Only this time it continued, not stopping for a full minute or more.

Aura trembled at the sound of it, burying herself against Payne as he turned and looked up, squinting into the darkness.

"Oh, God," she heard him whisper.

"What is it?"

"The sluice has collapsed," Payne shouted, hoping to warn Mailee and Wu. "Get back before we're crushed."

And then Aura felt herself being lifted and tossed over Payne's shoulder like a sack. He was running through the maze of tree trunks, panting with the effort, the thudding of his footsteps in the sloppy mess underfoot lost in the horrible cacophony caused by the logs of the mine sluice, freed to tumble down the hillside by the shifting mud, as they came crashing into the line of trees she had thought would shelter them.

Chapter Nineteen

The air filled with the shuddering, wrenching noise of trees crashing down to the ground and being crushed, a terrifying clamor that seemed to surround them and completely fill the night. The ground beneath them seemed to shake with it.

Payne put Aura down.

"Are you all right?" he asked her, shouting to be heard above the din of crashing limbs and cracking branches. "Can you run? It would be faster."

She peered up at him, squinting into the darkness. The noise was frightening enough, but under the canopy of the treetops, whatever little light there had been in the camp clearing seemed completely obscured. The rain continued in a steady downpour, and she couldn't see more than a foot or two in front of her. She had no idea how Payne thought he could run in the near total darkness, or how he hoped to keep his bearings.

Trust him, she told herself, you have to trust him. She nodded, almost too frightened to speak.

"As long as you don't let go of me," she told him, and reached for his hand.

He caught hold of it in his and squeezed it.

"Not on your life," he promised. "I've come too far

to find you to let you wander off and end up as some bear's dinner."

Aura sensed more than saw his grin, and knew he was laughing at her. He was, she realized, a complete bewilderment to her. Even at a time like this, still he could laugh at her.

He led her forward into the darkness. She had no idea how he managed to make his way through the maze of the trees and sodden underbrush or even how he kept his bearings. Branches and limbs seemed to her to be everywhere, reaching out for her, grasping her clothes, scratching her face and arms. But somehow Payne navigated a path through the thick growth. The noise stayed behind them, so she realized he'd kept his bearings after all, moving on in the right direction and leading them away from the havoc at the edge of the camp clearing. When finally they stopped, she was exhausted.

"I think we're far enough away now," he told her.

He reached for her, wrapped his arms around her, and pulled her close. She fell against him, exhausted and panting, was more than content to be still, to rest her aching legs and let herself feel comforted by the warm proximity of his body.

Eventually the sounds of trees being crushed started to become sporadic rather than constant. Finally it ceased altogether.

Payne held her still while he listened to the sounds of the night.

"Hear that?" he asked her.

She looked up and strained to hear whatever it was he heard, but all there was that she could find was the endless splattering sound of rain falling against leaves and mud.

"What?" she asked.

He grinned.

"Nothing. No more crashing noises," he told her.

It was over, she realized with a sigh of relief. It must have been her exhaustion that made her a little slow to understand what the sudden silence meant. Or maybe, she thought, it was simply the fact that her mind was a little clouded when she was with him.

"Do we go back?" she asked.

"No," he replied. "Not tonight.

"But what about Mailee and Wu?" she asked. "We have to find them. We can't leave them out here."

"It's useless to try to search now. It'd be impossible in this darkness," he replied. "All we can do is hope they keep their wits about them, and look for them in the morning."

The morning. Even the words sounded strange to her. After everything that had happened, it seemed impossible to think that the sun would actually rise again and a day would be born, clean and without any stain. It seemed almost too much even to hope for.

"Will there be a morning?" she asked in an exhausted murmur.

"I hope so," he replied. "Right now, though, we tend to your arm."

She glanced down at the dark stain on the sleeve of her blouse that she knew was her own blood. Her arm ached where the bullet had grazed it, but she didn't think it was serious.

"What can you do in the dark?" she asked him.

"Not much," Payne admitted, as he pulled out his shirt tail and began to tear off a long strip of the linen. "Just bandage it, I suppose. At least, all the rain will have washed it clean by now."

Aura unbuttoned her blouse and pulled her hurt arm free. It took only a moment for Payne to tie the makeshift bandage around her.

"How does it feel?" he asked, when he'd done.

She flexed her arm and then returned it to the sleeve of her blouse. "Achy," she replied.

"I wish there was something else I could do for it," he told her.

"There is," she said as she fell into his arms. "You could hold me."

He chuckled. "You do ask a lot," he murmured, as he tightened his arms around her.

"I don't care," she replied with an exhausted sigh.

He smiled and kissed the top of her head, pressing his cheek against the helmet of her rain-soaked hair. He couldn't understand why it felt so good to have her in his arms, why he felt such an unexpected wash of happiness drift through him. There was damn little that he could think of to be happy about at that moment, save for the fact that they were both still alive. Not that that was an inconsiderable point, especially taking into account everything that had happened in the previous few hours. Still, his horse had wandered off, they were as good as lost in a wilderness God alone knew how far from San Francisco, and as far as his job was concerned, he hadn't touched Hung Poh or in any way put a stop to either the counterfeiting or any of the dozen other illegal endeavors he managed. But despite all that, all Payne could think of was how happy he felt. As absurd as it might seem to him, he was happier than he could ever before remember being.

He led Aura slowly through the undergrowth until he found a large pine tree with wide, spreading branches.

"There," he said. "We won't be dry, but at least we won't be sitting in the mud. I'd say you could probably use a little rest."

"Now, that's a masterful understatement," Aura groaned, as she sank down to the ground.

She gratefully realized that Payne was right. She found herself sitting on a thick bed of pine needles that coated the ground beneath the pine's wide branches. Compared to the hard wooden floors she'd slept on the previous two nights, it was almost downy. It was wet, certainly, but then again, she was soaked already and hardly noticed anything beyond the cushiony softness of the heap. It even smelled nice, a clean, woodsy odor that grew stronger as her weight crushed the needles beneath her. Nothing had ever seemed as comfortable, she thought, as that bed of pine needles felt at that moment. She turned to Payne as he settled himself beside her.

"Not so bad," she murmured. "In fact, if this miserable rain ever stops, I could make myself quite comfortable here."

"Now, those are hardly the words I'd expect to hear from a prissy, pampered Easterner," he told her, as he put his arm around her shoulders and warmed her arms with his hands.

"Is that what I am," she asked, "a prissy, pampered Easterner?"

He chuckled. "A few weeks ago, that's exactly what I thought you. I'm not so sure anymore."

She rested her head against his chest, sighed with exhaustion and relief, and let her eyes slowly drift closed.

"Hmmm, being pampered," she murmured, as she snuggled close to the warmth of his body, "showered with flowers and bonbons. Toasted with champagne. That sounds inviting." She sighed. "Truth is, I'd settle for just lying down in front of a fire and sleeping for about a week."

She was tired, more tired, she thought, than she had ever been in her life. And it felt so good to lean her head against Payne's chest, to feel his body close to hers, to feel safe with his arms around her.

"I'm afraid a fire's out of the question, under the circumstances," he told her. "I don't suppose you might be satisfied with a kiss?"

By way of inducement, he lowered his lips to her neck and pressed them gently against the soft skin.

When she felt the warmth of his lips against her neck, when she felt the surge of heat that filled her at that touch, Aura suddenly found she wasn't quite as tired as she thought she'd been. She turned her face so that her lips found his, and brought her arm to his shoulder, pulling him close to her, drinking in the taste and the feel of him. She parted her lips and, with a sigh of pleasure, welcomed the probe of his tongue.

Suddenly nothing else mattered but the fact that he was there with her, that he'd come after her and saved her from Chaou Li and an odious fate. For the first time in days, she wasn't afraid. Whatever lay in front of them, she knew that as long as he was with her, she wouldn't feel so much as an echo of the terror that had haunted her since the evening she'd found Whit's body. She was in love, and Payne had proved his love by coming for her. Nothing else mattered.

She didn't feel the rain, or even the chill that had felt so miserably uncomfortable since the first moment she'd stepped out of the wagon and into the dismal world of the mining camp. Her body seemed to radiate heat, and she knew the cause of that heat was a fire Payne had ignited deep inside her.

She lay back on the pine needles, and he followed her, his lips touching hers, his hand warm and knowing on her breast. She thought of how close she'd come to never seeing him again, to never again feeling as she did at that moment. It startled her, lying as they were, unprotected in the rain, to realize just how lucky she was then, to consider all she'd gained by temporarily losing everything.

And then she deliberately closed off thought, tucking it away and shunting it aside. She wouldn't let herself think of anything, least of all the differences that separated them, all the reasons they had found to push one another away. She told herself that it had been too much thought, too much determination, that had kept them at odds in the first place. Let it be, a voice inside her advised, just let what is be.

She closed her eyes and let herself drift in the glory of the feeling of his lips on hers, of his hands against her breast, of the solid, warming weight of his body on hers. And she decided that this time the voice was right, that there were times to ponder and evaluate, and times to simply close your eyes and dance.

She wrapped her arms around his shoulders and pulled him close, thirsty for the taste of him. She found herself filling with a ravening hunger that was an alien thing, unlike anything she'd ever felt before, and yet something she knew that was rooted deeply within her. It was as though the previous days and nights had scrubbed her clean and left her naked to him, ready to be wakened to the guileless and prideless creature that she might have been had she been free of the so-called "civilized world" into which she'd been born. That world had served only to separate her from her feelings, to make her fear her own desire. She was past that now. Facing death had taught her how to savor life, to willingly embrace it.

The creature inside her was unashamed of the hunger, and more than willing to pursue the means of satisfying it. She pressed herself to him, reveling in the feel of his flesh beneath her fingers and the sharp taste of rain mixed with the salt of the sweat on his neck. She pulled his shirt free and pressed her lips against his

364

skin, acutely aware of the maleness of him, the hard muscles beneath the skin, the wiry curling hair on his chest, as she searched for the satiation of the mysterious hunger that seemed about to consume her.

Her transformation startled Payne at first, but hardly displeased him. This certainly was no priggish and proper "little woman" that he held in his arms, no frigid and civilized Easterner. Nor was she the frightened virgin who'd offered him solace when Whit died. No, this was a woman, eager and willing and ripe. Far from displeased, his body ached with the desire to satisfy the hungers he'd wakened in her.

He lay back and watched her intent expression as she unfastened first his belt, and then the buttons of his trousers, feeling her fingers against his naked belly like tendrils of sweetly burning fire. He'd had whores perform this service for him in the past, undressing him, kissing and caressing him, but never had his body reacted to those knowing hands the way they did to Aura's uncertain touch. And when he felt her lips pressed against his tumid member, he felt as though he would explode.

He closed his eyes and groaned with the sweet pleasure of the touch of her lips and tongue, adrift in an uncertain sea of unexpected and overwhelmingly pleasurable desire. But before the moment came, he pushed her away, grasping her shoulders and pressing her back against the bed of rumpled clothing and pine needles, determined he would not take his own pleasure before he showed her what the wild creature he'd released within her wished to find.

He pressed his legs between hers and parted them, then slid inside her, her body a sweet, silken glove to him, something so perfect it nearly stupefied him. It was then he realized that there was not one stranger wakened by the hungry fire they shared, but two. He'd never before felt as he did with her, and it shocked him to realize that she'd somehow roused something he'd never known had existed within him.

Aura gave herself up to the shimmering fingers of liquid fire that snaked their way through her body. She pulled him close, so hard her arms ached from the effort, wanting nothing else but to go on feeling forever the slowly growing turgid pleasure that swelled within her.

She'd nearly lost so much, and the realization that she'd been given a second chance was nothing less than miraculous to her. The recognition of that near loss made each sensation seem heightened, each movement a glorification of life. She pressed herself to him, pulling his body to her with a power that only the proximity to certain loss could generate. She'd nearly given herself up for lost, and now she reclaimed herself with the strength of her passion for him.

The release came to them both quickly, and with a shattering intensity that literally took Aura's breath away. It seemed forever before she felt herself breathe again, and then each breath was a ragged, labored gasp. She found herself clinging to him, trembling, lost in a world of heightened awareness, an afterglow that left her so sensitive to him that she trembled at his slightest movement. She held him close, not wanting to lose him ever again.

He pressed himself to her and kissed her, his breathing as ragged as her own. He was, he realized, lost in the same bewildering world her dazed glance showed her to be wandering, and all he could think was what a pleasure it would be to wander that mysterious place together with her forever. Odd thoughts, he told himself, for a man so determinedly independent as he was. Odd and probably disturbing. He told himself he would have to ponder that matter, that he would sometime have to find the answer to what seemed just then unanswerable and mysterious. For the moment, however, his thoughts were lost in other matters, and did not wish to be roused.

Gradually Aura's heart beat slowed to a steady, sharp thump and she found she could breathe almost normally again. She felt strangely distant from herself, oddly complete in a way she'd never been before. She sighed with sheer contentment, an oddity, she thought, as she was lying naked in the woods in the rain. But none of that mattered, she told herself, as she pressed her body close to Payne's.

"How did you find me?" she asked sleepily, not really ready for an explanation yet, but wanting to feel the rumble of his voice deep in his chest where she rested her head.

"It wasn't easy," he assured her. "There wasn't even any real reason to think you'd been kidnapped."

"But you knew," she said.

He nodded. "I knew. I don't know how, but I knew."

She smiled, a secret, knowing smile. He'd known, she told herself, because he loved her.

"And you came looking for me?"

"With Yang Wu's help. Grudging at first, I'm afraid, but I managed to rouse him to meet his nobler sentiments."

"But why?" She wondered why she asked, but once she had, she knew she wanted the answer more than anything, wanted him to put it into words, wanted to hear him say them aloud, to tell her that he loved her. "We parted on less than pleasant terms," she reminded him.

He chuckled softly. "Damned if I know," he told her, unaware of how much he was disappointing her. "I've been asking myself why since the moment I entered Hung Poh's friendly little opium den and found myself facing some very unpleasant-looking characters. I did manage to find the press the counterfeit currency was printed on, though."

Aura felt as though she'd been deflated and crushed. "Oh," she murmured.

She'd almost forgotten, that was what he was looking for, the source of the counterfeit bills. Perhaps finding her had been little more than a secondary excursion, an outgrowth of the search for the counterfeiters. Perhaps his coming after her had little to do with any feelings he might have for her, beyond a certain sense of obligation for his brother's sake. Perhaps it had nothing to do with anything save finding his precious counterfeiters.

She started to pull away from him, but he tightened his hold of her and began once again to kiss her.

"First lesson in surviving in the wilderness," he murmured, as he pressed his lips to her neck and her ear, "share bodily warmth."

And as though it was a smoldering fire just waiting to be stirred, the blaze inside her burst forth once again, searing away her doubts in a single outburst of flames. Let it be, the voice inside told her once again, and she told herself that, if only for the night, she would do just that. She wouldn't think about tomorrow, wouldn't torture herself with expectations of him she had no right to have. She'd accept whatever the fates saw to give her, and she'd content herself with that, no matter how little. Facing death had taught her the value of life, if nothing else.

"Share bodily warmth," she repeated softly, as she spread herself beneath him, grateful for the gift he offered her, even if it was only temporary protection from the storm.

* * *

Aura opened her eyes and stared upward. At first she was disoriented and confused, for there was no roof over her, only a seemingly endless number of tiers of pine boughs through which a bright shaft of golden sunlight edged its way downward.

"Good morning."

Startled, she turned to find Payne lying beside her, staring down at her, smiling at her. It slowly came back to her, the flight from the mining camp, the mudslide, the destruction of the mine sluice, and the havoc the falling logs had produced. And then the rest of it came back to her, lying with Payne in the rain on a bed of pine needles, making love out in the open. She would never forget that night, she knew, terror following terror that had ended in ecstasy.

But the ecstasy had given birth to an offspring of doubt, she reminded herself. Best be wary. Best not expect too much.

"Hello," she replied. She ventured a smile and found him only too willing to return it.

"Notice anything?" he asked.

She nodded. "It's not raining," she said. "I actually think there's sunshine somewhere up there."

He grinned. "Do you think that an omen?"

She shrugged. "I hope so," she whispered.

Or was hope a device only for fools, she asked herself. Perhaps it was wiser not to waste her strength with useless hope.

He moved toward her, lowering his face close to hers, and Aura felt her heart begin to beat faster. She could almost taste his kiss on her lips.

He suddenly pulled away. She could see confusion in his expression.

"What is it?" she asked.

369

"Shh," he insisted, and put his hand on her lips.

And then she heard it, too, sounds in the undergrowth, noises of twigs being snapped and branches moving. Someone or something was out there, moving through the woods, for the sounds were continuing far too long for it to be nothing more than the wind. Whatever was out there, she realized with an unpleasant lurch, wasn't very far away.

"Is it an animal?" she whispered. She remembered his joke the previous night and shuddered. "Not a bear?"

"There aren't any bears around here," he told her, even though he wasn't sure that was so.

He didn't want to frighten her, but he was worried. Either bear or human, whatever was out there might mean trouble, and he was unarmed. His fists were hardly protection against a bear. Nor would they mean much if it was one of Hung Poh's men.

He pushed himself to his knees and reached for the clothing that he had laid out to dry amid the pine needles earlier that morning.

"Maybe Mailee and Wu?" she asked hopefully.

"Maybe," he replied. "You'd better get dressed," he added, as he pulled on his trousers.

She nodded and stirred, then realized she was lying beneath a covering of her petticoat, the fabric decidedly dingy, but actually warm and dry. After all those days of rain, the sunshine seemed almost an alien thing, however grateful she was for it.

"Yes," she agreed, and hurriedly reached for her shift. Her arm was stiff, and it ached, she found, as she lifted the shift over her head.

"Aura," he said as she pulled her head free of the shift, "about last night . . ."

"There's no need to make any explanations," she murmured quickly, cutting him off before he could say

370

anything more, telling herself it was best not to wait for the words that would hurt her. "I don't expect anything—no promises, no pledges. It happened. After everything that went before, I suppose it would have been strange if it hadn't happened."

He sat and stared at her for a second, wondering if he ought to take her words at face value, if they meant that she expected nothing from him or if what she was really saying was that she wanted nothing. It hurt him to think that the latter was true, that what she was really doing was dismissing him, telling him that once they returned to San Francisco, she intended to sever whatever tenuous ties still bound them to one another.

Because the simple truth was, he realized, he had begun to consider the possible ramifications of giving things he had never before thought himself capable of giving, of making offers he'd never before so much as considered making. He hadn't realized it at the time, but it had started when he'd realized she was missing, a feeling of separation that was like a physical wound to him, and a realization that he didn't relish the prospect of a future without her. It pained him to think that he'd made that choice only to find her unwilling to accept what he had decided he was willing to offer.

But there was no time to explore any of that, at least, not now, not with the possibility that there still might be some of Hung Poh's henchmen somewhere nearby in the woods, stalking them. Whoever was thrashing about in the undergrowth wasn't bothering to take the effort to make his approach silent. Maybe he didn't realize they were so close. Maybe he didn't care if they heard him. Or maybe "it" wasn't even human.

The sounds seemed to be growing steadily nearer.

As Aura pulled on her blouse, she watched Payne dress, letting her glance linger on the lean lines of his torso as he bent forward to pull on his boots, the disturbing sight of thick muscle moving beneath the taut covering of flesh. What an incomparably strange thing a man's body is, she thought, as she pulled her skirt over her head, a mysterious and pleasurable thing to look at and to touch.

If only that was all there was to it, she mused, the looking and the touching. But life, it seemed, was never so simple as that, and finding her way through the labyrinth of the masculine mind seemed the most complex thing of all, something that was at that moment completely beyond her. Better to let it all go, she told herself, than try to find something that isn't there. She had memories, and he'd proved that he'd cared enough to come after her, to save her from Chaou Li. She'd have to satisfy herself with what little satisfaction that knowledge brought her, for apparently there would be nothing more.

She turned her attention back to the task of her own clothing, scowling at the torn and bloodstained blouse, at the decidedly dingy skirt. What was she doing here, she wondered, wandering around in the woods, frightened, filthy. This wasn't what she had come to California to find. Nor had she come to have her heart broken.

Payne stood waiting for a moment once he was fully clothed, watching her tie the laces of her still damp shoes.

"Stay here," he whispered. "Don't make any noise."

She turned abruptly and looked up at him.

"You aren't going to leave me here alone?" she gasped.

"I'll be right back," he promised. "Just don't move, and for God's sake, be quiet."

With that, he turned and walked into the undergrowth before she could object any further. Aura watched his near-silent disappearance, wondering if this was just his way of telling her that she must eventually resign herself to abandonment, that she might just as well begin to accept the feeling now. Leaving her alone like this in the woods, was that just a way to let her know that he'd come for her, not out of love, but merely a sense of obligation, an obligation that would be fulfilled once he brought her back to San Francisco? If so, it was a cruel lesson, one she would have preferred to have been spared.

Because being alone in the woods and hearing the sound of movement when she couldn't see who or what was making the noise was frightening her, and each moment that it continued, she grew more and more afraid. She tried to hide herself beneath the pine boughs, huddling under them, hoping that if she was alone when whoever it was out there stumbled across the pine that had sheltered them during the night, she could avoid being seen. She sat with her back against the tree's trunk, with her knees drawn up, hugging them and darting nervous glances into the undergrowth.

And then the noise stopped suddenly. After a moment of complete silence that was broken only by the intermittent cries of a bird perched somewhere in the branches above her, she realized that the absence of the sounds was even more frightening than the noises had been.

"Payne?" she whispered, afraid to cry out and afraid to remain alone much longer. She could think of any number of reasons why the noise had stopped, and none of them was the least bit comforting.

She edged her way out from beneath the shelter of the branches. She ought to go out there and look for him, she told herself. It was better than being caught alone like a frightened rabbit cowering beneath the tree. She began to examine the trodden leafmold and disturbed undergrowth, trying to discover in which direction Payne had gone.

And then there was a loud noise just behind her and she nearly screamed as she swung around.

Payne was standing a half dozen feet from her, grinning at her.

"Didn't frighten you, did I?"

"Yes, you frightened me," she snapped. She was angry, angry that he'd frightened her, angry that he couldn't see that she'd been worried about him and terrified. She stared at a large, dark, shadowy thing that stood behind him, obscured by the undergrowth.

"You'll be happy when I show you what I found," he told her, as he stepped aside and led his horse out of the shadows. "He was the one making all the noise. Must have been scared off when the mudslide started and then decided, once he was safe in the woods, to wait around and find the source of his oats. Anyway, he seems happy enough to see me." He turned and patted the animal's neck. "And believe me, I am delighted to see him. I didn't relish the idea of walking back to San Francisco."

Aura shrugged, aware that her anger would do neither of them any good at the moment, and that what she might vent would probably fall on deaf ears, anyway. She approached the animal. He whinnied when she put her hand on his mane, and then turned and nuzzled her shoulder.

"Meet Remy," Payne told her. "Short for Remington. He and I have been together for a long time."

"How do you do, Remington," Aura said, patting the animal's mane a bit more vigorously to show him that she was pleased to be formally introduced. She giggled softly when Remy pressed his nose from her shoulder to her neck.

"You're lucky he likes you," Payne told her. "Otherwise he might refuse to carry the two of us."

"Two of us," Aura said thoughtfully. She stared at him, evaluating, wondering. "That means you don't intend to look for Wu and Mailee?" she asked.

He arched his brow.

"I know you have your doubts about me, Aura," he said, "but at least give me a little credit."

He looked so genuinely hurt, Aura couldn't help but feel contrite.

"I'm sorry," she murmured.

"Good," he replied. "You should be. Let's get started." He looked up at the sun and the direction of the shadows it cast, trying to orient himself. "We ran into the woods south of the mining camp," he said, as he made his decision. "Unless the sun no longer rises in the East, that means we go this way."

He took her arm and they started off tramping through the woods.

Given the advantage of daylight, it took them less than a quarter of an hour to make their way back to the edge of the camp. Aura couldn't believe how the place had changed. A thick slab of the hillside was gone, with only a dark, rocky scar to show where it had been remaining. The mine shaft had collapsed, and what had been its opening was now indistinguishable from the remainder of the torn piece of hillside. All the cabins were also gone, those that the laborers had inhabited, as well as the one in which Aura and Mailee had been imprisoned. As for the lumber that had once been the sluice and its supporting members, it now lay strewn in the mire at the foot of the hillside, with much of it smashed amidst the rubble of uprooted trees at the clearing's edge.

"My God," Aura whispered, as she surveyed the damages. "I can't believe that rain alone could have done all this."

"Mother Nature is a deceptive creature," he told her. He watched two or three dozen people digging in the mud near where the laborers's cabins had once stood. "Deceptive, and very powerful."

Despite the calmness of his tone, it was obvious that he was shocked as well by the amount of destruction he saw. He took Aura's arm.

"Let's scan the edge of the woods and see if we can find Wu and your pretty little friend," he suggested. "Then we'll come back and see if we can help those poor souls."

Mailee and Wu had been lucky, finding their way out of the path of the falling trees at the clearing's edge to some safety further into the woods, just as Payne and Aura had done. And they, too, had returned to the mining camp in the hopes of locating their missing friends. It didn't take them long to find each other, nor to agree to Payne's suggestion that they offer to help the laborers dig out whatever of their belongings they could from the mud.

It soon became obvious that many of the camp's laborers had been far less lucky than they had been in escaping from the mudslide. The men worked steadily for the next two days, and when finally the rubble of the collapsed cabins had been completely searched, they found that in all, five had died, including one of the women who had come with Aura and Mailee from San Francisco. The sight of the bodies laid out on the ground at the edge of the treeline was a gruesome sight.

No one mentioned the fact that Jack Duran's body was not among those found, nor Chaou Li's. The wagon driver, too, was missing, although no one seemed to know where he might have gone in the storm. By tacit agreement, the cabin at the far edge of the camp was left beneath its layer of mud and rubble, its own gruesome contents remaining undisturbed. It was obvious that none of the workmen had been fond of the mine's overseer; they were all just as glad to be honorably freed of their obligation to him. They wanted nothing more than to bury their own and leave the miserable camp, salvaging what little they could of their belongings and hoping to find some easier way to face the remainder of their lives.

After the first day's digging, Aura and Payne sat together with the others around a smoky fire, exhausted and hardly satisfied by their portion of the three rabbits Payne had managed to catch in the woods. What little food the workers had found in the rubble was mostly spoiled, and they were more than grateful for the offering of meat. Mailee and one of the other women cleaned and cooked the carcasses, turning them into a kind of watery stew which was eventually doled out in meager servings.

If her stomach found little comfort in the arrangement, Aura at least found that Payne seemed only too eager to keep the peace between them. He was thoughtful and excrutiatingly polite with her, an effort Aura knew could not be easy for him. She accommodated him, determined to avoid any unpleasantness with him, frankly admitting to herself that she would sooner spend another night with his arms around her than spend it alone.

At first, she felt awkward about leaving Mailee and

Wu sitting by the fire and simply going off to sleep beside Payne. She hesitated, trying to think of some way to explain to Mailee her relationship with Payne, only to find she could think of no way to explain it to herself. But as for Mailee, she quickly realized that her worries were unfounded.

Much to Aura's surprise, Mailee seemed entirely taken with Wu, and almost awed by what she considered the wealth of courage he'd shown in going to face Chaou Li unarmed. She shyly nodded to Wu by way of invitation as she took up her blanket and moved off to the edge of the treeline. Aura realized she'd never even had the chance to broach the subject before it was settled without need of either her explanations or her reasons.

Early the next morning, Wu's horse wandered into camp, somehow finding its way alone. After that, Aura realized there was no reason, once the work of recovering the bodies was done, to stay on any longer in the camp. It was not a fact that especially pleased her.

At Aura's insistence, before they left, Wu informed the women who remained in the camp that the wife sale was illegal and that they might leave if they chose. At first, they seemed not to believe him, but when he insisted, they told him there was no place for them to go to, and that they had no desire to leave their husbands.

Aura was shocked by their attitude. With Wu translating, she tried to explain that the men who had bought them had no legal hold over them, but the effort was useless. She realized there was no way she could change their minds with regard to the rights they might have or those of the men who'd purchased them. It was painfully clear to her that an argument would not dislodge the beliefs with which they had been inculcated the whole of their lives.

Realizing there was nothing more they could do to help, Payne, Aura, Wu, and Mailee left the camp just as the rites for the dead were beginning. Aura left with mixed feelings. As eager as she was to be away from a place that had been nothing but a scene of unpleasantness for her, she was equally filled with trepidation about returning to San Francisco and what that would mean as far as Payne was concerned. She knew that once they returned, there would be an end to the quiet accord that had established itself between them, and she was sure the change would be for the worse.

Payne didn't notice her disquiet as they set out, for he had disturbing thoughts of his own to contemplate. Once they were back in San Francisco, he would have to deal with Hung Poh, and that, he knew, would be a far from simple matter, one hardly without dangers of its own.

Chapter Twenty

Aura leaned her head against the back of the tub, closed her eyes and inhaled the sweet scent of the bubbles mixed with the warm steam. It was a lovely, languorous feeling to lie there in the hot tub. Until that moment, she'd never before considered just how great a luxury a hot bath might be, but after having gone without one for longer than she wanted to think about, she found she'd gained a new appreciation for what had always been something she'd taken for granted.

In fact, she realized that there were a great number of things she'd always taken for granted—sufficient food, clean, dry clothing, the opportunity to laze as she now was in a tub filled with hot, scented water—things that she now realized much of the world's population would never have. She would, she told herself, never look at those things quite the same way ever again.

She sighed and let herself go completely limp. It might be pleasant, she decided, not to move, to simply stay as she was, for about a month.

"Now, that's about the most enticing thing I've seen in I don't know how long."

She opened her eyes and looked up to find Payne

standing beside the tub. He stared down at her and smiled.

"Hmmm," she agreed. "I can't even remember the last time I had a long soak. This must be what it's like in heaven."

"It wasn't the bath that I was talking about," he told her. His smile took on a decidedly lecherous cast. "The enticement isn't the water," he said as he knelt down, leaned forward to her, and planted a kiss on her lips. "It's what's in it."

Aura smiled tentatively and lifted a sudsy hand to his chin. He'd been so gentle and sweet to her during those long last days in the mining camp and on the ride back to San Francisco. More than once she'd found herself daydreaming about what it would be like to go on endlessly spending her days with him, wondering if it could possibly go on like this forever. And that, she knew, was a mistake. She'd let herself begin to count on the gentle concern he was being so careful to show her; she'd let herself fall into the folly of counting on him. But deep inside she knew all of it was about to come to an end, and worse, she knew she wasn't ready to face the fact.

"You could explore both," she offered with a slow smile, trying to postpone the inevitable by pretending it wouldn't come. "There's room for two in here. That is, two who happen to be very close friends."

She looked up at his eyes, wondering if that is what they might possibly have become, very close friends. More likely, she warned herself, they were still what they'd always been, strangers thrown together by circumstance, never destined to be anything more.

He was scanning the surface of the bubbles, or more probably, she thought, the outline of her body just beneath it. And for a moment, she thought he was about to accept her offer. She felt a shiver of excitement begin to rise inside her, a physical ache of anticipation that she'd found herself feeling whenever he was near her now.

But Payne disappointed her. Instead of gleefully joining her, he reluctantly shook his head and slowly wiped away the trail of suds her fingers had left on his chin.

"However regretfully, I'm afraid I must decline," he told her softly. "I have to go out for a while. I just came to tell you that while I'm gone, I want you to keep the shades drawn and the lights low. And whatever you do, don't open the door to anyone."

She raised an arch brow. "We're prisoners here?" she asked.

"Of course not," he told her. "But we both know that you won't be safe until Hung Poh is behind bars. So I don't want you to advertise the fact that you're here."

He stared at her face, watching her expression grow more and more withdrawn. They'd talked about it before, about how her testimony would put Hung Poh in jail on charges of kidnapping in the event he'd taken the cautious road after Payne's visit to the opium parlor and removed the evidence of the counterfeiting. He'd promised to try to keep her uninvolved if possible, but if the printing press had been made to disappear and there was no other proof to be found against Hung Poh, it would be left to Aura to testify. Payne knew she was willing, but not exactly happy at the prospect. He couldn't say that he blamed her.

"What are the chances that he's left the press?" she asked, even though she was well aware that he knew as little as she did. There had been little else he'd thought or spoken about during the long ride back to San Francisco.

He shrugged. "About even, I'd say. It's been more

than a week since I was there. He'd have expected something to happen right away, that day or the next. Or else, if Wu's suspicions are right, he might just count on his relationship with Sheriff Dougherty to protect him. I think there's a reasonable chance he thinks he's safe and has returned to business as usual."

"And he'll feel safe as long as he doesn't know there's someone in San Francisco who can accuse him of kidnapping and white slavery?"

Payne nodded. "That's why we don't go to the sheriff now and chance warning him off. We wait for the federal marshal to come."

"And in the meantime, I hide."

"And in the meantime, you hide," he agreed.

"And hope he doesn't find out what happened up in that mining camp."

He shrugged. "That's unlikely, Aura. At worst, he'd wait until Chaou Li was sufficiently overdue returning, and then send someone to find out what happened. Even then, he can't know that you escaped that mudslide."

"So I hide until the marshall arrives," she murmured.

He nodded. "Just a day or two more. Not long."

She was quietly thoughtful for a moment. It wasn't quite all over, she told herself. There's still a day or two left before the marshal arrives. It hardly seemed fair that she could have him only as long as the threat of Hung Poh remained. He would stay to protect her as long as she was in danger, but when the threat was gone, he would be, too.

"Where are you going?" she asked.

"To the Wells Fargo office," he replied. "I have a few arrangements to make."

"Will you be gone long?" she asked, begrudging every moment stolen from her by his precious job.

"I'll try not to," he assured her. "But the sooner I can arrange to get a federal marshal here and into that opium parlor, the better chance there is of catching Hung Poh with some real proof of the counterfeiting and the sooner all this will be over and done with."

"Yes," she murmured softly, her tone edged with real sadness, "the counterfeiting."

"That's why they sent me out here in the first place," he reminded her.

"Yes," she said, "I remember."

That was what really mattered to him, she told herself, catching his precious counterfeiters for his masters at Wells Fargo. An ache of regret and hurt had long since replaced the heady surge of anticipation. Now all she felt was lost—and the anticipation of being alone. She told herself she'd faced the prospect of being alone before, when Whit was killed, but she knew that this was not the same. As much as she'd liked Whit, she hadn't loved him. But she did love Payne. From the moment she'd seen him on the wharf, her life had become tangled with his, and nothing could change that. When it was over, when he left, she knew part of her would wither and die.

"Remember," he told her, "keep the place as dark and quiet as you can. We don't want it to be obvious that you've returned here."

She turned away, making a great show of searching for her washcloth among the soap bubbles, taking pains not to let him see the tears of disappointment that had sprung unbidden to her eyes.

"I'll remember," she assured him, in a voice so tight her throat felt as though it would crack.

Payne misunderstood the hurt he heard in her voice. He leaned forward to her once more and put his hand on her arm. It was sleek with the soap bubbles, and soft to his fingers, smooth and supple. He felt a stirring in his groin that made him wish he had the leisure to pursue her offer to share her bath. But when she refused to turn and look at him, the passion began to ebb.

"It won't be for long," he assured her. "A day or two of keeping out of sight, and then the federal marshal should be here. With any luck, it'll all be over as far as your involvement is concerned. Once Hung Poh is in jail, there won't be any reason for you to be afraid."

Just as there won't be any reason for you to stay, she thought miserably.

"I'll be fine," she assured him, still determinedly staring into the soap bubbles.

"Are you sure?" he asked. "You seem worried."

"I'm sure," she insisted.

But she wasn't, and he could see it.

"What is it, Aura?" he asked her softly. "Tell me. Let me help."

Aura felt a lump fill her throat, and tried to swallow it. Why was he doing this, she wondered, why try to make her admit she loved him when it would all be over as soon as he had Hung Poh arrested? Why couldn't he just let go and leave her with a bit of her dignity intact?

She swallowed a second time, and shook her head.

"There's nothing to tell," she insisted. "Nothing that needs help."

What was it, he wondered, why, when he seemed about to come close, did she draw back? It was becoming more and more obvious to him that, for whatever reason, she was building a wall around herself and shutting him out. Since the mining camp, she'd let him make love to her, but she seemed otherwise determined to keep him shut out. Part of him told him he ought to be relieved that she was asking nothing of him, but instead that fact pained him more than he'd have thought possible.

And the reason it pained him was quite simply that he'd come to the realization that he wanted her. She was, he realized, the first thing he'd ever really wanted in his life, wanted enough to make him reevaluate what had always been the givens of his existence. But now the need to remain without ties, the thirst for the uncertainty that gave his existence its savor, those things no longer seemed quite as necessary as they once had. He had no idea how she'd done it, but she'd managed to completely uproot his life.

The only problem was, he wasn't at all sure, now that he'd decided that he was willing to change his life in exchange for one with her, that she wanted him. In fact, despite the effort she seemed to be taking to keep the peace between them, she had let him know in countless ways, just as she was doing now, that there was a wall between them. Worse, he didn't know if he'd ever be able to scale that wall. Had she ruined his old life for him, he wondered, only to turn away and deny him what he needed for a new life? He'd never before had problems with a woman. How had he managed to fall in love with one who seemed to be constantly telling him that she didn't want him as a permanent part of her life?

He was silent for a moment, staring at her profile, trying to wish her to turn and face him, but unwilling to force her in any way. Finally, when it was clear that she had no intention of either unburdening herself to him or even turning to meet his gaze, he gave up. He removed his hand from her arm and straightened himself.

"Remember to stay away from the windows," he told her, "and tell Wu if you see or hear anything suspicious. I'll be back as soon as I can."

"We'll all wait up," she murmured, still intent on her search for the missing washcloth.

He stared at her a moment longer, then gritted his teeth and turned away. As he closed the door behind him, he told himself that dealing with Hung Poh might very well prove to be less difficult than dealing with Aura Randall.

"The federal marshal can be here by tomorrow afternoon. But I still don't understand why you need him. Why can't you just go to the local police?"

Payne clenched his jaw, but forced himself to control his anger. He eyed the stuffy little man sitting across the desk from him, one Richard Beal by name, with his starched shirtfront, fussy bowtie, and the spectacles that covered his rather beady dark eyes. He'd grudgingly done as Payne had told him, sending the wire to the authorities at Camp Roberts in the south and duly waiting for a response. But it was only too clear that he didn't approve of having to give up what had previously been his exclusive authority of the Wells Fargo office to the special investigator from the East, and he didn't have either the tact or the intelligence to keep his displeasure to himself.

Payne had to remind himself that Beal, after all, was little more than a glorified banking clerk, someone who knew how to count money and weigh gold dust. He was hopefully honest enough to keep fair and honest records of those transactions he made, and to dutifully forward it all to the head office of Wells Fargo in New York. Looking for any real help from him in a matter that dealt with something other than ledgers and measures, however, was beyond any rational expectation.

"The local police aren't equipped to handle this sort

of thing," Payne told him, keeping to himself Wu's suspicions that James Dougherty, sheriff or not, was in the pay of Hung Poh. "Besides, this is really a federal matter. The marshal would have to be called here in any case."

Beal scowled, but seemed, however grudgingly, willing to accept the explanation.

"I suppose you know what you're doing," he said, his tone suggesting that perhaps he didn't quite believe what he was saying.

Payne narrowed his eyes and smiled unpleasantly. But then he almost laughed out loud when he saw Beal's expression become frightened in reaction to his own. The little man obviously interpreted his displeasure as an outright threat.

"That's why they sent me here," he said. "Just remember to keep to yourself everything that's happened. We don't want any idle gossip getting back to our counterfeiters."

"And you're not going to tell me who these people are?" Beal pressed.

Payne shook his head.

"It's for your own good, Beal," he said. "You really don't want to know too much about this business. These men have already committed one murder that I know of. I wouldn't be surprised if there were more. The less you know about them, the safer you'll be."

That, at least, seemed to make an impression. Having a healthy interest in his own continued existence, Beal finally began to lose the edge of both his curiosity and his injured ego. He nodded.

"Yes, yes, of course," he murmured.

"I'll be here at noon tomorrow to meet the marshal," Payne told him. "If you need to get in touch with me before then, you can leave a message at the desk of the Palmer House."

It seemed a rational ruse, he thought. If Beal slipped and some unpleasant friends of Hung Poh came looking for him at the Palmer House, they'd come up empty. He'd stop there on his way back to the store and make arrangements with the desk clerk to take messages for him.

"You're staying at the Palmer House?"

Beal seemed bewildered by the thought that someone who worked for the same company that employed him at less than extravagant wages would allow such an outrageous outflow of expenses. A room for a single night at the Palmer House would cost more than he earned in a week.

Payne pushed himself out of the chair. He was tired, he realized, and just about every muscle in his body ached. He told himself that he was getting a little old for the sort of life that kept him in the saddle for days at a time, for the sort of life that required the frequent use of his fists. He'd already left behind that time in his life when those things had seemed adventurous.

As much as it pained him to realize it, maturity had begun to cast a dim shadow on such exploits, turning the adventure into drudgery and making the picaresque begin to seem little more than merely crude. At best, he realized, his life was rootless and rough; at worst it was beginning to seem meaningless and empty. Perhaps giving it up wouldn't be that great a sacrifice after all. He certainly wouldn't regret giving up the necessity of dealing with men like Richard Beal.

Funny, he thought, he'd never really considered his existence in those terms before. There had been times of late when he'd been discontented, certainly, but he'd never really thought seriously of changing things. Since he'd come to San Francisco to look into this counterfeiting matter, however, his thoughts seemed to keep drifting in directions he really didn't want them to go.

And the reason he didn't want them to travel where they seemed determined to go, he knew, was because they always ended with Aura. He thought about her now, his mind drifting to the way she'd looked in her tub, surrounded by a cloud of bubbles, a slight mist of steam rising into the air around her. He realized that in the back of his mind he hadn't stopped thinking about her invitation since he'd left her, nor stopped regretting that he hadn't accepted it.

Once this matter with Hung Poh was settled, he told himself, he'd get through to her, find out what was bothering her, make her realize that she needed him as much as he needed her. Because she *did* need him, he told himself. He couldn't feel as he did about her if she didn't love him.

But just now, he told himself, his job ought to be the object of his attention, not Aura. If he didn't keep his wits about him, he'd lose the small advantage he had, and if he did, Hung Poh would slip through his fingers. Finish the job, he told himself . . . once that's done, there'll be time to try to find the key to the enigma of Aurora Statler Randall.

"Just leave a message at the desk," he told Beal, evading the little man's question.

No need to let him know anything he didn't need to know, Payne decided. He realized Beal was hardly a man versed in the sort of discretion his own life demanded.

"Then I'll expect you at noon?" Beal called after him, as he started for the door.

Payne nodded.

"At noon," he said. "And then the fireworks will start."

"So soon?" Aura asked. "Tomorrow afternoon?"

Payne was startled by what seemed to be a hint of regret in her tone. He'd thought she'd be delighted to learn that by the next day she'd finally be free of Hung Poh.

"That's what the marshal wired," he replied. "Apparently, it's not so bad a ride from Camp Roberts, and presumably he's already received orders from back East to offer whatever cooperation is required. He'll be here with a dozen soldiers from the fort. It'll all be over before Hung Poh knows what's happening." He swallowed the remainder of the whiskey in his glass. At least, he hoped it would be over that easily. Experience had long ago taught him things were rarely that simple. He looked back at Aura, then at Wu and Mailee, who were sitting together by the fireplace. "So by this time tomorrow you'll all be free. No more hiding, pretending no one's in the house." He smiled at Wu. "You can begin to lead a normal life."

"None too soon," Wu grumbled.

Mailee glanced at Wu and blushed, and Payne could practically read her thoughts, that she was quite ready for a life as Mrs. Yang Wu. It seemed strange to him how quickly she and Wu had reached what to him had been the hardest decision in his life. But maybe that's the way it ought to be, he told himself. Maybe if it had been like that with him and Aura, there wouldn't still be the distance between the two of them, and the questions.

He turned his glance to Aura, wishing he could read her thoughts as easily as he seemed to be able to read Mailee's. She'd been watching him, he realized, and there was something dark going on in her thoughts,

391

but for the life of him he couldn't think what they might be.

Perhaps she wasn't thinking about him at all, he mused. Perhaps she was thinking about getting back to the life she'd begun to establish when Hung Poh had had her abducted. After all, she'd told him then quite pointedly she didn't need him. Perhaps she was just thinking about going back to running the store. Perhaps she was thinking about Howard Crofton.

Odd, he thought, how he kept running into the lawyer. He'd stopped by the Palmer House on his way from the Wells Fargo office to ask the desk clerk to hold any messages for him, and just as he was leaving he'd found himself face-to-face with Crofton, just as he had been after his sojourn to Hung Poh's opium parlor. Payne had been confused by the meaning of the look Crofton had given him as he'd asked to be remembered to Aura. An oddly knowing look, he'd thought, or perhaps it had been nothing more than sly and mean.

Or maybe, Payne told himself, he had simply been seeing things that weren't there. Maybe it was just jealousy that had gotten in his way, just as it was now. He ought to forget about Crofton, he told himself. Certainly Aura hadn't mentioned him. Perhaps he was looking for reasons to explain things he couldn't understand about her and was finding them in places where there was really nothing to be found.

Forget about Crofton, he told himself. At least for now, forget about him.

Instead, he looked at Aura and said, "I ran into Whit's lawyer. He asked to be remembered."

Whatever response he'd expected from her, it wasn't the absent surprise the news elicited.

"Really?" she said. "I'd forgotten about him." She shrugged. "But I'd think he would be angry with me."

That confused him.

"Angry?"

She nodded. "He stopped by just before I closed the store the day Hung Poh's men came for me," she replied. "He offered to take me to dinner the following evening, and I all but accepted his invitation."

Now, *that* was strange, Payne thought. Crofton hadn't mentioned that he'd expected to see her either time he'd run into him. Nor that he'd been left waiting for an engagement with her to which she'd never appeared. Not that a man with Crofton's ego would be likely to admit such a humiliation. Still, it was strange.

But what interested him more at the moment was the fact that Aura seemed completely disinterested in continued conversation regarding the lawyer.

"If you'd like, I'd be glad to heat some water for your bath," she offered.

Payne smiled. That was a hint he couldn't ignore. He put the empty glass down on the table and stood. He'd think about Crofton later, he told himself. For now, he had more interesting prospects in mind.

"And I'll admit it's decidedly overdue," he agreed. "I'll excuse myself, if no one objects."

"Oh, no one objects," Aura told him dryly, her expression adding that a shave and change of clothing wouldn't be inappropriate either, while he was about it. She pushed herself to her feet and started for the kitchen.

Payne grinned. He was, he knew, decidedly rank. He was surprised that she hadn't simply come out and told him bluntly to bathe if he planned to sleep in her bed that evening.

And he decided that he definitely did plan to sleep in her bed that night. He planned to make love to her, to try and show her how he felt if she refused to talk

393

about it. One way or another, he was determined to get through to her.

He didn't take his eyes off her until she'd disappeared into the kitchen, then he started for the bathroom, purposely ignoring Wu's low chuckle and Mailee's blushing smile.

The door opened and Payne turned to watch Aura slip into the room. She was carrying a steaming bucket.

"Planning to burn me clean, are you?" he laughed.

"If necessary," she told him.

"Close the door behind you," he said. "Don't want to let out all the heat."

She kicked the door closed behind her and approached the tub, aware of the way he was watching her, wondering if it was passion or simply lust she saw in his eyes, then wondering why she bothered to hope for anything more.

She set the bucket down on the floor beside the tub.

"I don't suppose you'd consider trying a bit of elbow grease before you resort to scalding?" he asked. He held out the scrub brush. "I'm getting too old and rickety to reach my back. And I do deserve it. I did save you from Chaou Li, after all."

She scowled, then laughed and began to roll up the sleeves of her blouse.

"I suppose I shouldn't have expected any less. But I guess you do deserve it."

He grinned, then leaned forward as she knelt beside the tub and took the offered brush. He sighed with pleasure as she slowly ran the soft bristles over his back.

"A little higher," he said.

"You certainly are demanding," she told him

primly, as she moved the brush upward. "I thought the object here was to get you clean, not to satisfy your every little whim."

He turned and found her eyes with his. Aura had no idea why, but those blue eyes of his had somehow found the means to mesmerize her. She froze. His glance held her, as if it had the ability to sap away whatever it was that controlled her independent movement.

"I don't remember discussing the matter of my every little whim," he told her softly. "But as you mention it . . ."

He put his hand on her arm and pulled her to him. His eyes still holding hers, he slipped his arms around her, his hands wet and warm against her back. Aura felt as though she was falling, and when his lips found hers, she knew, in a way, she was right.

Only this one last night, she told herself, as she felt the now familiar fire begin to rise within her. One more night with him and then the marshal will come and Hung Poh will be arrested and Payne's job will be done. And then he'll be gone, back to New York and his job and whatever else waits for him there.

Only one more night.

She began to kick off her shoes even before his lips left hers.

He was kissing her neck as he unfastened the buttons of her blouse, and she began to pull frantically at those of her skirt, hardly noticing when one popped and struck the wall. Reluctantly she pulled away from him, quickly shrugging out of the blouse and stepping out of the skirt, leaving it lying, a dark circle, on the floor. Heedless, she climbed into the tub.

He leaned back and reached up to her waist as she stepped in, holding her over him for a moment and staring at her before he pulled her down to him. He kissed her belly and her breasts, then pulled away the now wet shift and dropped it on the floor beside the tub. Aura threw her head back and lowered herself to him.

It was a sweetly aching pleasure to come to him like this, to feel the heat of him inside her and the hot water swirling around them. He put his fingers into her hair, pushing away the pins, freeing it to tumble onto her shoulders. She put her hands behind his neck and pulled him to her, losing herself to the feel of his lips on her breasts.

What had become of her, she wondered. How had she let herself become so wanton, so shameless? Never would the creature she'd been in Fall River have even considered doing what she was doing now. That woman would have been shocked at her thoughts, at her actions. And she would never have understood the need that seemed to drive her now, or the simple fact that she liked what he did to her, liked how it made her feel.

For there was no denying that she did like it when he touched her this way, that she dreamed of how it felt when her body welcomed his. If there had been any thought that he might stay, any possibility that it would last more than another day, she might excuse what she did now. But there was no excuse, except for the fact that she wanted him, and that this night would be her last.

One last night, the words kept repeating themselves over and over inside her head, one last night. She told herself that if she was to have nothing more, she would make this night last forever.

Chapter Twenty-One

Payne climbed out of the first of the two nondescript black carriages that had drawn to a halt in the street in front of Madame Charlotte's. A short distance away, Aura peered out from behind the hedgerow where she'd been trying to keep out of sight for the previous half hour. She'd begun to wonder if he might not appear and was starting to feel as though every eye in San Francisco was being leveled in her direction.

She breathed a sigh of relief when she saw Payne appear, stepping out from behind the hedgerow and moving quickly toward the carriage. She realized she'd grown tense and nervous in the time she'd been waiting for him and the marshal to arrive. But now that he was there, she found herself wondering how he would greet her sudden and unexpected appearance.

She realized she was right to be concerned. He stared at her for an instant with a totally blank expression, as if he didn't recognize her. It quickly changed, however. Aura didn't need to be clairvoyant to see that, much as she'd feared, he wasn't the least happy to see her.

"What the hell are you doing here?" he hissed.

The truth was, she realized as she watched the marshal and the dozen soldiers begin to climb out of the carriages, she didn't have any rational answer for that question. She really had no idea why she'd felt she had to be there, what had driven her to come to see it to an end. She'd even argued with herself after he'd left to meet the marshal at the Wells Fargo office, telling herself that a sane woman in her position would want to forget the whole mess, not pursue it to the end.

Despite the argument, however, she hadn't been able to convince herself to simply sit by the fire and wait for word that Hung Poh had been arrested. She found she had to be there to see it herself.

She glanced nervously at the hedgerow behind her, then back at Payne.

"I'm waiting for you," she told him.

"I told Wu to watch you," he said.

To guard me, she thought, not watch me; to act as my jailer. Perhaps that's what's driven me here, the feeling that I've been the prisoner, the need to know that I will finally be free.

"I told him I was tired and intended to take a nap," she told him, "and then I sneaked out."

Until that moment, she had been rather proud of her own deviousness. Not that the subterfuge had been all that difficult. Confident that the danger was past, both Wu and Mailee had begun busily planning what they hoped would be a far more pleasant phase of their lives. Aura had needed only to leave them alone together for a few minutes before they were completely oblivious to the world around them and then made her escape.

"Well, you can just sneak right back," Payne ordered.

It didn't take more than a glance at his face for her to see that he hadn't the patience for this sort of thing just now. She'd seen that expression before, and knew that he didn't want to have to think about her at the moment, that she was more annoyance to him than anything else.

Still, she refused to be cowed by his obvious displeasure. After all she'd been through, she had as much right to be there as he did.

"I'm as much a part of this as you are," she told him. "You can't send me away."

"I'm damned if I can't," he told her. "This is no place for a woman."

"That mining camp was no place for a woman," she snapped in reply. She was beginning to feel her own anger, and didn't care if she showed it. "This, on the other hand, is a whorehouse, and unless I've been sorely deceived, that makes it decidedly a place for a woman. For many women."

"Right you are, ma'am." A tall, uniformed man had exited the carriage behind Payne and now was standing at his side. The officer grinned genially, his tanned, moustachioed face, unlike Payne's, showing nothing more ominous than simple good humor. "It is a place for women, certainly, but not for a lady like yourself."

Aura nodded and returned his smile.

"You're very kind, Officer . . ."

"Marshall Craig Gates, ma'am," he said, willingly supplying the name and accompanying it with another smile.

Payne scowled, then grudgingly completed the introduction. "Gates, this is my brother's widow, Mrs. Aura Randall."

"A great pleasure, Mrs. Randall," Gates said, as he took Aura's hand. It was apparent from his expression that he wasn't merely being polite.

"You're very kind, Marshall Gates," Aura replied.

"Now," Payne fumed, staring pointedly at her hand until Gates dropped it, "if we're done with the social amenities, you can run along home, Aura."

399

She shook her head.

"I'm not going anywhere," she insisted.

"This really isn't any place for a lady, Mrs. Randall," Gates interjected.

"You don't understand, Marshall," she returned. "The man you're about to arrest had me kidnapped."

"I'm aware of that fact, Mrs. Randall," he told her.

"Then you ought to understand why I feel that I must see this through to the finish," she said.

He shrugged, apparently unwilling to take a side. After all, handsome young widows were rare in this part of the world, and he was not one to turn his back on an unexpected opportunity.

"Besides," Aura added, turning to Payne, "if he's gotten rid of the press, then you'll need me to press charges."

As soon as she mouthed the words, she knew she didn't want to think about that, knew she didn't want to consider what it would mean to her to have to testify at a trial and relive the whole horrible episode. She silently prayed that there wouldn't be any need.

Payne gritted his teeth. He was beginning to get an uncomfortable feeling that he was losing control, and he didn't like it in the least. He grabbed her arm and pulled her a few steps away from Gates and the others.

"This could be dangerous, Aura," he told her.

She stared at him, wide-eyed and ingenuous.

"Dangerous?" she countered. "This morning you said it would be a simple matter of walking in, finding the press, and arresting Hung Poh. He goes to jail, I go back to running Whit's store, and you go back to New York." There, she thought, she'd said it. Odd, that she'd simply blurted it out that way. Now that she'd said it out loud, it seemed to be closer, a little more real. She wished she could take back the words but knew that was impossible. She swallowed, feeling awkward and hurt as she fought to keep herself focused. "How can that be dangerous?"

Payne stared at her, surprised by what she'd said, wondering if she had finally told him what it was that had been bothering her.

"Aura . . ." he started.

"Please, Payne," she interrupted. "I have to see it. I have to know it's over." She stared at him, her expression becoming set and obstinate. "I don't intend to be sent away," she told him.

"Mr. Randall," Gates broke in. "I don't want to tell you your business, but we're going to cause a stir if we stand here much longer. And what the lady said makes sense: we may very well need her."

Payne scowled, but nodded. The marshal was right.

"I don't like this," he told Aura, but he realized there was little he could do about changing things. He certainly didn't stand much of a chance of arguing her into changing her mind. If he put her in one of the carriages and told her to stay there, he had no doubt but that she'd simply ignore his orders and follow. All in all, he decided, it would be better to have her where he could keep his eye on her. "Stay to the rear, with the soldiers," he ordered, with enough force to ensure that she'd comply, at least for the time being. He turned to Gates. "All right, this way."

They started forward, Payne directing four of the soldiers to the rear of the house, to the stables, to keep watch for any of Hung Poh's men who tried to escape that way. Once they'd disappeared around the corner of the house, he led the rest of the group directly to the front door.

It opened before Payne had the chance to knock. Payne was taken aback to see Howard Crofton step outside. Behind him, Madame Charlotte's black doorman stood gaping at the group of uniformed men. It was clear that he was far more accustomed to greeting men, including men in uniform, coming to the house for entirely unofficial purposes. The sight of armed, uniformed men with set and determined expressions on their faces staring back at him was obviously unsettling to him.

Crofton, on the other hand, was entirely unruffled by the experience. The lawyer smiled at Payne almost as if he had expected to see him there. He almost seemed amused, as if he was enjoying Payne's look of surprise.

"Randall," he said, offering his hand, then quickly dropping it when it was clear that Payne had no intention of taking it. He smiled again, a wide, jovial smile, as though he'd just heard a very good joke. "Odd, how we keep running into each other in the city's best social spots, don't you think?"

He glanced at the group of soldiers assembled behind Payne, his smile remaining firmly intact until he caught a glimpse of Aura standing toward the rear. It disappeared then, and he paled perceptibly.

Payne raised a brow at the change, wondering what had caused it.

"Is this one of the city's best social spots, Crofton?" he asked, as he watched Crofton's face. "Odd that a busy attorney like yourself has time for that sort of thing in the middle of the afternoon."

But Crofton had turned suddenly deaf to what Payne said. Ignoring Payne, who turned and watched him, he edged his way through the group of soldiers to where Aura was standing.

"Aura?" he muttered. He was clearly agitated by the sight of her, and equally confused.

"Hello, Howard," she replied.

She glanced at the front door to Madame Charlotte's house and swallowed awkwardly. She thought back to the evening when he'd called on her, just before she'd closed the store, to the way she'd tried to convince herself that he might prove to be adequate material as a husband. All that seemed totally distant now, and childishly shallow. The last thing she'd ever want in her life was a man like Howard Crofton, she realized. In fact, she knew there was only one man who could ever make her happy.

She took a step back from Crofton, trying to separate herself from both him and the circumstances of their meeting. "This is a coincidence, isn't it?"

"What are you doing here?" he demanded.

She shrugged. "Business," she murmured. She looked down at the leather case he was carrying. From the way he held it, it was clearly heavy. "You, too?" she asked, politely offering him a reason to explain his presence.

He swallowed, and shifted the case from his right hand to his left.

"Yes," he replied, "business." He stared at her for a moment more, as though he was assuring himself that what he saw was real. Whatever his confusion, however, that moment was all he needed. He quickly collected himself. He smiled. "Well," he said, "I'm afraid I must be going. I expect we'll see one another again soon."

With that, he touched his hand to the brim of his hat and started briskly off. Aura watched him for a moment, then turned to Payne.

He was watching her and smiling, a bit smugly, she thought. Crofton's appearance seemed to amuse him more than anything else, and from what she could see, he was delighted that she had been there to be witness to it.

"I suggest we get on with this," Gates said, as he moved to the door. He pulled a paper from his breast pocket and held it up to the doorman. "I am a federal marshal," he said, his tone briskly official, "and I have a warrant to search the premises. Stand aside."

"It was turning out twenty-dollar bills," Payne fumed. He pointed to one of the racks used to dry the printed sheets. "Look," he said, "smudges of green ink." He touched his fingers to one of the dark green spots and took it away stained. "It's still wet."

Marshal Gates nodded and frowned. "Unfortunately, I can't arrest him for the color of ink he uses." He lifted one of the damp sheets lying across the rack and stared at it in obvious confusion. It was covered in what were, to him, rows of completely meaningless characters.

Payne was beginning to feel like a fool. He'd been so certain when he'd led Gates into the room and found the press still there, just as it was when he'd been there before. But the certainty was gone now, and so was the elation that had accompanied it. He turned to glance at Hung Poh and swore under his breath.

Hung Poh was clearly amused by their conversation. And there was little question but that he was pleased by the predicament in which Payne now found himself.

"If you gentlemen pardon," he murmured with studied servility, "may inquire as to nature of search? Printing press used to make paper for Chinese community. Print news, much of interest. If gentlemen wish, would be most pleased to translate."

Payne glowered at him. Hung Poh was making a fool of him, and he knew it. Worse, he was enjoying his little act. He was exaggerating his accent, trying to impress Gates with the pretense of being an innocent, servile foreigner. The fact was, Payne knew, the last thing the man was was servile, and his act was far from

404

innocent. But to all appearances, Hung Poh was nothing more than an enterprising member of San Francisco's hardworking Chinese community. He had chosen the most convincing means possible of turning his press into a harmless enterprise, and he knew it.

"I don't suppose you'd care to explain why you tried to have me killed the last time I wandered in here?" Payne demanded.

Hung Poh tilted his head and stared at him in apparent confusion.

"Surely gentleman is mistaken," he said, his manner almost apologetic. "I fear I have never before made his acquaintance."

"No, of course not," Payne muttered.

He ought to have expected this. After all, it was his word against Hung Poh's with regard to their previous little fracas, just as there was nothing more than his word about the printing press. He had no physical proof that the press had been used to counterfeit greenbacks, and no witness to back him up. If only the plates for the twenty-dollar bills had still been in the press. But he ought to have known it couldn't be that simple.

Payne turned to Gates.

"No sign of the plates?" he asked.

Gates shook his head. "My men have been over the place with a fine-toothed comb. There's nothing here we can prosecute with," he told Payne.

"The opium?" Payne insisted.

Gates shrugged. "The bags don't have the tax stamps, but if he agrees to pay the duty . . ." He shook his head and shrugged again.

Payne realized he was grasping at straws. This was San Francisco, after all, not New York or Boston. Expecting import duties to be scrupulously paid and tax stamps to be affixed to every item the law pre-scribed was not only foolish, it was naive.

"Then we have no choice," Payne said.

"I'm afraid not," Gates agreed. He could see how reluctant Payne was, and he entirely understood that reticence. If everything he'd heard about Hung Poh was true, turning Aura into a prosecution witness was the same as turning her into a target. But as Payne said, they no longer had any choice. Gates motioned to one of the soldiers. "Bring in the young lady," he ordered.

For the first time Hung Poh's imperturbable man-ner faltered. His expression began to show signs of concern.

"Young lady?" he asked.

Gates ignored him, instead walking past him to the door and waiting for Aura to be brought to him. He watched her as the soldier led her along the corridor, listened to the rhythmic sound of her heels against the stone underfoot. Her expression was fixed, but she kept staring around her as though she was looking for a guidepost, for something familiar.

"I'm afraid we'll have to bring you into this after all," he told her, when she was finally standing in front of him.

She looked up at him and nodded silently. He could see the concern in her eyes, and the fear. But she seemed resigned, and when he stood aside for her, she stepped into the room.

She stood for a moment, feeling a surge of revenge fill her as she saw Hung Poh's face grow pale. The confidence in his expression leaked away as she eyed him. It was clear that he hadn't considered the possi-bility that she might ever return to San Francisco, that she ever might be in a position to threaten him.

Gates moved to her side.

"Do you recognize this man, Mrs. Randall?" he asked.

She nodded. "Yes," she replied. "That is the man who had me kidnapped." She glanced around the room, eyeing the walls, the press, and the other printing paraphernalia. She closed her eyes for a moment, remembering, letting herself feel the atmosphere of the place. It was well lit now, but she saw there was a lantern hanging from the ceiling in the center of the room, and there was something familiar about the scent, a mixture of opium smoke touched with the odor of printers ink. She remembered this room, she told herself, she remembered it as well as she remembered Hung Poh. She turned back to Gates. "They brought me here," she said, "to this place, and he questioned me about my husband and about a paper I'd found in one of Whit's ledgers. After that, he had me locked up in some storeroom at the other end of the corridor. The next day he sent me north, to be sold in what I was told was a wife auction."

"Thank you, Mrs. Randall," Gates said. He motioned to two of the soldiers and then faced Hung Poh and smiled.

"This woman is mistaken," Hung Poh sputtered, as the two soldiers took hold of his arms.

Gates ignored him.

"Hung Poh," he said, "you are under arrest for the crimes of kidnapping and illegal imprisonment."

The soldiers marshaled Hung Poh to the door. As he was led past Aura, he turned to her, and his eyes glowed with hatred. She backed away from him, remembering now the fear he'd instilled in her the first time she'd seen him. It was beginning to return now, a dull, chill feeling that settled uncomfortably into her belly. She stared after him as he was led away.

"You don't have be afraid of him, Aura," Payne

told her. He'd moved to her side, and now he put his arm around her waist. "It's all over. He can't hurt you any more."

"Can't he?" she asked.

"We won't let him," Gates assured her.

She shook her head. "It's not over," she told him, the calm of her tone belying the dread that was beginning to fill her. "There's still a trial to be faced, and all the unpleasantness that will go along with it. And there's no way you can make me believe Hung Poh will simply sit silently by and let me send him to jail."

She darted a glance at Payne, then at Gates. She didn't need to see them avoid her eyes to know that she was right. If Hung Poh had been anxious to be rid of her before, now he would stop at nothing to see her dead.

Neither Gates nor Payne said a word. She was right, and they both knew there was nothing either of them could say that would change what she was feeling.

Aura lifted the pen and stared at the document that Marshal Gates had placed in front of her. It was her formal statement, a complaint against Hung Poh, and signing it was the final formality left for her to complete. Once she put her signature to it, there would be no turning back.

The three men, Payne, Gates, and Sheriff Dougherty, all stared at her expectantly. She wished they wouldn't look at her that way, as though she held the key to their futures. Still, she couldn't really blame them, for in a way she did.

Dougherty, she knew, could only be thinking that the signature that was about to put Hung Poh in jail also was about to steal a major source of his income from him. Faced with the presence of a federal marshal, there was no way he could protect Hung Poh, nothing he could do but sit and watch and glower at her. As for Gates, he'd received orders to make an arrest that eliminated the counterfeiter who was operating in San Francisco, and her cooperation determined whether or not he would be able to carry out those orders. And Payne—well, she knew how determined he was to see Hung Poh punished, knew how he felt about seeing Whit's murderer finally jailed.

A fleeting thought passed through her mind, and she wondered what would happen if she didn't sign, if she refused to complete the complaint against Hung Poh. If she let him go free, she told herself, there'd be no reason for him to fear her. And that meant she ought not to have anything more to fear from him. There'd be no trial, no necessity to dredge up the whole mess again, no reason for her to continue to live through all the unpleasantness any longer. More than that, there would be no reason for Hung Poh's associates to want to remove the threat against their master.

For that's just what she became the moment she signed her name to the document, and she knew it. Despite Gates's assurances, and Payne's, she was certain that some of Hung Poh's men had avoided being arrested along with him. She also knew the man must have connections in San Francisco, men willing and anxious to do his bidding. If there'd been proof linking him to the counterfeiting, that would have been one thing, but as it stood, she was now the only obstacle to Hung Poh's freedom, and he knew it as well as she did.

She could still feel the cold fingers of fear that had gripped her when she'd seen the look in Hung Poh's eyes as he'd been led past her. She was afraid, and she knew she had good reason to be. The temptation to get up, to turn her back on Hung Poh and walk out the door, was so strong she could almost taste it. Let him go free, she told herself, and he would have no reason to want to see her dead.

It would also mean that Payne's counterfeiters would continue unchecked, and that, she mused, might mean he'd stay on in San Francisco in the hopes of finding his proof. The thought of holding him was almost as great an inducement to simply walk away from the complaint as was her fear.

But then she realized that even if it kept Payne in San Francisco, he would not be there for her. Wells Fargo might very well grow impatient and send another investigator to take his place. Even if the company let him continue on, she doubted it would change the fact that he would leave her. He would, she thought, have no feeling for a woman who had allowed his brother's killer to go free.

She could sign the complaint, go through the unpleasantness of a trial, and lose Payne. Or not sign it, live with the fact that she'd freed her husband's murderer, and still lose Payne. Whatever her choice, it didn't matter. In the end, she still lost Payne, and that meant she lost everything.

"Aura?"

She looked up at Payne's eyes, saw the question in them, and knew he was waiting for her to sign the statement. She swallowed, trying to marshal her determination. She put the pen on the paper and slowly signed her name.

"There," she said, and handed the pen back to Gates.

He took the pen and the paper, inspected her signature, and nodded.

"Thank you, ma'am," he told her. "There's no need to inconvenience you any further. I'll have two of the soldiers accompany you home. Mr. Randall and I have decided that it would be best if they stayed with you for the time being."

She nodded and bit her lip thoughtfully. Perhaps she'd been foolish to be afraid. They would keep her well guarded until the end of the trial. With soldiers protecting her, she'd have nothing to fear from Hung Poh. Her bout of terror had been nothing more than simple panic. She ought to have realized that both Payne and Gates would be completely aware of her position under the circumstances.

"Thank you," she murmured as she stood. She turned to look questioningly Payne.

"I have to make out a report to be sent back East," he told her. "I'll see you in a few hours."

She nodded. He was already beginning to grow distant, she thought. She shrugged. She ought to have expected nothing less.

Gates opened the door for her, and she saw that two soldiers were waiting just outside. They raised their hands in polite salutes.

"Sergeant Collins and Private Maloney," Gates introduced them.

"Ma'am," one murmured and the other nodded.

She nodded to them, smiled weakly, then darted a last glance at Payne before she followed the two soldiers outside.

"Well, I'll go check on our prisoner," Dougherty said, as he pushed himself to his feet.

Payne glanced at Gates and shook his head.

Gates took the hint.

"That won't be required," he said. "My men have everything well in hand. In fact, you might as well call it a day. No need for you to be bothered over this."

"No bother," Dougherty assured him.

Gates put a hand on his arm. "I insist," he said firmly.

"This is my town, my jail," Dougherty fumed.

"And I have a federal warrant to handle this matter," Gates returned. "That warrant makes my authority just a bit more potent than yours at the moment."

Dougherty glared at him for a moment, then shrugged, aware that, for the moment at least, he was in no position to argue. He lifted his hat from where he'd dropped it on the desk, and put it on his head.

"Have it your way," he said as he started for the door. He pulled it open, stalked out, and slammed it after him.

"Friendly fellow," Gates muttered. "I take it you don't feel the good sheriff is to be trusted?"

"I have it on what I assume is good authority," Payne told him.

"Which is?" Gates asked.

Payne shrugged. "An informer," he replied.

Gates shook his head. "I'm starting to like this whole situation less and less," he said.

"Not less than I do," Payne told him. He stood. "I have to get to the Wells Fargo office. I'll stop in here when I'm done."

"I don't suppose you'd care to invite me to have dinner with you and your pretty little sister-in-law?" Gates asked. He grinned. "I might even be convinced to stay the evening and help guard her."

Payne returned the grin. "I'll consider it, but I get the feeling that you'd enjoy that particular job a bit too much for your own good," he said. The grin quickly faded. "Can you get some more soldiers here from the fort?" he asked. "I don't know how many pies Hung Poh has his fingers in, or how many friends

412

he might have in the city. I don't want anything happening to Aura."

Gates clapped a hand to his shoulder.

"I'll wire for another dozen men and I'll see if we can't get a federal judge here as soon as possible," he said.

"The sooner, the better," Payne said. "If we could start the trial tomorrow, it wouldn't be soon enough for me."

"Don't worry," Gates told him. "We'll keep Mrs. Randall safe."

"We damn well better," Payne said. "I got her into this, and she's already been through enough because of me. I don't want to see her hurt."

"I'll have her guarded twenty-four hours a day," Gates assured him. "No one's going to get to her."

Payne walked out of the jail, wishing he felt as confident as Gates did. He wondered what he'd do if that confidence was ill conceived and Hung Poh somehow found some way to strike at Aura. The sooner the federal judge arrived and the trial was over and done with, the better he'd like it.

In the meantime, he told himself, he was going to see that Aura wasn't left alone for a moment.

Aura rapped at the door and waited. She turned to Sergeant Collins.

"That's odd," she said as she pulled her latchkey from her pocket. "Wu and Mailee should be here."

Collins shrugged. "They could have stepped out," he said. "Why don't I go in first and check?"

"Check what?" Aura demanded. What could he possibly suspect might be waiting up there for them, she wondered. Surely it was too soon for any of Hung Poh's men to have organized an assault. Who could possibly have known what had happened in the jail only an hour before?

Collins smiled reassuringly. "Just routine," he assured her. He took the key from her hand and fitted it into the lock. "I'll take a quick look around and be back before you know it."

Resigned, Aura murmured, "As you like."

She stepped away from the door as Collins pulled it open and glanced inside.

"Hello," he called loudly. There was no answer. He turned to Aura. "Looks like your people must have gone out," he told her.

With that, he unholstered his pistol and started up the steps.

Aura turned to the younger soldier, the one named Maloney. He seemed less confident than Collins had been, and she was beginning to get an unpleasant feeling that something was terribly wrong.

"How long should it take him?" she asked.

Maloney shook his head. "I don't know. A few minutes, I guess."

Aura turned away. She glanced up and down the length of the street. It was beginning to grow dark, traffic had become relatively sparse, and the shops were mostly closed. She walked the length of the front porch and back again, suddenly feeling very nervous.

She looked up at Maloney when she'd completed the tour.

"Oughtn't he to be back by now?" she asked.

Maloney swallowed nervously and nodded.

"Yeah," he said as he glanced up at the darkness at the head of the stairs, "I think he ought to be." He turned back to face Aura. "I think maybe I ought to take you back to Marshall Gates."

"But what about Sergeant Collins?"

Maloney shook his head. "My orders are to see you

aren't left alone," he told her. He put his hand on her arm and started to urge her toward the porch steps leading down to the street. But before they reached them, a tall man turned off the street and started up them. Startled, Aura jumped back.

Unaware of the effect he'd had, he looked up at her when he'd reached the top step.

"Hello, Aura," he said with a bright smile. "I told you we'd see one another again soon."

Aura exhaled a thick sigh of relief.

"Howard," she said. "You frightened me."

"Frightened you?" Crofton asked. He climbed the last step and stood facing her and the young soldier. "Surely there's nothing about me that's the least bit threatening."

"No, no certainly not," Aura replied, with a weak attempt to return his smile.

"I'm sorry, sir," Maloney interjected. "You'll have to excuse Mrs. Randall."

Crofton put his left hand on Aura's arm and put his right hand into his pocket.

"Surely there's no need to run off," he said, and smiled at Aura.

"I'm afraid there is, Howard," she replied.

"And I'm afraid I can't allow that," he said.

His hand tightened on her arm and she flinched, for his fingers were pressing on the sore Durand's bullet had left.

"You're hurting me, Howard," she told him, when he didn't soften his grip.

He ignored her and removed his right hand from his pocket. She glanced at it, shocked to see he was holding a revolver.

"Let's not make a scene," he said as he cocked the weapon. "Just walk inside like a good boy, eh?" he told Maloney.

415

"Howard!" Aura gasped in disbelief.

He didn't leave her any chance to react. He pulled her arm, spinning her around and pushing her forward as he pressed the barrel of his pistol into Maloney's ribs.

"Inside," he hissed, "or I'll drop you where you stand."

Chapter Twenty-Two

Maloney mounted the steps first, with Crofton hurrying Aura immediately along on the young soldier's heels. He said nothing, but Aura could almost feel his confusion and fear, and also his guilt, for it was apparent that he'd completely botched his assignment as a body guard and he was well aware of the fact.

Aura had no sooner stepped into the parlor than Crofton pulled her back and held her as an arm reached out in front of her and struck the back of the young soldier's head. He fell forward, sprawling to the floor. Aura registered a remote sort of dull resignation as she watched him land not more than a foot from the place where a second body lay. It was, she saw with a growing feeling of helplessness, Sergeant Collins, his face down, a wide gash on the back of his head and his neck covered with a thick coating of dark red blood.

Crofton pushed her past the two prostrate soldiers and into the center of the room. She felt her stomach turn with revulsion as she saw the ugly wounds on the back of their necks, especially Collins's. He seemed to be lying terribly still, too still.

She looked back and saw that it had been Sheriff Dougherty's arm that had struck down Maloney. She thought absently that his presence did not surprise her, thought that nothing would ever surprise her again, after the previous hours' events. She didn't allow herself to consider that there might never be another chance for her to feel surprise, or anything else, for that matter, that Crofton's and Dougherty's presence most probably meant they intended to ensure she never saw the opportunity.

Still holding the butt of the pistol he'd used to administer the blow to the back of Maloney's head, Dougherty lifted his glance from his two previous victims' prone bodies to meet her shocked stare. He smiled at her, his expression filled with a mixture of spite and smug satisfaction.

Crofton took her arm and pushed her toward a chair. As she stumblingly fell into it, Aura glanced up at him and realized she was not quite as beyond surprise as she'd thought herself. She considered him with dull shock as he turned to Dougherty and nodded his approval.

"I see you have everything under control," he commended the sheriff.

Dougherty nodded. "The two Chinese are in the bedroom, tied to one another hand and foot." He grinned. "I think they may even be enjoying the experience. The whole thing couldn't have gone off easier."

"And our friend at the jail?" Crofton pressed.

Dougherty scowled. That part, it seemed, hadn't quite gone according to his plans.

"I didn't get the chance to 'discover' the body," he said, "but it's all taken care of. I done him up fine, a nice, respectable suicide." He grinned then, remembering what he'd done and apparently not all that displeased with himself. "Easy as pie. I took care of it while they were getting the little widow there to give her statement. No one saw."

"Don't be so pleased with yourself," Crofton growled. "He could have talked."

"He didn't," Dougherty assured him. "He didn't have the chance."

Crofton nodded toward Collins and Maloney. "You better tie those two up before they come to."

Dougherty knelt by Maloney, expertly removing the young soldier's belt and using it to tie his hands behind his back, then stuffing a piece of cloth into his mouth and tying it securely before he transferred his attention to Collins. It only took him a moment, then he shrugged and looked up at Crofton.

"No need to bother with this one," he told the lawyer. "I must have hit him harder than I thought. He won't be no trouble to us now." He chuckled. "He won't be no trouble to anyone from now on."

Aura gasped. She'd been right. Collins was lying too still. She turned her glance away from him, unable to look at him, knowing he was dead.

She turned back to stare up at Crofton, remembering now how she'd sat in that very room and drunk her tea and thought about him. How long ago had that been, she wondered, a week? Ten days, perhaps? It seemed like a lifetime to her now. She couldn't believe that she'd actually told herself that the lawyer was safe and dependable, that she'd tried to convince herself that, unlike Payne, he was likely material for a comfortable and respectable marriage. How, she wondered, could she have been so completely wrong?

Even now, seeing him standing there with a pistol in his hand, still she couldn't understand what he was doing or why he was doing it. Payne had warned her that Dougherty was most likely in the pay of Hung Poh, but it was impossible for her to consider that courteous and proper Howard Crofton might be involved with counterfeiting or any of the rest of Hung Poh's unsavory practices.

"Why are you doing this, Howard?" she asked him. She darted an accusing glance at Dougherty. "How could they have trapped you into becoming a part of this insanity?"

He narrowed his eyes and he considered her for a moment with what she could only think was disdain.

"Such naïveté you display, Aura," he replied finally. "I admit I find it charming, but still it bewilders me that one so clearly innocent as you could have wrought as much havoc as you have."

"I don't understand," she murmured. "What have I done?"

"You pushed your pretty little nose into matters where it clearly did not belong," he replied. "And I, for one, truly regret that you found it necessary. You and I could have come to a far more agreeable arrangement if only you'd behaved as you should have."

"Behaved as I should have?" she repeated in a dazed murmur. "You're telling me that I shouldn't have tried to find out what happened to Whit?"

She was beginning to get an unpleasant inkling of what it was he was telling her.

"You ought to have contented yourself with the business of storekeeping, Aura," he told her. "You never should have tried to hunt down Hung Poh and his little establishment."

"But what has that to do with you?" she asked. "That paper I found in Whit's ledgers led to the opium parlor, to Hung Poh, not to you."

He shrugged. "A circuitous trail, I admit, but one that would eventually have led to me. If not by you, then by that damned Wells Fargo investigator." He turned away, thoughtful. "Did you really think a foreigner could accomplish what Hung Poh was supposed to have done in the last few months?" he asked. "An ignorant Chinese?"

"Then it wasn't Hung Poh behind the counterfeiting, after all," she murmured. She was beginning to understand it all now, and it was unpleasant enough to leave a sick feeling in the pit of her stomach.

"He made an adequate soldier, one who followed directions well enough, but I'm afraid, thanks to you and your friend Randall, his usefulness has come to an end. A dead end." He glanced at Dougherty and the two men laughed. "Luckily," he continued, "adequate soldiers are not difficult to find." He smiled. "And counterfeiting is easy, once you have perfect plates."

Aura shook her head slowly. She replayed in her mind what had taken place in front of Madame Charlotte's house, trying to remember what it was she'd actually seen that afternoon. It didn't take long for her to remember the leather case, her fleeting thought that, by the way he carried it, it must have been heavy.

"You took the plates away," she said, in dazed tone.

Crofton grinned. "I walked right past your investigator friend and all those soldiers," he told her. "That's the benefit of being above suspicion. I had those plates in my case, and no one even thought to question me about them."

"You've been behind all of it from the start," she murmured.

He nodded and smiled, his expression smugly pleased.

"The opium, the counterfeit twenties, the whole lot," he agreed, apparently delighted to reveal his brilliance to her, to show her just how far his talents reached. "I was the one who forced Charlotte to, shall we say, expand her business horizons. I arranged for the opium to be smuggled into California. And I was beginning to amass a tidy little fortune from those ventures. It pains me to realize I'll have to start over again from the start now. You've ruined a very lucrative little enterprise."

She felt a sharp pain of awareness in the pit of her stomach as she stared up at his inflated, superior expression. He was a monster, a monster who hid behind his mask of kindness and commonplace respectability. She felt a gnawing bite of suspicion, and it was growing stronger.

"And Whit?" she asked, hoping that she was wrong but somehow knowing she wasn't.

He shrugged and pursed his lips thoughtfully. Then he shrugged.

"That was unfortunate," he said. "But he mentioned he was doing a bit of digging around for his brother, that he had a lead to Hung Poh. It seemed expedient to make certain he was in no position to discover too much."

She gasped. He was standing there unshaken, calmly admitting that he'd committed murder in the same tone he might use were he discussing the weather.

"You killed Whit!" she cried.

He shrugged once again, clearly dismissing the importance of the matter.

"An unfortunate necessity," he agreed. "He was such a trusting fellow, only too willing to open the door to his diligent lawyer in the dark of night. He made it almost too easy." He approached the sofa and stood over her. "And now, I'm afraid, however much it pains me, I'm going to be forced to kill you, as well."

She stared up at him, horrified by the smugly assured way he looked down at her, by the fact that he could tell her he'd done these things and show not the slightest hint of remorse. She watched him remove a length of rope from his pocket, and she could only guess what he intended to do with it.

422

She'd been wrong, all along she'd been wrong, thinking that Hung Poh was the demon behind everything that had happened since she'd arrived in California. It had been Crofton who'd killed Whit, and now, he was going to kill her as well.

She told herself she had no intention of sitting there and waiting for him to put that rope around her neck and choke the life from her. She wasn't going to make it easy for him, as Whit had.

She pushed herself forward, out of the sofa, hitting his midsection with her shoulder and letting the full force of the weight of her body fall against him. Startled, with the wind suddenly knocked out of him by the blow, he stumbled backward. As he did, Aura caught her balance and started racing for the stairs.

And for a moment she thought she might actually reach them. Crofton reached out, trying to grab her as she darted past him, but she stayed just beyond his grasp.

"Get her!" he shouted to Dougherty.

She looked back, aware that Crofton might just as well have saved his breath, for the big sheriff was already lumbering after her. She kept running, sure now that she would escape as long as she kept her eyes on Dougherty and didn't let him reach her.

And that was her mistake, keeping her eyes on the bearlike advance of the sheriff as he stumbled after her. She'd forgotten about Collins and Maloney, forgotten that the path to the stairs was not without its own pitfalls.

She tripped and fell. And before she could collect herself to scramble back to her feet, Dougherty's hand was grasping her shoulder, but for a moment she was too horrified to recognize the fact. She screamed as she realized she'd fallen across Collins's body, that she was lying with her face only inches from his.

And then Dougherty was pulling her to her feet and dragging her back to where Crofton stood waiting with the rope in his hands.

He handed the length of rope to Dougherty. "Tie her up," he directed. "And then bring her friends out here."

She almost fainted with relief when she realized that Dougherty was not going to use the rope to strangle her, but to tie her hands. The relief was short lived, however, when she recognized that the reprieve would be only a temporary one.

"You do disappoint me, Aura," Crofton told her in a mournful tone, as Dougherty used the rope to secure her hands behind her back. "I'd hoped we could get past all this with as little unpleasantness as possible."

"What are you going to do?" she demanded. Try as she might, she could do nothing to disguise her clear terror.

Dougherty pushed her backward, into the sofa. She fell awkwardly. With her hands tied behind her, she couldn't catch her balance, and she banged her shoulder against the carved wooden back. Dougherty watched her wince, then turned away, unmoved.

"Just for now," Crofton replied, "we're going to sit here and wait. It shouldn't be long before your friend Randall comes back here, seeking whatever comforts you've seen fit to provide him. And then, once I have you all assembled, I think you're going to find this place is a tinderbox, ripe for a nasty little fire." He sighed and shook his head. "Such a terrible tragedy," he intoned with theatrical remorse, "how the unhappy young bride dies so soon after the death of her unfortunate husband."

She stared at him in disbelief for a moment, then started to scream. She didn't stop, not even when Dougherty put a thick gag in her mouth and tied it

424

securely. After that, she was the only one to hear the screams, and then she heard them only inside her head.

Federal Marshal Gates looked up at the sound of the jail door being opened.

"That didn't take you long," he told Payne. He deposited the papers he'd been reading into the top drawer of the desk and carefully locked it.

Payne shrugged. "Couldn't keep my mind on what I was supposed to be doing," he said. "The report can wait until tomorrow, I guess."

Gates nodded. He had a good idea of what Payne was feeling, for he, too, had had trouble keeping his mind on what he was doing. He kept thinking about what Hung Poh's friends might decide to do, wondering when and where they might strike.

"I'm going to check our friend one last time before we leave," he said as he stood. "Then I'll take a few men along and leave them to guard you and Mrs. Randall for the night."

"I've no objection," Payne agreed. "The help will be welcome."

Gates rummaged in the desk's side drawer until he found the keys to the cells.

"Care to accompany me?" he asked, as he stood and started for the stairs leading to the private cells on the floor above. He'd thought it expedient to hold Hung Poh there, rather than in the larger, communal cells which were now housing the half dozen employees of the opium parlor.

"Why not?" Payne agreed. "It'll do my heart good to see that miserable bastard behind bars."

They quickly mounted the stairs and entered the guard's room. The soldier Gates had left to guard

Hung Poh looked up from the newspaper he'd been reading.

"Everything quiet?" Gates asked him.

He nodded. "Not a peep since the sheriff was with him."

Payne wrinkled his brow in confusion.

"The sheriff was with him?" he demanded.

The guard nodded again. "Earlier," he replied. "While you were getting the lady's statement. Ain't been a sound from back there since."

As soon as he heard the words, Payne felt a sick feeling in the pit of his stomach. Somehow he knew that things were starting to go very wrong.

"Damn it," he shouted at Gates, "open the door."

Gates darted a puzzled glance at him, but hurried with the keys, unlocking the door to the cell area and pulling it open.

Payne darted through in front of him, and Gates hurried after. He nearly bumped into Payne, who had stopped outside Hung Poh's cell and stared in.

"Oh, hell," he hissed in disbelief. "He's committed suicide."

The two men stood in silence for a moment, staring at the body that hung from the ceiling of the cell, a wooden stool lying on its side on the floor only a half dozen inches from its feet. The body was very still, the head twisted oddly, the neck obviously broken, the face a vile shade of gray-blue.

The soldier who had been on guard had by now joined Payne and Gates.

"Hell," he murmured hoarsely, apparently choked with awe inspired by the sight of the body. "I didn't know he had any rope. No wonder it was so quiet."

"Dead men don't make a whole lot of noise," Gates hissed angrily. "How the hell could you have missed a

426

length of rope?" he demanded. "Why the hell didn't you search him?"

"It wouldn't have done any good," Payne said slowly. He turned around and faced Gates. "I'll lay odds that Hung Poh didn't commit suicide."

"He didn't have no visitors," the soldier insisted. "The only one in there with him was the sheriff."

Gates stared at Payne.

"You don't mean Dougherty?" he asked, incredulous.

Payne nodded. "I'd bet my life on it."

But why would Dougherty kill Hung Poh, he asked himself. Why would he shut off his source of income? Or maybe it wasn't Hung Poh who'd been keeping check on the actions of the sheriff, who'd been paying him to look the other way with regard to certain illegal activities. Maybe it was someone else.

The thought was a cold shower of sobering reality. He'd been looking at it all along, he realized with a start, and until that moment he hadn't really seen a thing.

He turned and began to run to the door.

"What is it?" Gates called after him.

"Aura," Payne shouted back to him. "For God's sake, man, there's no time to lose."

The parlor had an oddly eerie feeling about it, the two lamps that Crofton had lit casting only enough light to throw a troupe of threatening shadows onto the walls, not nearly enough to chase away the gloom. And the morbid atmosphere was hardly diminished by the sight of Wu and Mailee, bound hand and foot and left lying on the floor by the far wall, nor by that of the two soldiers lying near the stairs amid a small circle of Collins's blood.

Crofton, however, did not seem at all disturbed by the havoc he'd been responsible for creating. Nor did Dougherty, who sat nursing a bottle of Whit's whiskey, slowly emptying a thick crystal tumbler that he'd already refilled several times.

"I'll say this for your departed husband," the sheriff told Aura with a slightly drunken grin, loquacious with whiskey inspiration, "he knew his spirits. Look at this," he said, holding up the bottle and pointing to the label, "the best imported single malt Scotch whiskey. To hell with the expense, eh? Must be damned lucrative, being a lousy storekeeper." He smiled at Aura. "Maybe I should go into the business. Just take people's money, all nice and legal, and no bother to it." He leaned forward and pressed the bottle to her cheek. "How would you like a little taste, a nice little widow's toast, eh?"

Aura shrank back against the back of the sofa, but realized she couldn't go very far to flee from him. She could smell the whiskey fumes with each word he spoke, a thick cloud that grew stronger each time he exhaled.

"Leave her be," Crofton told him.

Dougherty leaned back into his chair, looked up at Crofton, and smiled.

"Still a little sweet on the pretty widow, are we, Mr. Lawyer?" he sneered. "You know, you're a damned fool, Crofton. It's a mistake, and I told you that from the start."

"You're drunk," Crofton said.

He glanced at the sheriff and his expression filled with disgust. He crossed the room to where Dougherty was sitting and grabbed the bottle away from the sheriff's hand, then set it down on the table near his chair. Dougherty grinned and retrieved it.

"I ain't so drunk I can't do your dirty work,"

Dougherty assured him. "Now, if you had let me do Randall in the first place, like I wanted to, I'd have done it right. I'd have taken care of the woman, too, I tell you. But no, not you, you're squeamish. And a pretty little widow—that's appealin' to you. So you don't listen to me and here we are, the woman still alive, and you with both feet knee deep in a pile of prairie pies." He raised the glass, drained it, then un-stoppered the bottle and refilled it. "Now, there's a half dozen more deaths that need doin', only these you can't take care of yourself. For these, you need ol' Jimmy Dougherty, dependable ol' Jimmy Dough-erty." He raised the glass in a mock toast and downed a fair portion of its contents. "Got dirty work needs bein' done, and you always turn to me."

Aura suddenly couldn't breathe anymore. The gag seemed to be choking her, only she knew it wasn't the gag but what she was hearing Dougherty say that made her stomach begin to heave.

Crofton took one glance at her and reached forward to her, about to loosen the gag. She reacted to his touch just as she had to Dougherty's offer of the bot-tle, pulling back in disgust and revulsion. At that, Crofton changed his mind and left the gag as it was.

"Shut up, damn it," Crofton hissed at Dougherty, his anger turning from Aura to the sheriff. "Shut up and sober up. Randall should be here soon."

Dougherty raised the glass in the air and waved it in mock toast. "The sooner the better," he said. "Get the whole lousy business over and done with, I say."

Aura felt tears of regret well up in her eyes. If only she'd remained still, Crofton might have removed the gag, she told herself. If only she hadn't reacted to him as she had, she might have had the chance to call out and warn Payne. She turned her stare to Crofton, hoping she could induce him to take pity on her, but he was looking away from her now, purposely ignoring her.

"Shut up," he told Dougherty again, his tone listless this time, and without much enthusiasm. He seemed to realize that he had no way to control the sheriff and that the effort was wasted. He stood and walked over to the window.

Dougherty scowled at him and raised the glass to his lips again, only this time he paused before he swallowed. His glanced sharpened and he looked up.

"What was that?"

Crofton froze and listened, as did Aura. There was a faint noise, she thought, that seemed to be coming from the roof.

Crofton shrugged. "It's a branch brushing against the roof," he said, dismissing Dougherty's alarm.

"I didn't hear it before," the sheriff told him.

"A wind's probably come up," Crofton told him, as he pulled the edge of the curtain aside and stared down at the dark and empty street.

Dougherty was completely undaunted. "You don't want to hear it, do you, Mr. Lawyer? To hear how I told you to stay away from that damned Chinee? I told you there'd be trouble, but you wouldn't have it. There's money in the opium, you says, lots of money, and he takes all the risks. Only it didn't turn out that way, did it? Too smart by half, that's you, Mr. High-and-Mighty Lawyer. And now you need ol' Jimmy to pull your ass out of the fire."

He raised his glass again and this time he emptied it.

Keep drinking, Aura silently prayed, swallow the whole of the contents of the bottle. If Dougherty was drunk enough, she told herself, he wouldn't be so great a threat. If he got himself drunk enough, she and Payne might somehow stand a chance of surviving.

Crofton dropped the curtain and stepped away from the window.

"For God's sake, shut up," he hissed at Dougherty, this time with clear urgency in his tone. "He's coming up to the porch now."

Dougherty carefully put the glass and the bottle down on the table and pushed himself to his feet. He edged his way to the side of the room, to the wall beside the opening to the stairs. Aura watched him, thinking how odd it was that he seemed entirely steady now, that there was no sign of the weaving walk or unsteady stance that would indicate just how much whiskey he'd consumed. A moment before, his drunkenness seemed the only chance she and Payne might have against him, and now it was, to all appearances, vanished. Despite all the whiskey, he was now surprisingly steady.

Crofton had returned to the side of her chair and was holding her firmly, his hands on her shoulders, making sure she did not have the opportunity to make any noise that might serve as a warning. It was so silent in the room she could hear Crofton's breath; the slight creak of a floorboard beneath Dougherty's feet sounded as loud as an explosion. She could hear the sound of Payne's key in the latch, and she cried out to him in her mind to leave, but it did no good. In the silence, she could hear the creak of hinges as Payne pushed the door open.

"Aura? Are you here?"

Crofton's hands tightened on her shoulders, warning her, although she had no idea what he was warning her not to do. She had never felt quite so helpless before, so completely incapable of doing anything that might warn Payne of the danger.

"Aura? Answer me!"

There hadn't been any noise on the stairs, she told

herself. That meant he hadn't started up, that he might still escape. Perhaps he'll go away if he thinks no one's here. She glanced up at Crofton.

But he had no intention of letting Payne escape. He grasped her arm and pulled her to her feet, propelling her toward the stairs. When they reached the top of the flight, he held her firmly and pulled away the gag.

"Aura?" Payne asked again, staring up at what seemed to him only a shadow at the top of the stairs.

"It's a trap. Get out," she screamed, before Crofton clamped his hand over her mouth.

"Leave and she's dead," Crofton called out quickly. He motioned to Dougherty to turn up a lamp so that he and Aura were bathed with the light and Payne could see them clearly. Then he took his hand away from Aura's mouth, took out his pistol, and pressed it against her neck. "You hear me, Randall? You have one minute to get up here or she's dead."

Payne stared up at the two of them, and even from the distance he could see the glint of the pistol in Crofton's hand and the fear in Aura's eyes.

"Let her go, Crofton," he said. He raised his pistol and let Crofton see it, let him know that it was aimed directly at his head. "Let her go or you're a dead man."

Crofton looked down at him and sneered.

"Put the gun down or I'll shoot her," he shouted at Payne.

"If I put the gun down, you'll shoot her," Payne told him. "And then you'll shoot me. No, counselor, it would seem we are at an impasse."

He put his foot on the first stair.

Aura heard the sound of his boot on the step and it was like a dagger being driven into her heart. She'd been the cause of all this, she told herself. Crofton had told her as much. And now she was about to be the cause of Payne's death as well as her own.

She squirmed, struggling against Crofton's hold of her, trying to edge away from the touch of the cold metal against the side of her neck.

"Don't, Payne," she sobbed. "Don't come up here. They're going to kill you."

He kept climbing.

"It's going to be all right, Aura," he told her, as he slowly mounted the stairs. "No one's going to kill anyone."

How couldn't he believe her, she wondered. Why was he still coming closer?

"Dougherty . . ." she started, but Crofton jerked her arm and jabbed the pistol barrel into the flesh of her neck. She gasped in pain, and for a moment until he released the pressure, felt as though she couldn't breathe.

Payne, though, didn't seem interested in her warning. He was halfway up the flight now, and slowly coming closer. She stared down at him, at the pistol he held aimed at Crofton. She felt as though she was staring directly down its barrel.

"I know," he told her. "Dougherty's up there with you. But don't worry. He's not going to shoot me, and the good lawyer isn't going to hurt you. Not unless they both want to die."

This was insane, Aura thought. How can he think he can defeat them both? She darted a glance to where Dougherty was standing, his back against the wall by the head of the stairs, his pistol ready in his hand and a vicious smile turning up the corner of his lips.

There was noise, a sort of muffled groan, and Aura glanced down to see that Maloney had regained consciousness. It did neither of them much good. Bound, he could do nothing more than stare up at Dougherty in obvious confusion.

Doughtery paid him no mind. He must have been counting the number of steps Payne had climbed, because now he began to move, aware that if he was caught in mid-flight there would be no place Payne could hide. And Aura knew that with his own weapon aimed at Crofton, Payne would have no chance to turn his attention to a second adversary.

Horrified, Aura watched as Dougherty carefully edged his way forward, aware that as soon as he reached the stair opening, he intended to open fire and empty his pistol into Payne's body.

Aura waited for as long as she dared, knowing she'd have only this one chance. She kept her eyes on Dougherty as he moved closer, praying he would come near enough for her single opportunity to have some value.

And when she could wait no longer, when he was only inches from the opening to the stairs, she ceased her struggle with Crofton, leaned back against him, and kicked with all her might to the side, to where Dougherty was raising his pistol and was about to take aim at Payne.

She couldn't have hoped for her effort to be better rewarded. Her shoe came into contact with Dougherty's hand, loosening his hold on the pistol. It fell, the impact releasing the bullet he had made ready in the chamber, the report filling the air with noise, and the bullet, striking him, sending him reeling backward with pain and surprise.

Crofton hadn't expected the sudden shift of her weight. Although it was hardly enough to budge him, it unsettled him, and he momentarily lowered the pistol he was holding against her neck. That moment was long enough for Payne to aim and fire.

And then it suddenly seemed as if reason was suspended, as if time stood still and things happened very slowly. Aura heard Crofton utter a garbled shout and felt him release his hold of her. She fell forward, to her knees, scrambling after the pistol Dougherty had dropped.

But the sheriff had regained control of himself, and despite the fact that his shoulder was covered with bright red blood that was flowing freely from a gory wound, he seemed determined not to give up. She found herself struggling with him for possession of the weapon. His hand was bloody from grasping his shoulder where the bullet had struck him, but it was only too clear that he was still far stronger than she.

He wrenched the pistol from her hand and then lashed out at her, his fury more than enough at that moment to override the pain from his wound. Aura felt the full weight of his fist and the butt of the pistol against her side and she tumbled backward, gasping and nearly blinded by the pain from the blow.

When she looked up at him, he was towering over her, hatred seeming to pour out of him as he glared at her. The pistol was shaking slightly in his hands, but not so much that if he fired he could possibly have missed.

"Hold it, Dougherty!"

"Drop the gun, Sheriff. You can't escape."

Aura forced herself to look away, toward the stairs first, to see that Payne was now standing at the entrance to the room, his pistol held in both hands and aimed at Dougherty.

"I said, drop it!" he shouted.

There was a series of clicking noises from the rear of the room and Aura turned to see that a half dozen soldiers had somehow gotten into the house and that they, too, were aiming their weapons at Dougherty. She realized now what the noises she'd heard on the roof a few minutes before had meant—soldiers climbing up to the roof and dropping down to enter the house by the back windows.

Gates had been the first into the parlor, and now he stood in front of his men, the furthest into the room.

"You haven't got a chance, Dougherty," he told him. "Drop the gun and you'll at least live long enough to stand trial."

Dougherty's hand trembled as his glance turned first to Payne and then to Gates.

"And then what?" he shouted at Gates in reply. "A public hanging?" He shook his head and returned his attention to Aura. "All because of a stupid woman's meddling," he hissed angrily. He looked up at Payne and smiled viciously. "I ain't gonna' stand trial, and I ain't gonna' hang," he hissed. "And I ain't gonna' die alone."

He steadied the pistol in his hand and aimed it at Aura's heart. And then he pulled the trigger.

Chapter Twenty-Three

There was the thunderous noise of the pistol being fired at close range, and then, immediately after, a half dozen more shots answered the first.

Aura closed her eyes, cringed, and waited for the pain. At first, when she didn't feel it, she thought she must have died instantly, that it had all happened too fast for her to feel any hurt. Dougherty had determined to die, and she was sure he'd succeeded in taking her with him.

Then she heard the shouts and felt the floorboards reverberate with the impact of running feet.

She opened her eyes, telling herself that ghosts don't feel. She was greeted by the sight of Dougherty's body, fallen to the floor not a half dozen feet from her. His eyes were open and he was staring upward, but it was clear that they no longer saw anything. Dazed, she pushed herself unsteadily to her feet.

And then Payne was beside her, and his arms were around her, pulling her close. Soldiers were swarming into the room, shouting, filling the space with noise and movement. But for the moment they might have all been a thousand miles away, as far as Aura knew. The only thing that meant anything to her was the warmth of Payne's body close to hers, the feel of his arms, strong and steady, holding her and making her feel safe.

"Are you all right?" he asked her.

She could hear his words rumbling through his chest, could feel their reverberation beneath her cheek. She closed her eyes and sighed, then nodded, too shaken to speak yet, too relieved to think.

But she soon realized there was to be no chance to savor the fact that she was still alive, that both she and Payne had somehow escaped. Despite her daze, she could not completely ignore the flashes of bright light coming from the far side of the room, or the fact that it had suddenly begun to grow very warm in the room.

"We can't put out the fire," Gates shouted to Payne. "Get her out of here."

Aura looked up. Flames were sprouting from the curtains at the far side of the room and rapidly climbing to the ceiling.

"What happened?" she cried.

Payne released her and started urging her toward the stairs.

"That young soldier rolled along the floor and against Dougherty just as he fired," he told her. "He staggered back and his bullet struck a lamp. It shattered."

She balked and looked back at the room. The lamp oil must have splattered onto the curtains and the upholstered chair near the window. Already flames were running along the window frames and beginning to eat at the floor.

"Maloney," she murmured as she darted a glance at the young man Gates was busily releasing from his bonds.

The young soldier was grinning, decidedly pleased with himself. Just then he glanced at her.

"I finally did something right," he told her with a broad grin.

"You saved my life," she said.

Payne nodded. "Now, let's get out of here before the fire ends it," he said. "You can convey your thanks when we're all out in the street.

He took her arm, but she didn't budge.

"Wu and Mailee?" she cried.

"There," he said, pointing to where two of Gates's soldiers were helping the now released couple across the room. They both moved unsteadily, their limbs numb from the ropes Dougherty had tied around their ankles and wrists, but the soldiers were helping them and they showed no indication that they intended to remain to die in the burning structure. "Come on," Payne told her. "The fire has already gotten at the floorboards. It won't be much longer before the whole place goes up."

He led her past Crofton's and Dougherty's bodies. Aura barely had time to think about what it was she was seeing, about the fact that the two men who had tried to kill her were lying in her parlor with the last of their lives streaming out of them and onto the floor.

Aura sank gratefully down onto the sofa and let herself shiver for a moment before she settled herself.

"Take," Mailee instructed and pressed a cup of hot tea into her hands. "Nasty weather. Foolish to go."

Aura sipped the tea contemplatively, then stared down into the amber liquid as though she might find in it some of the answers to the questions that still plagued her. She had to admit that Mailee was right. She should never have insisted that Payne take her to see the remains of the store. The still smoldering ruins had begun to hiss and moan in protest when a miserable drizzle began a few minutes after they arrived, and it had seemed to her almost as if the charred timbers were protesting their lost life. It had been a miserable and useless errand, and had done nothing but leave her cold and wet and unhappy.

Payne dropped the remains of what had been the hopeful sign Whit had made what now seemed like a lifetime before. It was charred, just as everything else had been, with only the last half of it still legible—"l & Sons, Provisions." It seemed so unfair. Whit was dead and there would never be any W. Randall and Sons. Now even the sign was gone, burnt along with the house and store Whit had worked so hard to build. She shouldn't have dug it out of the rubble, certainly she shouldn't have suggested to Payne that they bring it back here. It pained her to see his expression as he stood and stared at it. Even worse, it seemed like an accusation to her, a finger pointing at her, telling her that she had been the foolish and thoughtless author of the ruins that remained of her life.

"Are you not well, Mrs. Randall?"

She looked up to find Wu staring at her, his expression filled with concern. She knew she ought not to behave this way in front of him, knew she had no right to ruin his and Mailee's happiness. For the two of them were decidedly happy, pleased with themselves for having survived, and delighted with the prospect of beginning a life together. Aura had to stifle a pang of jealousy as she turned from Wu to Mailee.

She smiled and nodded. It made her glad to think that some good had come out of all the unpleasantness.

"I'm fine, Wu," she said, turning back to face him. "Just a little cold and wet."

He returned the smile, obviously relieved.

"Then you will not mind if Mailee and I leave?" he asked. "We have much to do before tomorrow."

"Of course not," she told him.

"Anxious to see new home," Mailee added.

"I've warned you," Wu told her, "it's not much of a home."

Mailee seemed unconcerned. "Together, it be fine home," she told him, with a smile that didn't require a mind reader to interpret.

"Go," Aura told them. She reached out for Mailee's hand and caught it. "You've spent a lifetime imprisoned," she told her. "It's time you had a taste of freedom."

"Freedom," Mailee breathed, saying the word reverently, as if it contained some magic property. It had never seemed even remotely possible to her that she might someday know the freedom to love whom she chose, to live however she chose. She was drunk with happiness.

Wu took her arm and they started to the door, but Mailee stopped and turned back to dart a glance at Aura.

"Not be late tomorrow," she said firmly.

Aura laughed. "I wouldn't dare be late for your wedding," she assured Mailee. "Go."

And then they were gone, leaving her and Payne alone in the room. It seemed unnaturally silent in their absence. The room felt alien to her, foreign in the way hotel rooms always felt. It as much as told her she was an interloper, that she had no place there. It was a painful thought, as was the realization of just how true it was, the fact that she no longer had a home. She swallowed uncomfortably. She no longer had anything.

She stared at Payne, surprised at his silence, at the way he kept looking at the charred store sign. She bit her lip, once again wishing she hadn't asked him to bring it back with them.

She put the cup down, stood, and crossed the room to him.

"I'm sorry," she told him. "I didn't realize what that might mean to you."

He didn't answer, and she put a tentative hand on his arm, not at all sure he welcomed her intrusion and yet unwilling to let him go on mulling over things that could not be changed.

He seemed startled by her touch. He started, then turned to face her.

"Oh," he said. "I'm sorry. I didn't hear what you said."

"It wasn't important," she told him, relieved that he'd finally looked away from the sign. "Just that I shouldn't have asked you to bring that thing back here."

He shrugged. "I'd have thought there'd be more than that bit of wood that might be salvaged," he told her. "Not much to show for a lifetime."

She nodded, unable to think of anything to say. He turned away, and his indifference was like a physical pain to her. She watched him cross the room to the window. He stood silent, looking down at the street.

"It's nice about Wu and Mailee," she ventured finally.

He nodded. "Yes," he agreed. "It would have been a real tragedy if nothing positive had come out of all this." He tore his glance from the street, turning and looking back across the room at the charred remains of the sign. "How many died?" he asked. "First Whit. And then those at the mining camp. Hung Poh, Crofton, Dougherty, that soldier, Collins. I've begun to lose count."

She wished he would stop reminding her, wished she

could somehow forget about it, at least for a little while. But even when he fell silent again, she knew what he was thinking, knew that neither of them would forget the events of the previous few weeks for as long as they had memories.

She swallowed, awkward with him now, not sure how to go about asking him the question that had been eating at her since she became aware that it was truly over now, that his job in San Francisco ended when Dougherty and Crofton died. The mere thought of asking pained her, but she knew she had to do it, and do it soon.

"When will you leave?" she asked finally. "After the wedding?"

He looked up and stared at her, apparently startled by the question.

"Leaving?" he asked.

"Marshal Gates said the formalities were completed," she replied, "that they found the plates for the counterfeit bills in Crofton's offices. Your job here is done."

"Yes," he agreed, "it's done."

The counterfeiters had met their own justice and there was nothing to hold him any longer. Nothing, she thought, except for her love for him, love she would never admit she felt for him. Certainly she would never beg him to stay.

"And you have New York and your job to return to," she reminded him.

He shook his head.

"No," he said slowly, his eyes on hers, "there is no job for me to go back to."

"I don't understand," she said. "Wells Fargo can't hold you responsible for what's happened. They can't fire you."

"They didn't fire me," he told her. He grinned, then

sobered and shrugged. "Not that they might not want to, when they receive my report. I decided to save them the cost of the wire, and included my resignation along with the expense chits for this hotel room."

"But why?" she asked, completely bewildered.

"Maybe I've just had enough of it," he told her. "Maybe after what's happened out here, I simply don't have the heart for chasing around the country after counterfeiters and train robbers any more."

"Oh," she murmured. She took a deep breath. "But what will you do?"

"I haven't really given it much thought yet," he replied. "It seems this town is in need of a new sheriff. I might apply for the job. Or I could rebuild Whit's store and see if I've the stuff to become a shopkeeper." He started moving toward her, his eyes on hers, holding them firm. "I suppose it depends on you."

He was close to her now, and she looked up at him, startled by his last words.

"Me?" she asked.

He nodded. "You don't expect me to just leave you here, do you, homeless, penniless and without any prospects?" he asked. "I think I owe Whit something more than that."

There was something about the way he said the words, something superior and knowing and judgmental. She hated it, she told herself, and she had no intention of allowing him to belittle her.

"Whatever you owe Whit is between you and his ghost," she told him, her anger with him growing a bit greater with each word, anger that he could think of her only in terms of his obligation. She'd sooner have nothing, she told herself, than take his pity. "As for me, I intend to take care of myself, so you needn't be concerned. I don't need your help."

She started to turn away from him, afraid that if she

didn't, she'd start to cry. The last thing she wanted at that moment was to appear a stupid little weakling in front of him. Now, more than ever before, she hated the thought of him considering her helpless and nothing more than a burden to be endured.

But he caught her, putting his hands on her arms and holding her in front of him.

"Why is it so impossible for you to admit you need me, Aura?" he asked her, his voice even and hard.

"Because I don't," she hissed in reply.

She knew as well as he seemed to that it was a lie. She was hurt now, aching inside, and fighting back the tears in the only way she could, by turning her pain into anger. She tried to turn away.

But he would have none of it. He tightened his hold of her and pulled her closer, so close that when he lowered his face, his lips were inches from hers.

"Yes, you do," he told her firmly. "You need me. Say it, say 'I need you, Payne.' Say it, and I'll let you go."

Her jaw hardened with fury. Why was he doing this to her? How could he be so cruel?

"You can go to hell," she spat out.

She pushed against him, wanting only to get away from him. But he refused to release her.

His expression hardened, and she could see the anger in his eyes, too, now.

"Hell?" he asked. He no longer sounded determined so much as distant, distant and angry. "It wouldn't make much difference. You've already pushed me into Purgatory."

That confused her. She stopped struggling with him and gazed up into his eyes. She was startled and puzzled to see there was hurt in them. How, she wondered, could she possibly have hurt him?

"What?" she whispered in hoarse confusion.

"Damn it, you've done everything you could to push me away from you," he told her. "Every time I try to get close, you turn your back on me and slam a door in my face. Well, I won't let you turn away this time, and I won't let you ruin both our lives. I know you need me, Aura. You need me and you love me. I know it because I need you more than anything I've ever needed in my life. And I love you a thousand times more than anyone I've ever loved, ten thousand times more."

For an instant Aura's heart seemed to stop beating, and she couldn't breathe. Then it started again, the beat so strong she could hear it; she could feel the blood flooding through her veins.

"You love me?" she murmured.

"Of course I love you," he told her. "Why do you think I went chasing off to that mining camp looking for you? Why do you think that when I saw Dougherty fire that pistol, I felt as though I was going to die? I can't live without you, Aura. I don't want to live without you."

It seemed impossible to her that she could hear his words so clearly despite the pounding that throbbed in her ears and filled her veins. She stared up at him, into his eyes, incapable of turning away from him even if she'd wanted to.

"You love me," she whispered. Her tongue felt thick and foolish in her mouth, barely able to form the words.

He was smiling at her now, and he slid his hands from her arms to her back and pulled her close. She could feel his heartbeat, too, now, and knew it echoed her own.

"And you love me," he told her. "Say it, Aura. Say you love me."

She gazed up at him and nodded.

"I love you," she repeated obediently, aware she didn't want to lie any more, not to herself and not to him.

"You can't live without me."

"I can't live without you."

"And you need me," he prompted.

She returned the smile, silently admitting her willing defeat.

"I need you," she agreed.

He touched his lips to hers then, softly at first, and then, suddenly, with a deep and searching hunger. When finally he released her, Aura was dizzy with the intensity of that kiss, breathless from it.

"Now, that wasn't all that hard, after all, was it?" he asked.

She shook her head.

"Easier than I ever imagined," she agreed.

He lifted her in his arms and she wrapped hers around his neck.

"It might be the perfect moment to suggest you make a resolution to abstain from being quite so argumentatively independent in the future," he said, as he started to move toward the bed.

She laughed softly. "I don't think that's quite so easy as you make it sound," she told him.

"Probably not," he agreed. "But it's part of the wedding vow, isn't it? Aren't you suppose to love, honor, and obey?"

"What wedding vow?" she demanded.

"The vow you're going to take when you marry me," he told her firmly. "Tomorrow, I think, will be time enough. For now, I'd hoped we might amuse ourselves despite a less formal arrangement." He put her down on the bed and lowered himself to her, his fingers on her cheeks, his eyes holding hers. "That is, if, for once, you have no objection," he added.

She shook her head and then pulled him close. "I've no objection," she said, before she pressed her lips to his.

Aura closed her eyes and let herself drift with the sensation of his body close to hers, of his lips touching hers. She could not believe how strangely fickle fate could be. An hour before, she'd been lost and alone, and now, she realized, she was holding everything she'd ever wanted in her arms.

He lifted his lips from hers and gently stroked her cheek. She gazed up at him and smiled.

"About that vow," she murmured.

He leaned forward, to press a kiss to her neck.

"Mmm?" he asked.

"Could we compromise?"

He lifted his head and stared down at her, his eyes slightly narrowed and his gaze sharp.

"Compromise?"

She nodded. "How about love, honor, and cherish?"

He considered her offer for a moment, then smiled. "I'm willing to be convinced," he told her.

She reached up for him and pulled him back down to her. She was, she realized, anxious to show him just how convincing she could be.